A

VOICE

within the

FLAME

THE SONG OF PROPHETS AND KINGS

A
VOICE
within the
FLAME

HENRY O. ARNOLD

WhiteFire
——PUBLISHING——

This is a work of fiction. All characters and events portrayed in this novel are either fictitious or used fictitiously.

A VOICE WITHIN THE FLAME

Published in association with the literary agency, WTA Media, LLC, Franklin, TN

Author photo by Ben Pearson

WhiteFire Publishing
13607 Bedford Rd NE
Cumberland, MD 21502

ISBN: 978-1-946531-91-9 (print)
      978-1-946531-92-6 (digital)

To my wife, Kay, who never stopped believing.

PART ONE

HANNAH LOOKED INTO THE CLEAR WATER INSIDE THE LAVER and saw her shrouded reflection. She gently rapped her knuckles against the outside of the basin disturbing the water so that her liquid features became distorted, then began to walk around the laver. The bustle of preparations inside the outer court of the Tabernacle for the upcoming festival made her invisible. No one noticed or cared that she was moving around this beautiful object that contained the water of purification. This laver had been fashioned from individual pieces of polished brass and copper used as mirrors donated by the women of Israel who served at the entrance of the Tabernacle after the Exodus. It had survived nearly a century of the wanderings of her people. This was a gift to Yahweh from the sisters of her faith.

She moved around the laver like her ancestors did around the city of Jericho. At the end of seven days of marching, as the shouts of the people of Israel and the sounds of the shofars by the priests and Levites pierced the air, the hand of Yahweh crushed the city walls. Hannah reasoned, if the walls of this great city dropped after only seven days of marching, why then, after years of pleading with the Almighty, Creator of heaven and earth, to grant her one request, could He not favor her with a child?

Hannah wracked her mind for new language. Maybe there were new words she could use, words she had not thought of to convey her appeal;

something that would strike Yahweh as a clever, new argument to get His favor. But her language skills were exhausted. She was verbally dry, only able to exhale vaporous sighs in hopes the sound of her grief would defy gravity, rise beyond the sky, and float into the ear of Yahweh.

Her fingertips caressed the outside of the basin as she put one plodding foot in front of the other, circling the laver. The dissonant sound of bleating sheep forced her to pause. Shepherds were herding flocks into temporary corrals set up inside the Tabernacle grounds. For those who could afford one of these unblemished lambs, they would be offered on the altars throughout the week celebrating the Feast of Tabernacles. Year after year Hannah and her family journeyed to the city of Shiloh for the holy days of this Feast.

Year after year her dear husband, Elkanah, would give Hannah a double portion for the proscribed offering for the family—two lambs, two baskets of fruit, two loaves of bread. Perhaps this double portion to honor Yahweh just might heal her aliment, they reasoned. But year after year, in spite of the same portions sacrificed, the same prayers uttered, the same sentiments expressed, these rituals yielded the same barren result. Her heart could only feel the grief of rejection, and there was no honor in such a human condition. How could the Almighty not hear and see? How could the Almighty not take pity? How could the Almighty ignore her?

The sheep broke through the fencing of an overcrowded corral and began racing around the outer court area. Shepherds leapt to repair the fencing while a group of priests tried to herd the frantic sheep back through the proper gates. Hannah might have found humor in the chaotic scene were it not for the state of her heart. The cries and the bleating only reminded her of the gossipy women in her village at home who, when not talking behind her back, were offering cures for her predicament: eat these vegetables, don't eat those herbs, grind up a precious stone and drink the powder, take pleasure with your husband on certain days of the month—a full moon was always preferable. Even the rabbi had come to the house looking for infections, and after numerous inspections and ritual cleansings, he threw up his pristine, koshered hands in hopeless resignation.

Was it hopeless? Would Hannah give in to hopelessness? Like the rabbi? Like the women in her village? Like her husband if pressed to speak the secrets of his heart?

Hannah looked at the stream of people and livestock flowing in and out of the Tabernacle's open gates. She should return to Elkanah who, even now, was overseeing the raising of the tent poles and setting up the family dwelling along the periphery of the bustling city square. He would want her opinion on the process. She folded her hands in front of her and felt the bracelet Elkanah had given her before the trip to Shiloh this year. She pulled back the sleeve and the gold band glistened in the sunlight.

Each year Hannah dreaded the trip to Shiloh. She dreaded the humiliation of having to enter the gates of the Tabernacle as the barren wife of Elkanah while his second wife with her boisterous brood of sons and daughters, scrubbed up for public display, clamored around them. Before Hannah had slipped away that morning to visit the Tabernacle, the second wife had said to her, "Who can know the mysterious ways of the Almighty?" It was a not so subtle reminder of her unproductive womb. Elkanah's generous gift she wore on her wrist could not take away the humiliation of this week.

Hannah dropped the sleeve over the bracelet and looked once more into the laver. The water vibrated from frantic sheep and the pursuing priests racing around the outer courtyard. The rippling water in the basin reacted with distress; a mirrored condition of her soul. Yet she could not quite give up on the Almighty. She could not quite give in to utter hopelessness. Not yet. Not while she had breath.

One

ELKANAH ENJOYED OVERSEEING THE CONSTRUCTION OF HIS FAMily's booth. The mini-tabernacle was always assembled on the premium real estate of Shiloh's city square. Elkanah was a perfectionist. Every cubit was measured with precision, and if his fellow tent dwellers to the right or left encroached onto his designated property lines with their tent pegs, he would hold up the signed document he bargained for year after year with the city council. They did not argue—they adjusted.

Elkanah's big family needed ample room for their creature comforts, including extra space for his servants, the livestock, and wagons of supplies parked behind the family encampment. While he might wince at the exorbitant price of the site, he was proud of the expansive plot his family required on the city square, proud to show off the increase of his bounty year after year from his vineyards and fields and his livestock, and yes, proud of his progeny.

He was a third generation landowner of the tribe of Levi. His grandfather had bought land outside of Ramah, the city where his family had been assigned to serve in the local synagogue and rabbinical school after the country was settled and the land divided up between the twelve tribes. His grandfather cultivated fields and raised herds of cattle, while his father had expanded the property and began breeding horses for the wealthy tribal chieftains. The weeks out of the year that Elkanah's father served at the Tabernacle in Shiloh, Elkanah was in charge of the duties at home. He loved being in charge.

When it had been time for Elkanah to serve at the Tabernacle, he found the menial services assigned to him complete drudgery. Waste disposal, laundry services, and cleaning the barrack housing lacked inspiration. And he quickly learned that these duties were permanent assignments. There was no requesting different tasks or hope for advancement within the system of services, something his father neglected to tell him. City life was not for him. He thrived in the outdoors, and he preferred the smell of the barnyard over the pungent solutions concocted to wash the laundry or clean the barracks. Each year once his term of duty was finished, Elkanah could not get home fast enough.

Though he had retired from his years of Levitical service, he maintained the tradition of coming to Shiloh once a year for the annual sacrifice. From their encampment, the family had a front row view of the city center where the nightly festivities would happen. Elkanah never quibbled over the cost to rent the space. The shekels he paid into the city coffers for such pricey frontage was a luxury he could afford. The event brought excitement and pleasure to his family who looked forward to the festival year after year, pleasure to all except his first wife, Hannah.

Elkanah scanned the city square looking for Hannah. It would be difficult to spot her in the energetic crowd. Citizens of Israel, those living near and far, who were able to travel to Shiloh, made the yearly pilgrimage for the Feast of Tabernacles. The family encampments dominated the perimeter of the city square, and each year, a contest was held for the best booth decoration. The competition was fierce, and the city council took the opportunity to charge a high entry fee to all competitors. At the end of the seven-day festival, the council announced the winning booth to great fanfare. A dated and signed document provided the declared winner a lifetime of bragging rights.

The family arrived two days before the festival began, rumbling into Shiloh in multiple wagons. It took them that long to set up and decorate the dwellings before the opening day. The main road leading into the city was lined on either side with booths: merchants and farmers set up to sell their crafts and pagan idols, farming equipment, household wares, trinkets, and food to all pilgrims arriving for the celebration.

Elkanah did not see Hannah, so he turned around and backed up to get a better view of the tent raising.

"Just tie it off, Mushi," Elkanah said to his house steward. "Hannah will want the peak to be as high as possible." There was no city restriction or penalty for tent height, so he would take full advantage of the airspace above this temporary dwelling. It could be an advantage to have the tallest structure on the square when it came to the competition. Elkanah signaled Mushi to stop.

"Tie it off at that height. I want Hannah's opinion."

Mushi ordered the servants to tie off the end of the rope onto a wagon wheel.

Elkanah wanted his wife's opinion in all things, especially when it came to beautifying a space. He trusted her artistic eye and the skills to execute an effect.

He looked back into the square, stretched up on his toes and craned his neck to see over the heads of the people in the crowd. When he saw her approach, she was not even looking at him, but instead, at the top of their tent. She stopped and turned in a circle, her hands placed above her brow to shield her eyes from the glare of the sunlight as she scrutinized the tops of the tents of the competition aligning the periphery of the square. Elkanah's face brightened when he saw the gold bracelet he had given her before they had departed on their journey hanging from her wrist.

"Two cubits more and our tent will tower above the others." Her hazel eyes were gleaming when she finally turned back to look at him.

"Another two cubits higher it is," Elkanah proclaimed.

Mushi clapped his hands for the servants to carry out the master's order.

Elkanah opened his arms for Hannah to ease into his embrace.

"You're determined to win." Elkanah chuckled and gently hugged her.

"This is my year." She gasped slightly at Elkanah's embrace.

They watched as the servants tugged on the rope and the center of the tent rose higher into the sky. Elkanah waited patiently for his wife's approval. It was not given until she had once more observed the other tents.

"It must be perfect."

Elkanah opened his arms for Hannah to make one last comparison of height of the other tents in the square. With one final look at the top of her tent, she smiled and nodded, and Elkanah told Mushi to secure the center pole at that elevation, and what he hoped would be an advantageous level.

"I believe this is your year." Elkanah gave Hannah a vigorous kiss on her cheek.

Elkanah knew that by the end of the day, his wife would have adorned the entire façade of the tent, top to bottom, with produce, flowers, and tree branches harvested from his bountiful vineyards and olive groves. Then she would fill in the empty spaces with cloth fabric and animal skins covered with crafted flags, banners, and ornaments all in keeping with the spirit of the Feast of Ingathering and the dwelling in provisional tabernacles. He had listened to her verbalize her plans for the tent's outside décor for weeks now, revising it every few days when she had a new idea or considered one of his suggestions. She made countless sketches right up to the day of their departure for Shiloh, but Elkanah knew that all her creative energy and artistic designs was only an attempt to mask the anxiety and dread Hannah felt year after year at this event.

Elkanah took a deep breath and began to cough. He pointed to the refreshment table Mushi had set up in front of the tent, and Hannah scooted over to fetch him a skin of water. Dust and smoke filled the air, thanks to the abundance of camp fires and thousands of feet stirring up the streets.

He took a deep swallow once Hannah handed him the skin of water. "Once the sacrificing begins tomorrow the air will only get worse."

Elkanah took a second swallow, and then offered the pouch to his wife. The pair looked out over the bustling city square.

"Let's hope for a cool, steady breeze." Hannah grasped the water skin and took a few sips before stuffing the top back into the neck.

"Do you see Peninnah and the children in this madness?" Elkanah waved his hand over the teeming, human masses in the square.

"Odds are we won't see them until dark."

"Patronizing every shopkeeper in Shiloh." Elkanah sighed, his head dipping forward in annoyance. "I'll need to hire an extra cart to get everything home."

Mushi waved to them after tying off the front entrance into the family tent. "My lady, the tent is now stable."

"Thank you, Mushi. Have the cart with the decorations brought to the front."

Elkanah smiled at how the brightness of the early afternoon sun made

15

Hannah's bronze skin shine. He ran a finger underneath an errant strand of curly hair hanging between her eyes and tucked it into the silk headband. A decade of marriage and his love for Hannah had only grown; a reality that was a constant mystery for him. Perhaps his love was fueled in part by the harsh reality that their union had produced no children...another mystery.

"It's not her fault. It's not her fault," he declared to anyone who wagged their head in sorrow at their plight. Once after a Sabbath service, Elkanah nearly came to blows with an insensitive rabbi who hinted that this problem could be a sign of Yahweh's disfavor against Hannah. "How dare the fool suggest such a thing?" Elkanah said as he pressed his sobbing wife close to his side on their way back home.

By the end of their third year of marriage, the inevitable had to be faced, yet Elkanah refused the alternative of a second wife. It was Hannah herself who changed his mind by asking him to agree to this arrangement for her sake. "Think of Jacob's wife, Rachel. If a second wife can bear you children, then perhaps I might have Rachel's joy and have my own with you."

So the matchmaker found Peninnah, the second daughter of a good Levitical family from Mizpah with all the right pedigree. The additional marriage bond served a purpose, yet the transaction was empty of romance. Within seven years, Peninnah had provided three sons and two daughters while Hannah waited patiently to see if Yahweh might remember her.

"I must get to work." Hannah kissed her husband's hand before heading off to meet the cart loaded with decorations rumbling around the corner of the family tent.

From her position on the ground in front of the tent's entrance, Hannah could see Mushi struggling to maintain his balance on the top rung of the ladder. Sweat was pouring from him, creating large rings of moisture under his arms and stains around the rim of his headdress. He kept wiping his eyes while struggling to secure the multicolored flag bearing the family and tribal insignia on top of the tent's center beam. This completed the finishing touch on the outside of the family tent. At this hazardous moment, Hannah wondered why she had not ordered one of the more agile, less rotund servants to climb the ladder to the top of the tent and tie off this banner. But Mushi had insisted on completing the last of the decorations. He had done it every year. And Hannah had always trusted him with the job.

Hannah pulled back the tent flap and stepped just inside the opening. She saw Peninnah and her children sprawled on carpets and cushions eating their evening meal. They were transfixed as they looked up and watched the tinctured form of Mushi's extended body making its bulging impression through the canvas as he lay across the top of the tent. Hannah noticed when it dawned on Peninnah that any second Mushi might crash down on top of her and her children, she ordered her brood to take their plates of food and scoot out of range of the impending human boulder that might fall from above.

An impending disaster forced Hannah to call out to Mushi from inside the tent.

"Mushi, are you close to finishing?" She tried to keep her voice free of concern. She would never want to imply that Mushi might no longer be able to do this job. But still there was the chance for catastrophe.

"About to tie off the banner now, my lady."

She could hear him gasp and grunt as he inched his body closer to the tent pole. Any sudden or extraneous move might loosen the security lines and unearth the tent pegs holding the family tabernacle in place. Hannah held her breath and willed him on. She tried not to imagine the tent collapsing and crushing an innocent child below with his bulky figure, or for Mushi to tumble backward off the ladder and his corpulent rump land on her husband who was bracing the ladder below him.

Hannah stepped back outside the tent. She watched Mushi stretch his arms almost out of their sockets and tie the leather straps around the tent pole. When Mushi finished knotting the straps around the top of the pole, she breathed in relief.

Mushi carefully turned his head toward his mistress. "My lady, the banner is secure." It was impossible for him not to wheeze when he tried to take a deep breath.

There was no way Hannah was not going to be pleased even if Mushi had tied the banner upside down. His legs were shaking uncontrollably, but she had to take a few steps back to take in the full view of the tent for Mushi's sake so that he might know that he had fully satisfied his mistress's eye for artistic perfection. She quickly viewed the whole and pronounced it perfect.

"Yahweh be praised." The relief in Mushi's voice was explosive.

"Excellent, Mushi." Hannah added applause to the pronouncement. "Now come down and let's have our supper."

Just as Mushi began his descent, a gentle gust of wind from the north brought the banner to life.

Hannah scooted over to the ladder to hail the hero. She gripped the opposite side of the ladder from her husband. The ladder wobbled as Mushi descended.

"Yahweh, don't let him fall." Hannah spoke only for her husband's hearing.

She would not look up. The indignity would embarrass them both if Mushi knew she were watching. The bouncing ladder was difficult for her to grip.

"This is the last year for him to do this."

Elkanah nodded his head in agreement, and then he waved for her to step away from the ladder.

When Mushi stepped down off the bottom rung, Hannah and Elkanah each took an arm to help him regain his balance.

Hannah smiled at Mushi's brave face, proud of his daring and pleased to see the approval he had brought to his mistress. She removed the scarf from her neck and began to pat his perspiring face.

"I am so proud of you, Mushi." She would not show any concern for his well-being, or inform him that this would be the last time he would do this task. She would not hurt him in any way. She would not let Mushi ever believe that she thought he was no longer capable of performing any request for her. It was another year before the next festival, and she would give Mushi time to realize on his own that this laborious task could be handed off to another.

"Glad to be of service, my lady."

Hannah gave Mushi another short round of applause before kissing him on the cheek. It was a great relief to all to have Mushi back on solid ground.

Elkanah gave Mushi a slap on the back for a job well-done. The two men were the same age and had become fast friends. Mushi and his family were city dwellers in Ramah. Impressed with him as a young man, Elkanah's father had hired Mushi and began grooming him to become the house steward. Elkanah and Mushi had developed a strong bond over the years, and when Hannah had been brought into the family as Elkanah's wife, Mushi greeted her with joyful welcome. The bond he had with her husband was instantly extended to her, and it had only grown in the time since.

"I'll put the ladder back in the supply wagon, my lady."

Mushi reached for the ladder.

"The ladder can wait." Hannah tucked her arm under Mushi's and escorted him into the tent.

Elkanah and his family heard the sound of the shofars from inside their tent. The evening's festivities were about to begin. The shouts and cheers of greeting from the crowd began to fill the air. All but Elkanah leapt from their cushions and rushed out the entrance of the tent. He was the last one to exit as the volume of excitement from the crowd rose to greet the contingent making its way into the city square. All eyes were turned toward the road leading up to the entrance of the Tabernacle. Elkanah meandered up behind his family while the servants dashed to the edge of their rented space facing the square to watch the festivities. Elkanah looked down at his youngest daughter, Dinah, hopping around her father's feet begging to be picked up to get a better view. He bent down and lifted the little girl onto his shoulders.

A company of Tabernacle guards armed with polished shields and spears cleared the last of the pedestrians from the street for the double line of musicians leading the parade. The sound was more the staccato noise of drum, cymbals, and tambourine piercing the ears than any sort of pleasing musical cadence as they marched into the city square. Eli, the High Priest, carried upon a litter, followed behind the company of musicians. He wore a seamless blue robe over his bulky frame. Tufts of white hair flowed from beneath the flat gold cloth turban on his head and down the sides of his face. He sat on an elaborately carved wooden throne and barely acknowledged the crowd as six stout Levites lugged him through the multitude toward the city center.

"Looks like his holiness has been pilfering extra fat from Yahweh's altar." He did not bother to muffle his voice or disguise his disgust.

People in closest proximity turned their heads toward him.

"Last year it only took four Levites to carry him on his throne."

Elkanah saw Hannah's finger race toward his lips to silence him, but he jerked his head away, unfazed by the scornful stares caused by his words.

Elkanah's sneer turned to a scowl as Hophni and Phinehas, Eli's two sons, rode behind their father, each on a milk-white stallion and dressed in silk garments with purple mantles flowing down their backs and covering the flanks of their steeds. Ornate gold chains hung around their necks and bounced off their chests, and on their heads they wore turbans of gold and crimson.

"And look where our hard-earned offerings go. To clothe two peacocks."

The stern look Hannah gave him did nothing to silence him.

"They pretend to be noblemen and not priests of Yahweh." He pointed directly at the two brothers. "Yes, I served in menial positions at the Tabernacle in my time as a Levite, but I served well and with honor, even when these two sons had me empty their slop bowls each morning. They have grown in power over the citizens of Shiloh and wield their religious authority over the faithful who try to serve Yahweh. And the old man does nothing to stop them."

Elkanah plucked Dinah from off his shoulders and set her in front of Peninnah before storming back inside the family tent.

Eli clutched the lion heads carved onto the front of each armrest with his arthritic fingers. He knew his hands would pay a painful price once the Levites set the litter down and he could free his grip. Eli looked into the strained faces of his litter-bearers. He was sure they resented having to bear this burden. It had not been so long ago that he refused such cumbersome duties, that he walked in the parade on his own two legs. But his sons' rise in power among the citizens of Shiloh and the slow aging betrayal of his body had forced him upon the litter to be transported for any distance.

Eli looked behind him at the smaller contingent of Tabernacle guards marching behind his sons followed by the seven-member city council straggling in last place in the parade. He may be the High Priest of Yahweh, the direct descendant of the priesthood of Aaron, but he knew all eyes were on the brothers as the procession spilled into the city center, and that he was only a figurehead.

He turned back around to see the musicians gathering in the performance area in front of the stage. The first group of Tabernacle guards split into two lines and surrounded the elevated platform in the middle of the square facing the crowd. The stage was adorned with brightly colored draperies along its bottom. Positioned on each of its four corners, stood a decorative column with a large iron basin perched on top of its flat base. A fire burned in each basin, providing illumination and spectacle.

Eli's throne was set on the ground to the side of the stage, his burden-bearers forming a semi-circle behind him. Hophni and Phinehas rode right in front of him and dismounted from their steeds right onto the stage not bothering to take the stairs. They began waving to the cheering masses. It was no accident that the sons always maneuvered to have their positions elevated above their father. It was a constant reminder to Eli that the older generation would acquiescence to the younger.

The seven members of the council scrambled up the steps behind Eli to join the brothers on the platform. The chief of the council of seven stepped forward, welcomed the pilgrims to Shiloh for the Feast of Tabernacles, and announced that the judging for individual booth decorations would begin tomorrow, the first day of sacrifice, with the winner declared on the last day of the festival. Everyone knew that whoever received the coveted prize had probably spent more in bribes to the city council than on decorations for their dwellings.

The chief of the council finished, and the crowd became silent. Eli dreaded this moment when all eyes would turn to him. He had not yet released his hold on the lion heads. He would not let go. Nothing would happen until he let go, but he waited, if for nothing else than to frustrate his sons. He would force them to turn in his direction and glare at him for his peevish stubbornness. It may be the only power he had over his sons. When they finally did turn to him with twin masks of frustration on their faces, Eli raised his arm into the air but paused. He had to drop it before the festivities could continue. He smiled at the consternation pinching the faces of his sons. After he had waited long enough to build the anticipation, Eli dropped his arm and offered his sons a satisfied smile for milking his one moment of power longer than was prescribed. At the signal from the

High Priest, the entertainment began. Eli knew he would be completely ignored for the duration.

The drummers began a driving beat, and the guards twirled their spears into a horizontal position and pushed the crowd away from the stage, clearing a space in front. Dancers and acrobats leapt out from behind the stage and began the dance in celebration of bounty. Women carried baskets overflowing with fruit and vegetables above their veiled faces. Their sheer billowy skirts allowed the freedom of movement for their rounded thighs and curved hips, which they playfully exposed. Their bodices were clusters of grapes barely covering their flesh. The young female dancers gave special attention to the men and boys in the front row, flirting and teasing them with items from their baskets. This intentional torment brought laughter and cheers from the crowd. Whenever an unruly young man attempted to reach for a female dancer, he found himself knocked to the ground with the shaft of a guard's spear.

The male dancers carried sheaves of wheat bound in twine and branches of olive, willows, and palm trees into the center of the circle. After passing in front of the stage and receiving a wave of approval from Hophni and Phinehas, they weaved their way through the female dancers and began to deposit their produce on the ground.

Acrobats raced up to the columns on the stage and lit their torches from the fires in the basins. Then they circled back around the heap of produce and began to hurl the torches into the air lighting up the night sky, catching them just before they hit the ground. One-by-one the acrobats tossed their torches onto the pile of wheat. The flames began to consume the offering and the dancers and acrobats circled the pyre, their limbs and body a frenzy of motion, enthralling the audience by the spectacle.

Eli could remember when this festival was a solemn expression of thankfulness for a bountiful ingathering of harvested produce. Slowly under his leadership it had devolved into a pagan entertainment devoid of all ceremonial worship. He had listened to his sons' reasoning that the majority of the people no longer wanted dry, stale ceremonies. They wanted amusement, diversion.

When Hophni and Phinehas brought their proposals before the council they quickly silenced all protests by those citizens concerned with the moral decline in the festivities; those who wanted to return to more of a sense of holiness to the celebrations. This was an opportunity to expand the concept of the Feast beyond the religious to include competitions, parades, and nightly entertainments in the city center—all designed to infuse the glut of shekels into the coffers of the Tabernacle, the brothers argued, as well as their own private accounts. The economy from the inflated taxes and fees the pilgrims had to pay for remaining in the city for the required seven days would grow beyond what anyone could believe.

And when Eli saw that this was so, when the shekels increased with each year's financial success, the High Priest knew the complaints against the commercialization of the Feast of Tabernacles would become whimpers and finally cease altogether. Such revels had become acceptable practice, turning the worship of Yahweh into meaningless words and hollow theatrics.

Eli kept his head lowered. He did not want to fill his eyes with the sensual displays of jubilation happening in the city square. He rubbed his sore fingers, swollen from clutching the armrests to keep from being thrown from the litter as he was carried from the Tabernacle and placed beside the stage. He did not know which was more painful, the joints of his fingers or the throbbing ache ballooning inside his skull. He cast his eyes at Hophni and Phinehas prancing around the stage and leading the crowd in raucous applause as the music and dancing reached its crescendo. His sons led these people like they were blind and stupid lambs.

Eli could not pinpoint one moment in his memory when his sons' took control of the Tabernacle. It had been gradual, even trivial, just under the surface, then picking up speed until it convulsed the sea, drowning the High Priest in misery. Eli had been unable to see it, then unable to stop it. He had been silent until his preference became silence. He preferred having little or no responsibility. He preferred complacency over conflict. And if the people preferred his sons' leadership, then let them have what they deserved. While it disgusted him, it also exhausted him, so let his sons have free rein. Let them deal with the people. Let them carry out the duties for Yahweh. He knew in his soul the flame for Yahweh had burned out, and he couldn't remember when or how it happened. It just went out. His heart went silent. Now he just wanted to be alone in the silence of his chambers. The next seven days would be grueling, and he wanted solitude more than anything.

From his throne, Eli waved to his Levitical burden-bearers. He was not going to sit through any more of this high spirited choreography and ordered them to take him back to the Tabernacle. Eli was indifferent to Hophni and Phinehas and disgusted by the revelry. The rest of the throng hardly noticed his departure. Perhaps he could feel some relief in the silence and solitude of his chambers.

Each morning, Hannah was awakened by a band of Levitical musicians blowing their silver trumpets, announcing the beginning of the sacrifices. With the englut of people swarming into Shiloh there would be an excess of sacrifices beginning at dawn and continuing nonstop until sunset as each family brought their offering before Yahweh. The families who could afford the premium spots for their booth in the city center were automatically entered into a lottery. For an additional fee, this drawing gave those families the opportunity to be first in line each morning and avoid the midday crush with its seething mass of people and the pungent odor of animal offal, blood, and thick smoke from the sacrificial fires choking the air. The eldest son of Peninnah drew for the family and secured an early morning spot on the second day of the festival.

Hannah dreaded this day. She carried her year-round sorrow for being childless with a degree of dignity and resolve, and for the weeks leading up to the festival, she distracted herself by creating designs for the family booth in hopes of winning the competition. But when the day came for the family sacrifice and her precious husband honored her with a double portion to offer Yahweh; his generosity broke her heart. *Double the offering and double the chances of finding favor with the Almighty,* Elkanah had told her. Year after year Hannah's hopes were raised that Yahweh might be inclined to grant her favor, and year after year, her hopes were dashed. Winning the coveted "Best Decorated Booth" seemed more likely than being favored with a child.

She stood before the altar, her soul trembling as she watched the Levites slaughter her double portion, separate the breast and the right leg, the allotted portions for the priesthood, toss the remaining parts upon the altar fire, and see the smoke rising into the air. She wondered if this sweet aroma would be pleasant to the nostrils of Yahweh.

Hannah felt faint as she leaned her body against her husband. She had hardly eaten in the days leading up to this moment. She had no hunger; all hunger itself devoured by hope. The sight of the streams of blood running down the sides of the altar, drenching the rock piles at each corner and pooling around its base made her nauseous. She wrapped her arms around Elkanah's waist and dug her head into his chest, finding his strength a comfort to her trembling body.

"May Yahweh, the Almighty remember you and bless you, small and great alike," intoned Eli as his two sons stood at either side with their hands raised in their direction as if channeling the blessing directly from heaven. "May the Lord make you increase, both you and your children. May you be blessed by the Lord, the Creator of heaven and earth."

Hannah wept as she listened to the rote, priestly blessing. How foolish to expect the Almighty to remember, to make her fruitful like the land her husband cultivated, or like Peninnah whose babies appeared as regular as the seasons. This was a sterile incantation uttered from the lips of the High Priest. Hannah pressed the side of her head deeper against Elkanah's chest and put her hand over her other ear. She could not bear to hear the prayer spoken for another year.

Elkanah guided Hannah away from the altar and headed straight for the entrance of the Tabernacle, ignoring the rest of his family and pushing his way through the crowd. He would spare his wife further grief. It was not a lack of piety that made Elkanah disgruntled or his sorrow for Hannah. He loved Yahweh with all his heart and had been faithful in his service when his rotation had come up and required his time at the Tabernacle. What Elkanah despised was the fact that the Feast of Tabernacles was little more than a lucrative commercial enterprise for the entrenched system of Levitical power. Eli and his sons had manipulated this structure to their benefit. All sacrifices had to meet the Mosaic standard to be acceptable to Yahweh, and only the Levites could appraise such standards. They offered the "unblemished" creatures conveniently for sale at highly inflated prices in the makeshift corrals at the entrance to the Tabernacle.

Under the leadership of Eli and his sons, these holy days had become a meaningless repetition of sacrifice and empty prayers, with the desired effect of an overflowing treasury. Eli might wear the robes of the High Priest and bear the twelve-gem breastplate with its pouch containing the precious stones of lights and perfections that were supposed to reveal the mind and heart of the Almighty, but it was obvious to Elkanah and any other observant, discerning eye, that Eli and his sons had long since given up any communion with or commitment to the Almighty. The forms and rituals were consistent with the religious traditions, but absent of any real presence of Yahweh.

When Hannah saw Mushi waiting at the entrance of the family tent, she let go of her husband and rushed toward him, falling into his embrace. She began to heave as if trying to expel some unnameable toxin buried deep within her heart. She knew she might soon faint, so Mushi lifted Hannah into his arms and carried her limp body inside the tent, laying her upon a couch. Without requesting it, she heard Mushi set up the dressing screen to shield her from view. Then Hannah listened as Mushi ushered Elkanah and the family out of the tent, suggesting he take them on a guided tour of the city or hire a wagon for an outing in the surrounding countryside. Their absence was a mercy for all.

Mushi knew what to do to care for her. He always had. Each day while the family took their sightseeing excursions, Mushi was never out of earshot of his mistress. He doted on her, and did not allow Peninnah or her boisterous children to disturb Hannah when they returned to the family tent in the evenings. Mushi suffered with her. When Hannah would crack open her eyes after a fitful sleep, often she would find Mushi quietly whispering his prayers to the Almighty on her behalf as she lay on her couch.

After days of not eating, Mushi finally got Hannah to drink some broth, gradually adding bits of fruit and honey cakes to her diet. Mushi had witnessed Hannah's infrequent bouts of low spirits for years and had always been able to restore her to her cheerful, engaging self. "This might be the worst we've seen, dear friend." Hannah had said, but Mushi just patted her hand, softly shushing her and encouraging sleep.

On the last day of the festival, when the city council announced that the tabernacle of Elkanah, of the tribe of Levi, from the hill country of Ramah, had won the "Best Decorated Booth," even this prize failed to revive her.

Hannah asked Mushi to stand beside her as she peeked through a crack in the screen to watch Peninnah skipping through the tent. She had accepted the award on behalf of the family, and she waved the scroll tied with colored ribbons in the air, chortling with glee as if she had won the award.

"I know who won the prize, my lady." His whispered words were gently spoken, but brought her heart no comfort. Even his sensitive touch upon her shoulder brought no positive effect. Hannah moved away from his hand, lay back down on her couch, and silently wept. She felt Mushi drape a silk covering over her before he slipped around the screen to join the rest of the family.

Two

THAT LAST NIGHT OF THE FEAST, HANNAH STARED AT THE CEIL-
ing of the tent from where she lay upon her couch. The sole oil lamp in the
center of the tent cast faint shadows along the white fabric drapes above
her. She could hear the calm and peaceful breathing of her family deep in
slumber. She strained to hear the familiar, erratic sounds of Elkanah's distinct breathing above the others, but could not detect it.

Hannah swung her legs off the couch and forced herself to stand. She
had to brace herself upon the screen, hand-painted with her own design of
wheat stalks, until she got her balance. She stepped around the screen and
saw Elkanah sleeping peacefully next to Peninnah, his bare arm slung over
her bare shoulder. The sight pinched her heart with jealousy, but what could
she expect? She had put herself in exile from him and the rest of the family,
and Peninnah had seized the opportunity to garner Elkanah's affections.
Perhaps if Peninnah continued her winning streak, child number six would
be a child of the festival.

In a startling burst of energy, Hannah threw off her gown and got
dressed in her finest garments, the ones she wore to the Tabernacle to
present her sacrifice that second day. She tiptoed to the entrance of the tent
as she slipped Elkanah's gold bracelet over her wrist. Before unlacing the
straps of cord that fastened the tent flaps, she looked at Mushi, her savior

and healer, lying dead to the world, and whispered a blessing upon her friend.

In the last hours before sunrise, the tents around the square were quiet, the inhabitants asleep within. The fires in the columned basins on the stage still provided enough light to expend a warm glow around the square. Along the stage and on the ground where the musicians had played and performers had danced, a throng of people lay sprawled out, sleeping off the excesses of their revelry. When Hannah walked by the stage she saw a trio of thieves foraging through the garments of their victims, taking advantage of their inebriated state and helping themselves to whatever they could steal. The bandits paused in their scavenging and eyed Hannah as another potential victim, but she glared back at them in defiance. It was a simple group decision to return to easier picking by robbing the intoxicated than troubling with someone who refused to show any fear. Hannah continued to make her way through the city center, stepping around the debris and sleeping bodies strewn across the grounds.

The brothels on either side of the road leading to the entrance into the Tabernacle still showed signs of life. A stream of clients flowed in and out of each establishment. During the festival, proprietors of each brothel brought in additional personnel from the countryside to meet the demand. The oil lamps and fires blazed inside each shop. A din of music and laughter left Hannah's ears ringing as she passed between them, but she did not give even a cursory glance through the open windows and doors of each brothel. She kept her focus clear and direct, not contaminating her imagination with the hot brightness of these images.

Just before reaching the entrance of the Tabernacle, Hannah was forced to stop in the middle of the street as a cadre of loutish Tabernacle guards burst out of the largest brothel onto the street and began pushing aside the people milling about in front of the brothel. Two splendidly dressed men stumbled out of the entrance with a pack of half-naked women clinging to their drunken bodies. The mass of writhing humanity stopped in front of Hannah. She could not avert her eyes, but froze in place, holding her breath and hoping her stillness would make her invisible. The laughter turned to animated squeals when the two men dropped shekels into the eager hands that pawed and fondled them. Hannah's body stiffened as she waited. Dust from the street stirred up by the muscular legs and sandaled feet around her began to sting her eyes and burn her nose. Still she did not move and the guards took no notice of her, looking over her head and scanning the perimeters of the street for potential dangers.

Hannah realized these two noblemen were the sons of the High Priest when they began a lewd dance to the delight of their admirers. When the two brothers collapsed into the arms of their female audience, one of the brothers stared right into Hannah's face. She could tell his eyes were too bleary with wine to bring her features into sharp clarity. The guards set the brothers upon their feet and began to guide them toward the Tabernacle as the prostitutes dashed back into the brothel, cheerfully counting their shekels. The sentries posted at the entrance of the Tabernacle removed the barrier, opened the partition into the Tabernacle and snapped to attention as the bodyguards hustled the brothers past them. Once the group was inside, the sentries set the barrier back in place and resumed their positions before the entrance.

Left unharmed in the middle of the street, Hannah forced her legs to move toward the Tabernacle. She did not want to be standing in front of a brothel when the sun rose. She approached the entrance and there waited until the first light appeared in the east and the gate was opened. Long ago she had learned the pain and power of waiting, so waiting a little longer for the morning to dawn and for Eli to make his way to the entrance of the Tabernacle gave her the time to quiet her soul before one last outpouring of her heart.

The Levites parked the High Priest's throne at the entrance and set a large bronze chest in front of it. All worshipers had to pass before Eli and the opened chest and each was expected to drop an offering into the coffer. Eli stepped up onto the throne, releasing a rumbling groan as he settled himself onto the seat. Once comfortable, he then nodded for the guards to open the gates and allow the people to enter. All the pilgrims, eager for one last opportunity to pray for Yahweh's favor for the coming year before leaving town, began to stream into the Tabernacle.

The High Priest did not look at the people moving before him, and most ignored him as they tossed coins or jewelry into the open chest before passing through the entrance. He nestled deeper into his ornate throne, a slumped craven. Fixing his dark eyes on the open chest, he listened to the clink of coins and jewelry filling the inside as the devout passed before him. A flow of human shadows cast flickering light and shade over the chest.

When Eli noticed that one human shadow had stepped out of the flow and paused before the chest, he sensed he was being watched and raised his deep-set eyes. He had to shield them from the glare of the sunrise before they could adjust to the bright light. He gazed upon the gaunt but beautiful form of a woman smiling at him. Eli determined her smile to be one of pity for the cheerless man on his throne. He felt a sudden tremor inside his rib cage. He slipped his hand beneath his breastplate and massaged his chest to relieve the rising pressure. The woman pulled back the sleeve of her robe and removed a golden bracelet from her wrist. She brought it to her lips and kissed it before dropping it into the bronze strongbox, and then she bowed her head at the High Priest before joining the other pilgrims. Eli was accustomed to most people ignoring him or giving him obsequious looks as they walked before him. But this woman honored him with a smile and a bow, which meant much more to him than her deposit into the treasury.

Eli adjusted his elegant robes and sat up straight. He stretched out his upper body, craning his neck to watch the woman as she fell into the current of people flowing into the outer courtyard. Once Eli lost sight of her he leaned back and adjusted the purple-colored turban that had slipped down over his brow. When he lowered his arms he saw that his fingers were trembling, intensifying the pain in the joints. He slipped them behind the breastplate and clutched the pouch containing the two divination stones, the Urim and Thummin, in an attempt to conceal his shaking hands.

Hannah eased along the queue of chanting priests lined across the front of the entrance into the Holy Place, their arms and hands extended toward the crowd, protecting Yahweh from the rabble. No one could get past them. No one could enter the Holy Place but the ordained, and inside the sanctuary, beyond the veil, only the High Priest was allowed once a year into the Most Holy Place to stand in Yahweh's presence. She wondered why it was that Yahweh was so inaccessible.

As she waited her turn to cleanse her face and hands with the sacred water from the laver, Hannah watched while the priests inspected the last of the creatures to be sacrificed in this final act of worship, signifying the end of the festival. There must be no blemish on these lambs that Yahweh would find offensive. Hannah knew her own soul was blemished, an unacceptable offering to Yahweh, yet she believed only Yahweh could move beyond the deep recesses of her imperfect heart and understand her desperation. She had to make one more attempt to break through. She had to make Yahweh listen to her pleas one more time.

When her turn came, Hannah splashed her face and hands with the sacred water and stepped away from the laver with her face sparkling from the moisture. It was futile for her to locate a private spot to pray, so Hannah knelt at the bottom of the steps of the portico under the shadow of the droning priests. If she could not enter or even peek inside the Tabernacle, she would at least face in the direction of the Most Holy Place. Perhaps the Almighty, enthroned on the Mercy Seat between the wingtips of the twin Cherubim on the Ark, would extend mercy to her. Before she even parted her trembling lips something caught in her throat, a tiny blaze that took her breath. What was this fervid sensation? Hannah looked around to see if anyone was watching, but the crowd was absorbed by its own yearning for Yahweh, and took no notice of her.

"Oh Lord Almighty, do not forget me. Look upon your servant's misery with compassion. I sink in an ash pit of despair. Do not forget me. My eyes stream with tears. Do not forget me. My feet stumble. Do not forget me. My heart has turned to dust. Do not forget me. My bones waste away. Do not forget me. My strength is sapped, baked in the heat of the sun. Do not forget me. The floods cover my head. Do not forget me. I am your servant. Surround me with songs of deliverance. I am your servant, and I declare the righteousness of the Almighty. I ask, Almighty One, Creator of heaven and earth, to give your servant...to give her...give her a..."

Rushing from between her lips on a stream of stricken passion—the bay of a beast, the howl of a dog, the wail from a wounded heart—the vow burst forth; words never conceived before, never uttered before: "A son. Give your servant a son, and I will give him back to the Almighty for all the days of his life. He shall be consecrated before you. No razor shall cut his hair. You, Almighty One, shall be his crown. He shall be yours and yours alone."

She said it and kept on saying it. "A son. Give your servant a son, and I will give him back to you," repeating the promise over and over, her lips and tongue forming the words but her vocal cords too weak to coat the language with anything but a whisper. She couldn't believe she was thinking it, saying it, imagining the very reality of such a vow. But she couldn't stop herself from uttering the vow. She was amazed such a proposal came to mind. The very thing she wanted most from the Almighty, she now stated her willingness to give back. It was a hard bargain, too hard, borne from a laden misery, yet it sprang from a veiled place in her soul and was impossible to deny. This vow was deeper than a momentary burst of religious fire. It bore the substance of heavenly power and light, eternal light, and she burned, her heart and mind and spirit aflame, healing years of anguish that had persistently clawed at the lining of her soul.

Eli did not need to push people out of his way or have a vanguard of Levites clear a path. The people stepped aside as he weaved an erratic lane through their midst clasping the pouch of sacred stones beneath his breastplate. His frantic eyes searched the outer court; something had touched him; something in her look, her smile, the radiance of her eyes. He had been yanked from his watch-dog position outside the Tabernacle. Vibration from a wild bolt shot through the hard-coating of stone encasing his soul. He felt a heat coming from the pouch soothing the pain in his fingers, burning the dross in his heart. Was this heat emanating from the precious stones or from this burst of energy circulating through his blood? He had to know.

And there he saw her, kneeling at the foot of the steps. This woman was making a spectacle of herself before the row of Levites, swaying back and forth, a single fist rapping a bitter rhythm against her breast, lips moving with no vocal sound. Eli felt light-headed and anxious. Could he have misjudged this woman's fervor and holy piety for intoxication? Could she have deceived him into believing he had received some uncanny communication that caused this resurgence in his blood? That a long-silent Yahweh had mysteriously come back to life in his heart? He bent down close to her ear.

"Dear woman, please say you are not drunk, that you have not been drinking."

The instant he spoke the words, he knew he had misjudged her and regretted the accusation.

It took a moment for the woman to stop swaying and come to herself. When she opened her eyes, Eli hoped that the earnestness of his expression would not frighten her.

"No, my lord," the woman gushed as she wiped the moisture from her lips. "I have not been drinking. I only pour out my soul to the Almighty. It is from grief that I plead with the Almighty."

Eli did not know how to respond to such direct sincerity; would that all God's people speak with such honesty. He stared into the moist light of her eyes, unsure what this exchange in the middle of the congested Tabernacle courtyard might mean to him, to her. Why had he, the High Priest of Yahweh, singled out this lowly woman and been drawn to follow her, compelled to speak to her, only to find out that in her misery and grief she had been pouring out her heart to the Almighty? In this unexpected moment of connection, Eli's whole body grew warm, his soul exhaling out of his lungs and taking shape in the air before him. He felt a bare vulnerability, an exposure of his heart. Had he forgotten this feeling? Had he ever felt something like this in his lifetime? What was it about this woman, this moment, that made him believe they were not strangers but companions in the mysterious plans of Yahweh?

Eli released his hold of the pouch beneath his breastplate, his hands no longer alive with tremors or pain, and he placed them upon the woman's covered head.

"Go in peace, and may the Almighty grant you the asking of your heart."

The woman rose to her feet, her body a bright essence of herself.

"May your servant find favor in your eyes," she said, bowing once again to Eli.

There was a charge in his heart that only intensified as he watched the woman depart. Eli looked down upon his hands and observed his twisted fingers that he had placed upon her head. He felt no pain. When he stretched each finger to its full extent, he felt no pain. He balled them into a fist and stretched them again, and again, no pain. There was no pain in his fingers, no pain in his head, no pain in his body. He began to laugh, and he did not care who might see him express such inappropriate pleasure in such an inappropriate place. He had no pain, and this was worthy of such a joyful utterance.

The blessing of the High Priest accelerated Hannah's heart, and she felt her spirit pulsating with the charge of her vow as she dashed out of the Tabernacle. No prayer she had uttered before—an exact count abandoned long ago—had left her so quickened.

Hannah felt a hunger emerge—no, more than a hunger, a ravenousness bordering on the predatory. If she did not eat soon she might do something desperate. She raced through the city square. Something was different, something that would be impossible for her to explain. A surge of power had replaced her despair. Her soul was strong. Her face was no longer downcast. Her eyes shone with brightness, no longer averted in shame. Something was definitely different.

When she approached her family's encampment, she saw Elkanah overseeing the disassembling of the tents and the packing of the wagons. He patted his leg with a rolled parchment. Hannah paused to catch her breath, then eased behind him and curled her arms around him, embracing him from behind. She saw the parchment fall to the ground, and then felt Elkanah grip her wrists before turning around. She could tell that he was relieved yet mystified at her sudden appearance after being absent all morning.

"Where have you been?"

"The Tabernacle. One last prayer before we left."

He gave her a puzzled look, but then looked down at her bare wrist.

"You have lost your bracelet."

"Not lost. An offering."

She offered no more of an explanation. How could she explain to her husband what she had done, or the kind of outrageous prayer she had just uttered to Yahweh to accompany his gift of the gold bracelet? She could not explain it to herself, and Elkanah made no further inquiry. Instead, he cocked his head and saw the parchment on the ground. He let go of Hannah's wrists and knelt down to retrieve it.

"Here is one prayer the Almighty answered."

Elkanah held up the ribbon-trimmed parchment awarded to the winner of the best decorated booth of the festival. He remained on one knee and raised the document in his hands like a subject presenting a gift to a queen, but the queen did not accept it.

Hannah could tell that her husband was proud and happy his wife had received such an honor, but she no longer felt she needed this prize to raise her spirits. She reached down and lifted him to his feet. Hannah could not have cared less about the award.

"You are absolutely glowing. What brought this on?" Elkanah's look silently asked what inspired Hannah's shining countenance.

Hannah could think of no rational explanation for her bright appearance or her complete lack of interest in the very thing for which she had worked so hard to acquire.

"I'm starving." It was the best explanation she could come up with. And then she wrapped her arms around him, crushing the parchment between their bodies.

Hannah stood on the roof of the house in the lingering sunset and watched as Mushi hustled Elkanah straight to the bathhouse once his master had come in from the fields. She could not make out their full conversation, but could tell that her husband was protesting the purpose for this middle of the week bathing. Mushi brooked no nonsense, and spun his master around, firmly pushing him through the door of the bathhouse. Once he closed the door, he looked up at his mistress on the roof and waved.

Hannah had worked it out well in advance: a table of favored cuisine and wines, fresh flowers plucked just hours before the occasion and tactically arranged for visual effect, scented oil lamps, red and blue petals of Scarlet Crowfoot and Grassy Bindweed scattered over the plump cushions and pillows, all encased in a circular, curtained partition on the roof to ensure intimacy. Hannah and Mushi had conspired for days.

Once Hannah saw Mushi emerge from the bathhouse with her husband in tow and point him in the direction of the outside steps leading to the roof, she slipped inside the curtains. Elkanah could find his way on his own.

Hannah pushed aside the edge of the curtain to watch as her husband appeared on the landing of the steps. In the light of the torch he carried, she could see the dawning realization travel over Elkanah's face. Hannah pulled back the curtain to reveal herself and extended her hand in welcome. It thrilled her to see him smile at her beautiful scheme and then approach, a willing prey of her plot.

It was as if Hannah had transported them back to the night of their wedding, yet with a decade of experience navigating the arcs and crevices of their bodies. Words were unnecessary. Hunger for food was light. Thirst was quenched with a few sips of sweet wine. The heat from the fire burning in the metal basin on the floor was sufficient to warm against the slight chill in the autumn night air. Still neither Hannah nor Elkanah could keep from shivering when their fingers untied the cords around each other's robes and gently guided the folds of cloth off their shoulders. The garments cascaded downward and pooled around their feet. Hannah knew this moment beneath the radiance of a full moon was more than just a night of amorous pleasure. It was not an instance of consoling a broken heart or the attempt to heal after an argument. It was a clean, absolute passion of passing life into life—eager, knowing, a rush to embrace her husband into the hope of a future happiness that had thus far been denied her.

Three

HANNAH LOOKED INTO THE BABY'S WIDE BROWN EYES AND smiled as she entered the synagogue to the congregational greeting: "Blessed be he that cometh in the name of the Lord. We bless you out of the house of the Lord."

There had been no doubt in her mind it would be a son. She knew it the moment she had finished her prayer in the Tabernacle at last year's Feast of the Tabernacles. She knew it the night she and Elkanah spent on the rooftop. She knew it the moment she realized her normal blood flow had ceased and the formation of a child had begun in her womb. She knew. She had always known the child would be a son. And in the months leading up to his birth she would speak to her son growing inside her. She would stroll to the top of the hill above the family dwellings and sit beneath the olive trees, lay her hands upon her swelling belly and tell her son the story of her struggle, the years of praying to Yahweh, pleading for a child and hearing only silence. Now her prayers were answered, and her son, her firstborn, would be dedicated as a son of Yahweh. And on occasion, as a reward for her stories, the child would turn inside her, causing her to wince in pain before a smile of joy settled upon her face. She was sure he was listening.

Hannah put up no argument as to which rabbi would perform the circumcision. Elkanah was adamant in his refusal to allow the senior rabbi of their village near the child; the same one who had insinuated years ago that Hannah was in disfavor with Yahweh because she was unable to have a child. Hannah secretly enjoyed her husband's sweet revenge against him. The older rabbi would be present for the ceremony, yet sidelined as an observer forced to watch as a younger rabbi led the service. Hannah did encourage her husband, for propriety's sake, to allow the senior rabbi to have some role in the ceremony.

"He can ask for the name of the child, that he can say. But he pronounces no blessings, and he's to go nowhere near my son's manhood with his flint knife."

That was Elkanah's only concession and his only directive.

The hard-faced, old rabbi could stand in the corner wearing his hurt feelings and stern theology on the sleeve of his robe.

"I wait for Thy salvation, O Lord." The young rabbi took the child from Hannah, placing him on a cloth-covered pedestal.

Hannah slipped around behind Elkanah sitting in a chair beside the pedestal.

"Great are Thy compassions, O Lord. Quicken me as Thou art wont. I rejoice at Thy word as one that findeth great spoil. I have hoped for Thy salvation, O Lord. And have done Thy commandments."

When the rabbi finished his blessing, he picked up the child and laid him upon the cushion in Elkanah's lap, a cushion Hannah had made just for this occasion.

"Happy is the man who Thou choosest and bringest near that he may dwell in Thy courts." The young Rabbi waved his hands to the congregation for their response.

"May we be satisfied with the goodness of Thy house, the holy place of Thy Temple."

After the response from the people, the rabbi dipped his hands in a laver of water and raised them to the Almighty. "Blessed art Thou, O Lord our God, King of the Universe, who hast sanctified us by Thy commandments, and enjoined us to perform the commandment of circumcision."

Hannah gripped her husband's forearms to steady him when he stood, bearing the child upon the cushion. Together they approached the pedestal. This was their son, eleven years in the making, Yahweh's gift to them...a gift the Almighty would reclaim.

The child gave a short cry as the quick operation was performed, but the moment Hannah clasped her warm hands around his tiny feet, he began to calm.

When it was time for Elkanah to pray, he paused to compose himself. He looked into Hannah's eyes and laid his hand upon the boy's head. There had been no guarantee of this blessing, only the hope, and now they touched with their hands this visible, human soul of Yahweh's favor. Hannah smiled and nodded for her husband to begin his prayer.

"Blessed art Thou who hast sanctified us by Thy commandments and hast enjoined us to make him enter into the covenant of Abraham our father."

That was the cue for the old rabbi. He stepped out of the corner where he had been placed and gave Elkanah a self-satisfied expression before he spoke.

"And what name shall be given this child?"

Once he asked the question, the old rabbi stepped back into his designated spot in the shadows, driven more by Elkanah's glaring eyes than by the completion of his duty.

"His name shall be called Samuel."

Hannah had asked of Yahweh, had begged and pleaded with the Almighty. Her soul had writhed before Yahweh—and Yahweh had heard ultimately...perfectly. She had chosen his name, "God has heard."

Hannah folded the blanket over her son's nakedness then scooped him into her arms before the young rabbi uttered the final prayer.

"Our God and God of our fathers, preserve this child to his father and mother, and let his name be called in Israel 'Samuel, the son of Elkanah.' Let the father rejoice in him that came forth from his loins, and let the mother be glad in the fruit of her womb; as it is written, 'O give thanks unto the Lord, for He is good, for His mercy endureth forever.' And now let the child named 'Samuel' increase in greatness."

Hannah begged off going with the family that first year to the Festival of Tabernacles—the child was just a baby; the journey would be too strenuous. Or the year after that: the child was not yet weaned. Or the year after that: the child was still too young. On the morning the family left for Shiloh without them, Hannah held Samuel's little hand as they stood in the courtyard of the dwellings and waved good-bye to Elkanah and the departing caravan of wagons. Hannah looked into her son's worried face, knowing he could not understand why his abba and his siblings and Mushi—all of them—were leaving without them. Hannah patted his head and assured him they would return.

"Next year we shall all go together."

When Samuel's lip began to quiver Hannah knew this promise of next year was insufficient. She knew that her son was beginning to understand the uncertainty of parting, the pain of seeing someone leave him behind and not understanding if they might ever return or if he might ever see them again.

"Come, let's go to our special tree on top of the hill."

Samuel reached up for his mother to take him into her arms.

"No, you are old enough to walk on your own two legs."

It was time now for her to explain. The inevitability of fulfilling her vow could no longer be avoided, and while the physical weaning was nearing an end, she needed to begin preparing her son and her own heart for the hard truth of separation. She had waited until this moment to have this conversation. Who could blame her? She did not know when would be the proper time to begin the emotional weaning of mother and son, but the boy's inability to understand why he and his mother had been left behind by the family seemed as good a time as any.

Certainly, Hannah had spoken of Yahweh to Samuel even before he was born, and afterward, she had told him stories of how she had implored Yahweh's favor for a child, and Yahweh had blessed her with a son, this tiny salvation. An affectionate kiss on his forehead always followed this story to assure him that he was the promised child Yahweh had given to her.

As she nursed him she often repeated his name, "You are my asking. You are Samuel. I asked Yahweh for you, and He heard." At night as she rocked her son asleep in his cradle, she sang to him of what she imagined Yahweh's call might be for his life. Would he be a great rabbi, a great scholar and teacher of the Law, a great judge, a great prophet? In the end, Yahweh would determine her son's gift and task. She had only to fulfill her vow to release him. Before his conception, he had been given to Yahweh, and soon the handing over would be complete.

No sooner had they entered the olive grove did Samuel bolt toward the tree. Mushi had a stool constructed for Samuel to stand on to help him reach that first branch. He bounced from the stool onto the branch, then swung his legs up and over it.

"Look, Ima." Samuel was pleased to have made the branch in one attempt.

"You are growing so. It won't be long before you will not need the stool."

Hannah gasped. The words caught in her mouth. The boy was growing, growing too fast. These playful moments would soon come to an end. The vow was beginning its slow process of consumption, and the explanation must begin. But how did one prepare a child to say farewell to his ima at such a tender age? How did you tell a child that you were giving him to Yahweh, the Almighty? How did she tell her son that a vow was made with the Creator of heaven and earth, the One who had kept His side of the bargain and now awaited fulfillment from the other party?

"Do you know why Abba and the family went to Shiloh?"

"Why?"

"To worship Yahweh, the God of Israel."

"The Yah you tell me about?"

Hannah watched Samuel reach for the next branch on the tree and begin to pull himself up.

"Yes. He is the God of our people. There is no other God but Yahweh. There is no one like Yahweh. He is holy. He is the Almighty. He is the Creator of heaven and earth. He loves and protects His people."

"Yah loves me, Ima?" Samuel was out of breath from the exertion. He perched on the second branch to catch his breath. He wiped the sweat off his face and smudged his cheeks with crumbs of tree bark and grime. Hannah would have immediately wiped away the residue from his face, but she was not within reach.

"That is high enough. Now I want you to jump to me from the first branch." Hannah raised her arms to Samuel as she approached the tree. She could see the fear begin to surface in his eyes at her request, a request she had never made of him.

"Drop your feet onto the first branch while you hold the branch you are sitting on. You will be fine."

She watched Samuel's gradual obedience as he leaned forward and gripped the branch he sat on and then slowly dropped his feet onto the branch below. The ascent had been daring. The descent more cautious.

"Now turn around and face me."

"Ima?" Samuel hesitated.

Hannah knew he was doubtful of her command.

"You will not fall." Hannah's surety gave her son the confidence to turn.

Once he had made the half-turn, Hannah positioned herself right below him.

"Jump, Samuel. Jump into my arms." She nodded her head for him to know that she was ready to catch him. Their eyes were completely locked together. Hannah saw the strength in her son's sweet face begin to wain and his little legs begin to tremble. "Do not be afraid."

With a pinched cry, Samuel dropped into his mother's arms. It was more of a fall then a leap.

Hannah caught her son and pressed him so tightly that his trembling became her trembling. She held the back of his head.

"I jump, Ima. Tell Abba."

"We will tell Abba how brave you are."

Samuel leaned back in Hannah's arms and saw the tears in his mother's eyes. "Ima crying."

"You asked me if Yahweh loves you." Hannah ignored Samuel's comment on the state of her eyes, and though he nodded his head in response, Hannah knew he was perplexed by her words. "He does love you. You are Yahweh's child. And He loves you enough to ask you to do hard things sometimes, and then holds out His arms to catch us when we fall. Yahweh has set the foundation of the world, and He will guard the feet of His people who walk upon it. You must always trust Yahweh, always love Him. You are a gift from Yahweh, Yahweh's special gift to me. What Yahweh does with you, with us, will be wondrous, beyond our understanding. And we will never be the same."

These words poured out of her unrestrained and unexpected. She knew this was too much for her son to bear. It was too much for her, and she hurriedly began walking out of the olive grove. Samuel made no attempt to wiggle out of her embrace as she made her way down the hill toward the family dwelling. She wanted to carry him, and she knew her son wanted to be carried.

The following year flew by, and Hannah devoted much of her time to reinforcing her conviction that Yahweh—the Lord of Hosts, the Almighty, the Creator of heaven and earth—was a God who loved His people, who heard their cries and saw their afflictions, as He had heard her cries and saw her affliction and was moved with compassion to act on behalf of His people and His maidservant. There was a cost, a cost that neither she nor her son realized the value of its price. Her focus had been to prepare for the eventual parting. All Hannah knew to do was to speak well of Yahweh in the presence of her son and to encourage Samuel to love the Almighty with all his heart and soul. That belief would sustain him when everything else would fail.

Samuel tried stuffing clothing and food into the travel bags, but his mother seemed unhappy with everything he was doing to be helpful. She was not this way most of the time, except when she was upset with the other mother or his brothers and sisters. He ended up being sent to bed. He had begged to stay up all night to be sure they did not accidentally leave him behind, but his mother assured him that would never happen. In the last few days, Samuel had noticed that Abba and Ima did not speak much to each other. They did not hug each other, and they did not smile. He was sure that it had something to do with taking this trip to see Yahweh that had caused them to be mad. But he could not understand this because his mother always said nice things about Yahweh, singing to him about Yahweh, preparing him to meet Yahweh, telling Samuel that he was special to Yahweh. The family was always happy about going to the place where Yahweh lived, and this would be his first time to get to go. He was excited to meet Yahweh, so why weren't Abba and Ima? And why weren't the rest of the family going with them like they always did?

His mother insisted he kiss her before going to bed, tapping her right cheek with her finger as if he stopped kissing her long ago and had forgotten where to place his lips. He always kissed her good night, and on the same side of her face. How could he forget? But this time she hugged him a little harder and a little longer than usual. And when he walked in front of his father toward his bedroom, instead of the expected tussle of his hair, he was scooped up into his abba's arms and squeezed with as much fervor as Ima had used. His going to see Yahweh for the first time must have made them act in this strange way, which only raised the level of anxiety in his little heart.

He lay still in his bed, eyes adjusting to the shadows and shapes in the darkness of his room, and listened to the edgy voices of his parents. Samuel saw the light spilling in around the base of the heavy curtain separating his bedroom from the common room. He could see shadows moving about from the common room and hear footsteps and the sound of packing supplies for the trip. He rose and crept to the entrance of his bedroom.

Hannah paused in wrapping the loaves of flat bread and putting them into sacks when she looked up and saw Elkanah with his ear cocked toward Samuel's room, listening for any physical sign of sleeplessness.

"You saw how agitated Samuel was when you sent him to bed." Elkanah stepped back into the center of the room.

Hannah did not respond, but resumed her focus on covering loaves of flat bread in cloth and putting them into sacks.

"You can't be happy with this decision."

"We've been over this. Over and over."

Elkanah was silent. Hannah sensed he was watching her mechanical movements.

"You are packing enough food and clothing as if the whole family was going to the Feast, like the days when we went for the week."

"I don't know what they will feed him." Hannah's hands were aching from the repetition of wrapping food and she lay them in her lap. "I don't want him to be hungry."

"We never thought through the consequences. We never even discussed the possibility that our minds could change, that we...that you might feel differently when it came time for us to take this journey."

"It was a vow. I made a vow."

"Made impulsively...under duress."

"I was not under duress. No one forced me."

"Then you just did it without thinking."

"Perhaps I wasn't thinking how much I would come to love my son or grow more in love with his father, or if I really believed my prayer would be answered after all those years of waiting, or how conflicted I would feel, or face the unimaginable thought of what our lives will be like once...once we..."

Hannah could not finish. Her mouth was open but a sob replaced the words, and she put her wrist to her lips to contain the groan rising in her throat.

Hannah saw Elkanah open his hands in deference to her attempting to stifle her sob before he stepped back toward Samuel's bedroom and listened. They heard no sound. She suddenly realized this was what it would be like when they returned home. There would be no sound coming from his room, no boisterous wrestling with his father before bedtime, no more multiple openings of the thick curtain to look in on her sleeping child.

"Have you told him what is going to happen to him?"

Hannah heard the unnatural strain in his voice as he turned back into the room.

"Have you explained to him...?"

Hannah cut him off by violently shaking her head and pressing her wrist harder against her mouth, holding back waves of grief. Her grief was blinding, worse than the grief she experienced in ten years of barrenness. This answered prayer felt more like a punishment than a blessing from the Almighty. A vow she was forced to keep and would regret the rest of her life. A vow that had become a curse. A vow that would age her quicker than the natural ravages of time. The sleeve of her gown was soaked with saliva and tears when she took it away from her mouth.

"I have explained to him that he is a child of Yahweh." Her mind was unable to comprehend the meaning of those words.

"Isn't every child a child of Yahweh?"

Hannah nodded, her hands now covering her face.

"You don't see anyone else giving their child to Yahweh. No one is sending their sons to the Tabernacle just after they've learned to feed themselves or barely stopped wetting the bed. What are people going to say when we don't come back with our son? What kind of monsters are we? How could we thrust aside our child like that?"

Hannah knew the gossip in the village would be vicious. What kind of a woman went to such lengths to have a child and then abandoned him the moment he was weaned? And why now? Couldn't she wait until he was older? She was a terrible human being. No, she was not even human. The Evil One had taken possession of her heart. This was worse than when the Destroyer took the firstborn in Egypt. Pure malevolence, there was no other explanation. Elkanah should send her away before she did something harmful to his other children. Fulfilling a vow to Yahweh? Who would believe she was motivated by love for Yahweh? Was there any chance of a reprieve from this dreadful vow? She could not go through with it. At the last minute her mind would change.

"We must talk to the rabbi. Somewhere in Mosaic Law there must be a way out, an escape clause, some sacrifice or offering we can make instead, some way to appease Yahweh and your conscience."

"It is not my conscience that is in conflict. It is my heart."

"There must be some way we can keep the boy at home."

"Not if I am to remain faithful to my vow."

"Do you realize who is to take charge of our boy: a half-blind old man and his wicked sons? Do you know that at last year's Feast, Hophni and Phinehas had their own stable of prostitutes parading in front of the entrance to the Tabernacle. They've gone so far as to purchase their own brothel on the street right in front of the Tabernacle. They sacrifice and pray during the day and whore at night. And where do they get their shekels? From the treasury of the Tabernacle. Our yearly tithes and the gouging prices they exact for sacrifices. They don't have real jobs to make their own shekels. They take my shekels. The shekels of Israel pay for their whores, and their father does nothing. Is that who you want to take charge of our son?"

Hannah felt an arrow pierce her heart. Was this a warning to her? A sign that the penalty of her vow would destroy her son, her marriage, her very life? She took a few deep breaths to calm her heart. She placed her hands upon her chest as if to push the arrow out the other side of her heart.

"I am not giving my son, our son, to Eli or his two horrible sons. I am giving him to Yahweh the Almighty."

"Since when has Yahweh been in the child-rearing business? Since when did the Almighty feed our son or make his clothes or teach him to walk or comfort him in the middle of the night when he wakes from a bad dream? Why doesn't Yahweh just get rid of the evil that's in His house? Why does He have to take my son?"

"Maybe, just maybe, that is what the Almighty is doing, beginning to rid His house of evil and replacing it with something good."

She could only hope that her words were one clear message that made Elkanah think. Could her husband hear its potential truth, attach his fears to it and release the life and soul of his son to the will of the invisible Almighty?

"If Hophni and Phinehas grieve my son in any way—if they try to lead him astray—if they so much as look at him cross-eyed, I will disembowel them and throw their severed parts on the altar. And I will laugh while their little members burn in the fire...that's the sacrifice I would be happy to make."

Hannah saw her husband extend his hand toward heaven as if to give Yahweh a physical sign of his promise to not hesitate to carry out this judgment. It caught Hannah by surprise. Her eyes widened and she held her breath, waiting for him to move or speak to break the silence. Hannah covered her mouth again, but this time to stifle her amusement. She watched Elkanah lower his arm, and he too began to chuckle. She waved for him to be quiet, pointing toward Samuel's bedroom. Hannah was grateful for this shift in mood, and she began to feel a softening of her features.

Samuel stood still behind the curtain of his room for fear his parents might find him out of bed listening to their quarrel. Why were they fighting? What had he done? He did not want to go to the city where Yahweh lived if this is what it did to his ima and abba. He did not want to meet Yahweh if Ima and Abba were going to quarrel. He crawled back into bed and pulled his blanket over his head. If he just went to sleep then what he had heard would come to nothing. This is what happened in the world of the big-people, never in the world of a child, never in his world. Whatever Ima and Abba were talking about, it had nothing to do with him. He would wake in the morning and everyone would be happy again.

Hannah did not argue with Elkanah when he made the decision that the rest of the family would stay home. She let him make all the arrangements and decisions. This trip would not be their traditional holiday to celebrate the Feast of Tabernacles. It was a mission. They would arrive a few days ahead of the official opening of the festival before the city swarmed with merchants and pilgrims. There was no pitching a family tent, or decorating it, or staying to enjoy the week-long festivities. He and Hannah would go to the Tabernacle, fulfill her vow, and depart. Her husband saw to everything. She only had to think of what she had done and what she was about to do.

Hannah held onto the back of Samuel's garment as the boy gripped the wooden guard on the back of the wagon. The tailgate was locked in place, but Samuel could still see over it and potentially bounce out should the wagon hit a large rut in the road. Protective as always, Hannah kept a tight grip on his garment. Elkanah rode his stallion ahead of them while Mushi drove the wagon with three bulls tied to the back lumbering behind it. Hannah allowed her son to hop around on the cushions and blankets inside the wagon, but the last thing she wanted was for him to accidentally fall out of the back and be trampled by the bulls. Her offering to Yahweh would be unblemished.

There was a joyful boisterousness about her son. After all, her over-excited child was seeing the wide world for the first time. And he had an inquisitive spirit about the nature of Yahweh. She knew his energy would soon be channeled in service to Yahweh, and the scope of his mental imagery would begin to be filled with the wonder of Yahweh. In her little boy's mind, Hannah knew her son was anticipating an encounter with Yahweh. She had always tried to steer her son's imagination toward Yahweh in their conversations, but now her son's jabbering slew of questions were difficult for her to answer. Where does Yahweh live? What is a Tabernacle? What does sacrifice mean? Will we see Yahweh at the Tabernacle? Was Yahweh scary or nice? Could he touch Yahweh?

And the one question that most often broke her heart: Why do you always call me "Yahweh's child?"

On this bumpy ride to Shiloh, on this mission to the house of Yahweh to leave "Yahweh's child," the mother of "Yahweh's child" struggled to answer all the questions of the young boy. She would keep her promise and fulfill her vow, but the worst fear she harbored was what would Samuel think of her when he was older? Might he resent her for the choice she made?

This vow was her idea, not his father's, not his. What would he think of his mother when he came of age and realized what she had done? Would he ever understand the bargain she had struck with the Almighty? She prayed for the ten-thousandth time that she would live long enough to see the heart of "Yahweh's child" come to a place of peace and accept the risk she took by making this vow with his life.

Once they arrived in Shiloh, Elkanah guided them to a stable and had Mushi tend to the mules and his horse. He wanted them well fed and watered and ready to depart once they returned from the Tabernacle. Elkanah hired the stable keeper's two sons to lead the three bulls straight to the Tabernacle, along with a bushel of meal and skins of wine, so the priests could have them ready to be sacrificed when the family arrived. Two of the bulls were for the sin and peace offerings, but the third was to be offered for his son's dedication. It was a double sacrifice; a bull and his son given to the Almighty. He could not allow himself to ponder what this meant. He remained focused on the details, the actions required to accomplish the mission. If he paused even for a moment then his heart would overwhelm him.

Elkanah hustled his family through the city center past the stage with a giant arch behind it that would be soon festooned in colorful fabrics and flowers. Elkanah saw his son's wide-eyed stare at the sights and sounds and bustling crowd. He did not scold or explain, but pulled him closer to his side as they marched toward the Tabernacle.

When they moved past the brothels in front of the entrance to the Tabernacle, Elkanah scooped his son into his arms, cupped the back of his head, and pressed his face into his chest. While his son was still in his care, he would not allow his innocent eyes to register the images of such blatant perversion flaunted in front of the entrance into the house of Yahweh.

During the sacrifice of bulls, Elkanah and Hannah squeezed their son between them, keeping a safe distance from the heat and light of the conflagration. Elkanah felt his son dig his face into his side like a burrowing mole. He had to peel Samuel from his side and hand him over to his mother before he could walk up the stairs of the portico to where Eli slouched in his luxuriant chair, gazing out over the outer courtyard with Hophni and Phinehas flanked behind their father.

With each step Elkanah felt pressure rising in his chest. He struggled to form the words in the ear of the Levite guard, requesting an audience with the High Priest. These were his assignments. These were the details he had to carry out. And it was beginning to skin the flesh of his soul.

He waited for the guard to deliver the request, and when Eli waved for Elkanah to approach, he turned to his wife and son. Elkanah motioned for Hannah to join him. When Elkanah heard Samuel ask his mother if this was Yahweh sitting in front of them, it took everything within him to keep from scooping his wife and son into his arms and racing out of the Tabernacle.

Yahweh could hold this against him. He would accept the consequences. He would buy every bull in the market and sacrifice them if it would make Yahweh happy. He would lose all he possessed to keep his family together. How could he go through with this? There had to be another way. But when he looked into the stone-cut yet tender face of his wife coming up the steps with their son clutching her side, he knew there was no turning back. The course was set for "Yahweh's child" to be given to Yahweh.

Eli remembered Hannah the moment she began to explain her purpose. He remembered the woman who had prayed so intently in the Tabernacle years ago. He recognized the tone and timber of her speech, the same quality of humility. It was she whom he mistakenly thought her fervent praying was an excess of wine. It was she whom he had hoped might return to the Tabernacle. He reached behind the breastplate for the pouch containing the sacred stones and inched forward in his seat.

"I have been waiting. I have been waiting. My dear woman, I have been waiting for you to return."

His voice filled with a heaving rasp, a floating awareness that what he had felt years ago was returning. As he rose from his seat the warmth from the sacred stones once again warmed his hands.

"I believed Yahweh...I knew in my heart...I knew that someday, somehow you would return. I knew, and now I know."

But what did Eli know? What had he been waiting for? A child? Hannah's child? What was Yahweh communicating to him?

"Is the boy the answer to your prayer to the Almighty?" Eli released his hold of the pouch and pulled his hands from behind the breastplate of precious stones. He uncurled his heated fingers and stretched both hands toward Yahweh's answered prayer.

The woman nodded, and then she turned Samuel to face Eli so the High Priest and the child could get a better look at one another.

The boy turned his inquisitive eyes back toward his mother.

"Ima, is this Yahweh?"

Hannah knelt behind her son and gripped his shoulders. Mother and son faced the High Priest. Then she spoke into his ear.

"Listen to me, my son. Hear with your heart and mind what I am about to say to Yahweh, the Almighty. My prayer is for you. My praise is for Yahweh. These words I speak are from the heart. Yahweh looks upon the heart. Yahweh knows the heart. Listen now to the words of my heart. And know that from this day on, you are for Yahweh and Yahweh is for you."

This was the passing of the gift. This was the giving back to the One who gave. This was the sacred completion of her sacred vow. What she had fervently prayed for so long ago would now be offered to the Almighty with the passion of gratitude. She rose to her feet and stood behind her son, hands clutching his little shoulders, her body flushed with strength she had never experienced, and the words poured from her lips.

"My heart exults in Yahweh. My power is lifted in praise to Yahweh. My lips speak of Yahweh's deliverance over my enemies. There is no one holy as the Lord Almighty. There is no one besides Yahweh, no Rock like Yahweh. Do not be proud. Do not boast. For Yahweh is the Lord of all knowledge and He weighs the actions of us all."

Hannah watched Eli raise his arms to heaven, his face luminous with awe. She continued her adulation of the Almighty.

"The strength of the mighty is broken, yet those who stumble will find strength. Those who are full will go hungry, yet those who are hungry will hunger no more. The one who was barren will bare seven children yet the one who has many sons will languish. Yahweh brings life and death, the grave and resurrection. Poverty and wealth are sent by Yahweh. He humbles and He exalts. The poor and needy He raises from the dust of the earth, from the ash pit, and makes them sit with princes on thrones of glory. Who can do this but Yahweh who created the pillars of the earth and set the world upon them? It is Yahweh who guards the feet of His holy ones, but the wicked shall be silenced in darkness."

Hannah saw the quick reaction from the sons of Eli by her prophetic affront calling out their wickedness. Yet she gained strength from their dismay and anger. She would not grow weak or feeble in this moment but continue speaking. Her words were no sanctioned blessing, no designated priestly prayer. Her words bit down on the claws of wickedness. The claws of the sons of Eli. She wanted to assure them that Yahweh was placing her child, Yahweh's child, in their midst, and there would be a reckoning if any harm were to come to him.

When the sons motioned for the guards to remove them, Hannah would not be moved. Nor would her husband who raised a threatening arm to the advancing guards. Nor would her son who stiffened his shoulders beneath her grip.

Hannah's final words broke like thunder in the ears of those poised to harm her. "The force of man shall not prevail. Yahweh will shatter those who oppose Him. Against them will Yahweh thunder in heaven and the ends of the earth will be judged. Yahweh will give strength to His king. Yahweh will exalt the horn of His anointed."

Hannah suddenly felt weightless. The words had been spoken and all the strength flooded out of her. She did not know if she had fainted or a gust of wind had lifted her off her feet, but she found herself floating above her son. There seemed to be a tumult of bodies and shouting around her, their actions slowed down, their words spoken in muffled roars. She looked into the astonished eyes of the High Priest who broke through this thickened dimension to say, "Your son shall be safe with me."

Hannah reached out her weak arm toward her son and saw Eli place his hands upon Samuel's head to keep the boy from turning. She felt the firm arms of her husband carry her away. It was as though she was floating above the courtyard, an observer of all actions, unable to participate any longer in this incomparable moment. Her role complete.

Hannah became rigid the instant she heard Samuel wail. The mother knew her son sensed she was leaving without him. The mother knew the screams of her terrified child, and his cries echoing above the noise in the courtyard were a sudden threat to her vow. What had she done? What was she doing? What madness was this? If she wrested free from her husband's strong arms, if her feet touched the ground, if she looked back at her son she knew she would defy Yahweh and race to liberate him. But she had no strength against the vow. The vow was unyielding. The vow had been spoken and acted upon. The vow was a living thing with a power of its own.

Inside the firm hold of her husband's arms, she looked into heaven as they passed out of the entrance of the Tabernacle and cried out, "Into your hands, Almighty. Into your hands. Your child now. Your child."

PART TWO

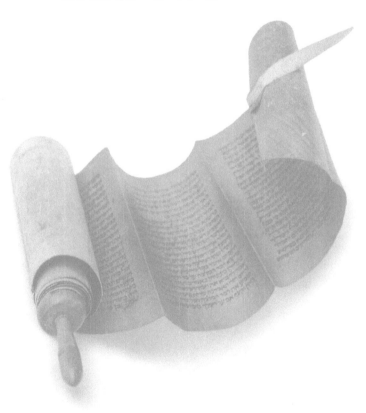

Four

SAMUEL SEPARATED THE DISINTEGRATING BONES AND SPENT coals from the burning embers with his rake. This was all that remained of the sacrifice he had placed on the golden altar from the night before. Samuel volunteered for this job when a fellow Levite had gotten ill and been unable to perform his duty to keep the sacral fire burning throughout the night.

The air inside the Holy Place was heavy with wispy curls of incense and charred animal fat. Candle smoke formed transparent clouds on the curtained ceiling before soaking into the layers of wool, linen, camel's hair, and animal skins sheltering the hallowed space from the weather and climate. Together, it all concealed the sanctity of the Almighty from the impious eyes of the curious. The smoke had no chance of seeping out into the environment. Rather, it was absorbed and distilled into an atmosphere of holiness.

Samuel scooped out the bones and ash, dumping the consecrated waste into a bronze basin at the foot of the altar. He brushed away the ash that floated onto the ephod, which was draped over his shoulders and tied with a sash around his linen robe, before spreading the cooling cinders along the edges of the altar and pushing the hot embers into a pile in the center. He stacked the new wood in a circle around the embers and then cast his eyes around the sanctuary. The other young Levites were engaged in changing out the candlesticks on the lamp stand and replacing the twelve cakes of unleavened bread with fresh ones. A few priests were facing in his direction but were on their knees, heads bowed and eyes closed in prayer. Samuel positioned himself between the altar and his fellow Levites. He faced the curtains embroidered with angelic creatures sewn into the front and hanging behind the majestic columns separating him from the Most Holy Place. How artisans, in the middle of the desert, could create such beauty so long ago was a marvel to him.

But it was what the curtains concealed to be the true beauty of Yahweh, a beauty so holy and glorious that to behold it could cause instant death. The great prophet Moses had asked to see the beauty of Yahweh, but for this to happen, the Almighty had to protect the prophet. He placed him inside a cleft in the rock and shielded the prophet's eyes with His hand so that the prophet did not see the face of Yahweh as the glory of the Creator passed by.

Behind those curtains, once a year the High Priest would enter the Holy of Holies; once a year the High Priest took his life into his hands when he parted the veil and approached the Almighty to sprinkle the sacrificial blood of the scapegoat upon the top of the Ark of the Covenant where Yahweh sat enthroned between two golden-winged Cherubim. Eli confessed to Samuel that he had never seen any sign of Yahweh on his yearly foray into the Holy of Holies, nor did he ever want to meet the Almighty face-to-face. That was in the early days of our fathers, Eli had said, when the Presence of Yahweh was more visible. He would perform his duties as High Priest, but wanted Yahweh to keep His distance and remain in the past times of the fathers.

Not Samuel. In the fifteen years Samuel had served in the Tabernacle since his arrival, he longed for the Presence. He longed for the sight of Yahweh. He had learned in the sacred writings of the Laws and Blessings that Yahweh knew the name of Moses. Did Yahweh know his name? His mother had boldly asked Yahweh for a son and her pleas and cries were answered. Samuel was the son of the asking, but dare he ask Yahweh to show Himself? To speak to him? Each year when his family came to Shiloh for the annual festival, his mother pulled him aside and asked if he had heard Yahweh speak his name. His answer was always the same. Hannah would not let him be discouraged. "The days of Yahweh's visions and words are rare," she would say. Wait. Be patient.

It was difficult for Samuel to be patient. His young man's heart was always vibrating like a plucked bow string, waiting to see some manifestation of Yahweh—a glimpse of the glory the prophet Moses beheld in the safety of the rocky sanctuary. Samuel believed that one day he would be the one to enter the Holy of Holies to represent the nation of Israel before Yahweh, and sprinkle the blood on the Mercy Seat. Perhaps then the Creator of heaven and earth would speak his name. Perhaps then Yahweh would cover Samuel's face with His hand and pass over him. He trembled at the prospect of his fulfilled hope.

Samuel looked back over his shoulder. No one paid him any attention. He tilted his head covering back before leaning over the altar. Through his pursed lips he funneled a stream of air onto the coals. He filled his lungs again, and his second breath sparked the wood shavings, inspiring them to catch fire.

From the flow of his breath, he began his prayer, his secret moment with Yahweh. A private prayer taken from the traditional chants, his own words to draw him closer to the Presence, closer to the Divine Name, a Name unspeakable, a presence just beyond the veil.

"Blessed are you, Yahweh, our God, King of the universe," he said, his quiet voice low enough to attract only the attention of Yahweh. "You are holy. You can only abide in holiness. I am not worthy to speak your Divine Name. I am not worthy to be in your Tabernacle. Sanctify me in the divine lights. Sanctify me so that I might be your servant. Burn your holiness within me. Purify my soul in your divine flame. Divide the light and darkness within my heart and fill me with the abundance of your faithfulness. Speak my name, O Lord, that my tongue may speak of your glory."

He blew another breath beneath the layers of cut wood, and his face began to sting from the heat of the ignited flames. He had to turn aside to keep from burning his skin, but his heart felt as though it had become pure spirit.

Eli stood just inside the entrance of the Holy Place of the Tabernacle, quietly observing the Levites carrying out their routine duties while other priests prayed. When his eyes caught sight of Samuel leaning over the golden altar, his face brightened. This young man, always reliable, always busy about the Tabernacle, a star student in the Levitical studies, never complained about menial tasks. Eli had taken Samuel under his wing at such a young age. He had promised Samuel's parents that he would be safe under his care. Such a boisterous boy, Eli thought it would be difficult for him to adjust, but after the initial shock of being left by his parents at the Tabernacle subsided, and once the boy learned to read and write, he naturally took to the life of a young Levite in service to Yahweh. How he had matured these last fifteen years. A smile crossed Eli's lips as he stepped toward his favored student, his wobbly frame balanced by the use of his staff.

"You think blowing on the embers in the direction of the Holy of Holies will get the attention of the Almighty?" Eli kept his voice low so as not to startle Samuel.

"I am sorry, Rabbi." Samuel backed away from the golden altar to make room for the High Priest.

Eli stepped beside the altar and waved his hand above the flames, directing the smoke toward the curtains.

"The Divine Presence...perhaps one day Yahweh will come out from behind the veil." Eli shivered at the thought. "How terrifying that would be."

Eli could see that Samuel's eyes were fixed on the curtain and his body poised as if he might dare to enter the veil.

"Do not be hasty, my son. It is dreadful enough to walk through that veil once a year to sprinkle the blood of the scapegoat." Eli cupped his hand over a puff of smoke and drew it toward his head.

"What is there to fear, my lord? Did not Father Moses stand before the Divine Presence at the burning bush while a shepherd in Midian?"

Eli placed his hand upon the young man's shoulder, amused by the impetuousness of youth. "Yes, my son, and look at the world of troubles that came into his life when he approached and heard the voice of Yahweh. Be cautious about what you hope for."

Samuel lowered his eyes at Eli's mild scold.

"Be patient. In time I will gladly give my job over to you." Eli nodded his head toward the Holy of Holies, indicating he would one day grant Samuel's wish to meet with Yahweh. Eli squeezed Samuel's shoulder and a sharp pain ran up through his arm. He yanked his hand away and winced.

"What is it?" Samuel raised his eyes to the High Priest.

"When you are my age pains appear out of nowhere and for no reason." Eli saw the look of concern on the young man's face and was appreciative. His mind was a scramble of a thousand reasons to explain the quick sting shooting through his arm but chose to blame his age. "Are you done here?"

"I need to put the lamb shank on the altar and dispose of the sacred ash."

"Yes, well, be quick about it. The cock has crowed and the sun is rising."

"I must change as well." Samuel reached toward the lamb shank.

"Change." Eli's face turned into a quizzical frown that halted Samuel's movements.

"My clothes, Rabbi."

Eli saw a lighthearted smile on Samuel's face as though they were playing a child's guessing game. Still, Eli could not guess what Samuel meant.

"Remove my holy garments and change into the common ones to dispose of the sacred ash."

Eli became annoyed, more with himself than with his young charge. How easy it was to forget all the regulations. How easy it was to overlook details that at his age had become irrelevant or inconvenient. How easy it was to slip into complacency when his sons were indifferent to everything about the sanctity of priestly life and sought out only that which brought them personal pleasure or gained them wealth and power. Eli looked at Samuel, the turban on his head and the ephod draped over his shoulders. Beneath the ephod Samuel wore linen leggings and a shirt that reached just above his knees. It was too short and needed to be replaced. He was growing too fast for his wardrobe to keep pace. The sash was tied perfectly around his waist with the knot slightly off center.

It was nearing the time of the Feast of Tabernacles and Eli knew Samuel's family would be traveling to Shiloh, and that his mother would deliver new clothes for her son. Eli knew that the clothes she fashioned each year for her son was always of the finest quality. He had never seen any of Samuel's clothes blemished with mud or dung or stained with blood. Eli often pointed out to the other Levitical students and priests of Samuel's meticulous care with his garments, a commendation that too often brought ridicule for others. Each year when his mother brought him a new set of clothes, Samuel took the old clothes outside the city and burned them.

"Yes, yes, of course." Eli tapped his forehead as if it were a lapse in memory and then began to lumber toward the entrance of the Holy Place.

"Was there something you needed for me to do?"

"Yes." Then Eli paused, realizing that he had spoken impulsively. There was nothing urgent he needed Samuel to do for him. He just wanted the young man's company. He could not explain the unusual circumstances of how Samuel came to the Tabernacle, and at such a young age. But since Samuel's arrival, a peace had settled upon the old man's heart. He felt more confident, more assured that there would be a future for the priesthood as long as Samuel remained. That Yahweh may be silent, but not absent.

"No, my son. No. Just continue with what you are doing." Eli held up a hand by way of blessing the young man, and then shuffled toward the Tabernacle door.

Samuel finished his duties, smoothing out the glowing coals on the altar with his rake, and then picked up the lamb shank off the plate beside the altar, carefully placing it upon the grill-work. The juices began to sizzle the moment the flames touched the fresh meat and Samuel began to salivate. Did Yahweh's mouth ever water when inhaling the aroma of the cooking meat?

Samuel held the basin of sacred residue away from his body, careful to keep the ashes from flying up into the air or settling onto his garments as he made his way to the front of the Holy Place. He had to change his clothes in the chambers adjacent to the Holy Place where the Levites stored the priestly robes they wore to perform their Tabernacle duties before he could dispose of the contents of the basin. He could hear Eli in heated argument as he made his way out of the entrance of the changing room. When Samuel emerged into the sunlight he saw Eli on the portico blocking Hophni and Phinehas with his staff, struggling to keep them from entering the Holy Place.

"You cannot enter." Eli was trying to push his sons back down the steps.

Samuel had witnessed his share of confrontations between Eli and his sons. These types of incidences were becoming more commonplace, and recently, more public. Samuel had always been hesitant to interfere, but his heart was struck with pity toward the High Priest. Enough was enough.

There was never a reason for these reprobates to attack their father, and certainly not in plain sight of the whole courtyard. The commotion was drawing everyone's attention.

Samuel rushed over and stood beside the High Priest. The sons stood on the steps below their father, both with a firm grip on Eli's staff. They toyed with him and pulled on the staff, causing Eli to lose his balance and finally crumple to his knees.

"Hophni, Phinehas, please not here. Please stop." Samuel kept his appeal under his breath hoping to keep from making the scene any worse.

"Please, please have mercy, oh Samuel the great and wonderful." Hophni released his hold on the staff and raised his hands in mocking supplication.

Samuel had been the object of the brothers' scorn for some time. When he was younger, he ignored them or just hid from their sight whenever he could. At every opportunity Hophni and Phinehas ridiculed Samuel for the way he had been brought to the Tabernacle years ago, and the prayer his mother had prayed over him. They took his mother's words of warning as a personal attack, and threw them back into his face as the hysterical prattling of a raving woman. It was becoming more and more impossible for Samuel to hold his tongue.

The sons of Eli were not dressed in the garb of priests. Instead of turbans, they wore gilded circlets of naked graven images over their unkempt hair. Instead of white robes they wore multicolored linen costumes. The fronts of their disheveled garments bore the stains of wine and filth. Instead of pious expressions appropriate for someone about to enter the Holy Place, their puffy faces were masks of derision.

Samuel set his legs apart and raised himself to his full height. Allowing for the fact that Eli's sons were a step below him, his straight posture made him appear taller. With a deep breath Samuel expanded his chest, and for the moment he could see that his inflated stance had given the brothers a wide-eyed pause. But then Hophni looked down at Samuel's skinny legs exposed to the world and burst into laughter.

"My, my, how the little brat has grown. His ima must have forgotten to bring her little boy another set of clothes." Both brothers laughed and pointed to Samuel's legs.

When Samuel realized his attempt to intimidate the troublemakers with his puffed up stance had failed, he bent over to help lift Eli to his feet, trying not to spill any of the ash from the basin in the process.

"Samuel the usurper, our father's alleged successor comes to his rescue again." Phinehas grabbed Samuel's arm to keep him from helping his father to his feet. "You are not of the natural line, boy. Stand aside."

Samuel would not easily yield and resisted Phinehas's attempt to push him aside.

"You reek of wine and whores." Eli fought to get back on his feet on his own. "You shouldn't even enter the courtyard let alone the Tabernacle."

"Please Phinehas, we can discuss this somewhere else." Samuel saw that it was best to let go of Eli's arm, and he opened his hand in supplication toward Phinehas.

Phinehas spun around on the steps, raising his voice for all to hear.

"Why not here on the steps of the Tabernacle where everyone can see how the High Priest and this Levitical school boy are preventing the true heirs from entering the Holy Place to perform their duties?"

The crowd in the courtyard stood motionless, none of them sure what to make of this public family squabble. The Tabernacle guards stopped the flow of people from entering the front gates. The Levites around the laver stopped their ceremonial washing. Those at the altar ceased scrubbing the dried blood from its base. Even the sacrificial lambs in their pens stopped bleating and remained still. Those Levites who had finished serving inside the Holy Place and were exiting out the Sanctuary door, froze in place. It was as though the universe had paused to watch.

"No one disputes your rightful place in the priestly line." Samuel put up his hand to stop Phinehas's sudden aggressive advance.

"Rightful place, is it? You speak of a rightful place. What do you know of it?" Phinehas knocked away Samuel's raised hand. "Your parents disposed of you on these very steps with your lips still wet with breast milk. What sort of a mother would do that?"

"You are nothing but a baseborn, cast aside on our doorstep." Hophni spit at Samuel's feet, coating his legs with his curse.

Samuel's limbs went slack and the blood rushed to his head. To be accused of being illegitimate was beyond his comprehension. His mother had pleaded to Yahweh for him. His mother had vowed to Yahweh to return him. His mother had faithfully spoken in favor of Yahweh's gift of him to her: the asked of Yahweh; the heard of Yahweh; the name of Yahweh. His name. Samuel.

And yet hearing these curses, having heard them for years, and looking at the spittle running down his bare legs, drained all his strength from his body. The bronze basin slipped from his fingers, the smoldering ash scattered at his feet as the basin tumbled down the steps of the portico. The shock for Samuel to see the smoke and ash ascending his legs and feel the warmth of the sacred radiance only made the trauma to his heart even worse. It took a moment for the sound of the two brothers' laughter to reach his ears, and when the laughter pierced his momentary deafness, it sent a wrenching shock wave through him.

Samuel collapsed into Eli's arms, forcing the High Priest to drop his staff. The weight of Samuel's limp body was too much for the old man's feeble strength and they fell together onto the portico. Samuel held onto Eli's arms wrapped around him, and through his sobs he heard the High Priest whisper into his ear.

"You are my true son. My true son. You are my true son."

Samuel lay inside the comfort and safety of Eli's arms, and through his tears, he watched Hophni and Phinehas swagger through the stunned crowd, their crony escorts trailing behind, as they made their exit out of the entrance of the courtyard. Samuel's legs lay outstretched along the steps. He wiped his eyes and caught sight of his bare legs covered in spit and ash. His linen robe was also soiled with ash and the sacred embers had singed the material. His ears were ringing. Not with the derisive laughter of the brothers, but with Eli's declaration. Eli had never spoken these words to him. Was this an answer to his prayer? Was the Almighty speaking to him through the High Priest avowing his future? Had Yahweh scorched his clothing with purifying fire, and whispered in his ear of his rightful place?

Five

SAMUEL WAS GROWING WEARY AS HE TRUDGED UP THE MOUNtain. The front part of his robe was shredded and bloody from his constant stumbling over the rocks and falling upon the hard ground. His hands were also covered with grime and blood. He paused on all fours to catch his breath. He tried to swallow but the dust had caked his mouth and throat and he had no saliva to moisten his dry, cracked lips. Why had he not brought a skin of water? He forced himself to his feet and looked out over the landscape below while standing on his unsteady legs. The land was barren. No forests. No cities. No inhabitants or creatures. He looked down at his soiled and bloody clothes. He was wearing the vestments of the High Priest, the attire worn to enter the Holy of Holies. He did not remember clothing himself in these priestly garments. And why would he wear them to climb this mountain?

Looking up the path leading to the top, he saw an outcropping of rocks and the appearance of something bright and burning in the middle of a crevice. The sky was clear blue with no trace of smoke. He stumbled on, over the loose rocks, and as he neared the outcropping there was a rumbling sound like that of a furnace. He felt a consuming heat. His thirst intensified and his strength began to fail, but he lurched onward. Then as he neared the crevice, he heard a voice speak his name. The voice reverberated all around him. The earth shook and the loose rocks began to tumble down the mountain. He was sure he was going to fall, but his feet and legs remained firm. Then he felt a firm hand upon his shoulder, the fingers digging into his skin shaking him.

"Samuel. Samuel, wake up. Wake up."

Samuel awoke with a start. The light from the windows filled the classroom with its brightness. For the moment he was unsure where he was until he looked down at the pile of scrolls scattered on the table and the opened one before him. The light in the clay lamp was burned out and the vessel was empty of oil. He pressed his hands upon the table to stop the spinning in his head.

"Did you sleep here all night?"

Samuel turned and looked into the face of his friend, Eleazar.

"I must have fallen asleep." Samuel wiped his mouth then reached for the clay bowl and drained the water inside it. In spite of the stale, warm taste, the liquid felt soothing as it flowed down his throat.

"I thought you would return to our room before I went to bed, but I could not stay awake." Eleazar patted Samuel's shoulder and went to open the last remaining windows along the southern side of the academy building to let in as much light as possible.

Samuel rubbed his eyes before he focused them upon his friend. Even though he and Samuel were close to the same age, Eleazar had not come to Shiloh until a few years ago. His father, Abinadab, was a Levite from the village of Kiriath-Jearim. Eleazar had come with Abinadab for his father's time of Levitical service. Eleazar came as an apprentice to learn the services of the Tabernacle and also to study the scrolls of the Laws and Blessings of Moses. Samuel had befriended Eleazar during his apprenticeship, and Eleazar decided to stay behind after his father returned to the village.

Eleazar was lanky and tall, like Samuel. He had a plumage of curly dark hair, and his olive face was covered with a rash of brown splotches. He had a natural ear for music and could sing the dedicated songs of worship and praise with a power and grace that entranced those who listened. Samuel would often slip into the musician's room to listen to the chorus of Levites rehearsing sacred songs, but it was really to listen to his friend's beautiful singing.

"It must be nearing time for class." Samuel covered his mouth to conceal a ferocious yawn. "And I'm starving."

"You do not have time to eat. The High Priest sent me ahead to open the room. He could not find you, so he is leading the other students from the barracks here."

"Ah yes. He will be upset with me."

"That is doubtful." Eleazar propped the last window open with a wooden rod. "The High Priest is never upset with his star pupil." Eleazar could not help but mimic Eli's whistling voice with his last statement.

Samuel smiled at his friend's impression of the High Priest. "You sound exactly like him."

"What are you studying?" Eleazar walked back to where Samuel was sitting and looked down at the open scroll.

"Stories of the judges. After the conquest came the occupation of the land of Promise, and few judges were worthy of the people's trust, not to mention Yahweh."

"Much like today." Eleazar tapped his finger on the open scroll.

"Please, Eleazar." Samuel spread his arms over the scroll as if to protect it.

"Tell me it is different now. Tell me our leaders devote themselves to Yahweh and the Laws and Blessings. Tell me Yahweh is pleased with His people and her leadership. Nothing has changed, Samuel."

Samuel felt Eleazar's eyes burning into his soul. Samuel did not avert his eyes from his friend's combustive glare, but he did not want to encourage the direction he knew Eleazar would take if Samuel responded to this incitement of thought. Eleazar was as studious as Samuel, but he was always asking Samuel for answers and understanding to difficult passages in the writings of Moses. Samuel knew Eleazar looked up to him, as did many of the younger Levites, but Samuel knew in his heart that he was not in a position to be leading any sort of challenge against the religious authorities.

"I agree with you, Eleazar, but it is not my place to—"

"To do what? Nothing? Watch in silence? Sit in silence?" Eleazar shook his head in dismay. "The sons of Eli might as well be the sons of Belial for all they are worth. And their father is as worthless as they."

"Eleazar, please do not speak ill of the High Priest."

"The High Priest's sons use their sacred office to steal, extort, and whore. They know nothing of Yahweh, and yet they carry out their priestly duties as if Yahweh was turning a blind eye, or worse, approved of their actions."

"Eleazar, I just woke up. I have had nothing to eat. My head was about to stop spinning and then you start." Samuel looked in the bowl, hoping for a final drop of water, but found it dry. He watched Eleazar walk back to the open windows and look out.

"How long have you been here, Samuel? In Shiloh, in service to the Tabernacle?" Eleazar kept staring out the window, not looking back at Samuel.

"It feels as though since before I was born. It was in the courtyard of the Tabernacle that my mother made her vow to Yahweh that I should be His. And then...and then my world turned over at the age of four when my parents left me here." Samuel still had trouble remembering that moment. His hands began to tremble, and he placed them under the table and clasped his fingers together.

"I have been here three years, and I came when I was in my fifteenth year, well after pleasant years of growing up, long enough to know I did not want to live at home."

"I never had that choice. My life has been bound to the vow." Samuel lay his forehead on the edge of the table and closed his eyes.

"I cannot imagine all that you have witnessed in that time. I cannot imagine that your heart is not stirred up after all these years, that you do not come against the immoral priests, that Yahweh has not—"

"Not what, Eleazar? Spoken to me? No, He has not. I do not know Yahweh. The Almighty has not been revealed to me. I have not heard even a whisper. I go about my Levitical duties as faithfully as I know how. I read and study the scrolls. I pray the prescribed prayers. I do not make noise or complaint. I am quiet so I can hear if Yahweh ever speaks."

Eleazar turned away from the window and looked straight at Samuel. "We all know of your mother's vow. I came initially because I wanted to get away from my provincial village, but I chose to stay. The others come because of their Levitical responsibilities, and many stay because something in our heart draws us to Yahweh. But you, you are a child of the vow. Do you remain here enslaved to the grip of the vow or do you stay because your heart compels you?"

Samuel jerked his head off the table and glared at Eleazar. "Do not ever question my mother's vow or my commitment to be obedient to it."

Samuel saw his outburst had subdued Eleazar, stopping his advance toward him.

"I did not mean to offend you, Samuel. If I have, I am repentant. I only ask the child of the vow why he endures the flagrant wickedness of those among us who know not Yahweh nor care to?"

"What would you have me do, Eleazar?" Samuel threw up his hands and held them out toward his friend.

"That is not a question you should address to me."

"Then who? What are you saying?"

They both looked out the window when they heard Eli and the flock of Levitical students chattering merrily as they began to enter the academy building that housed all the copies of the scrolls of Moses and the histories to date of the people of Israel.

"They are coming." Eleazar pointed to the scrolls in front of Samuel. "Do we need to put the scrolls away?"

"I think the High Priest will be teaching from these texts today."

Samuel knew their conversation was only temporarily stalled. He knew that Eleazar spoke for other Levitical students in the school. He knew that many citizens in Shiloh, many citizens throughout the twelve tribes of Israel, were also disheartened by the disregard of Yahweh among many of the religious leaders led by the sons of Eli. He knew within his own heart that the unknowable and yet to be encountered Yahweh must be aware of the conditions in His house. He must see. He must listen. He must speak for the sake of the Name if nothing else. And yet the Almighty had not spoken to him, and so, he too would not speak.

Eli meandered at a deliberate pace along the edges of the wall, listening to the Levitical students take their turn reading from the scrolls as they sat around the table in the center of the large room. It was the classroom where he felt most invigorated. It was here in the study of the Laws and Blessings and Histories that his old bones felt stronger, where the joints in his legs and arms were not as stiff, nor did they ache. He walked more upright, not with his normal stoop. Even his eyes let in more light, and the haze around objects and people lifted.

"And when he, the Levite reached his home in the hill country of Ephraim, he took a knife, and laid hold of his dead concubine, and divided her, limb by limb, into twelve pieces, and sent her throughout all the borders of Israel. And it was so, that all that saw it said: 'Such a thing has not happened or been seen from the day that the children of Israel came up out of the land of Egypt unto this day; consider it, take counsel, and speak.'"

Eli paused at an over-sized window. From the vantage point of the second story room, he could see beyond the city walls and into the wheat fields and vineyards of the eastern valley. When he did not hear the resumption of the reading, he looked back at the table of students.

"Why did we stop?" Eli looked around the table. No student spoke. Surely someone would have a reaction to this event. When he looked at Samuel, not even his prize pupil had anything to say. "You are surprised by this bloody action? Yes, one of our own committed this awful deed. One who wore the robes of a priest of Yahweh cut his dead wife into twelve pieces. This is what happens when the heart of man gives in to evil. Read on. The story is not finished." Eli signaled with a wave of his hand to continue.

The students lowered their heads and the reading proceeded. Eli braced himself against the windowsill and gazed out over the valley. It was a nice vantage point from which to watch a sunrise, and he wondered why after all this time he had never thought of it. He was not too old to discover something new. Perhaps in the morning he would come to this spot and await the sun.

Eli remained at the window until the reading was done. He knew the story. He knew the bitter ending. He remembered his grandfather telling him the tale when he was just a boy. A Levite and his dower-less second wife had domestic troubles, and she walked out on the Levite and returned to her home in Bethlehem. After months of separation, the Levite left his home in the hill country of Ephraim and went to fetch her. He persuaded her to return with him and while traveling back to their home, they stopped in the town of Gibeah for the night. One of the citizen-elders of Gibeah invited the couple to spend the night in his home. When a gang of drunken Benjamites discovered these strangers were in town, they came to the house where the Levite and his wife were lodging and demanded the Levite be brought out so they could sexually abuse him. The citizen-elder refused, but the Levite in his cowardice offered these criminals his wife instead. The wicked men committed so heinous a transgression against the woman she died of the abuse, and when the elders of Gibeah refused to turn over the perpetrators of the offense, the sons of Israel rallied to avenge the crime and the entire tribe of Benjamin was threatened with extinction.

Eli's grandfather had his left forearm severed in the first battle. It kept him out of the fighting and probably saved his life. The Benjamites were fierce warriors and slew thousands of the sons of Israel before the tribe was defeated in the third battle. In that last battle, the sons of Israel slaughtered all but six hundred of the Benjamite militia, and Eli's grandfather, along with other tribal leaders, pleaded with the military commanders not to completely wipe out one of the tribes of Israel.

When the reading was over, no one stirred. The students sat quietly at the table. When Eli noticed the silence, he pulled away from the window and approached the class and began to lecture.

"It was the madness of violence, the blood lust of revenge that drove the sons of Israel to almost annihilate one of our tribes. The tribe of Benjamin brought a curse down upon its own head because of their evil deed, but it would have been a greater curse on the nation of Israel if we had extinguished the flame of one of our tribes, awful as those Benjamites were, and still are. The disgrace remains to this day. They will be forever remembered as the tribe who brought the wrath of the Almighty upon itself. A Benjamite is never to be trusted."

While he had been High Priest, Eli had not allowed any male of the Levitical order who happened to live in the cities and villages of the tribal land of Benjamin to come and serve in the Tabernacle. Those Levites could serve in the synagogues in those towns, but were not allowed to enter the gates of the Tabernacle. Eli brought his family prejudice and tribal bias into the job with no apology, and the edict would remain in place as long as he held the office.

Eli waited for a response from the class but none came. He liked to provoke the minds of his students, stir up their inquisitive natures, but this story had muted them.

"Such a story should sober all who hear it, and its ending should leave a lasting impression. It is why I had it written. But there is more to this story, more to be written."

Eli paused behind Samuel and patted his shoulder before he began to circle around the table of students. He had captivated their imaginations.

"My grandfather witnessed it all. After the third battle that left the city of Gibeah in ruins, the sons of Israel went back through the land of Benjamin, putting every living thing to the sword—women, children, domestic beasts—and burning every town to the ground. Nothing was spared. None but the six hundred captured Benjamites who survived the slaughter of tens of thousands of their kinsmen in this vicious civil war.

"But slaughter begets slaughter. The sons of Israel grieved and cursed. They grieved the near destruction of one of the twelve tribes and then proclaimed a curse on anyone who would give a wife to a Benjamite. They nearly destroyed a tribe of Israel with the sword and yet set a path for its inevitable extinction with a curse: 'Cursed be anyone who gives a wife to a Benjamite,' was the saying. What a dilemma. How to provide wives for the remaining six hundred men?

"There was a great assembly of tribal rulers, and when they realized no warriors from the city of Jabesh Gilead had come to fight in the battles against the Benjamites, the leaders elected to put to the sword every man, woman, and child of the city, sparing only those young women who were still virgins. Twelve thousand warriors were chosen to go to Jabesh Gilead with a mandate for slaughter. Four hundred young women survived that bloodbath. Imagine the horror. Imagine the hearts of those young women who watched their families butchered before being forcibly removed from their homes. To provide wives for the surviving Benjamites, Israel had become a wanton, depraved matchmaker.

"And yet the account was not balanced, four hundred brides for six hundred Benjamites. The tribe of Benjamin must survive at all cost. It must have heirs, so a tribe of Israel may not vanish from the earth. An ingenious plan was devised. Years ago, before you were born, at the annual Festival of Tabernacles, young maidens of Shiloh would perform a dance at the harvesting of the vineyards. The vineyards just outside our city walls, the vineyards you walk through, the vineyards whose grapes and wine we enjoy became the scene of the great abduction. The Benjamites hid in the fields and forest surrounding the vineyards, and when the young women were in the frenzy of their dance, the Benjamites rushed out of their hiding places and seized a wife. A few complaints were raised by fathers incensed that their precious daughters were so poorly treated, but most were silent. There had been enough bloodshed. In those days of upheaval, Yahweh did not intervene, and we in Israel did what was right in our own eyes."

Eli found himself standing back at the east window looking out at the fields of abduction. He imagined that scene in the vineyards so long ago. Perhaps he would not watch the sunrise from this vantage point after all. Perhaps that was why he had never done so in the first place.

One of the students cleared his throat, which drew Eli's attention.

"There is a question?" Eli asked without looking away from the window.

"So you are saying, Rabbi, that all of this destruction and death was brought on because a married couple could not get along?"

Eli continued to hold his gaze out the window a little longer before turning and facing his class. His students looked uneasily at one another, waiting for him to respond. Eli saw that Eleazar was standing behind his seat at the table.

"Ah Eleazar, it is a fearful choice to leave Yahweh and make our own crooked paths." Eli said this more to himself than in answer to the question. He knew his own comments were like sharp teeth biting into his flesh, but he had to speak truth and finish his thought. "We become cowards; madness takes hold and a nightmare is unleashed."

If he spoke the truth nowhere else, he would do so in his classroom. There was a residue of truth in his heart, and in his classroom it would be revealed. He made a swift turn from the window, his arms jabbing at invisible phantoms, and marched toward the circle of students who began to recoil at his approach.

"To serve the people of Israel, you must know the people of Israel. Know our dark hearts and corrupted minds. Know that we are broken and fearful. Know that the longer Yahweh is kept at a distance the more craven we become. In all Israel, I am most guilty."

Eli stood still, out of breath and red-faced by the vehemence of his answer, an answer no one in the room expected would get such a forceful response, not even Eli.

"Rabbi." Samuel whispered as he rose to his feet.

Eli looked at the young man and his breathing began to calm. He realized that his arms were extended, aimed toward the ceiling. He lowered them to his side. Eli looked into Samuel's face that expressed nothing but concern for him.

"Could the Almighty break His silence to reveal His glory?" Samuel asked.

"We can only hope." Eli dropped his head trembling at the prospect. He kept his eyes closed, almost in hopes of detaching himself from this room, his students, his life. He did not even notice the appearance of the priest bursting into the room until he spoke.

"Forgive the intrusion, Rabbi, but there is commotion in the courtyard in front of the altar." The priest was barely able to control his panic. "I thought it best…"

"Yes. Yes." Eli raised his hand to silence the priest and nodded as if he expected this intrusion. Why should he not expect chaos in the courtyard when he lacked the courage to discipline his sons or lead the people to righteousness or seek the Almighty? He did not want to hear any more from the priest, and he asked Samuel to take his arm and lead him back to the Tabernacle. He no longer felt the strength he had enjoyed while lecturing. Now his frail heart sank. He knew what was happening in his absence, and he dreaded the prospect of what he was about to face.

Samuel was prepared to enter the courtyard of the Tabernacle with Eli, but the High Priest stopped at the entrance. The rest of the students who had rushed out of the academy building following behind Samuel and Eli were forced to stop behind them. Samuel held onto Eli's arm. It did not take an expert in the Law to grasp the nature of the scene. Everyone in Israel knew the legalities and customs of this infraction of the traditional sacrifice of the peace offering.

In front of the altar, Samuel was shocked to see Tabernacle guards restraining a man while a third beat him mercilessly. A woman holding a baby stood off to the side with two other children clutching her robes and crying. The woman was begging the guards to stop beating her husband.

Hophni and Phinehas stood to the side munching on charred beef they peeled from a short, wooden, three-pronged spear. They were enjoying the meat and the beating.

Hophni raised the trident with the meat in the air.

"When you dare to insult the priests of Yahweh, this is what happens." Hophni pointed to the brutalized man. Then he lowered the forked beef to share another mouthful with his brother.

Samuel looked at Eli to see if he would do something to stop this. But before the High Priest could react, the accused man broke from his captors and charged toward them. Blood was smeared on his lips and flowed from his nose. His tunic was rent down the middle, exposing his undergarment. Samuel stepped in front of Eli to keep the man from hurling himself at the High Priest, but the man dropped to the ground at their feet.

The man began to scream at them. "You are the cause of this. Before the fat is burned on the altar to Yahweh, your wicked sons steal the choice cuts from our peace offering. I tried to stop them. They disgrace our offerings. They dishonor our nation."

"Praise the Name, the Name of the Almighty!" Eli shouted to the heavens.

"Rabbi, what are you saying?" Samuel was dumbfounded by the High Priest's response to such brutality. He could not believe what he had just heard. "Rabbi, your sons are stealing the peace offering of this man and eating the choice meat before the fat is burned in honor of Yahweh. How can you praise the Almighty for such offense?"

"I praise the Almighty that the mother of my sons rests in Sheol and cannot look upon this horrible scene," Eli spoke in a moaning voice as if proffering a confession to the failures of his character.

Samuel released his hold of Eli's arm just as two Tabernacle guards grabbed the victim of their beating and began dragging him back toward the altar.

Samuel stood perfectly still. Beneath his turban, he felt the hair on his head rise and prickle. He felt a shaft of sunlight come out of him, incinerating his eyes without burning them. He drew a single deep breath, as if from the bottoms of his feet, and the heat from the light burned through his legs, into his chest, and flowed into his arms and hands. There was no thought of attempting to reason, nor was there any consideration of walking away with the High Priest in tow. There was no turning back.

Samuel sprang forward and was upon the two guards, ripping their hands off the man's shoulders. He jerked the man to his feet and rushed him over to his family. When the Tabernacle guards attempted to regroup and retrieve their victim, Samuel pushed through them, knocking both guards to the ground. They made the decision to remain on the ground. But Samuel did not stop. He could not stop. The task was not done. He ignored all the witnesses to this scene and headed straight for the two brothers. By their horrified expressions, Samuel knew they were too frightened to move.

Samuel yanked the three-pronged fork out of Hophni's hand and pulled the meat from off the tines. He went over to the altar and tossed the meat onto the flames with the rest of the burnt offering. Then he turned back to the brothers and snapped the small spear over his knee, tossing the broken pieces at their feet. Samuel just stared at them, daring them to speak or order the guards to attack. He knew they would not attack themselves. His lungs were snapping like bells buffeted by a high wind, and though he might have lost the power of speech, he had not lost his hearing.

Samuel felt an arm rest carefully upon his heaving shoulders. He did not flinch, nor did he react in defense as if the guards were attempting to take him from behind. He knew they were as cowardly as the two brothers. No one would approach him in such a way except a friend, and when he heard this friend speak, he knew it was Eleazar.

"The child of the vow has awakened and come to life."

Six

THE MASTER WAS NOT HIMSELF. HE HAD NOT BEEN FOR WEEKS. Shira knew something was unusual about Elkanah's behavior when he asked her to divide her time between caring for the horses and helping Hannah prepare for their upcoming trip to Shiloh for the Festival of Tabernacles. Elkanah had to go into isolation, he told Shira, and gave no more explanation. She should also prepare to take the journey with them. Shira saw very little of him after that until nearer the time for them to depart.

Elkanah rarely spoke to Shira of his firstborn with Hannah. When he did speak of him, it was with pride and wonder. It was Hannah who spoke of her son to Shira, telling her how they would play together as small children. Hannah had only a few years to bond with her son. What Shira often heard Hannah express was the painful years of waiting she endured before Yahweh blessed her with a son. But as painful as that was, it paled in comparison to the day she and Elkanah left him at the Tabernacle. Since then, Hannah only saw Samuel once a year at the time of the festival, but each time she met him at the Tabernacle her heart would anguish at the memory of that day. Still, Hannah was convinced she had done what she knew she should do, and every time she returned from Shiloh, she could not wait to tell Shira what a man of Yahweh he was becoming, what he was studying in the Levitical school, and all the responsibilities he had working for the High Priest. She knew her child of the vow was being prepared by Yahweh for some great purpose, perhaps High Priest.

Shira had no memory of Samuel. In her mind, the image of this young man was solely formed by what Hannah shared with her. She could not understand a mother making a vow with the Almighty to have a child that required her to give him back at such a young age. But all this talk from his mother, year after year, about her son was creating quite an impressive figure of Samuel. Now that she had been invited to accompany the family to Shiloh, she began to anticipate her first encounter with this mystifying child of the vow. She would finally get to see for herself if Hannah's version of her son was deserving of his mother's praise and expectations.

This trip to Shiloh was her first. Shira rarely left the property except for Sabbath at the synagogue in Ramah, or on a trip to help Elkanah deliver a horse to a wealthy chieftain. Shira's father, a fellow Levite, had gone into business with Elkanah to raise horses after Elkanah had purchased the land outside the city of Ramah for such a venture. He had accidentally been killed from a fall off a horse when it was spooked by a sudden rock slide. Shira had been his only child when he died, so it was natural for Elkanah to embrace the role of surrogate father. Shira grew up living with her widowed mother in housing quarters nearest to the stables, and like her father, she was a natural with horses. She learned to ride at an early age, and bore a calm and comforting demeanor with a mare who was foaling or horse who was skittish.

Shira appreciated Elkanah's resolve in allowing her to decide her future, and like her father, she chose horses. Elkanah's reputation for breeding and raising a quality of horse had only grown over the years, and his success was due in large part because of Shira. Those wealthy tribal chieftains who purchased horses from Elkanah were always surprised to find that a woman was a skilled equestrian. It was the cultural norm for the women of Israel to be in the house not the corral. But on occasion, a father would inquire of Elkanah on behalf of his son if the young woman might be given to marriage. Shira's answer was always the same, "Why leave paradise, my lord?"

Shira had never seen Hannah anxious about anything, but she confessed to Shira that this trip to Shiloh was a double anxiety, for her husband and her son. Samuel had sent word weeks ago that the High Priest had chosen him to assist him in the first official sacrifice of the festival. This news arrived around the time that Elkanah had chosen to sequester himself, a separation from the family that continued even as they traveled to Shiloh.

Shira drove the family wagon with the wives and all the children. The supply wagons following behind. Mushi led the caravan driving a smaller wagon with a tent set up on the wagon bed and the solitary Elkanah sitting inside it. Shira thought it all very strange, looking at the tent swaying in the wagon bed containing her master whom she had barely seen for weeks. Hannah's anxiety at the peculiar behavior of her husband and the hoped-for success of her son's performance with the High Priest had created a level of anxiety in her own soul. She knew it all centered around the child of the vow, this cryptic young man she had heard of all her life, but never met. A man given by Yahweh to parents only to be given back to the Almighty. A man who must possess a soul greater than all other human souls.

Elkanah insisted the tents be pitched outside the city and not in the city square, as had been the family tradition. He had refused to enter the city before the opening ceremony at the Tabernacle on the Day of Atonement. If Hannah and Peninnah and all the children were to enjoy the festivities leading up to the High Holy Day, they would do it without him. Elkanah would not even venture outside the tent. He remained confined in the private booth he had Mushi construct behind the two large tents pitched just off the main road leading into the city. The family had grown. The two wives and their increasing number of offspring required segregated living quarters.

While Elkanah waited beside the wagon for Mushi to oversee the construction of his single-chamber tent, Hannah had approached him with a plate of food, but he refused, citing that he had no appetite except for silence and solitude. He told her he needed to listen. When Hannah asked him what he needed to listen to—or for—Elkanah did not speak. He just raised a hand to the sky as if pointing to the answer. He saw the perplexity and anxiety in her eyes, but how could he explain to her, to anyone, what he himself did not understand?

"I will see Samuel when he comes. I must speak to him, but no one else."

When Elkanah saw that Mushi had the tent ready, he had Hannah follow him behind the family tents out of public view. They stood in front of his goat-haired chamber, and Elkanah disrobed and gave Hannah his clothes. He wrapped his naked body with the linen sheet and kissed her forehead. "I wait for Samuel," were his last words to Hannah before disappearing inside the tent.

Elkanah spent each day sitting on his wooden stool, naked except for his linen blanket wrapped around him; his face held a fixed stare into the flames of the altar fire set in front of him. His lips recited or chanted words for his ears only. The only accessories besides the small altar were a skin of water, a basket of twigs and shavings, and a wooden bucket for his waste. In this modest space was a makeshift bed and pillow for Elkanah to sleep on when he became weary. He refused all food and fresh clothes. Each morning, Mushi was allowed inside to resupply the water skin and basket of kindling and to clean out the waste bucket. Elkanah refused Mushi's offer of a plate of bread and vegetables until his servant stopped asking. He knew Mushi, like his beloved wife, was despairing over his odd behavior, but he must keep himself clean and pure. He knew this process of cleansing must not stop until his task was brought to completion. Whatever that was. Whenever it would happen. Until then the altar was aflame and the basket was kept supplied with fuel. He knew the fire must never go out...never go out.

In the years Samuel had lived in Shiloh attending Levitical school and training as a priest in the Tabernacle, he was never able to travel home. Home for him was the Tabernacle. While pleased to see his family when they came to Shiloh during religious holidays, he had to acknowledge the tension he felt with each visit. He had yet to reconcile in his heart that at such a young age he had been dedicated to Yahweh. He appreciated not having any distractions from his devotion to Yahweh, but he wondered what it would have been like to grow up in the love and nurturing home of his parents. His life was contained within a system designed to educate and train young men in religious duties to Yahweh. The love he might have received and given within his natural family, Samuel showed in his faithful and obedient service to Yahweh.

There were many demands on Samuel's schedule during the week leading up to the Day of Atonement ceremony, but this year was exceptionally busy. He could only see his family for a brief time each day. His mother had three more sons and two daughters in quick succession after she fulfilled her vow. A blessing of fruitfulness Eli had pronounced upon his parents at one of their yearly visits after leaving Samuel at the Tabernacle proved true. Samuel had been replaced, a reality he struggled with if he allowed himself to dwell on it for too long. He found it difficult to act naturally around his mother. He felt foolish and awkward. And he had no genuine attachment to his siblings except in the abstract as distant relations from the same bloodline.

Samuel felt a stronger kinship to his father for one reason: Elkanah had opposed the fulfillment of his mother's vow and argued against it. He had risked an alternative to his mother's vow by offering to give specified sacrifices or pay a redemption price as a trade-off for their son. Surely the Levitical codes could be interpreted in his favor. His father had placed himself in the gap for him. The faithfulness of his mother to keep her vow to Yahweh and the faithfulness of his father to keep his son at home were powerful realities that Samuel grappled with. Though Samuel knew that the vow his mother made those many years ago could not be paid by a sacrifice or redemption price, he still felt a wound in his heart, a wound that perhaps only Yahweh could heal, if the Almighty ever were to reveal Himself to him.

Samuel had secured two seats for his parents in a special section in the courtyard of the Tabernacle for the first festival sacrifice of the bullock and seven lambs that began the week-long Atonement rituals. The courtyard was always packed with hordes of citizens and this section of privileged seating near the altar was offered to the elite citizens from the twelve tribes of Israel at exorbitant prices, a clever scheme devised by Hophni and Phinehas to profit from sacred traditions. The increased tensions between Samuel and Eli's sons had only gotten worse since Samuel confronted them at the altar for their thuggish tactics in stealing from the sacrifices of innocent people. When Samuel pointed out that their latest scam was never prescribed in the Law of Moses, the brothers threatened him with violent retribution. Given his relationship with Eli and his prominent role in the ceremonial observances, Samuel chose not to argue the point. He did not want anything to overshadow the holy sacrifices on the opening day of the festival, so he accepted the gift of the two coins from Eli for these special seats for his parents. He wanted only to please Yahweh and make his parents proud with this opportunity to assist the High Priest on this Day of Days.

The news of his father's strange behavior only added to his anxiety. If word got back to Hophni and Phinehas, he would be ridiculed mercilessly for a father who sat in a tent refusing to attend the most important day of his sons' Levitical life. The tightness in his chest grew more intense as his mother dragged him around behind the family tents. They stopped before getting too close to the entrance of his father's tent and kept their voices low so as not to be overheard.

"At moments I think he has lost his mind. I have never seen him like this. He will not talk to me or to anyone. He just stays in his tent."

Samuel's attention was drawn to the tent when his mother cast her eyes toward it. "And you say this began at home?" Samuel massaged his chest.

"The day we received the news you would be helping the High Priest in the public ceremony, he announced that he felt a rising pressure in his chest, and he asked Mushi to take over running everything. Each morning at dawn he went to the synagogue. The rabbi tells me your father never asks for him to read with him or explain the words of Moses. He sits and reads alone. He comes home. He barely speaks. He's always staring into the horizon even if I am standing right in front of him."

"You're sure he wants to see me?" Samuel looked uneasily in the direction of his father's tent.

"You he will see. He will not come out of his tent until he has seen you. I pray Yahweh will give me back the old Elkanah. I don't know what to do with this new one."

Hannah pointed to the tent where his father sat waiting for him.

Samuel looked into his mother's unquiet face. He did not know how to react in a way that might comfort her. Physical warmth was not a normal reaction. Instead, he dropped his hands into the pockets of his tunic. When he felt the coins, he remembered, and pulled out two bronze coins with a bull and a lamb insignia on either side.

"Show these to the guards when you arrive tomorrow at the Tabernacle, and they will show you and Father to the reserved seating in the courtyard." Samuel dropped the coins into his mother's hand.

"Thank you, son." Hannah folded her fingers over the coins and held them to her breast. "Regardless of what is going on with your father, we are very pleased with you."

Samuel managed a gentle pat on her shoulder before stepping over to the entrance of his father's tent. He looked back and saw Hannah scoot around the corner of the family tent. Before she disappeared, she lifted her hands in a gesture of prayer.

Samuel cracked open the tent flap and peeked inside. In the dim glow of the light he saw his father's bare back; the linen blanket loosely flowing over his legs. Elkanah was stoking the fire on the altar with a stub of wood and blowing on the embers. Samuel noticed his father's back tense and straighten. He must have sensed Samuel's presence.

"Come in, my son." Elkanah reached over to collect some cuts of wood stacked in the corner.

Samuel pulled back the tent flaps and stepped into the dank chamber. The odor of human sweat, musty heat, and smoke made him choke. His eyes began to water and he raised a hand to his mouth to stifle his recoiling stomach.

"Mushi has the same reaction every time he enters." Elkanah dropped the handful of sticks onto the fire. He picked up the skin of water that lay at the foot of his stool. "He should have warned you. It has been many days since I've been outside. I don't know how many. Once a day, Mushi brings me a fresh skin of water and removes my bucket of waste. That's how I know another day has passed."

"It's almost a week, Father. Mother says you refuse to come out until... until..."

"Until I saw your face." Elkanah offered Samuel the skin of water.

Samuel reached for the skin. The swallow of water was hot in his mouth and throat, but helped to settle his stomach. He put the leather plug back into the neck of the skin and stared at the man he barely knew. His father looked much older than last year: pinched eyes, skin sagging around his face and neck, stiff and tussled hair, arms and shoulders no longer muscular but soft and flaccid, his chest blotchy and concave. Samuel could not hide the visible discomfort this vivid exposure caused in him.

"I have no seat to offer you." Elkanah lifted the blanket up onto his shoulders, covering his nakedness from neck to foot.

Samuel set the water skin beside the altar and sat down upon the rumpled quilts. The small fire snapped and popped at the movement of fresh air Samuel had brought with him into the tent. Samuel looked into the fire. He could not disguise his awkwardness at being held captive in this dreamlike encounter, nor could he understand any hidden essence of truth in this moment.

"I could have asked for incense or could have bathed, but this is a time for afflicting one's soul, and I wanted my stench to remind me of my wretchedness."

Samuel ignored his father's mystifying words and his choice to live in these conditions.

"Father, tomorrow is the Day of Days. The High Priest asked me to aid him in making the kosher cut on the first sacrificial bull after the morning trumpets. I have been given a great honor."

"To be sure. I'm sure it is a great honor."

"And I want you and Mother to be there. I want you to see me standing next to the High Priest and all the—"

Elkanah raised his hand, stopping Samuel. "All the firstborn males belong to the Lord." He closed his eyes. "*And it shall be when the Lord shall bring you into the land of the Canaanite, as Yahweh swore unto you and to your fathers, and shall give it to you, that you shall set apart unto the Almighty all that opens the womb, every firstling that is a male, every son and every beast. Every firstborn beast you shall redeem with a sheep. If you do not redeem it, you shall break its neck. Every firstborn son you must redeem. And it shall be when your son asks, "What does this mean?" you shall tell him, "By the strength of the hand of the Almighty who brought us out of Egypt that place of slavery. When Pharaoh stubbornly refused to let us go, Yahweh slew all the firstborn in the land of Egypt, both the firstborn of man and the firstborn of beast. That is why I sacrifice to Yahweh the first male that opens the womb, and why I redeem every firstborn of my sons."*"

Samuel took a deep breath. It felt as though listening to the spoken words of Yahweh had refreshed the dense air of smoke and sweat with a cleansing lightness.

"You have been studying the words of Moses, Father. It is good to study the sacred texts." Samuel was surprised by Elkanah's feverish recitation of Scripture.

"On the day your news arrived at home, I walked out of the fields and into our synagogue. For too long my eyes read only the signs of livestock and vegetation or parchments of business transactions. Before my eyes failed me, I had to let them drink the holy words as written by the prophet Moses." Elkanah went silent and cupped his hands over his eyes as if pained by the glare.

Samuel waited to see if his father would continue, but the only sounds in the tent were the hiss and crackle of the fire. Samuel could not hear his father breathing. He could not hear his own breathing.

"This is good, Father...good to study—"

"No, my son. It is not." Elkanah let his fingers descend from his face until his hands dropped into his lap and disappeared into the folds of his blanket that had slid from his stooped shoulders down to his waist.

"Mother is afraid you are ill, or worse."

"Worse." Elkanah's expression was creased with a bemused curl of his lips. "This drinking of holy words has become a heavy burden. The Presence...the Presence of the Almighty who brought our people out of Egypt, who wandered in the desert with our forefathers, who is with us in this universe of our chosen people, of blood, of broken necks and redemption, of guilt and atonement; the Presence is always..."

The words drifted into silence as Elkanah darted his gaze around the interior of the tent as if Yahweh had suddenly entered the confines of this bubble of animal skins.

"I do not understand, Father." Samuel gave a sigh of irritation at his father's enigmatic words, and he did not appreciate being forced inside this hot chamber to listen to his father's incoherent thought process.

"You do not belong to yourself, Samuel. You are the firstborn of my dear Hannah. I am the firstborn of my firstborn father. We are Levites. In the days of our desert sojourn, Yahweh set apart the tribe of Levi to serve in the Tabernacle. The firstborn sons of our tribe are the ransom paid for the firstborn sons slain in Egypt when Pharaoh stubbornly refused to release the chosen from bondage. Yahweh warned, and Pharaoh would not listen. Yahweh warns us still, but we will not listen. The Law of Moses tells us we are all slaves to sin and death, yet the Law by itself is impotent to deliver us. We deserve death, but we live in Yahweh's pardon and favor. You do not belong to yourself."

Elkanah removed his arm from beneath the damp, soiled linen wrapped around him and stretched out his hand toward Samuel.

Samuel leaned back, resistant to the touch of his father. He feared that should he touch his father he might catch this strange infection. He had to be clear-headed tomorrow, not possessed of this malady, holy or not.

"Do not be afraid, my son." Elkanah retracted his hand, slipping it back into the folds of the blanket. "Yahweh has reserved a sacred seed from His people. Yahweh treasures this seed and will not let it escape Him. Yahweh is jealous. Yahweh is deadly. Yahweh will purify all things. Do not be afraid."

Elkanah reached behind him and removed a blanket that had concealed a long pouch wrapped in goat hair. He turned back to Samuel and stretched out his arms, offering it to Samuel.

"What is this, Father?"

"It is the sword of our family."

Samuel took the sword from his father and laid it upon his lap. He pulled back the top flap. Its sheath was covered with Egyptian symbols. Just below the top rim where the bronze hilt of the sword rested was the symbol of the Aket, the sun nestled between two mountain peaks. On the other side was the Ankh, the symbol of eternal life.

"Father, this is your sword. I cannot..."

"The story is that when our fathers left Egypt, it was given to our ancestor by an Egyptian captain. It could have been stolen for all I know. But it has passed down through the generations of our family. You must have it now."

"But, Father—"

"It is a fitting gift for the Day of Days when my son makes the kosher cut for the High Priest." Elkanah exhaled a massive breath of air and bowed his head. He seemed exhausted by his fierce candor. "Tell Mushi I am hungry and ready for my bath. And tell your mother to lay out fresh clothes for me in the morning."

"Does this mean you will be coming with Mother to the Tabernacle, Father?" Samuel rose to his feet. He shivered from cold, a cold within him, for the air inside the tent was sweltering. He looked to leave, but could not move. He looked down at his father's bowed head, but Elkanah did not look up. Samuel could not get his legs to move. They were locked in place, his body immovable, unable to exit.

"I will be watching tomorrow. I will be proud of you. I am proud of you."

His father kept his head lowered, his eyes closed. He began a serrated whisper of reverent praise.

Only then was Samuel released from this invisible constraint. He tucked the sword under his arm and sidled to the entrance of the tent. He did not look back at his father, but yanked open the tent flaps and burst into the cool, night air. Samuel's head was spinning, and he held onto the pole supporting the entrance into the tent to get his bearings. The sound of his father's raspy voice praying to Yahweh drove him away. He did not want to hear any more words from him. He had heard more words spoken tonight from this man than he had in years of annual family visits. Their past conversations had always centered on farm life or tribal politics or the systemic corruption of the priesthood and the shameful way Eli allowed his sons to bilk and bully the people of Israel.

His father never inquired how it felt to live without his parents all these years. He never asked Samuel how difficult it might have been to adjust to Levitical life. He never spoke to him on a human level until this startling expression of pride taken in the son he had left to Yahweh's charge. And now he was speaking of Yahweh, speaking for Yahweh, speaking as if Yahweh had direct communication with him. And the gift of this sword. Centuries of family history, the history of Israel. Such a gift to honor him.

Samuel dashed around the family tent, and when he rounded the front corner, he ran right into his mother.

"Well?" His mother had gripped his face with her hands, and Samuel could not move. "What did he say?"

He knew he could not hide the fact the encounter with his father had distressed him. Samuel's body trembled and his breathing was rapid. The locks of his hair protruding from beneath the outer rim of his turban were plastered to the sides of his perspiring face.

"What did he say?" she repeated, her tone emphatic, her fingers pinching.

"He said to tell Mushi he was hungry and ready for a bath."

"That is progress. Yes, and what else?"

Samuel felt the burn of her eyes into his heart. His mother had never looked at him like this before. It was almost as confusing as the way his father had stared at him.

"And he wanted you to lay out his clothes for the ceremony tomorrow."

Samuel offered no more, and within an instant, he saw his mother's face unfold from patient inquisition to anger. He knew it was cruel of him to make her pry information from him when she was desperate to know of

Elkanah's well-being. She must think that his father's outlandish behavior had possessed Samuel as well.

"The whole time you were in there that's all he said?"

"There was more, but I didn't understand most of it. He quoted the prophet Moses. He talked about Yahweh. He said…he said…"

"He said what?"

"He said he was proud of me."

Samuel had never heard these words spoken by his father. He was shocked by their effect on him. Pride was something to be shunned. Pride was a vice that could lead to one's downfall. He now saw why. In spite of the conflict of feelings he bore for his father, Elkanah's words had made Samuel's chest expand, allowing room for his enlarged heart.

"And he gave me his sword." Samuel held it up for his mother to see.

Samuel watched as his mother stepped back and threw up her hands in frustration. He could see his mother's lips moving and her arms fluttering about like a wounded bird, but a new sound entered his hearing, a voice singing a melody of Yahweh, to Yahweh. Not his father's voice—that jagged voice had vanished—but a voice so clear and virtuous it drowned out his mother's scolding. Samuel felt a tingle of pleasure at this new sound.

> "Hear us, O Yahweh of Israel.
> Awaken your might and save us.
> Restore us, O Mighty One.
> Make your face to shine upon us,
> That we may be saved."

The singer must be an ethereal creature announcing a claim on the world. Samuel felt his stamina return. His head cleared. His eyes could see in the cool night, through the smoke of the fire, between the shoulders of the people huddled around the singer rapt and silent. He could see her shadowed beauty enhanced by the flickering oil lamps and candles: her dark flowing hair bound in colorful ribbon with loose strands of curls caressing her face in the gentle night breeze. Her oval eyes sparkled in the glow of the fire, her full lips uttering pleas to Yahweh.

> "O Adonai, how long?
> How long will you be deaf to our prayers?
> You feed us with the bread of tears.

We drink our tears. We drink our tears."

She sang a serenade that required no accompaniment. The melody was simple enough with a slow pulse that made it serene. Yet her voice built in power, reaching a crescendo and holding a high, piercing note with the last word. The note she held cast a shaft of sound into the air almost unbearable to hear.

"Are you listening to me?"

He felt his mother grab his arm and try to turn him toward her, but he would not budge, he could not. The singer had full control over him.

"No, Ima, I'm not listening to you." Samuel removed his arm out of her grip.

> "Return to us, O Adonai.
> Look down from heaven
> And watch over us.
> Restore us, O Mighty One,
> Make your face shine upon us,
> That we may be saved."

The initial pleasure Samuel had when first hearing her voice turned to pain, pain expressed by the singer, a united pain. But what was this pain of dejection she sang of? What was this desperate need that she begged Yahweh to fill? His heart burst as he began to circle around behind the crowd, making his way toward the main road. After finishing her song, she opened her eyes and saw Samuel staring at her.

When Samuel realized she had caught him staring, he began to run. It was her face that followed Samuel through the city to the quarters for the Levites. It was her face that lingered above his bed as he tried to drift off to sleep. He could not think of her. He should not think of her. His thoughts had to be of Yahweh and his duty to the High Priest and his performance at the sacrifice tomorrow. But her face refused to depart. It was her face that made his dreams fitful, and it was her face he awoke to the next morning.

Seven

SAMUEL STOOD INSIDE THE ENTRANCE OF THE HOLY PLACE holding the silk cushion bearing the sacrificial knife in a golden scabbard. The light from the menorah reflecting off the knife's jeweled handle made Samuel's eyes glint. He watched as Eli, flanked by Hophni and Phinehas, made their way around the Holy Place, performing the ordinary rites that began each day. These rituals were typically carried out by Samuel and other younger priests, but not this day, the Day of Days. Eli and his sons must maintain the traditions of today. Hophni dressed the lamps of the eternal flames; Phinehas emptied the ashes from the basin of incense and dropped fresh cubes into the smoldering coals. Then they dutifully followed their father as he approached the altar.

Eli paused in front of the thick curtains concealing the Holy of Holies. He placed one hand on his breastplate with its twelve sparkling stones and raised his other hand toward the Mercy Seat concealed behind the curtains. Samuel could not hear what the High Priest was praying but could see the movement of the old man's lips and hear the faint, incoherent mutter of his speech. He observed Eli's raised hand trembling before the curtain. He knew Eli dreaded the moment when, on this Day of Days, he alone would have to part those curtains and come face-to-face with the Ark of the Covenant and the Mercy Seat of the Almighty—a prospect that would rivet the heart and soul of anyone.

Samuel watched as Eli lowered his arms. Hophni and Phinehas stopped snickering behind their father's back when he turned around and faced his sons. They dropped their heads as if shamed for their irreverence, but Samuel knew they had no shame. Eli bent down and picked up the shank of the year-old lamb and carefully laid it upon the grate in the altar. It instantly began to sizzle. That morning, Samuel had made sure there was plenty of fuel for the holy fire. Eli wiped the residue of the lamb shank from his fingers and thrust the cloth into Hophni's reluctant hands, which elicited another snicker from his brother. Eli disregarded them both as he marched between them and made his way toward where Samuel waited. Along with the sound of the jangling bells sewn into the hem of his robe, Eli's bare feet made a smacking thud with each step across the hardened surface of the Tabernacle floor.

Samuel watched as the sad old man haltingly approached. His breath caught in his throat. For the first time, he felt sympathy for Eli. Samuel was not thinking of his own nervousness, but of this all, too-human man in the exalted place of High Priest, today the bearer of a nation's sins. Samuel bent down, and with one hand he straightened Eli's rough, leather sandals placed on the floor so he could easily slip into them.

Eli was dressed appropriately for the Day of Days. Hophni and Phinehas had chosen to wear unauthorized clothing: scarlet shoes with golden tassels laced around the ankles, footwear matching their linen tunics dyed scarlet with a bright purple sash draped over one shoulder. Both wore necklaces and earrings created for this occasion—costumes designed to draw attention to their wealth and power. Outside the Tabernacle doors was a courtyard full of the elite from the twelve tribes of Israel plus prominent citizens of Shiloh, all gathered for this holy festival. The brothers were more concerned about impressing these prestigious people than displaying any humility toward the Almighty.

Samuel braced one knee upon the floor so Eli could maintain his balance by resting his hand upon Samuel's shoulder while he slipped his crooked feet into his sandals. Samuel glared up at Hophni and Phinehas who stared at him with a shared look of disdain. Samuel quickly averted his eyes, focusing instead upon the knife lying on the cushion. Samuel needed to dispel his unholy thoughts and replace them with holy ones.

When he felt Eli tap his shoulder, Samuel rose and faced the High Priest.

"The Day of Days has begun." Eli ran his fingers delicately over the knife sheath, a reverent caress. "May Yahweh look with favor upon us this day."

"Step aside, boy." Hophni dropped the cloth Eli had used to wipe his hands at Samuel's feet. "We shall walk beside our father."

"You will not." Eli's unexpected rebuttal startled his sons.

"But father, you need help getting into place at the altar."

"Samuel will aid me." Eli added a growl to emphasize to his sons that his decision was final, and then looked back at Samuel. "Am I presentable?"

Samuel reached up to secure the golden plate attached to Eli's turban with the inscription "Holy to Yahweh" engraved upon it.

"Everything in place." Samuel then slipped his hand back underneath the cushion.

"Don't be nervous. You'll do fine." Eli gave Samuel a reassuring pat on his arms. Then he turned to his sons. "Open the doors."

Samuel turned with Eli to face the closed doors and waited as the brothers stepped around them and took their positions, one on each door. Samuel could not stop trembling. He did not want to show any weakness or give any more reason for Hophni or Phinehas to hold it against their father for choosing him to assist in the first sacrifice to begin the Day of Atonement. When the sons were in position, Eli nodded his head and they pulled open the doors. Samuel felt the hand of the High Priest rest upon his shoulder and dig into his flesh and muscle with his crooked fingers. It was a calm grip to balance both heart and body. Samuel took the first step, and together they walked into the morning sunlight with Samuel reverentially carrying the silk cushion bearing the jeweled blade.

When the two of them stepped out of the Holy Place, a double line of Levites snapped to attention. One line of priests began to blow their shofars while the other line began chanting prayers to Yahweh. The double line led from the entrance into the Tabernacle to a ramp leading up to the large altar in the center of the courtyard.

Samuel and Eli paused on the portico to take in the view of the courtyard. Worshippers packed the inside of the Tabernacle with hundreds more just outside the gates, clogging the main street.

Samuel glanced at the section of reserved seating, looking for his parents. Instead of finding his parents in their assigned seats, he saw his mother, but not his father. Next to his mother was the young woman whose voice the night before had pierced his heart and whose face he had worked so hard to drive out of his mind. In the bright sunlight, he saw his mother put her hand to her mouth and tip her head in the direction of the young woman, a signal of some kind, he determined, that something had changed. Had his father decided not to attend? Had he become ill from all his self-inflicted purification?

Samuel felt Eli's gentle prodding which brought his attention back into focus, and they started down the steps between the two lines of priests. Samuel found Eleazar leading the chanting in his line and acknowledged him with a quick smile. The noise was deafening. The shofars and vocal praise from the chorus of Levites, the frightened lambs choking out their last terrified bleats, the roar of the fire blazing in the altar, were all an assault on the senses.

Samuel and Eli paused before the laver. The High Priest dipped his hands in the holy water to cleanse them. Then he raised his purified hands to heaven for Yahweh's inspection before proceeding the short distance to the animals chosen as the opening sacrifices of Atonement. Seven lambs and two goats huddled in the pen beside the altar. A year-old bullock waited at the foot of a wood and stone ramp that led up to a level platform at the edge of the altar. Eli would confess his sins over the year-old bullock before it was offered to Yahweh. The platform was wide enough to accommodate the two Levites who led the panicky bullock up to the rim of the altar with thick, coiled ropes around its neck and then maneuvered the beast into position to face the High Priest. The bullock had been blindfolded to reduce the risk of potential disruption to the ceremony.

While the two Levites were positioning the bullock, Samuel took another moment to glance in the direction of his mother and the young woman seated next to her. His mother only smiled as if to encourage him to continue his duties without concern. Only this did not settle Samuel's heart. He looked about for his father, but the crowd was too dense for Samuel to spot him.

Once the bullock had been steadied, Hophni and Phinehas dashed up the ramp, ordering the two Levites who flanked the beast to stand aside. Eli gave Samuel a confused look as the two Levites descended the ramp with their own bewildered expressions. This substitution had not been planned or discussed. But the brothers were now in place, and there was nothing to be done but proceed with the ceremony. Between not finding his father in the reserved seating with his mother—instead, the young woman—and now this unexpected shift by Eli's sons, Samuel's heart began to falter.

Eli nodded to Samuel and the two of them ascended the ramp as the shofars and chanting reached their climax of worship. Once in place in front of the bullock, Eli placed his hands on its head and all sounds of adulation ceased. What immediately punctured the eerie silence was the deep bellows of a fretful beast.

Eli dug his fingers into the bullock's hide and raised his voice to the heavens.

"I pray, O Eternal! I have done wrong, I have transgressed, I have sinned before you, both I and my house; I pray. O Eternal! Forgive, I pray, the iniquities, and the transgressions, and the sins, which I have wrongly committed, and which I have transgressed, and which I have sinned before you, both I and my house, as it is written in the Law of Moses, Thy servant, 'For on this day shall atonement be made for you to cleanse you; from all your sins you shall be clean before the Lord.'"

Eli released his hold of the beast's head and turned to Samuel who offered him the sacrificial blade. Eli gripped the handle and removed the knife from its sheath. He held it before Samuel for one final inspection of any irregularities, any dents or nicks that would render it unholy. The sacrifice must be without blemish. The instrument used in this sanctified fatality must also be without blemish. After Samuel gave his approval, Eli raised the knife and listened. There was no sound from man or beast. The pause was in honor of the Angel of Yahweh. He might intervene as he had centuries ago when he stopped Abraham from sacrificing his son Isaac upon the makeshift altar on Mount Moriah. When sufficient time had passed for divine intervention, Eli lowered the knife.

"Be my eyes, my son," Eli whispered to Samuel. "Be my eyes so the cut will be clean and death will be instant."

Samuel set the silk cushion on the edge of the platform next to the silver bowl that would collect the blood from the bullock, which would be sprinkled later that day onto the Mercy Seat. Samuel then gripped the hands of the High Priest and guided them beneath the neck of the bullock. Hophni loosened the ropes around the bullock's neck in preparation for the cut. It had to be a single cut across the throat at a precise depth, severing all arteries and causing instant death to avoid undue suffering. Samuel looked for the mark on the neck of the beast where he would need to plunge the blade to prevent any mishap. The night before he had gone to the pen where the bullock was kept and had a small, yellow mark painted on the precise spot on the beast's neck. He knew he would be nervous, and now given the unusual nature of the changes happening around him, he needed the assurance that his mark was in place. But it had been smudged out. He looked at Hophni who cocked his head, sneering and taunting Samuel by coiling the loose rope in his hand like a snake ready to strike.

"Why do you hesitate, my son?" Eli asked. "The time is now."

Samuel took a deep breath and thrust the blade into the beast's flesh. He held the knife at the point of entry for a moment, time for the beast to grunt in surprise, and for Eli to release his hold of the handle, and then, on his own, Samuel drew the blade across the bullock's neck, opening the arteries as he drew the deadly instrument to the opposite side. The blood cascaded down the throat of the beast, drenching Samuel's hands and forearms.

Phinehas grabbed the silver bowl, holding it beneath the slit in the bullock's neck to collect the rivulets of life-blood pouring from the open wound.

Samuel stepped back as the bullock's front legs crumpled. The sight of the dying beast came almost as a surprise. The operation had been precise. In spite of all the unforeseen distractions, what he had feared had been quick and straightforward. He had performed a flawless surgery, and he felt an exuberant rush of triumph. He might have shouted, but someone else beat him to it. The shout did not come from the seated area for the special guests, which was where Samuel first looked. When he saw his mother rise from her seat, a look of shock on her face, and turn toward the entrance into the courtyard, he felt as if his own blood began to flow out of him like the throat of the young bullock he had just sliced. He recognized the voice, and when he looked in that direction, the same direction every eye in the courtyard was now looking, he saw his father, one arm raised to the sky, the other pointing at Eli.

"Yahweh, the Almighty, speaks!" he shouted. "Yahweh, Creator of heaven and earth says this, 'Did I not reveal myself to your father's house when they were in Egypt under bondage to Pharaoh?'"

There was no doubt. Samuel's father stood just outside the entrance, and when he began to move into the courtyard, instead of the Tabernacle guards attempting to stop him, they moved away, almost fearful to approach him. His father wore a simple robe and tunic. Samuel noticed a drastic change in his father's voice. It was a bold and clear roar, not the raspy, semi-coherent whispering of the night before inside the rank tent.

"'Did I not choose your father out of all the tribes of Israel to be my priest, to go up to my altar, to burn incense, to wear the ephod in My Presence? And did I not give your father's house all the offerings made with fire by the children of Israel?'"

Samuel watched in awe as his father stepped forward—keeping his arms in the same formation as if channeling energy from heaven toward its intended objective—and moved toward the altar. Samuel looked to his mother. He could see in her eyes the dawning of understanding for Father's recent behavior. She reached for him, but then retracted her arm. The young woman rose to her feet, and her mother embraced her. What was happening? What did this mean? The words his father spoke were holy, prophetic. But what was the source and origin of these words? Could this be Yahweh?

"'Why do you scorn my sacrifices and kick at my offerings, which I commanded in my Tabernacle? Why do you honor your sons above me, making yourselves fat with the choice parts of every offering from Israel, my children?'"

Samuel took his eyes off his father and watched as Eli stumbled down the ramp in an attempt to flee. When he reached level ground, his knees buckled. He crouched into the shape of a fearful child, thrusting his hands beneath his breastplate.

"Therefore the Lord, the Almighty, the God of Israel, declares: 'I swore that your house and your father's house would serve before me forever.' But now Yahweh declares: 'Far be it from me! Those who honor me I will honor, but those who despise me, will be held in contempt.'"

The High Priest looked frantically to the Tabernacle guards for aid, but they, like him, were powerless. From his place on the platform, Samuel watched as those standing between his father and the High Priest began to back away in alarm as Father made his way toward the cringing High Priest. They did nothing to stop the forward progress of his father, the prophet. The Levites who had been clustered around the High Priest also stepped away. Who would want to be close to the object of Yahweh's renunciation?

The hind legs of the bullock finally gave out, and as it fell on its side, the beast crashed into Hophni and knocked him onto the platform, trapping his legs beneath its dead weight. He screamed from the unexpected shock.

"'The time is coming when I will cut off your strength and the strength of your father's house, so that there will not be an old man in your family line, and you will see distress in My Tabernacle. Although good will be done in Israel, in your family line there will never be an old man. Every one of you that I do not cut off from My altar will be spared only to blind your eyes with tears and to grieve your heart, and all your descendants will die in the prime of their lives.'"

Samuel's heart no longer feared what he had imagined his father might do or was doing. He silently rejoiced. He felt an immediate bond with his father. He was acting as Samuel had done when he confronted the brothers for desecrating the offerings, in the very same courtyard, before the very same altar.

Eli bellowed as if to echo a final gasp of the bullock lying dead upon the platform with Hophni writhing in pain trapped beneath the crushing weight. He begged for someone to help lift the beast off his legs, but no one moved.

Samuel crept down the ramp, the bullock's blood running down the blade of the knife and dripping from his fingers. The long, white skirt of his priestly robe was smeared with streaks of red. He watched as his blood-father drew nearer to his spiritual-father with calm and deliberate steps. Samuel said nothing to either man. He did not try to stop his father from speaking. He did not rush to help Eli to his feet. He could not intervene. He dared not. He was spellbound just as all those gathered in the courtyard. One thought entered his mind. He knew intuitively the words spoken by his father were divine. He knew they must be remembered. He knew they must be written down. *These words, this moment must be recorded. They must be written and remembered.* And he knew he was the one who would write the record of this event.

"'And this shall be a sign for you: your two sons, Hophni and Phinehas, they will both die on the same day.'"

Hearing his doom, Phinehas dropped the silver bowl in his hands onto the platform, splashing the sacred blood on the planks and across the front of his new clothes.

Father came to a stop before Eli just as Samuel reached the bottom of the ramp. Samuel stood between the two of them; his father's face a fixture of resoluteness and charity; the face of Eli, bloated and quivering with foreboding.

Father lowered the arm he had extended to heaven and rested his hand upon Samuel's shoulder. He looked into his son's face, their eyes locked in reverent wonder.

"'I will raise up for Myself a faithful priest who will do according to what is in My heart and mind. I will build him a sure house, firmly established, and he will walk before Me and minister before My anointed forever.'"

A surge of energy rushed through Samuel's body. His heart beat with such force his rib cage felt as though it might break apart at any moment. His legs drove his feet into the hard ground as if to stake a permanent hold on the earth. Whatever his lifespan would be, he knew in that instant, the course set for him was immutable.

Samuel watched as his father knelt down beside Eli. He lowered the arm he had pointed in the direction of the High Priest with the accuracy of truth and rested it upon Eli's slumped back. His voice dropped in volume, but not in power. He spoke now with pity as if regretting the last words that had to be said.

"And then it shall come to pass that everyone left in your family line will come and bow down before him for a piece of silver and a loaf of bread and shall beg, 'Pray, give me some priestly office so that I may at least have food to eat.'"

Though gently uttered, it was a curse he spoke. Whoever remained in Eli's family would be dependent on the mercy of the faithful priest whom Yahweh would raise up.

Samuel watched Eli remove his hands from beneath the breastplate. They were red and blistered, and raised in supplicant gesture for mercy. Samuel cast his eyes up at the platform at the condemned sons of the High Priest. Hophni lay half-buried beneath the heaviness of the dead bullock, cursing those around him for not coming to his aid. Phinehas clutched his stained robe, his agitated fingers wringing out the wet blood. If these words uttered by his father were true, with the death of Hophni and Phinehas, the degenerate progeny of Eli's loins, the legacy of Eli's house, would bear the curse his father spoke as long as the chosen people of Yahweh existed.

Once Father stood, Samuel was unsure what to do. He looked down at Eli whimpering at his feet, and then into the face of his father. He felt helpless. He could do nothing. He wanted to comfort Eli. He wanted to embrace his father. But he was too awed to do anything but remain still.

His father seemed to sense the conflict in his eyes and made it easy for him. He smiled at Samuel, and then began moving toward the gates of the Tabernacle, leaving behind the aftermath of the spoken word. His father had not called for fiery destruction nor armed revolt. He had been only a voice of the word and the Day of Days had come to a standstill. As he passed by the reserved seating, Father reached out for Samuel's mother. She went straight for her husband and the young woman who sat with her followed at their heels. The trio moved through the stunned crowd like departing angels immersed in the bristling daylight.

Eight

ONCE HIS PARENTS AND THE YOUNG WOMAN LEFT THE TABERNA-
cle, Samuel helped Eli to his feet. Hophni and Phinehas offered no assistance to their father, nor did they give a public denunciation or religious
explanation to the bewildered people in the courtyard as to what the crowd
had just witnessed. The two men had no idea what had just taken place
other than personal humiliation. Samuel knew the prophetic words meant
nothing more to them than babbling from a lunatic. Their only rebuttal was
to curse.

Phinehas helped his limping brother down the ramp, condemning
Samuel, the son of a "madman" and the madman himself, and swearing
revenge as they stumbled through the courtyard toward their private
quarters under heavy escort by the Tabernacle guards. Samuel did not see
them in the Tabernacle the rest of the day.

Samuel remained with Eli, helping him carry out the functions of the
High Priest for the Day of Atonement. It was a day of sacrifices. It was a
day for Yahweh to forgive the sins of Israel and the sins of the individual.
It was a day for the scapegoat to be sent into the wilderness. It was a day
for the blood of the unblemished slain to be sprinkled onto the Ark of the
Covenant. It was the day the High Priest must step behind the veil and,
through clouds of incense, come face-to-face with the Almighty, and pray

for atonement for the people of Israel with their God. It was a day of terror and dread for Eli.

Samuel looked into Eli's eyes and saw the panic. His breath was labored and his whole body trembled as Samuel ushered the High Priest across the floor of the Holy Place toward the curtain. It was time for him to enter the Holy of Holies. With each creeping step, Samuel felt his own heart breaking for this old man. He had been denounced and humiliated in the courtyard, his sons condemned to die, and now the Almighty waited behind the curtain. Samuel's soul bore an almost unbearable pain for Eli. His father's words still rang in his ears, and yet an awareness of compassion he held for Eli could not be denied. These sensations awakened within Samuel's heart was something new to him, never felt before. He never knew he could feel such emotion.

When they stopped before the curtain, Eli's hands trembled so violently as he dipped the spoon into the bowl of blood that he splashed much of it onto the floor and over his ephod. Samuel had to steady his hand and help him sprinkle the blood against the curtain so the entrance into the Holy of Holies could be purified.

"I can never go in there." The perspiration soaked through Eli's turban and dripped off his earlobes. "I will never be pure enough to stand before Yahweh."

Who of us is ever pure enough? Samuel put his arm around Eli's shoulders in his hope to comfort. Before Samuel and the other Levites were required to leave the sanctuary to wait outside while the High Priest officiated in the Holy of Holies, Eli made Samuel tie a rope around his leg. If he were to die while sprinkling the sacred blood onto the Ark of the Covenant, then Samuel and the others would have a way to remove his body.

But Yahweh was merciful. When Eli emerged from behind the curtain in a thick vapor of incense, he stumbled out the doors of the Holy Place onto the portico, broken and exhausted, and fell into Samuel's arms.

It was after dark when Samuel arrived at the family tent pitched outside the city gates. He paused when he heard her voice. She was leading his sisters and brothers in a children's song; the same voice that had stirred his soul the night before with its beauty and power was now playful with its tune and lyric. In the aftermath of the day's events, he had nearly forgotten her. Now it all came flooding back—the passion of her voice, the glimpses he stole of her lovely face that morning before his father stopped the world with his prophetic utterance.

Samuel stepped back from the entrance of the tent and saw the dancing shadows of his family cast onto the fabric by the firelight inside. He could not believe their reverie. After what had happened that morning, he was surprised they were still in Shiloh. He thought that his father would have ordered everyone to pack and leave the moment they returned from the Tabernacle.

A communal fire burned on the ground outside the tent where the families from Ramah had gathered the night before to listen to the singer, but there was no one around this fire. Samuel moved over to the fire, taking a seat on a discarded stool. There was only a dribble of traffic venturing in and out of the city gates. The first day's celebrations had ended and most everyone camped along the highway was settled in for the night. Samuel was surprised to see the encampments on either side of his parents' tents were vacant spaces. The night before the tents of other families had been crowded around them. Samuel figured his father's performance that morning had influenced their relocation.

Samuel extended his hands toward the warmth of the flames.

"I knew you would come."

The voice startled Samuel, and he leapt from the stool, knocking it on its side.

Father emerged from the far corner of the family tent. "I did not mean to frighten you."

"Father, I didn't know if you would still be here. I didn't expect you to be." Samuel picked up the stool and held it to his chest as if to shield himself from his father.

"I told your mother we would wait...he will come, I said." Eli looked at Samuel holding the shield in front of him. "Do not be afraid. I will not harm you."

Samuel set the stool down by the fire. He noticed that his father had changed into more casual attire, something he would relax in at home. His father's head was uncovered and his long, gray and black hair was braided down his back and tied with a red band around his forehead. He looked strong and vigorous, so different from the night before.

Samuel looked into his father's face for any leftover signs of this morning's zeal, but he appeared calm and natural, as natural as Samuel thought he might be given his limited access to his father over the years.

"It seems our friends decided to find new locations for the rest of their holiday in Shiloh." He pointed at the deserted spaces around his tent. "I don't blame them for not wanting to keep our company."

"It feels dangerous. You are exposed like this, unprotected. After what happened today, I worry. I want you to be safe."

"We are safe, my son."

Samuel brightened when his father called him *son*. This claim of sonship brought a solace to his soul that he had not expected. Still, he was fearful.

"Many are upset by what happened today, angry even. Eli's sons want revenge."

His father appeared amused by this. "They are frail, mortal men. Their threats of revenge are empty."

"Eli was barely able to finish his duties today. He was terrified to enter the Holy of Holies. I have never seen him so shaken."

"A fitting response given what he had to do. Still, I pity the old man."

"Father, I do not understand. What happened today?"

"I tried to explain last night, but I could not explain what I did not understand. It seemed clear to me one moment, and the next, it was as if I had sunk into a dark cloud and had to fight my way out. It brought me no pleasure to speak these words. In spite of my feelings toward Eli and his sons, I did not speak from personal revenge or judgment. That is not my place. I do not regret what was spoken or fear the consequences."

"But these words...these words. Help me to understand. Was this from Yahweh?"

"This is where the cloud sinks into my mind. It was so clear to me this morning as I walked to the Tabernacle, through the crowds, their empty religious bleating and braying about the sacredness of the Day of Days. And when I saw you assisting the High Priest, it broke out of me like a storm in my soul."

"It?"

"A mixture of pity and anger, of righteous justice, of courage and sympathy all boiling up in my soul. It has been building for weeks now. I didn't know when it would spill over, but I knew it would. This morning it broke out of me. I had to express the heart of the Almighty with the feebleness of language."

"You spoke for Yahweh?"

"I spoke, that I know. For Yahweh? I believe I did, but time will be the test."

Samuel could no longer look into his father's face and shifted his gaze to the flames of the fire. Had Yahweh really broken through the vast distance of heat and light and volumes of air between earth and heaven and given His voice to his father?

"And the curse you pronounced on the High Priest and his sons." Samuel searched the burning embers as if he might find some understanding behind his father's reasoning revealed in its inferno. "I knew you didn't approve of them, nor do I, but to say such things, to say that Hophni and Phinehas would die, and that Yahweh...that this is the will of Yahweh. Such things have not happened in Israel for some time. Our people have not heard from Yahweh since..." Samuel's voice trailed off as he pondered what he was about to say. "Heard from Yahweh since the days of Samson the Judge when Yahweh appeared to his childless parents and announced they would have a son."

"Do you hear what you are saying?"

Samuel saw his father step closer to him, but he did not give an answer.

"I pray you do not suffer for what happened today." Father paused his advance toward Samuel. "It is as vexing to me as it is to you, but I can only say I felt this iron hand between my heart and stomach."

"Samson's childless parents." Samuel muttered this quietly to himself.

His father nodded slowly, his eyes a bit dazed. "I had forgotten this."

"I have been studying the scrolls of the judges. Yahweh came to them, spoke to them, and left them with the promise of a child."

"Who would lead Yahweh's chosen people for twenty years."

"This was Yahweh's answer to the prayer of a childless couple." Samuel began to tremble like Eli before the curtain of the Holy of Holies.

Father resumed his approach toward Samuel. "Yahweh is not indifferent to His people. What was said today may have been an announcement...an end of indifference. I just know the iron hand on my gut was released once I walked out the gates of the Tabernacle. I can breathe now."

Samuel could not believe what he was hearing. "Did you plan to offer a lamb for the atonement sacrifice?"

This was all Samuel could think to say. Preparation for sacrifice and atonement to Yahweh was all that had been on his mind for days, it was the reason the children of Israel gathered at the Tabernacle in Shiloh, and his father had turned it all upside down.

"I did not." Father was close enough to lay his hand upon Samuel's shoulder. "I have sacrificed enough."

The declaration stunned Samuel, and he looked into his father's gentle eyes free from the blaze of this morning. Samuel had been quietly serving in the Tabernacle for years, in the middle of the darkest times of Eli's priesthood, studying the sacred scrolls, fulfilling all the Levitical services, and in this dawning moment—outside all Tabernacle rituals and prescriptions—Samuel realized that Yahweh might be drawing him into... into...into what?

"I have sacrificed my firstborn son to Yahweh. That is enough. You are of more value than a lifetime of sacrifices."

His father's confession finished him. Samuel felt the earth beneath him crack open and he feared he would be swallowed whole.

"There you are."

Samuel did not have time to step away from his father before his mother burst out of the tent and rushed past Elkanah and wrapped her arms around him. When he saw that she was followed by the young woman from the night before and who sat next to his mother this morning, he was thankful for his mother's embrace because he was near to losing his balance. Samuel saw the woman's eyes drop. She kept her distance, holding back from intruding on this moment between mother and son.

"You are shivering." Hannah began rubbing her hands over Samuel's bare arms, trying to generate some heat. "Here, step closer to the fire."

Samuel resisted being pushed by his mother as she tried to gently guide him toward the flames.

"Shira, please fetch Samuel a blanket."

Once she ducked back into the tent, Samuel whispered to his mother, "Who is she?"

Samuel thought that the blanket must have been placed at the entrance of the tent, because Shira reappeared in an instant. She remained at the entrance, waiting to be summoned, and Hannah immediately waved for her to come forward.

"Thank you, Shira." Hannah took the blanket from the young woman and placed it over her son's shoulders.

This time Shira did not step back to the tent. She remained in front of him, looking right at him, and he wrapped the blanket around him more to conceal the rapid beating of his heart that must be bursting from his chest, than for the warmth.

She was more beautiful up close than Samuel expected. His view of her from the night before and from a distance at the Tabernacle that morning, had not given him the detail of features that this bright firelight offered. Her hair was pulled back and the skin of her face and arms were a light bronze, enhanced by the flames to a burnished shine. Her brown eyes were like two deep wells of omniscience. Samuel knew he could not hide from these eyes, and what's more, he did not want to. He wanted to remain the object of her focus forever.

"You remember Shira?"

Samuel shook his head in spite of his mother's prodding elbow into his side.

"You played together as very small children before..."

"...Before I was taken to the Tabernacle."

Samuel blamed Shira's eyes for blurting this statement of fact. He saw only truth in her eyes and only truth could be spoken in her presence.

"Yes, yes...before." Hannah removed her arm from around her son's shoulders. "Shira lives with us. She is a great help in all manner of things."

Samuel completely ignored his mother. He was not even the least bit curious as to why she had not bothered to mention what had happened that morning.

"You are beautiful. Your voice is beautiful. Your eyes, your hair..."

He could not stop his mouth. He could not keep silent in her presence. He did not know how to act. He just exclaimed the words that erupted from his heart. Her lithe body draped in this gown, her face in this firelight bordered on sculpture. When Shira lowered her head and parted her lips in a blushing smile, Samuel thought he would dissolve inside the blanket.

"Samuel, do you think you might be able to come home with us? Give time for things to settle here. Carry on our conversations."

This invitation came from his father, the only thing that would force him to tear his eyes away from Shira. He looked at his father opposite the fire, his arms open to him.

"Home. Perhaps after the festival. I would need to speak with the High Priest."

Home was a beautiful word. Samuel repeated the word over and over in his mind as if to convince himself of its existence and the sincerity of his father's request and the fact that this beautiful singer would be there and he could see her again. He was suddenly shy, and laughed to cover this foolish feeling. He felt an awakening in his heart, a newness of something he had never experienced...joy...yet he had no idea of the implication of this sensation. It had instantly replaced the wonder of what he had expressed with his father. He hoped this feeling of joy might continue if he were to go home.

A man cleared his throat. "Samuel." Everyone turned toward the sound of a gruff voice and saw three members of the Tabernacle guards standing just off the main road in front of the family encampment.

"What do you want?" Samuel squinted in their direction.

"The High Priest has taken a fever. He is asking for you."

"Yes, yes, of course." Samuel began to remove the blanket from his shoulders and hand it to Shira.

"No, you need it." Shira extended her hand in refusal. "It will keep you warm on your way back to the Tabernacle."

She was wrong. Her image, her voice, her eyes would be warmth enough for him.

Samuel wrapped the blanket around his shoulders, pleased by Shira's suggestion. He moved toward the guards, but then paused to turn back to his father.

"Father, you really want me to come home?" Samuel's voice was plaintive, soft, like a hopeful child not wanting to risk a possible rejection or that this moment might vanish like a dream.

"Yes, my son."

There it was again...my son. *Yes, my son.* He would go home. Perhaps to study with his father, learn from his father, hear Yahweh through his father. Perhaps something good had come from his father's mystifying submission to Yahweh.

Samuel had to trot to maintain the brisk pace set by the guards as

108

they hustled through the city center. The air was pungent with smoke from the fires, the blood and dung of animals, and the stench of human hordes. Samuel's feet squished with every step as he and the guards got closer to the Tabernacle. The animal blood from all the sacrificing that day had flowed into the street. The raw, well-trod earth was unable to absorb it all, leaving a skim coating on the top. Samuel had to stop to clean off the bloody clods of earth caked onto his sandals.

When he removed his sandals, he felt himself lifted into the air, the blanket Shira insisted he take pulled over his head, shrouding him in complete darkness. A rope was lashed around his arms and tightly secured. His sandals fell from his hands when his abductors began to carry him away from the street. Samuel kicked his legs, trying to touch solid earth with his feet, but it was useless, and he gave in to this assault.

When Samuel heard the sound of laughter and music he knew he had been taken inside some structure but did not recognize any one voice and had no idea what it was. He was forced onto a seat but no one untied the rope or removed the blanket from covering his head. He heard someone shouting to draw the attention of the boisterous crowd, and then say, "Watch," just before wine was poured onto the outline of his face. Samuel was already finding it difficult to breathe through the shroud, but once the fabric was soaked with wine, he gasped for air.

"Don't waste good wine on the likes of him."

Samuel knew immediately it was Hophni, and he began to swing his head back and forth, trying to create slack in the rope and blanket so he could get more air.

"He's suffocating. Remove the blanket. We don't want to kill Father's darling."

"Why not? His father wants us dead. He said so today."

Hophni and Phinehas were inseparable, never one without the other, always each other's best audience.

Pain exploded on the side of his face and nearly knocked him out of the chair. There was a ringing in his ears followed by a chorus of voices encouraging the attacker to inflict more punishment. Samuel was bent over to one side, and then violently jerked upright.

"Remove the blanket. Let him see my face."

Samuel felt the rope loosen and the covering yanked from his head. His turban came off and his long locks fell below his shoulders. Samuel's first impulse was to gulp down some air, filling his restricted lungs, and then dash for the door, but the strong hands of the Tabernacle guards pressing down upon his shoulders made escape impossible.

Phinehas grabbed Samuel's jaw in his thick fingers and brought Samuel's face directly in line with his own. His breath was sodden with wine, eyes rheumy with intoxication. He twisted Samuel's face from side to side, giving it a curious examination.

"Look at this unblemished lamb. Yahweh would approve of this sacrifice. Unless we scar him up a bit."

Phinehas held Samuel's jaw firmly in his grip, then pulled back his other arm and smashed his fist into Samuel's right eye. The crowd erupted with squeamish praise at the brutal act. Phinehas bowed before his appreciative audience, but instantly fell to his knees, too drunk to keep his balance. His crash to the floor raised the volume of laughter.

When the room stopped spinning inside his head, Samuel could see the men and women crowded around a large table in this well-lit and spacious public house, all looking in his direction, pointing at him with amusement and derision. The musicians in the corner had stopped playing, also enjoying the torturous entertainment.

Hophni lurched from the table, knocked over the bench he sat upon, and had to be caught by the people standing behind him. Once he regained his balance, Hophni reached across the table, fumbling with his cane and gripped it with his fingers. He slammed the tip onto the floor and hobbled over to Samuel. He yanked Samuel by his hair and observed the swelling above his right eye.

"How sad for you." Hophni then lifted his own robe. "Look at my legs, boy. Our injuries don't compare, do they?"

Samuel looked at Hophni's bruised and swollen legs, the damage done them when the dying bullock pinned his legs on the platform that morning.

Hophni secured his footing and then rammed the end of his cane into Samuel's stomach. The recoil from the blow caused Hophni to fall on top of his brother who still struggled to get to his feet.

Tears burst from Samuel's eyes and all the air bellowed out of his lungs as he doubled over in his seat, his body in shock at the sudden loss of oxygen. The guards yanked him back in the chair and one of them took a handful of Samuel's hair, pulling hard to keep it taut. He whipped a knife from his belt and raised it to the crowd who began to chant, "Shear the lamb! Shear the lamb!" The guard cut Samuel's hair so close to the scalp that it began to bleed.

Hophni scrambled to his feet with the help of one of the prostitutes. A jeweled necklace secured the top half of her robe; the fabric was decorated with inky pagan images. Slits were cut in the see-through fabric, exposing her breasts.

Hophni slung his arm over the woman's shoulders and kissed her willing lips in appreciation for her assistance. Then he looked back at Samuel—blood flowing down the side of his face, his right eye swollen shut—and pointed his cane at him.

"Let's see how good a job the rabbi did when he circumcised the boy."

Hophni looked at the crowd for encouragement, which they willingly offered.

"You know these country rabbis. They're not very good with a knife."

The crowd howled with laughter, which motivated the musicians to begin pounding their drums and inspiring the woman to move her hips in erotic rhythm as she danced over to Samuel and straddled his lap with her long legs.

"See if he got a kosher cut or if the rabbi sliced off the whole thing." Phinehas shouted into his brother's ear while holding onto his brother to control his lack of equilibrium.

The delight from the crowd exploded when the woman kissed Samuel hard upon his lips and then forced his head between her breasts. Then she rubbed her hand over his loins and turned around and gave the crowd a quizzical look.

"I can't find his barley stalk." She feigned a look of puzzlement which made the room erupt in laughter.

Hophni yanked the woman out of Samuel's lap and pointed for the guards to bring Samuel to his feet. Hophni held out his hand for the knife used to cut Samuel's hair.

"Could he be a limp-vine eunuch?" Hophni pointed for the guards to stretch out Samuel's arms.

Samuel had little strength to fight back. If it were not for the guards propping him up, he would have collapsed.

Knife in hand, Hophni cut Samuel's long shirt down the middle, from neck to knee, and ripped it apart. Then he sliced the lace tied around his waist and pulled it through the hollow hem of his linen breeches, throwing it onto the floor.

Samuel attempted a feeble struggle with his legs and hips to keep the loosened breeches from falling from his waist, but he could not free himself from the firm hold of the guards. The underclothing slid down his legs, exposing his nakedness to the room.

"He's got a kosher cut after all." Hophni turned to face the hysterical crowd applauding his performance and mocking Samuel's uncovered loins.

Hophni spun back around and slapped Samuel on the side of his face. The sound brought the mirth in the room to a sudden stop, and his pleasure took a sinister turn.

"Where is your father now? Where is Yahweh now?" Hophni then spat in Samuel's face, and the room held its breath, waiting to see if there would be a response, but Samuel remained silent. "Take him out of my sight."

The guards dragged Samuel out of the room as most of the clientele rushed to the windows and door to watch.

Samuel was tossed onto his back in the middle of the street. A guard stood above him, holding Shira's blanket in his hands. He spat on Samuel's prone body then slung the blanket onto his chest and walked away.

Once he knew he was alone, Samuel gingerly lifted one arm and held his hand in front of his face until his fingers came into focus. He brought the other hand to the same eye level and moved all his fingers to see if they would function. He took the blanket and wiped his face and chest. He could feel the moisture of the blood-soaked dirt seep into his skin. When the tingling in his limbs had subsided and he felt his strength begin to revive, he rolled onto his side and got to his feet. He teetered in place until he felt steady enough to take a first step, then another, and another before he realized he was naked. He wrapped the blanket around his body and looked into the heavens. The words burned as they formed in his throat and fell from his lips.

"Where were you, Yahweh? Where was my father?"

Nine

SAMUEL HELD HIS BREATH AND LAY BACK IN THE COPPER trough, allowing the hot water to envelop him. He held the blanket to his chest. It had to be cleansed as well. He had scrubbed his body twice, and now for a third time had drained the dirty water, boiled fresh pots, and plunged himself beneath the soothing liquid. He might clean his body and this blanket, but the images in his mind could not be so easily washed away with boiling water, a scouring brush, and scented oils. His ribs reacted with stabbing pain every time he tried to take a deep breath. His eye was now swollen completely shut. His chin felt as if it had been wrenched out of its hinges. The gap on the side of his head where the lock of hair had been cut away was so tender he had been unable to cover it with a bandage.

He had become an untouchable corpse. Better to drown rather than live with these vivid and disturbing memories, or to face Eli, to face his sons, to face his parents and Shira, to face Yahweh. But his sore body overruled his mind. He broke the surface of the water, rising with an agonizing gasp and exhaled in a cry of severe pain.

It will pass, he told himself. *It will pass*, and he dug his fingers into the thick wool blanket and began to stretch and rub the material, loosening the particles of filth and blood ground into the fabric. He remained in the tub, washing out the blanket until the water cooled and he began to shiver.

He stepped out and hung the blanket over the metal rack near the fire.

He wrapped himself in his towel and stood beside the fire until the shivering stopped. The bathing room was empty. At this late hour, all the Levites had either gone off with their families or were asleep in their quarters, exhausted after serving in the Tabernacle for the Day of Atonement. He was grateful for the solitude. He would eventually have to explain his damaged body, but not tonight. Tonight he hoped to be spared any more face-to-face encounters.

Drying off was painful. Getting dressed was excruciating. Walking back to his room with the speed of a hundred-year-old man grew more agonizing with every step. He set his oil lamp on his side table and looked down at his bed. He knelt down and pulled out the goat-hair pouch his father had given him the night before and laid it on the bed. He pulled back the flap and grabbed the hilt of the sword and carefully removed it from its sheath. The muscles in his arms trembled and his thoughts turned deadly. He could return to the brutal scene and wield a sword of vengeance upon his enemies, lie in wait, strike when least expected. But these were not the thoughts he wished to have. They were not the thoughts of the child of the vow. It became painful to hold the sword, so he returned it to its sheath, folded the pouch back inside the goat hair, and placed it back underneath his bed.

He braced his hands upon the bed to help him rise to his feet. He welcomed the thought of lying down. It would ease the pain, but he could not. His heart was too broken; his wretched soul was in more agony than his body. Samuel knew he would just lie there and relive each vicious moment of what had happened in the brothel. Better to move, occupy his mind with other activities, and create distance between the present and recent past, so he snuffed out the flame of his oil lamp and slipped out of his room.

Samuel went to Eli's private quarters to look in on him. He found Eli asleep in his bed, his fitful breath passing through his lips in sputtering moans. In the flickering light of the small fire, Samuel looked upon the High Priest. How would he explain what had happened without causing the old man more pain and regret? What good would that do?

Samuel moved from Eli's sleeping quarters into the adjoining chamber where the holy clothing was kept. Samuel paused in front of the sacred clothing of the High Priest mounted on a stand in the center of the room.

Draped over the ephod was the pouch containing the famed oracular stones used to inquire after the will of Yahweh. Samuel wanted to know his future. Before today, he thought he would always be subject to his mother's vow, the child of the vow, defined by her choice to dedicate him to Yahweh. He had come to accept this destiny with a level of anticipation and dedication, finding assurance and even pleasure in his service to Yahweh. But now his world had turned over and become uncertain. He had lost his bearing. What had been a solid point of reference for his life turned hostile and left him bruised in body and broken in spirit.

Samuel imagined himself dressed in the garments of the High Priest. Had not his father's prophecy spoken of a faithful priest replacing the old guard? Samuel was faithful. He had proven himself. Once Yahweh removed the obstacles, could he be the one chosen to serve? He raised his arm and extended his hand toward the pouch containing the divine stones of revelation and perfection, but blanched in agony. He desired revelation. He wanted to be perfected, for his soul to be washed clean, for the racking pain in his body to cease. It was too painful to extend his arm any further and he lowered it to his side.

Samuel made his way out of the chamber and shuffled through the High Priest's private entrance into the Tabernacle. He kept his head down, shielding the side of his bruised face with his hand, away from the eyes of the Levite posted in front of the doors into the Holy Place. He was grateful when the door was opened for him to pass through.

He felt a sense of peace the moment he was inside the Holy Place and the door closed behind him. Here he was safe. No one, nothing, could harm him while he remained in this sanctuary. Samuel hobbled toward the altar. The Levite attendant had fallen asleep and the fire in the altar was on the verge of going out. Samuel took a handful of fresh coals, dropped them onto the altar, and gently blew his breath on the cooling embers to reheat them. His ribs reacted sharply and cut short Samuel's exhalation of breath. He tapped his fingers on the shoulder of the sleeping Levite, rousing him from his slumber. When he saw that it was Eleazar, he quickly shielded his bruised face. He did not want to explain to his best friend what had just happened. Eleazar was too drowsy to recognize who it was, and when Samuel offered to relieve him from his post, he made no argument and scooted out of the Holy Place as reverentially as possible.

He was alone. When Samuel bent over to get a fresh lamb shank to place on the altar, his body reacted with a thrust of pain. He moved with caution, gritting his teeth and trying to minimize the throbbing jabs. He sat on the stool exhausted, closed his eyes, and allowed his head to fall forward. His neck muscles hurt too much to keep his head elevated. When he heard the meat begin to sizzle, he knew the fire had taken.

"Samuel."

A voice spoke his name, and his body jerked in response, forcing a cry of pain.

"I am here, my lord." He gasped air through gritted teeth. "Here I am."

Samuel waited and listened. He blinked his swollen eyes and looked around, expecting to see the High Priest somewhere in the room, but he was alone. Had he fallen asleep? He stood to look at the lamb shank on the grate. It was barely singed, yet the flame around the meat burned brightly. It could not be, not from the altar or the flame. The pain in his body was surely playing tricks with his hearing. He limped across the room and pushed open the door. The High Priest needed him. He had called his name. In spite of the pain, in spite of abandoning his post, in spite of his uncertainty, he had to return to Eli's chamber.

When Samuel entered the bedroom, he found Eli stretched out upon his bed just as he had been when Samuel first passed through on his way to the Tabernacle. Perhaps Eli had cried out from a dream and, to Samuel's ears, it sounded like he had spoken his name, but he had to be sure, so he tapped Eli's foot, softly calling his name.

"My lord. My lord, it's me, Samuel. You called for me?"

Eli rolled over disoriented by the arousal from his sound sleep. "Samuel, is that you?"

"Yes, my lord. You called me. I was in the..."

"I didn't call for you. I was asleep, as you should be. Go back to bed." Eli lifted the cover over his shoulder and instantly fell asleep before Samuel left the room.

Once inside the Holy Place, Samuel looked about the sanctuary. He dismissed hearing his name spoken to fatigue and bodily pain and emotional shame. He returned to the altar and examined the lamb shank on the grate. It was a sizable portion, and the fire was burning slow enough for this perpetual sacrifice to burn until morning, so he sat back down upon the stool and allowed his eyes to close and his head to droop once again.

Everything was in order. He would take a few minutes of sleep before offering prayers.

How long it was before he heard his name called a second time, he could not say. His eyes had trouble focusing, and it took him a moment to remember where he was. Perhaps Eli had awakened after he left and remembered he did have something he needed to tell Samuel. But Eli was sound asleep when Samuel entered the room. He wasn't sure if he should wake him or not, but finally decided he must.

"My lord, here I am. You called me."

"What! What is it?" Eli blurted his exasperation while swinging his legs off the side of the bed. "I'm in desperate need of sleep and you keep waking me."

Samuel was forced to step back, a confused and foolish expression on his face, and Eli instantly looked remorseful for his harsh manner.

"My lord, forgive me, I could have sworn you called to me."

"Look at me. Step closer." Eli yawned and rubbed his eyes for a sharper focus.

Samuel moved toward him, and Eli reached out and lifted Samuel's head. Eli sucked in his breath when he saw the dark discoloration on the side of Samuel's face.

"Who did this to you?"

"No one, my lord." Samuel's answer came too quickly. "I fell on my way back from visiting my parents. I slipped coming up the steps of the portico."

Eli let his hand fall to his lap. "I will not press you for the truth, but I believe you shield the cause of the wound behind the protection of a lie."

Samuel remained silent and would not confirm the High Priest's discernment.

"I did not call you. Now go back to bed."

"I was not in bed, my lord. I've been keeping watch at the altar."

"This is not your normal time of duty, is it?" Eli was surprised to hear that Samuel was keeping guard over the perpetual sacrifice to Yahweh.

"I just did not feel like sleeping, so I relieved the Levite on duty."

"Yes, yes...well." Eli grumbled and scratched the back of his head. "Then go back to your post."

"Yes, my lord."

Samuel tried to make his exit from the bed chambers without Eli questioning his painful limp. When he hobbled out of the room, Samuel was thankful he did not have to give another false explanation for his body's battered condition.

Samuel had just set foot back inside the Holy Place when the voice spoke a third time. The day had already been filled with events too strange to explain. Why shouldn't he hear voices as well? But the voice had spoken his name and there was no one here. Was Eli toying with him? He looked around the room. He did not want to return to Eli's chambers a third time, but what else could he do? He was being called. He knew it. There had to be some explanation. He had to risk Eli's irritation.

Eli was still sitting on the side of his bed when Samuel reentered the room.

"I had a suspicion you would return." Eli's feet were planted on the floor, his hands nestled in his lap. "Kneel before me, my son."

Eli could see the pain on Samuel's face when he bent down before the High Priest.

"You heard the voice again. Three times now?"

"Yes, my lord. The voice speaks my name. I am confused and frightened."

Eli tucked his fingers underneath Samuel's chin and raised his head. He took the oil lamp from his bedside table to aid his examination of Samuel's bruised and distended face. He noticed the bloodstains on the edges of Samuel's turban and removed it, setting it beside him on the bed. He held the light over the bare scalp on the side of Samuel's head.

"These injuries did not come from a fall on the steps of the portico. They did this to you, my sons."

When Samuel began to weep it was all the response Eli needed to validate what he knew to be the truth. He put the lamp back on the table and exhaled a weary sigh. All Eli had wanted to do at the end of an exhausting day was sleep. He had fallen asleep the moment his head struck the pillow. He could have slept for days he was so exhausted, exhaustion so heavy he could feel its weight pressing him into the straw mattress. Earlier that day, in the shine and heat of the morning sun, he had lain on the ground whimpering like a child and quaking beneath the weight of the prophetic words of this young man's father. He had grasped the pouch next to his heart containing the stones of light and perfection and felt the rising temperature on his skin. If a thick darkness could have covered him or if the earth swallowed him, he would have welcomed the judgment, but the horrible, morning light blazed around him. There was no escape. There was no solace. There was no hiding place. Even sleep was no protection now. Eli had the attention of heaven and earth. He knew then as now that the voice of Yahweh was speaking, that the Presence was making Himself known.

This voice, this calling of Samuel's name, Eli knew he could not take credit for uttering it. When had Yahweh last spoken and to whom? Not to him. Rare had been the visions of Yahweh. Not in his lifetime. Not since the great prophet Moses had Yahweh been a regular Presence among His people. Eli had never heard the Almighty utter his name. Certainly his sons had never heard the voice. Eli knew he could be looking into the battered face of his replacement. He felt a stab of disgrace that the Presence had passed over him and his sons and spoken to someone outside his family line. But perhaps the long silence was over. Perhaps with this young man Yahweh would restore the honor due Him.

"Yahweh is introducing Himself to you. It is time you faced the Divine. Go back, and if the voice calls your name again, say 'Speak, Lord, for your servant is listening.'"

Eli took Samuel's turban and lowered it upon the young man's head. His hands began to tremble as he gently secured it over the wound.

"Do not be afraid, my son."

Samuel got to his feet and began to leave.

"Samuel, whatever the Almighty says to you, you must tell me. Every word."

"Yes, my lord."

Eli watched as Samuel limped from his bed chambers. Deep in his heart, Eli knew that Samuel was hobbling toward the Presence. Samuel was about to face the Presence and Eli knew he would not escape unscathed. What had happened that morning was only the beginning of Yahweh taking righteous action. He knew the young man would return from the Presence with news of the intent of the Almighty. The news of that morning would be confirmed by the news of this night. Father and son would speak to Eli the truth of Yahweh. He felt a doubling of his weight, the weight of the Presence upon the weight of his body. At least Yahweh was coming to him, even by the indirection of Samuel. Yahweh had seen and heard, and Eli would not die without contact with the Creator of heaven and earth. No matter how dire the news, Eli would welcome the words of Yahweh for these words were solely for his ears. In the mercy of Yahweh, he would receive the word of Yahweh before his soul would depart this world. Whatever the word, whatever the outcome, he could be at peace.

All was the same when Samuel returned to the Holy Place. He stood just inside the closed doors, scanning the room. Nothing was out of place—the table of manna, the candles on the menorah burned brightly, the incense smoldered in the dispensers, the altar fire gave off its heat—everything in its place. All was just as he had left it. All was just as it had been since he had been serving in the Tabernacle as a child. All was as it had been since Yahweh, the Almighty, the Creator of heaven and earth, had chosen Israel for His people and made His dwelling with them during the wanderings when the Tabernacle was built and the Presence took residence.

When the voice spoke his name, Samuel dropped to his knees. When the voice spoke his name the second time, he fell on his face. The voice paused, and Samuel lifted his head and tried to speak but could only produce a blunt, hoarse cry. He crawled toward the altar and in the effort found his own human voice.

"Speak. Your servant can hear you."

His power of speech was a flea's response to a voice of thunder. Why had not the High Priest and other Levites come bursting into the Holy Place at the sound of this voice? Why had not the Tabernacle collapsed upon him? Why had he not disintegrated when the voice spoke his name?

The hiss of the sizzling meat on the altar fire intensified, and the flames began to rise above the grate. Samuel tried to lift himself, but a weight pressed him to the floor. He could only inch his prostrate body forward with his face in the direction of the altar. So he dragged himself toward the altar as the flames began to gyrate upward to the ceiling. Samuel tried calling out to the guard at the door to warn him of the danger and to run for help, but his lips and tongue could not shape the words. Samuel was sure the Tabernacle would be enveloped with smoke and burst into flames. Then the voice spoke from out of the flame.

"Behold, I will soon move in Israel in a way that will make the ears of everyone who hears of it tingle."

Samuel's ears went beyond the sensation of a minor prickling. They were roaring tunnels, clear passageways for the word of Yahweh to enter.

"At that time I will carry out against Eli all that I spoke against his family from beginning to end. For I told him that my judgment would be on his family forever because of the sin he knew; his sons made themselves contemptible and he failed to restrain them. For this, I swore to the house of Eli, 'The guilt of Eli's house will never be atoned for by sacrifice or offering.'"

The word his father had spoken was now confirmed. His father had been driven to abandon his normal life and pursue the Almighty, to be in fellowship with the Presence, to prepare to be the voice of the Divine. How could he have ever doubted him, and now, how would he ever explain this divine confirmation of Yahweh's prophetic word to anyone? Eli? His fellow Levites? Who would believe him? Who would understand? His father. Only his father.

The voice said no more, and the flame of the altar fire returned to normal, burning beneath the grate with its slow, steady flame. If there had been more to this visitation than voice and flame, he would not have survived.

The doors of the Tabernacle flew open and sunlight flooded into the Holy Place. Samuel heard his name called again, but this time spoken with the tone and timbre of the human voice. He lifted his head toward the altar to confirm it was not a return visit from the Almighty and realized he was still lying on the floor. He had not been able to rise. He had not made the effort since the departure of the voice, but how long had that been? Had he fallen asleep? Had he let the altar fire go out?

He felt his body being lifted off the ground by a pair of hands with extraordinary strength. When the hands spun him around, he looked into the face of Eli.

"What did He say, my son?" The urgency of his question bordered on desperation.

Samuel looked at the ceiling of the Tabernacle, sure he would see the burnt fabric charred by the shaft of fire, but there was no damage. He wanted proof of the voice. He didn't want to just repeat the words spoken to him. He wanted to show the High Priest a physical sign of the curse that would come upon him, but there was nothing he could point to that would confirm the visitation. He had to speak the words. He had to trust the words, but what he had to retell would be unbearable to speak and unbearable to hear.

"I know it was Yahweh. I know. I never went back to sleep. I remained awake the rest of the night waiting for you to return. Did Yahweh appear? Did He speak?"

"Yes, my lord. The fire from the altar...Yahweh spoke from the fire of the altar, and the flames rose all the way to the ceiling."

Eli could not believe what he was hearing. He looked over Samuel's shoulder at the altar, burning as it always had. He lifted his eyes to the ceiling above the altar expecting to see the evidence of Yahweh's appearance, but there was none.

"Yahweh was in the altar fire, you are sure." Eli searched Samuel's puffy face for any hint of deception.

"Yes, my lord. I thought the Tabernacle would burst into flames."

Eli began to sink to his knees, taking Samuel down with him. "My son, do you realize Yahweh no longer remains behind the veil? He has come out from hiding. The Presence revealed Himself...to you." The thought of this miracle was impossible for Eli to comprehend. His whole life had been devoted to maintaining a Levitical tradition without any sense of who he was serving...until now.

"Yahweh spoke. Tell me what Yahweh said to you?"

When Samuel kept silent, Eli clamped his twisted fingers around Samuel's throat, not caring if it was painful to the young man.

"Do not hide it from me. May Yahweh deal with you, be it ever so severely, if you hide from me anything Yahweh told you."

Eli knew what Samuel would say before he uttered a word. He knew he would confirm what his father had proclaimed the day before—and so he did, in a choked, regretful whisper. There was no hiding from it, no changing it. Both father and son confirmed Eli's failure as a father and the death sentence for his offspring. No sacrifice could atone for the guilt of Eli's dynasty.

Eli heard the laughter from his sons, but was blinded by the sunlight streaming through the open doors as he turned his head toward them.

"Look, brother. Our father is going to kill the boy for us." Hophni pointed to Eli's fingers clasped around Samuel's throat. "When you're done, Father, we'll cut him into parts and burn him on the altar."

Eli released his hold on Samuel's neck and looked him in the eyes. "Yahweh is the Lord. Let Yahweh do what is good in His sight."

Eli pushed Samuel aside, rejecting his attempt to help him stand. "I need no help. I feel stronger than I have in years; my eyes clearer than ever."

Eli rose to his feet with the strength of a man half his age. He charged his two sons standing in the doorway of the Tabernacle like an old bull, taking them by surprise as he gripped their throats, one in each hand. He pushed them out of the doorway and slammed them down upon the floor of the portico.

"You should be dead." Eli snarled as his sons flailed their arms, squirming desperately beneath the strangle hold of their father.

All the Levites in the courtyard and the citizens of Israel stood dumbfounded, watching Eli attack his sons.

"You will die." Eli's snarl turned into a God-roar—an extended, unbearable wail to the heavens, no longer silent, ever watching. "You will die."

Eli released the hold on his sons and ripped his garment asunder, bellowing the name of Yahweh in anguished sobs, begging for any drop of hope for his family that might be wrung from the Almighty's famished mercy.

Shira stirred the contents of the cauldron suspended over the fire with a wooden spoon. She scooped a small portion into the spoon and raised it to her mouth. The smell of cooked lamb and vegetables was always pleasant. After blowing on the contents to cool it, she carefully placed the spoon to her lips for a taste. She determined a little salt would enhance the flavor, so she reached into her herb pouch, pinched a moderate amount into her fingers, and sprinkled it into the stew while she stirred the pot. Soon, Shira would have the stew ready for the family whenever they decided to rise. They had not yet begun to stir.

She watched the people moving up the road toward the city. After yesterday's opening sacrifices, the regular family offerings would begin and continue day-and-night all week. One of the travelers who struggled against the flow of the people with a hitch in his step caught her eye. When he came to a stop on the road in front of the family tents, he did not look at her, but kept his face pointed to the ground. The hood of his robe concealed most of his profile. *He may have gotten a whiff of the stew.* She would offer him a bowl should he turn toward her.

To her surprise, the pilgrim did just that, but he kept his head bowed, leaving much of his face hidden as he approached her, only his chin visible. When he came to a stop in front of the fire he did not speak. His breathing was raspy, labored by his hobbled gait. Shira thought that once he caught his breath he would speak. But when his breathing calmed, he still did not speak to her nor raise his head.

"Are you hungry? I have plenty and can offer you a bowl." Shira reached down and took a wooden bowl from out of the crate beside the fire.

"Is the family awake?"

Strange question from this stranger. But his voice had a familiar ring to it, though halting and slightly damaged.

"No. They are still asleep, though I expect them to—"

"Please do not wake them."

When the stranger raised his head and removed his hood, Shira dropped the wooden bowl into the fire and covered her mouth with her hand to stifle her gasp.

"Please say nothing, Shira. Please do not awaken them, or...or run from me."

"I would never run from you." Shira took a deep breath and slowly brought her hand away from her mouth. She looked into his swollen, discolored face. His eye was nothing but a slit with a flow of water trickling down his cheek.

"I have a message for you, for my parents." Samuel raised the sleeve of his robe and carefully wiped the stream of water spilling from his cheek. "I will not be returning home with you as I had thought. As I had hoped. Tell my parents that I am no longer the child of the vow. I am the son of the vow. I am the firstborn son of my parents. I am the ransomed price. It was confirmed last night by the voice of Yahweh."

Shira stepped back. The boiling stew in the pot was a momentary distraction, but it matched the strange motion in her own stomach. Not a sickness, but a sensation of nourishment and strength.

"The voice of Yahweh spoke to me out of the flame of the altar in the Holy Place. The Almighty confirmed all my father spoke yesterday. The line of Eli will end with the death of his sons."

"Your face...Yahweh did this when He spoke?" Shira regretted the question the moment she asked it, but how would she know unless she asked? And how would she explain to Elkanah and Hannah?

"This was done by the enemies of Yahweh. When the Almighty spoke last night, I had already suffered these wounds."

"What will you do?"

"I shall return. I shall turn my face toward Yahweh. My parents will understand. It is the true fulfillment of what my mother vowed. It is what she prepared me for. It is what my father resisted at first but has now confirmed by his own encounter with the Presence. Now I will begin living my life for Yahweh as the son of the vow...the son of Elkanah and Hannah."

Samuel started to turn away.

"Shall I tell them what happened? Your...your..." She caught herself, and waved the spoon in front of her face, indicating his bruised condition.

Even through the discoloration and swelling around his lips she could see he was attempting to smile.

"This is a momentary condition." He pointed to his face. "I will heal. There is no need to concern them with this."

Samuel began to move back toward the road. She wanted to stop him. She wanted a few more moments in his presence. If she were honest, she thought she wanted a lifetime of moments with him, but this was impossible. He was returning to Yahweh, this son of the vow was limping back to the Tabernacle, the Holy Place of Yahweh. She felt herself begin to let loose her breath which turned to heaving. She dropped the spoon to the ground and noticed the wooden bowl aflame in the fire. She did not bother to get it out. Was this a sign? Was this burning bowl a sign that confirmed to her she might have a place in the life of the son of the vow? She heard her name spoken, but she knew it had not come from out of the flame. She looked up and saw Samuel standing at the edge of the road about to join the other pilgrims heading to the Tabernacle.

"You have a voice of beauty. A voice that honors the Almighty. I will hear it again, and soon."

She watched him pull the hood of his robe over his head and begin to make his way up the road. *Yes, yes you will hear my voice again,* she thought. *And soon.*

Ten

BY MID-MORNING SAMUEL REACHED THE ENTRANCE TO THE courtyard of the Tabernacle. There was a constriction in the line of families waiting for their turn to offer their sacrifice. They were haggling with the livestock merchants over the price of a lamb or calf that would soon find its throat slit and its carcass grilled on the altar.

The prices these greedy merchants charged were outrageous. The shekels brought into the Tabernacle helped finance the religious activities of the Levites, the school of the Levites, and above all, the continual worship of Yahweh in the Tabernacle. The Law of Moses mandated that all Israel support the tribe of Levi and the religious devotion to honor Yahweh. Only the priests who profited from Hophni and Phinehas's schemes could determine what sacrifice was acceptable, and when a family's "blemished" offering was rejected, they were forced to pay the higher prices from the livestock corralled just off the courtyard of the Tabernacle that these dishonest priests had blessed. No one wanted to come to the Atonement Festival to have their sins forgiven only to be turned away at the gates of the Tabernacle, unable to offer their atoning sacrifice.

The practice of charging so high a price for the lamb or the calf or bull was not financing worship of Yahweh. This outright robbery went into the pockets of Eli's sons and the priests in league with them, and the coffers of the Shiloh's city leaders. For too long this was the accepted co-mingling of religion and politics, greed and power. No one stopped them for this illegal and immoral conduct. No one confronted them. No one thought Yahweh was watching. Until now. Even Samuel wondered how Yahweh could be so long-suffering.

He kept the hood of his robe over his head, concealing his identity. After yesterday's public event, he knew he might be more easily recognized. He did not try to maneuver his way through the crowd, but stood back and observed the whole swarm of activity inside the courtyard and on the portico steps leading up to the entrance of the Tabernacle. Sacrifice and worship were being offered by tribal clans gathered from all over Israel for the days of Atonement.

Smoke from altar fires and large basins of incense filled the air. The jumble and noise from the hordes of humans and livestock were an assault on Samuel's eyes and ears, and he pulled the front of his robe up over his nose to aid his breathing. The linen cloth did little to filter the polluted air.

He saw Eli seated in the chair of the High Priest on top of the portico observing all the controlled pandemonium going on from his vantage point. Samuel was surprised and pleased to see the old man. Eli had been the unfortunate recipient of very distressing news the day before from Samuel's father and then from him earlier that morning—a public humiliation followed by a private one, both messages ending with the promise of death. This news was devastating, and the High Priest could have remained in his chambers to avoid any more public shame. He could have hidden out on the grounds of the Tabernacle. He could have fled Shiloh all together. But he had stayed, and he had perched himself in clear view of everyone. His disgrace had been in the open, but he had not hidden in the shadows. Eli was fulfilling his obligation as High Priest, overseeing the public sacrifices. Samuel admired him for his spirit.

Hophni and Phinehas should have been on either side of their father, offering praise to Yahweh and peace to the people of Israel, but Samuel could not find them anywhere on the grounds of the Tabernacle. Their absence was not surprising. Mortification and the pronouncing of death did not inspire repentance. Just the opposite.

The raucous laughter coming from the brothel owned by the brothers drew Samuel's attention. He saw Hophni and Phinehas cheerfully greeting and welcoming guests into their establishment. It was the city leaders who sanctioned the brothels located at the very gates of the Tabernacle, and who profited from the increase in tax revenues. Not to mention the free access to the services as regular customers. Families of Israel in line to sacrifice were forced to stand before the entrance of this brothel with guards from the Tabernacle posted at the gates. The children of these families stared wide-eyed at the people entering and exiting the fenced-in area and eating and drinking with exotic looking women employed to bring them pleasure. This was not a scene that would turn the hearts of these families toward the Tabernacle and Yahweh. Samuel saw mothers shield the eyes of young children and fathers pull their sons away from the entrance. Samuel began to walk through the people toward the entrance, but then stopped. Witnesses, he remembered. The prophet Moses insisted on witnesses to verify the truth of an action, and few witnesses could be trusted in this situation. How well he knew that.

Samuel turned around and entered the courtyard of the Tabernacle. He saw the Levitical chorus on the steps below the High Priest and made his way over to them. When he found Eleazar, he pulled him aside and removed the hood of his robe. Eleazar flinched at the sight of his face. It took his dear friend a moment before he even recognized him.

"What happened to your face? Who did this to you?"

"There is a story here." Samuel waved a hand in front of his face. "And yes, my face feels as bad as it looks, but we do not have time for that now. Come with me."

Samuel slipped the hood back over his head and bounded up the steps to Eli sitting on his priestly chair. He looked back at Eleazar, who was lagging behind, and waved for him to hurry. Then he knelt before the High Priest, took the hem of his priestly robe in his hands, and raised it to his lips.

Eli reached down, perhaps thinking him a humble stranger. He pushed the hood off his head and gasped when he saw it was Samuel.

"My son, I should be the one kneeling before you." Eli put his hands on the armrests of his throne and began to push himself to his feet.

"No, my lord. That would not be right." Samuel rose to his feet and laid a hand upon the shoulder of the High Priest for him to stay seated.

"I want to hand authority over to you. I want all of Israel to know that Yahweh has a prophet in our midst." Eli waved an arm over the crowd in the courtyard below.

"I do believe Yahweh has begun to make Himself known again among His people, my lord, but your sons will resist the change that is coming."

"They will fail at this." Eli sat back in his chair. He looked beyond the courtyard to his sons' brothel outside the gates of the Tabernacle. "As I have failed as High Priest. I have chosen my sons over Yahweh. They are my sons, and I will love them for the rest of the days Yahweh has appointed for me, but Yahweh has spoken and His word shall not fail. The arrow has been shot from the bow of Yahweh and will soon strike its target."

"My lord, allow me to speak with them. Perhaps their hearts will be touched while there is still time."

Eli cast his eyes to the ground and breathed a long hopeless sigh. "We both know what the outcome will be, but Yahweh may yet be merciful."

"My lord." Samuel bowed to Eli one last time.

He waved at Eleazar to follow him. Samuel raised his hood over his head as he descended the steps, and he and Eleazar made their way out of the courtyard.

Samuel approached the gate of the brothel with a self-assurance he had never known. His confidence was so real he could taste it. The night before he had been carried onto these polluted grounds next to the Tabernacle against his will, beaten and abased by the sons of Eli. Now he would enter the premises under his own strength and with the wind of the Almighty billowing his heart.

The hand of the guard slammed into Samuel's chest as he tried to enter the gate.

"Let me see your coin purse, Levite. No one enters without a deposit of shekels."

Samuel kept his head bowed. The guard held his hand firmly against Samuel's chest, waiting for his demand to be met.

"I wish only to speak with the proprietors."

"Talk or not, you must pay to enter."

"Sir, you should know Levites have no shekels." Eleazar raised his empty hands as proof of a Levite's chronic poverty.

Samuel smiled at his friend's response to the guard's demand.

"Then go back to your sacrifices."

"Come, Samuel. We should not be here." Eleazar put his hand on Samuel's shoulder as if to pull him away.

Samuel felt the pressure of the guard's hand upon his chest begin to slacken. He pulled his hood back, and instantly, the guard's face went from stern to trembling.

"I have paid already with this." Samuel pointed to his injured appearance.

The guard's hand fell to his side, and he stepped back. Samuel knew this man recognized him, that the guard's sudden lack of force was from a weighted heart for previous wrongs he had done against Samuel. But Samuel was not here for the guard, and he moved forward without further hindrance.

"What has your face got to do with any of this?" Eleazar inquired as he stumbled behind his friend.

Samuel paused when he reached the entrance and turned back to Eleazar. "Everything."

Eleazar threw up his hands, a perplexed expression on his face. "Must we enter this place, Samuel? I do not want to see what is inside, especially during the days of Atonement."

"What is inside is the brokenness of Israel. It is the result of our hearts turning away from Yahweh. It is time to return. Atonement begins today."

Laughter could be heard coming from inside the large structure. Samuel could see that Eleazar still struggled with the idea of following him into the brothel.

"I was here last night. It will be nothing like that experience."

Eleazar's eyes widened when he heard that his friend had been here before. Samuel put his hand upon Eleazar's shoulder.

"Do not be afraid, dear friend. I need a witness. You are my witness."

Samuel turned and went inside. When he walked through the curtains and entered into the open space, the memory of the night before came back to him. But this time he had entered on the strength of his two legs. He looked around the room filled with patrons and those in service to their trade. In any other circumstances, these elite citizens of Israel would never mingle with such people, were it not for their lust and pleasure. Samuel walked to the center of the room where the night before he had been tied to a chair, beaten, and verbally abused. He stood silent and waited to be recognized.

"Guards, surround them." The double-voiced command flew above the noise of the dense crowd like an echo and brought an instant silence in the room.

Samuel had trusted that Eleazar had followed him. With this order shouted by the sons of Eli, he knew.

The guards responded as they were instructed, and then Hophni and Phinehas stepped out of the crowd of revelers and approached Samuel. They stood on either side of Samuel, sneering at him, but Samuel did not speak. He did not need to. He could wait.

"You have come back for more, I see." Hophni raised a fist, threatening to repeat his physical strike from the night before.

Samuel did not give him the satisfaction of flinching.

"With a face in this condition, it is questionable if you have enough money to find anyone who would agree to take you." Phinehas pointed to Samuel's face and looked around the room for any prospects. There were none. "I see the little lamb is too blemished for any of our ladies at any price. Go back to the house of Yahweh. Maybe the Almighty will overlook your blemished face."

"Come with me, Phinehas, Hophni, back to the house of Yahweh. Leave all this behind. Seek the mercy of Yahweh. Seek to change the mind of Yahweh. Come back."

The brothers looked at Samuel, then at each other, then around the room.

"Where is Yahweh? Who is Yahweh? Anyone here ever seen Yahweh, ever heard His voice?" Phinehas raised his arms to welcome any response from the crowded room.

The people were silent, even when Hophni tried to encourage them to laugh, the few that complied squeaked out barely a chuckle.

"Yahweh is real, my brothers. The God of Israel will rule His people regardless of her leaders. Come back. Do not be destroyed."

"You and your father hear voices in your heads and say you speak for Yahweh." Hophni made an expression of madness which got a few more people to laugh.

Phinehas took a determined stance in front of Samuel. "You have spoken your words, you and your father. We are not so easily frightened or fooled as our father. You have him believing you speak with the voice of Yahweh. I read the Law of Moses too, little lamb, and it is written in the scrolls, 'If a prophet speaks in my name anything I have not commanded him to say, he must be put to death.' I will enjoy watching you tossed into the stoning pit. The first stone to hit your head will be the one I throw myself."

"And I the second." Hophni slapped his chest to affirm his brother's word.

"Now leave." Phinehas took a step back. "You are not welcome here."

Samuel glanced over his shoulder and caught the shocked eyes of Eleazar.

"Did you bear witness, Eleazar?" Samuel spoke forcefully.

Eleazar opened his mouth but could not speak.

"Did you bear witness?" Samuel repeated with a gentler tone.

Eleazar swallowed hard before he spoke. "I have borne witness."

Samuel looked back at Eli's sons. "I tremble at the words of Yahweh. They will not fall to the ground like spilt wine. You have chosen your way. You delight in your transgressions. May the mercy of Yahweh crack your hearts of stone before it is too late."

Samuel turned his back on the brothers and started to make his exit. Before he and Eleazar parted the curtains to leave, Phinehas screamed at him.

"We will destroy you, little lamb!"

Samuel did not bother to turn to face the one who threatened him. He spoke loud enough for everyone in the room to clearly hear his voice. "For as long as Yahweh desires, I will serve Him in the Tabernacle. I am going nowhere."

Samuel walked out of the establishment. He departed as he had entered. He was not carried by Tabernacle guards or flung into the mess of the street, a broken soul. He walked in a new strength, a strength not of his own creation, but the strength of Yahweh.

When Samuel made his way up the stairs of the portico with Eleazar beside him, Eli rose to his feet to greet them. He waved to the Levites to blow the ram's horns as if in welcome of champions. The air blasted with the sound of the shofars, and Eli indicated for Samuel to stand next to him.

"Remove your hood, my son."

Once Samuel pushed back his hood, Eli raised his arms before the people to draw their attention. Eli declared in a powerful voice for all ears to hear, that Samuel, son of Elkanah and Hannah of Ramah, even he who has served faithfully in the Tabernacle since a tender age, he is a true prophet of Yahweh. That he, High Priest of Israel, declares to all citizens from Dan to Beersheba that Samuel has been raised up as prophet of Yahweh and that none of his words would fall to the ground and become waste or empty.

Samuel felt discomfort listening to Eli declare him a prophet of Yahweh in Israel. He stood before these people a blemished lamb—his face proved it. But if Eli could hold himself up before the people, himself disgraced the day before, and give glory to Yahweh for reestablishing the Presence among His people, then Samuel could bear the embarrassment of everyone looking upon his marred face. His face would soon heal. His face would soon be known in Israel. His face would soon reflect the glory of Yahweh.

PART THREE

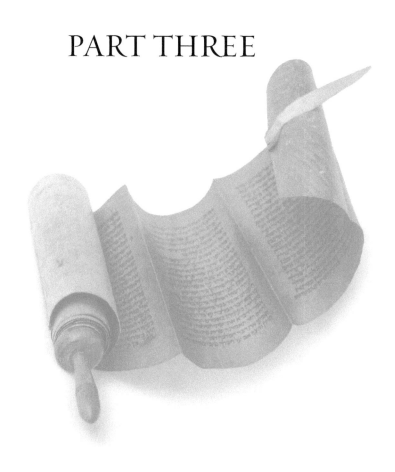

Eleven

THE BROILING AFTERNOON SUN BEAT DOWN UPON THE PROCES-
sion. The funeral cart, pulled by a team of oxen, swayed back and forth
along the dirt-packed road. Saba had made sure the weight inside the cart
was distributed evenly to keep the sarcophagus from shifting, assuring the
deceased a smooth ride. He guided the team with a purple rope decorated
with colored flags and silver rings strung through the nasal septum of the
oxen. The deceased had requested Saba be in charge of the entire proceedings. He offered to pay extra for the service, but Saba refused. "It is my
honor to start you on your journey," he had told Lord Ib.

On his last visit to Saba's shop, Lord Ib was so sick he could not walk
or stand. Saba stood outside the door of his artist's studio to greet the Fifth
Seren's litter when it arrived at his shop in the heart of Aphek's commercial
district. Saba had not wanted to cover his nose and mouth out of respect for
his patron, but Lord Ib insisted, not wanting to risk infecting his favorite
artist. Saba bowed low as the muscular slaves lifted the frail body of Lord
Ib out of his cushioned litter and carried him inside.

The design on the sarcophagus was Lord Ib's vision. He wanted images
of dancers, musicians, scholars, and poets painted within rows of vineyards
and groves of fruit trees around the circumference of the sarcophagus
with enough room inside to hold the many offerings and gifts he would
take with him on his journey to the underworld. He was a man of peace,

137

educated and refined in manner, not like his counterparts who ruled the other Philistine cities and had more quarrelsome temperaments. Those lords celebrated power and wealth; Lord Ib, the mind and spirit.

"It won't be long now, Saba."

Lord Ib only spoke in hoarse bursts. He coughed bloody phlegm into a clean cloth as he wheezed the shop's dusty air into his lungs. He wiped the sweat from his bald head with the soiled cloth before tossing it into a sack held open by a dutiful physician.

"I'm laboring day and night, my lord." Saba pointed to his work on the hardened plaster with his paint brush. "The face piece lacks the final touches of paint."

The slaves carried Lord Ib around the stone vessel so he could study the intricacies of the carved and painted images.

"It is a thing of beauty."

"Fit for a member of the Seren." Saba bowed his head, touched by his sovereign's praise, though the design on the front piece was a bit grotesque for Saba's taste.

Lord Ib paused at the head of the coffin to admire the bas-relief of his visage carved into the top of the lid. The feathered headdress burst around Lord Ib's face like rays of the sun.

"I should look this good when I arrive in the Abode of Souls and meet the Mother Asherah and Ilu, the Father of Years." Lord Ib ran his scaly fingers over the image.

The Fifth Seren's physical dissipation was most apparent in the reddened and deflating tattooed images on either side of his face: on one side an inflamed emerod blossomed in the center of the storm cloud; the other, Baal, a once lusty god of fruitfulness, was now cursed with sagging virility.

"Saba, you are a true artist; the only one I trust to send me to the underworld in a proper manner. I will praise your name to all I meet on my eternal journey."

"You are too kind, my lord." Saba smiled at the Fifth Seren's admiration of his work, though it was concealed behind the mask over his face.

That was the last time Saba saw him alive. Lord Ib died within a month, and the other four Serens arrived in Aphek shortly afterward for the funeral.

Saba hired laborers to cut a tomb out of the rock base in the side of a mountain to fit the sarcophagus. For the Fifth Lord, Saba respected every detail of the last wishes of the deceased for one reason: he wanted those who made the westward journey to the underworld ahead of him to speak well of his work and his character. He prayed the Fifth Lord would remember to keep his promise.

The citizens of Aphek lined the road from the city gates all along the half-league march to where Lord Ib's tomb had been cut into the mountain base. Every six feet a soldier in full military regalia stood at attention. Each soldier slapped his sword against his shield as the body of their lord rumbled by them. Merchants, public servants, and nobles stood behind the soldiers and would bow as Saba led the oxen down the road. Ahead of the procession, dancers and musicians were celebrating Lord Ib with music and song, raising such a dust cloud in their frenzy that Saba had to cover his nose and mouth with the hood of his robe to filter his breathing.

Behind the ox cart marched the four surviving Lords of the Philistines, each imperial head bearing a fluted crown of sun rays and embossed with religious icons. Behind each lord, train-bearers held the ends of their flowing robes to keep the splendid garb from touching the ground. Their exposed torsos bore the ink representations of a history of their exploits written on fleshy parchment. Each lord carried an offering to be placed inside the encasement to sustain Lord Ib on his excursion through the underworld.

A chorus of priests and poets awaited the convoy beside the altar. Once Saba parked the oxen in the designated spot before the tomb cut into the mountain, they burst into their unison ode:

> "Oh ye gods of the heavenly skies, lift up your heads.
> Oh Mot, the god of death, awake from slumber.
> Draw your eyes to the prince of Aphek.
> He comes to the gates of the underworld in splendor."

Saba handed off the guide rope to a soldier and moved quickly to oversee the special military detail as they removed the sarcophagus and set it on the flat, stone altar in front of the open tomb. It took eight soldiers to slide the receptacle out of the cart and place the weighty object upon the altar. Then Saba ordered the stone covering removed. He had them prop the heavy lid upright beside the cutout tomb, like a tongue removed from an open mouth, so everyone who passed in front of it could behold Saba's handiwork carved into the top of the lid.

Saba bowed to the four lords as they proceeded to the altar, each one taking his position at one of the four corners of the sarcophagus. Once the wives and children of Lord Ib were positioned behind Lord Ib's honor guards, each lord, in turn, raised his gift before the assembly and then to the heavens.

"To keep thee from hunger on your journey!" Lord Arioch cried, and then set his silver tray of roast pork in his corner.

"To keep thee from danger on your journey!" Lord Ashur exclaimed, before setting his jeweled short-sword in his corner.

"To keep thee from thirst on your journey!" Lord Shinab shouted, and set his skins of wine in his corner.

"To keep thee from darkness on your journey!" Lord Tidal yelled, and he set his lamp and oil in his corner.

For their offerings, Lord Ib would speak well of them to Mot, god of death.

The four lords bowed their heads in reverence and the priests' ode continued:

> "Mother Asherah, Lady of the sea, rejoices.
> Lord Baal stands when he sees Lord Ib arrive.
> The gods of Canaan rise from the banquet table in greeting.
> El Elyon opens the store house of his treasures."

Saba took the opportunity to usher the four lords from the altar to a designated area just far enough away where they could observe the proceedings and still have relative privacy. He had been a member of Lord Ib's court long enough to understand the importance of taking advantage afforded by such an event for the lords to discuss the nation's business. Saba arranged for a banquet-size table laden with food and drink for the lords to consume while the funeral continued.

> "From the seat of his dominion did Lord Ib rise.
> From the throne of his kingdom did he take flight.
> The Rider of the Clouds departs for the eternal kingdom.
> Like the mighty eagle, he doth take flight."

Once the four lords held a goblet of wine in their hand, Saba motioned to the commander of the honor guard for the wives and children to approach the sarcophagus of Lord Ib. The family swarmed around the open receptacle, keening and wailing as they lay their gifts around the dead body in royal attire to meet the pantheon of Philistine gods.

Saba remained with the four lords during the noisy lamentations. He was thankful that they had required his presence and that he did not have to be in the middle of such clamorous familial grief. Saba had instructed the stewards to have the parchments of his maps and sketches spread out for the lords on the opposite end of the table from the food and drink. The four lords ignored the wailing and quickly became engrossed in the parchments of maps and sketches as Saba had suspected.

Lord Ashur tapped the parchment he was examining with his finger and looked over at Saba standing off to the side. "You are the artist?"

"Yes, my lord." Saba bowed his head. "It was Lord Ib's last request of me, to provide his fellow lords with this knowledge when you gathered in Aphek."

"And when did you make these drawings?" asked Lord Ashur.

"At a recent festival in honor of the Hebrew god."

"What was your ploy? What did the Hebrews believe you were doing in Shiloh?"

"I had an artist's booth in the merchant's section of the city. The Hebrews like my miniature carvings of the Baals and the Ashtoreths. There are so many people in Shiloh for the festival, the officials take little notice of one artist's booth or of me."

Lord Ashur studied the parchment with Saba's drawing of the Tabernacle in Shiloh. Then he looked over at the sarcophagus of his dead friend.

"You are a talented young man, Saba. I may commission you to design a funeral vessel to carry my soul to the underworld."

"I would be honored, Lord Ashur, though may the gods keep you safe and well for one thousand years."

"Let us not hope for too much blessing." Lord Tidal smiled at Lord Ashur as he stepped away from the table long enough to pour some wine from his jeweled goblet onto the ground in honor of the dead. Lord Tidal paused to glance at the wailing women and children circling the altar and reaching inside the sarcophagus to make physical contact with the dead one last time. Then Lord Tidal returned to the drawings on the table. "Based on your drawings, Saba, we may have an opportunity."

"How were you able to canvass the city?" Lord Ashur poured out a portion of his wine but did not bother to step away from the table.

"Morning and evening while my booth was closed, I moved about the city. At night I drew what I observed with bits of dried charcoal." Saba glanced over his shoulder to check on the family. They were still engaged in saying their farewells to Lord Ib.

"I say strike now." Lord Arioch poured some of the contents of his goblet onto the ground behind the table to honor Lord Ib. "The nation of Israel is disordered with no centralized government or strong ruler; the tribes have no loyalty to anyone."

"May I speak, Lord Arioch?" Saba bowed his head in honor of his request.

Lord Arioch extended his goblet toward Saba by way of permission.

Before he spoke, Saba pointed to the wine steward and signaled for him to refill Lord Arioch's goblet.

"Lord Arioch, the Hebrews may have someone to unite them; a rising young priest. The High Priest of Israel acknowledged him during the festival at the Tabernacle."

"All the more reason to strike now, I say," Lord Arioch said before he drank deeply from his refilled goblet. "Before this Hebrew gains strength."

Lord Shinab took his turn to pour a libation. "This is for the One-in-Five passing from us into the underworld." He poured a portion onto the ground, and then raised his goblet again, but not to be refilled. "And this is for our dead citizens crying out from their tombs for revenge for their murder by Samson the Judge in the temple of Dagon just five years ago. May their voices be silenced by the spilling of Hebrew blood. I say we are gathered now. I say we should strike now. I say we silence the cry of our people now."

Lord Shinab emptied his wine upon the ground, and the other lords did the same.

"It is good to remember the Hebrew god is defensive if you harass his people." Lord Tidal handed his empty goblet to a servant, refusing the steward's attempt to refill it.

"Yet he likes to turn the Hebrews over to their enemies whenever they displease him." Lord Shinab turned his empty goblet over on the table.

"We cannot underestimate the power of this god." Lord Ashur was never hasty for war. "The Hebrew god is not to be trifled with."

"Having one god is too cumbersome." Lord Arioch raised his glass to Saba, and Saba pointed to the steward to refill the goblet. "I am thankful for many gods. Should we offend one, many others may rush to our aid."

Lord Shinab held up the parchment of the painted images of Shiloh's defensive walls and gates. "Based on your sketches the city's defenses are in need of repair," he said.

"Yes, my lord. And the eastern and northern gates appear the weakest."

"The Hebrews are fierce fighters." Lord Ashur continued to advocate for caution. "We need unity among the Seren if we go to war. We need the Fifth Lord."

"My lords." Saba risked interrupting the Serens' talk of war and directed their attention toward the altar. "Son firstborn of Lord Ib is approaching."

A young man, his head bowed in respect, carried an ornate chest and advanced with deliberate steps toward the four lords. The lid was closed on the gold chest and covered in precious stones. The man's garb was plain, suitable to the occasion of mourning, yet revealing of his statuesque physique. His leggings and vest were plain linen. His boots were old and worn. The bands around his long, muscular arms were bronze and bore the engraved image of Baal. Belted onto his side was an iron sickle-sword. His head was shaved except for a tail of black, braided hair reaching the middle of his back and bound with a strip of leather. A cluster of three purple desert flowers bloomed from the top of his woven hair. His exposed skin bore no ink drawings. He was only a prince and had yet to do anything worthy of historical notation drawn onto his skin.

Saba handed each lord a gold coin collected from them before the ceremony. They came around to the front of the table to meet the young man. Then Saba pointed for the young prince to kneel in front of the lords and open the chest.

"For the expense of my father's journey." He made his humble appeal, and the lords dropped their coin into the chest.

The chest was already full of coins provided by Lord Ib's treasury, but by custom, the surviving lords were to make a donation from their personal coffers. They were only allowed to donate one coin so as not to give the impression of enticing Lord Ib's favor.

After the young man thanked the lords, Saba began to lead him back to the altar.

"Prince Namal." Lord Arioch called out, and the young prince turned back to face the lords. "You are the firstborn male child from the loins of Lord Ib. I ask, are you your father's son or are you your own man?"

Saba saw that Prince Namal was unsure how to respond. He instructed the prince to bow to the lords and continue on toward the altar with Saba.

The family made room for the prince to step beside the coffin. Saba signaled for the priests and poets to cease the verse prayers. When all was quiet, Prince Namal held aloft the jeweled chest of coins and gave his public supplication for his father to those immortals about to receive him.

> "Oh, celestial gods, look upon this housing of gold.
> Let the wealth of this treasure prepare the feast.
> Let the tables be set with plates of fruit and meat.
> Let the flagons be filled with wine.
> Receive these offerings with gladness,
> And may there be rejoicing from all the gods,
> When Lord Ib enters the gates of the everlasting."

Prince Namal lowered the chest into the sarcophagus and gestured for the family to move back to their place behind the honor guard. He would oversee the final proceedings. When the family was behind the barrier, the prince nodded to Saba that he could begin.

Saba pointed to the honor guard to restore the lid back onto the sarcophagus. Once it was in place, Saba instructed the metallurgist to fill the crack between the lid and coffin with molten lode. The artisan carefully poured the boiling ore along the edge of the coffin from his iron pot. Then Saba invited the four lords to join Prince Namal at the cut-out tomb at the base of the mountain.

Prince Namal stood alone at the opening and watched as the honor guard labored toward him under the weight of this burial vessel laden with eternal treasures, carrying it from the altar to the tomb.

Each lord placed his hand upon the vessel as it passed before them.

Saba offered Prince Namal an opportunity for a final, private farewell to his father before inserting the sarcophagus into the cut-out rock, but the prince declined to speak a blessing or prayer over the vessel. He kept his stoic face focused upon the citizens of Aphek over whom he would now rule. Prince Namal was about to launch his father into eternity, but he kept his eyes toward his own future dominion.

Once the sarcophagus was placed inside the carved indention into the mountain base, Saba ordered the cut stone covering hoisted into place, and then directed the metallurgist to seal the tomb. While the artisan filled the gaps along the line of chiseled rock with the molten sealant, the oxen were unhitched from the funeral cart and brought before the altar. Saba signaled to another military detail to chop the cart into pieces and place the wood upon the altar. Saba then doused the altar with flammable oil as the broken cart was arranged onto the flat surface. When the altar and bed of wood glistened with the oil, Saba instructed the priests to light their torches.

Prince Namal stepped over to the oxen and raised his iron sword above his head. The force of the blow was so powerful the head of the beast was severed with one cut. Prince Namal repeated the execution of the second beast with the same effective potency. Once the animals were heaved upon the altar, the prince took one of the torches and tossed it between the bleeding carcasses. A blaze quickly engulfed the sacrificial plinth.

Spattered in blood, his wild eyes bulging, Prince Namal turned to the four lords and thrust his bloody sword into the air. "May the citizens of Aphek rejoice in their new lord. May the Sea Peoples of Canaan sing the exploits of the Seren. May the enemies of the Five Lords tremble at the mention of their names. May the nation of Philistia cut down her enemies with the sword. May the gods raise the kingdom of the Philistines above all the nations of the earth."

The new Fifth Lord ended his declaration by repeating the name of his father. Saba watched as the Four Lords of the Seren were caught up in the chanting of the name of the deceased, adding their own voices to the praise. Saba allowed himself a contented smile for doing his part in perfectly executing Lord Ib's departure into the afterlife and providing the other lords with the information he gathered on his mission. Then he joined with the others echoing his lord's name and shouted into the heavens.

Twelve

ELI SAT ON A CHAIR IN A CORNER OF THE HOLY PLACE, LISTENING to the shuffling activities of the Levites going about their duties and to the quiet chants and prayers of the priests. His old eyes were failing him. His old body was failing him. He had been chastened by Yahweh for years of excessive quiet, ignoring his sons' wrongdoing. But in recent days there had been a spark of revival in his heart. He knew his time was coming to an end, his remaining days were few in number, and he wanted to spend them quietly, out of the public eye. His body would turn to dust and his soul would pass on to Sheol. Until then, he would sit still before the Presence in the Tabernacle. He wanted peace. He wanted to wean himself from the troubled world. He wanted his heart to be open and receptive to any communication from Yahweh.

Eli knew that Samuel had Yahweh's favor. His tired soul was relieved by the relinquishing of spiritual authority to Samuel's position as the prophet of Yahweh. The Almighty appeared to Samuel. Revelations from the Creator were given to Samuel. Eli need not stand in the way of this divine connection. But he did secretly hope that Yahweh might whisper to *him*. That Yahweh might take pity after the doom pronounced on him and his family line. He would be still and silent. Eli would take the scraps of any whispers Yahweh might drop before him. He would worship in his heart the great name of Yahweh, recite the prayers of the priests, chant the songs of the Levites. The world outside the Holy Place was in turmoil. The enemy of Israel had gathered on the plains between Aphek and Shiloh. But inside the sanctuary of the Almighty, Eli could rest and worship, wait and listen.

When the doors of the Tabernacle burst open, Eli was jolted out of his tranquil frame of mind. It was the hour for the doors to be opened, greeting the dawn with reverence, but noise and chaos rushed in. The voices were angry and insistent.

"What is the cause of this disturbance?" Eli shifted around on his stool, but unable to rise on his own strength.

Eber, a young Levite, serving in his first duty period as aide and guide for the High Priest, rushed over to Eli and stood beside his charge.

"I do not know, my lord." Eber held an empty receptacle where he had just replenished the oil for the flame burning in the menorah before the doors flew open.

"Stand back. We are here for the Ark."

Eli's eyes might have failed, but his ears had not. He heard the unmistakable voices of Hophni and Phinehas.

"Help me to my feet, Eber." Eli reached out his arm, and Eber lifted him onto his unsteady legs. Eli gripped Eber's shoulder, and with his staff in his other hand, allowed Eber to guide him to the open doors of the Tabernacle.

"What is the meaning of this outburst?" Eli could see the animated but blurry forms of his sons standing at the entrance into the Holy Place.

"Out of the way, old man!" Hophni shouted. "We are here for the Ark."

"Go." Phinehas gave the command to the Tabernacle guards who began clearing the way for the Levites ordered to bear the Ark out of the Tabernacle.

Eli and Eber were nearly trampled by the small horde that rushed into the Holy Place, heading straight for the Holy of Holies.

Horror overtook him. He could not believe how the world was out of control and had invaded the Holy Place of the Almighty.

"Do not do this, my sons. You will be struck down for this desecration."

"We do not have time, Father." Phinehas knocked Eber's hand off his father's shoulder and pulled him outside onto the portico.

"We need the Ark to rout the enemy." Hophni followed the Levitical Ark bearers into the Holy Place.

Eli held onto the doorframe and looked back into the darkness of the Holy Place. He could only make out ghostly forms swarming around the blue, purple, and scarlet veil.

"You are not allowed!" Eli shouted. "You are not allowed!"

When Eli heard the sound of the Levites and guards yank the curtain from the four pillars of acacia wood and the gold and silver clasps and sockets clatter onto the floor, he bellowed as if from a spear thrust straight into his heart. When he was able to get his breath, he violently pulled away from Phinehas and bolted across the portico. He did not care that he could not see where he was going. His only thought was to find Samuel. Before reaching the top steps, he felt a hand upon his shoulder. He was about to spin around and strike the assailant with his staff until Eber quickly identified himself.

"Guide me to the academy of Levites, and make haste."

Samuel and Eleazar stood at the shoulders of the Levitical students, monitoring the progress of their classifying and filing new copies of Moses's account of the early wanderings out of Egypt, when they heard the sound of commotion through the open windows. They barely had time to look out the window when the High Priest and his aide burst into the large library of scrolls and writing tables. Sweat had soaked through the turban on Eli's head, and both he and his aide were panting.

"My lord, what is the matter?" Samuel rushed to Eli's side.

"The Ark." Eli struggled to speak between labored breaths. "They are taking the Ark. My sons. The Ark bearers. The Tabernacle guards. When we left, they were tearing down the veil before the Holy of Holies."

Eli could not contain his sorrow and began to wail.

"There were soldiers waiting outside the entrance of the Tabernacle," Eber added.

"Where are they taking the Ark?" Eleazar stepped from behind one of the scribe's writing tables and moved toward Eli.

"To the battlefield." Eber bore a bewildered look. "I do not know."

"Stay with the High Priest." Samuel gave his instruction to Eber as he ran out the entrance of the academy. "Eleazar, come with me."

Samuel ran toward the Tabernacle. He could only imagine that the brothers were using the Ark as a way to gain power. What did they care about the Ark of the Covenant or its sacred contents? This attempt to use Yahweh was to force the Almighty to act on Israel's behalf, not for the honor of Yahweh. And should Israel defeat the Philistines, then they would take all the credit.

When Samuel and Eleazar arrived at the Tabernacle, there was a crowd of citizens gathered around the entrance. They forced their way through the throng, but the soldiers would not let them pass into the courtyard. When Samuel insisted they be allowed to enter, he was told that it was for their own safety.

"We do not know what will happen when the Ark comes out of the Tabernacle."

"We are Levites and priests of Yahweh. No one can move the Ark without the consent of the High Priest." Samuel's declaration caused a stir among the soldiers.

A military leader pushed through a cohort of soldiers and stood in front of Samuel, giving him a pugnacious glare.

Samuel was not intimidated. "Who are you?"

"I am Jediael, commander of the host of the tribe of Benjamin. The Philistines engaged us in battle and four thousand sons of Israel were lost. The sons of the High Priest gave instruction to bring the Ark of the Covenant to the battlefield. They said the sign of Yahweh's covenant will change our fortunes and we will defeat our enemies."

Trumpets and shofars split the air with their blasts, and all attention was turned toward the entrance of the Tabernacle. As soon as the bearers of the Ark came out onto the portico, Jediael barked his order. "Push back the crowds from the entrance."

The soldiers brought their shields to their chests and began to push the people away from the entrance. Hophni and Phinehas appeared first and raced down the steps of the portico. Horses were waiting for them at the bottom of the steps, and by the time they climbed into their riding seats, the Ark emerged from the Tabernacle. Once the fathers had conquered the land of Promise and divided the territories among the tribes, Shiloh became the city for the holy shrine of Yahweh. Now the Mercy Seat of Yahweh was being removed to the battlefield and used as an object of war.

"That I should live. That I should live. That I should live."

Samuel and Eleazar turned to see the crowd behind them begin to part and make way for Eli. Eber carried Eli's turban and staff as the High Priest held onto Eber's shoulder. Every few steps Eli bent down and scooped up a handful of loose dirt. He threw it into the air, creating a cloud that rained dust down upon his bare head.

"That I should live to see the glory of Yahweh depart."

The howling cry of the High Priest pierced Samuel's heart. The lament did not rise from a single voice. It rose from the voices of all Israel, the living and the dead—from the desert wanderings, from the days of slavery, from the ancients before there was a people of Yahweh's choosing. The flung dust of the earth floating in the air, tiny grains of dust, reminded Samuel it was from the dust that Yahweh shaped them and it was to the dust they would return.

When Eli stopped in front of Samuel, his knees gave out and he collapsed into Samuel's arms. Samuel was unable to bear the weight, and he fell to the ground in the arms of the High Priest, their shared lamentation rising into the sky.

Samuel did not see the Levites carry the Ark out of the courtyard of the Tabernacle and load it into a wagon. He was lying on the ground next to Eli in the middle of a throng of citizens. It was Eleazar who reported that Hophni and Phinehas were escorting the Ark to the battlefield under the protection of Commander Jediael.

"Help me, please." Eli's voice was a raspy whisper.

Samuel, Eleazar, and Eber helped the High Priest to his feet. It took all three of them to support Eli as they slowly guided him into the courtyard. Eli stopped when they reached the first steps of the portico leading up to the Tabernacle. He looked up at the open doors leading into the Holy Place and began to tremble.

"What is it, my lord?" Samuel asked.

"I cannot look upon the desecration. Go, my son. Be my eyes. Go and look inside and tell me what you see."

Samuel and Eleazar left Eli and Eber at the bottom of the portico steps and dashed up to the open doors of the Tabernacle. They pushed through the cluster of Levites and priests. They would not venture inside but were huddled at the entrance, weeping and praying. The curtain that separated the Holy Place from the Holy of Holies lay in a pile on the floor with two of the four pillars resting on top of it. The menorah and the altar had been set to the side near the table of consecrated bread. The flame of the menorah had gone out. The sacrificial fire of the altar had been spilt, ash and coal and burning flesh lay scattered on the floor of the Holy Place. Sunlight filtering through the doors cast shadows on the emptiness of the Holy of Holies. A numbing clarity descended upon Samuel's soul. After centuries of containing the Presence, this sacred space had not been ransacked by a pagan army, but by Yahweh's people. The chosen of Yahweh had ripped out the heart of their faith, turning this sanctuary into a hollow cavern.

Samuel and Eleazar returned to Eli sitting at the bottom of the steps of the portico. When Samuel reported what he had seen, it only intensified Eli's grief.

"That I should live. That I should live." Eli began to rock forward and back.

"What should we do, Samuel?" Eleazar looked at his friend.

Samuel was unsure how to answer. The Tabernacle lay open and violated. The High Priest sat broken and weeping on the steps. The city was in chaos. The army of Israel had suffered a defeat from her enemy and hoped to turn this into a victory with the aid of a hallowed treasure of the Almighty. What should he do?

"Follow the Ark. Follow the Ark. Save it from the hands of our enemies, from the hands of our own people. Bring it home." Eli's sobbing words seemed fitting to Samuel.

"My lord, Eleazar and I shall go to the battlefield. Would you like to return to your chambers?"

"No." Eli was emphatic, his voice strained but assertive. "Take me to the city gates. Set me beside the road. I fear for the Ark. I want to hear the news of the Ark's safe return as soon as possible."

Samuel and Eleazar helped Eli to his feet while Eber raced up the steps to fetch Eli's chair where he had left it inside the Tabernacle. As they started to move out of the courtyard, Samuel remembered the sword his father had given him.

"Eleazar, I must return to my room. I will join you at the city gates."

Samuel rushed to his room and grabbed the goat-haired pouch beneath his bed, tucked it under his arm, and ran back to the courtyard.

Eli's slow and plodding steps gave him time to retrieve the sword and join Eleazar and Eber with the chair by the time they moved out of the courtyard of the Tabernacle and into the city center. Citizens of Shiloh were rushing in all directions like senseless sheep, fleeing as if pursued by an invisible enemy, panic etched on everyone's faces.

When they reached the city gates, Eber pointed to a spot on the side of the road and placed the chair for Eli.

Once Eli sat down, Samuel knelt in front of him. "My lord, shall we bring you some food and drink while you wait?"

"No, my son. I shall not eat or drink until I know the Ark of Yahweh is safe and returning to its rightful place." Eli placed his hands upon Samuel's face and leaned forward and kissed him on the forehead. "Now go...return with the Presence."

By the time Samuel and Eleazar were marching toward the battlefield, the sun had reached its high point in the sky and was beginning to descend toward the west. Samuel's only concern was the Ark of the Covenant above all else. The Ark must be protected. It must be defended. It could not fall into the hands of the Philistines. It contained the two tablets of Yahweh's Law, a pot of manna preserved from the desert wanderings, and the staff of Israel's first High Priest—that miraculous staff that turned into a serpent before Pharaoh and blossomed to stop a plague ravaging the people of Israel. From the time Moses instructed the artisans to create the Ark from plans given him by Yahweh at Mount Sinai, this holy object of the Presence had never been out of Israel's possession. Now it risked becoming a spoil of war, the holiest of plunder captured.

Samuel and Eleazar could smell a change in the air as they drew nearer to the encampment. They were met with a headwind, a vile stench of blood, smoke, animal and human entrails, and waste that became thicker the closer they ran toward the battle lines. From a distance it looked as if the road connecting Shiloh with the plains had become a black river flowing toward them, but the closer they came, they could make out distinct images of human beings running, walking, limping, crawling, and being carried. Bodies piled high on wagon beds were being hauled by teams of oxen and donkeys. Even men strapped in harnesses were pulling carts of the dead and dying, the wounded and exhausted, stretching from east to west.

Women and children were running against the tide of retreating warriors, crying out the names of husbands, fathers, and sons and shrieking when they discovered a slain loved one.

Samuel shielded his eyes from the sun with his hand as he scanned the road for a sign of the Ark. "Do you see it, Eleazar?"

"No. We must get closer to the front lines."

Samuel could not believe the current of humanity flowing back to Shiloh. By the look of the number of exhausted soldiers coming their way and the countless wagons piled beyond capacity with the dead, it appeared a front line no longer existed.

Samuel and Eleazar stayed off to the side of the highway, going against the surge of people. They did not want to be an obstacle in their flight. The bedraggled soldiers had their clothes torn and were covered in dust and blood; the fortunate ones were able to walk under their own strength or help a fellow comrade whose wounds were not life threatening. It was the wagons of the dead that disturbed Samuel the most, heaps of bodies and body parts bouncing along the road. Samuel suddenly became ill. He had to stop, lean over and wretch. If only he could as easily dispel the images playing out before him.

Once Samuel stood up, Eleazar handed him a water skin. He took a long drink to settle his stomach and quench a raging thirst. When he handed the skin back to Eleazar, they heard shouting up ahead. They looked in the direction of the voice and saw two bodies dressed in priestly robes, their legs dangling off the back of a wagon about to fall onto the road. A soldier was running behind the wagon, shouting at the driver to slow down, but the driver did not hear. The two bodies bounced off the bed onto the ground before the soldier could reach the back of the wagon. The driver did not stop. None who marched behind the wagon stopped. The bodies were stepped over and ignored. Only the soldier who had been shouting at the driver stopped and knelt down between the lifeless corpses. Samuel raced back onto the road and leapt in front of the team of donkeys, causing the driver to yank on the reins.

"What are you doing?" The irate driver shouted and raised his whip ready to strike at Samuel.

The donkeys bobbed their heads in irritation for this sudden stop.

"Two bodies have fallen off the back of your wagon." Samuel pointed to the rear of the wagon.

"Then they can lie in the road. I've got too much weight as it is. It's hard enough for my donkeys to keep pace without having to stop and start."

"The bodies are priests of Yahweh who serve in the Tabernacle. Surely you can wait until they are loaded back onto your wagon."

Samuel looked around to the back of the wagon and saw the soldier lift the dead priests off the road and hoist them upon his back, one over each shoulder. The warrior strained under the weight of carrying two dead men. He grunted with each step until he reached the back of the wagon. Samuel and Eleazar dashed over to help the soldier. Out of respect, they did not want to just sling the bodies back onto the bed. Samuel dropped his sword on the road, and he and Eleazar took the body draped over the young man's left shoulder and eased it onto the wagon. Since the deceased was in priestly attire, Samuel immediately identified the dead man. What he saw brought him to his knees.

"O Yahweh. Dear Yahweh. Have mercy, Yahweh. Save us, O Yahweh." Samuel beat his chest and threw dust in the air over his head.

Eleazar helped remove the second body off the warrior's shoulder and laid it next to the first one. Then he helped Samuel back on his feet only to watch him react in similar fashion when he looked at the face of the second man.

The soldier watched in amazement as Samuel crumpled to his knees in the middle of the road and began to fling the dust above his head and weep aloud the name of Yahweh. Eleazar braced his hands on the back of the wagon while he wept.

The disgruntled driver climbed down the front of his wagon and marched to the back, whip in hand, ready to use it on man or beast.

"What is the delay? The Philistines are breathing down our necks and I want to be in Shiloh by—"

The soldier withdrew his sword, thrusting it toward the driver's face, the lethal end just short of puncturing the driver's right eye. The driver threw up his hands and began to backtrack, and the young man put up his sword and extended his hand to Samuel.

"These were your brothers or your friends?" The soldier offered Samuel his hand, but he did not take it at first.

"Neither brother nor friend. These are the two sons of the High Priest. We served together in the Tabernacle. Have mercy, O Yahweh. Have mercy."

"All of Israel should weep like you. Thirty thousand sons we have lost today. The Destroyer has found us and turned against us. Great was the slaughter."

Samuel covered his ears with his hands and rocked back and forth on his knees when he heard the staggering number of dead at the hands of the Philistines. Those hobbling by were oblivious to Samuel's and Eleazar's lamentations in the middle of the highway. Samuel took the offered hand and got onto his unsteady legs. He wiped the tears from his eyes and looked into the young man's muscular, hairy chest. Samuel had to raise his head to look into the soldier's eyes staring down at him with pity and fatigue. The young man's broad shoulders and large head towered above his fellow soldiers as they streamed past. A leather strap was tied around his head with a silver plate attached to the front and the menacing face of a wolf engraved upon the plate. *He is from the tribe of Benjamin.* A Benjamite, the sign of the wolf. A Benjamite, acting so noble. Samuel never thought that possible. The soldier's dark, matted hair was coated with dirt and blood. There was no wound on his muscular chest or arms. His warrior's skirt was frayed and ragged, but below the hem a bloody cloth was tied around his thigh.

"You were injured." Samuel pointed to the moist rag.

"We must go." He ignored Samuel's concern for his wound. "When the Philistines are finished picking over our dead they will march on to Shiloh."

"I don't know how I can tell him." Samuel looked at the dead brothers lying side by side in the back of the wagon, shafts of broken arrows protruding from their chests.

"These are the dead sons of the High Priest," Eleazar stated, then he asked the warrior, "Where is the Ark?"

"The priests were standing before the Ark when the Philistine archers let fly a barrage of arrows."

Could they have been defending the Ark? Could their final act in this world be one of bravery? Samuel prayed it be so, but the Ark proved no security for the sons of Eli or for Israel. The fatal decision to bring it into the encampment was a vain confidence. Yahweh had withdrawn from the throne of His Mercy Seat, and Samuel did not have the courage to tell this to Eli.

"Are you with your fellow soldiers? Are you from this area?"

"My commander was slain, and few survived in my unit. We all scattered when the onslaught became so great. Any soldier not on this road has fled to his own home. I'm going to Shiloh to get what supplies I need before returning to my home in Gibeah to protect my wife and newborn son. If the Philistines have captured the Ark, they will push into Shiloh by nightfall and begin their blood lust and plunder."

"You must tell him." Samuel gripped the warrior's brawny arms. "You must find the High Priest and tell him the Ark has been captured and his sons are dead."

"That is not a task I'm suited for. It is too great a burden."

"We are just on the outskirts of the city. Go into Shiloh, give the message to the High Priest. And here"—Samuel bent down and picked up the pouch with his sword—"take this sword as a gift for you. It's all I have."

Samuel folded back the flap and offered it to him. The eyes of the young man widened as he looked upon this exquisite sword. Still, it came with a steep demand.

"I will do as you wish." The young man did not linger long over his decision but folded the flap over the hilt and tucked it under his arm. "How do I find the High Priest?"

"He will be sitting in his chair by the side of the road at the main entrance into the city. He is very old, nearly a century, and his vision is gone."

"Yahweh be with you." The soldier bolted around the wagon and broke into a run on the side of the road out of the flow of human traffic racing toward the city.

"Your name. What is your name?" Samuel had cupped his hands over his mouth to funnel the sound, but the young warrior was out of earshot.

Eleazar walked around to the driver and told him to move on while he walked alongside the wagon.

Samuel squeezed in between the lifeless bodies of the brothers. He would ride the rest of the way to make sure the sons of Eli made it back to the city. He held onto their bloody robes to keep the bodies from falling off the end of the wagon. Within his grip he held the fulfillment of Yahweh's prophetic word.

Israel was routed and beaten. Who could stand before the Almighty? Samuel never imagined the fulfillment of Yahweh's word in such a fashion—the slaughter of over thirty-thousand men, the capture of the Ark of the Covenant, the chosen people laid waste and scattered before her enemies.

All Samuel could think of was the warnings and curses from the scrolls of Moses should Israel turn aside from the ways of Yahweh: "The Almighty will cause you to be defeated before your enemies. You will come at them from one direction but flee from them in seven, and you will become a thing of horror to all the kingdoms on the earth. Your carcasses will be food for all the birds of the air and the beasts of the earth, and there will be no one to frighten them away." It was impossible to fathom such an act of divine will by Yahweh.

Samuel heard a great hue and cry as the wagon bounced toward the entrance of the city. Soldiers and civilians behind the wagon quickened their pace, dashing past him. In a moment, the driver stopped the wagon, and Samuel hopped off and raced to the front. He saw Eleazar dash to where the High Priest sat at the side of the road. Standing head and shoulders above the crowd was the young man he had sent ahead. Samuel forced his way through the people until he stood before the young man and the prone body of Eli.

"I spoke all you had me say." The young warrior's voice quivered with fear, his face awash in horror as he looked down upon Eli struggling for breath. "He stood, rent his garment, and fell backward off the pedestal. I never touched him, I swear."

"It is not your fault." Samuel forced the young man to look into his eyes. "You are not to blame. Do you understand? You are not to blame for any of this."

Samuel released the young man's arms and fell down beside Eli. The old man's eyes were glazed over, but his soul had not quite taken flight. Samuel leaned into his ear and identified himself, and Eli immediately raised his hand in the air for Samuel to clasp.

"It is true, my lord. Everything you were told has come to pass." Samuel pulled Eli closer to him.

"The sacred scrolls...protect them." The High Priest's lips bubbled over with foam. "And the treasures of the Holy Place."

Eli wheezed, and then a seizure forced its way through his massive chest and his hand went limp within Samuel's grasp.

"The glory has departed from Israel." Samuel gently closed Eli's blank lifeless eyes, and then leaned back to release his own howl of grief.

There was no time to mourn. The bodies of Eli and his sons were taken back to the Tabernacle. Eli was laid on his bed in his chambers while his sons were placed on the portico outside the doors into the Holy Place. Samuel instructed Eleazar to load all the sacred objects in the Tabernacle, including the attire of the High Priest, into wagons and meet him at the south gate of the city. Samuel then commandeered wagons and had them brought to the academy. Within a short time, the Levitical students had placed the sacred scrolls into jars and crates and loaded them onto the wagons. He then instructed all of them to leave Shiloh immediately, return to their own homes and remain. Word would be sent to all the tribe of Levi throughout Israel once Samuel had heard from Yahweh.

Samuel made one last inspection of the library. A calfskin, unrolled on its spindle upon a table in a far corner, caught his eye. Before rolling it up, he read the words, "Be strong and courageous, because you will lead these people to..." The scribe had gotten no further with his copying than these early words of Yahweh to Commander Joshua before leading the conquest into the land of Promise. There was still room on the skin to continue writing the story. The story would continue, and Samuel quickly rolled up the skin and raced out of the building with the spindle tucked beneath his arm.

Once outside, he leapt onto the lead wagon and had the driver head for the south gate. Eleazar, and the wagons carrying the sacred objects, were waiting for him. As the driver led the caravan of wagons out of the southern gate, Samuel stood in the wagon and looked back at the city of Shiloh, a city in turmoil, its citizens fleeing, the Philistine army approaching. Over two decades of his life had been confined within the walls of the city. And within those walls his work had kept him within the perimeters of the Tabernacle, and inside the Tabernacle he had moved within the small space of the Holy Place, all in service to Yahweh. He had peered into the Most Holy Place after the Ark had been taken, but he did not venture into that empty space. It would have been a sacrilege to him despite the fact that it was no longer inhabited by Yahweh. Samuel was leaving everything behind and venturing into the wider world. All that had happened for the last few centuries in this city, in the Tabernacle, to him, to his family, to the people of Yahweh, were about to be overrun by the enemies of the chosen. Would the city be restored or the Tabernacle rebuilt? Had the glory of Yahweh departed forever? Once outside the city gates as night was beginning to fall, Samuel turned around and sat next to the wagon driver. He faced south. He was headed toward Ramah. He was going home.

Thirteen

SHIRA DISMOUNTED IN THE COURTYARD OF THE MAIN FAMILY dwellings and led her horse into the stables. The sky was bright with a slight easterly breeze that cooled the air. Each morning before the household awoke, Shira would ride out onto the property, a routine broken only by poor weather or the rare absence from home. She and her mother lived in their small dwelling on a hill just down the well-worn pathway from the stables. The road was wide enough for a wagon and a team of donkeys to pull it.

On the other side of the pathway was the corral where horses were taken when it was time to break them. Beyond the corral were the fenced pastures for the small herds of horses and donkeys to graze. Farther on toward the western hills were the vineyards, and continuing to the top of the hill was the olive grove with trees that were over one hundred years old. From the groves at the top of the hill the view looked out over the property and the valley beyond.

Shira barely had time to remove the riding blanket and bridle and begin washing the sweat from her horse when she heard wagons rumbling into the courtyard and loud voices calling to the occupants inside the house. She slipped the feed bucket over the ears of her horse and made her way out of the stables. The sight of six wagons and teams of mules or donkeys coming to a stop in the courtyard amazed her. A few of the beasts had crumpled to their knees in exhaustion and appeared as though they might expire.

When Shira saw Samuel standing in the lead wagon parked in front of the house, she could not believe her eyes. He did not wear his turban, and his dark, windblown hair fell below his shoulders. His leggings and tunic were filthy and smeared with streaks of blood. Was it his own or another's? She moved toward the wagon and was about to call to him when the door opened on the family dwelling and out came Elkanah and Hannah.

Young men were slowly climbing down from the wagons as Shira made her way toward the entrance of the family dwelling. Each man looked weary and disheveled, in need of food and drink, fresh clothing, and days of sleep. She watched Samuel painfully climb down from the lead wagon and hobble alongside it, gripping the panels to keep from falling like an old man or one seriously injured. He moved in a similar way the last time she saw him when he bore the markings of trauma. She wondered if bodily injury was a common occurrence for the son of the vow. When Samuel stopped behind the wagon and fell to his knees, he cried out, though to her ears, it sounded more like the cry of an anguished soul than of physical pain.

Shira moved quickly around to the back of the wagon just as Elkanah and Hannah came from the opposite side. Samuel opened his arms, and father and mother fell to their knees before their son and embraced him. Samuel's back was to Shira with the arms of his parents wrapped around him and their faces buried into either side of their son's neck. Shira felt as if she were an unraveled thread of this familial fabric, connected to the whole yet loosened and floating away from the central weaving. She felt the tug of being drawn into this scene of weeping, the wonder of it, the bewildering expressions of sorrow, and she did not resist. She reached out her hand and laid her fingers upon the top of Samuel's head, then slowly extended her fingers and pressed her palm onto his crown. Her hand could console children, could calm a mare about to foal, so perhaps it could comfort a broken man. Though he did not turn to face her, she felt the slightest reflex of response pass from the back of his head into her hand.

Samuel did not want to let go of his parents. Kneeling with them on the ground where he spent his early days gave him an unexpected feeling of safety. Nothing would harm him here. The enemies of Israel would not pursue him here. He could shelter here, have time to restore his soul and hear from Yahweh. The world he had known had disintegrated right in front of him. He could do nothing to stop it. He could only react to the violent shifting of events, the mayhem and death, and what was sure to be the destruction of the city where he had lived from his childhood until this instant. He had made decisions in the heat of each moment, and did not spend precious time wondering whether they were good or bad choices, wise or foolish determinations. He had been forced to be decisive to an onrush of conditions beyond his control and had ended up back home. It surprised him, bewildered him, and yet deep down, this earth he knelt upon, the arms of his parents that embraced him, and knowing that his first steps taken in this life were on this ground, produced within him a balm of peace.

What Samuel did know was in this hailstorm of events that had befallen the citizens of Israel at Shiloh, he must try to save everything he could that identified the people of Yahweh. The Ark of the Covenant had been lost, and in the process, perhaps even Yahweh. But by saving all he could from the Tabernacle and the Levitical library, a large portion of what it meant to the chosen—the people of the covenant, the twelve tribes being one nation—would be protected and kept alive for future generations. If nothing else good came from this awful destruction, preserving the words of Yahweh and the instruments of worshiping the Almighty, might uphold the nation.

Samuel held onto his parents as they all three rose to their feet. When his parents released him to step back for a better look, he saw the horror in their eyes.

"This is not my blood," Samuel said, looking down at his stained tunic. "I am not harmed. There is much to tell you, but first we must protect the wagons."

Samuel turned around to give Eleazar instructions and found himself face-to-face with Shira. All words flew from his mind. His mouth went dry. The woman whose voice had stunned his ears with her singing, the one whose beauty he had held in his memory since the moment he saw her, the first one he shared with, after Eli, that Yahweh had spoken to him out of the flame of the altar, had stolen his ability for speech.

"May I help unhitch the teams from the wagons? They are exhausted."

Samuel was still unable to speak to her, so he just nodded his head.

"I thank Yahweh for your safe return."

Samuel only found his voice when the driver of the first wagon Shira approached was resistant to her aid.

"Do whatever she tells you." Samuel was surprised by the force of his command, but the shocked driver gave Shira the reins to the team and stepped off the wagon.

Samuel eventually came around to the decision to allow Eleazar to take the holy objects of the Tabernacle home with him. At first he had been reluctant, until Eleazar pointed out that in these uncertain times, with the Philistine victory at Shiloh and the capture of the Ark, their enemies might be embolden to attack more cities of Israel.

"Our country is in turmoil with no designated leadership," argued Eleazar. "Not everything of such value should be hidden in one location."

Samuel saw the wisdom in such a conclusion, and so only the wagons with the sacred scrolls of the library and writing supplies for the scribes were unloaded and put into one of the stalls in the barn that Shira had cleared out. When Shira closed the stall gate and draped a blanket over it, Samuel realized that the written words of Yahweh were his sole responsibility. For the time being, there was no Levitical academy with scribes to copy the sacred texts; all had fled to their own homes. At this moment, he was the last scribe. He must protect this library at all cost. These crates and clay jars of the sacred words of Yahweh were more important than the objects of worship in the Tabernacle.

"Do you realize what we have hidden here in this stable?" Samuel pressed both hands on the blanket covering the gate of the stall and leaned his weight upon it. Shira did not answer his question, so he looked at her. "The collected words of Yahweh given to the prophet Moses, from the scrolls of the beginnings to the histories of our conquest of Canaan. We have even gathered the latest stories of our judges and had begun copying them into a collection. All here. All consolidated in one place. I alone must continue to record and copy these words."

"You will not be alone." Shira spoke with a confidence Samuel had not expected to hear. "Yahweh will not abandon the son of the vow."

Samuel and Eleazar spent the night on his parents' roof while the drivers and other Levites took shelter in the storage room above the barn. The two of them discussed what should be done next. Samuel and Eleazar hoped that the Philistines would be so happy to have captured the Ark of the Covenant and killed over thirty thousand warriors of Israel, that after sacking the city of Shiloh, they would not mount further attacks.

The next morning Eleazar left for his home in Kiriath-Jearim to hide the worshiping objects of the Tabernacle. All the drivers and Levites went with Eleazar to protect the wagons pulled by fresh teams of donkeys. Neither of them knew when they would next meet.

It only took a few days for Samuel to realize that it would be impossible for him to live in the house with his parents. It was not for lack of room. Father's second wife, Peninnah, had been dead for some time, and her children had married and moved away. Of Samuel's other siblings, the ones born of Hannah, the youngest ones had died and the others had also married and begun their own families in other cities. It was not as if Samuel knew them. He only saw them for a brief time once a year so the bond was not strong or deep. There was plenty of space in the house for Samuel, but it was difficult for Samuel to know how to communicate with his parents in a domestic setting. Yearly visits to Shiloh had been his only context for their relationship, that and the shared knowledge that he was the son of the vow and Yahweh had established him as the prophet of the Almighty. But he found this new and drastic change in his living arrangements was difficult to maneuver.

He did not wish to hurt his parents. He needed them. He needed time with them. There was a part of him that longed to have what his siblings had enjoyed, time to grow up in this nurturing home. He had no real memories of the early days in his birthplace. Shiloh and the life of the Tabernacle were all the memories he had.

Samuel struggled to know how to communicate to his parents his own wounded heart. He did not know how to tell them what he had experienced growing up as a Levitical student and priest in Shiloh, the persistent cruelty at the hands of Hophni and Phinehas, or even this recent event of seeing the massacre of Israel's army at the hands of the Philistines. Most important, how could he explain fully that Yahweh had witnessed to his heart and fulfilled what he had spoken? He needed time to understand what had taken place in his life and how that might shape his heart and mind for the future.

It was his father that suggested they convert the sizable storeroom on the second level of the barn into private living quarters. So Mushi, Father, and Samuel cleaned up the storeroom, repaired damaged walls and floor, and constructed floor-to-ceiling shelving onto one whole wall so Samuel could store the crates, clay jars, and pouches of scrolls and documents he had brought from Shiloh. There was sufficient natural light through the windows to brighten the dingy space. The east window was large enough for him to climb out onto the barn roof and stretch his legs without having to go up and down the flight of steps in the back of the stables. The furnishings were simple: straw mattress and several blankets, a trunk for clothing, a table and two chairs, three oil lamps.

When Hannah entered the room carrying a bundle of curtains to hang in the windows, she gasped when she saw her son sitting on the edge of the windowsill with his legs dangling over the side.

"Samuel, be careful."

Samuel turned his head back through the window and looked her. "Ima, I have windows. I never had windows in my rooms in Shiloh. I can see the house and the courtyard and valley and the corral and the horses. The sun will wake me every morning when it rises. Come and see."

Hannah heard the excitement in his voice. It was the excitement of a small child looking at the world with the eyes of infatuation and wonder of everything it beheld. This was what she had missed after taking him to the Tabernacle. Moments to enjoy with her son as she watched him discover the newness of the world. Her maternal instinct surprised her when tears began to well up in her eyes. She, of course, had these motherly impulses with her other children, but not with the child of her vow. The nurturing urge was renewed for him. But the small child she remembered all those years ago was now her grown son. How different it would all be was something she could not have imagined. This grown son of hers was home.

"I have brought curtains for the windows." Hannah moved up behind him and lifted a corner of the material for him to see.

Samuel gave the material no more than a glance. "I do not want curtains."

"You can leave them open. And it would add some color to this drab space." Hannah stepped into the middle of the room, shaking her head at the lack of color.

Samuel spun around in the windowsill and set his feet on the floor. "I have a better idea."

Samuel dashed out of the door and scrambled down the back stairs. Through the flooring in the room Hannah could hear him rummaging around in the stables.

"What are you doing?" she called to him through the flooring.

When he did not answer, she walked over to the open door and saw him struggling up the steps, carrying a heavy crate of scrolls and writing materials. She backed away from the door to allow him to enter. Samuel set the crate upon the table and paused to catch his breath. Then he opened the crate and lifted out an armful of scrolls, placing them on one of the shelves. The ends of the scrolls came to the edge of the shelving.

"Now let's see if this works."

Samuel took one of the curtains from his mother, shook it out, and held it up to the wooden frame of the top shelf. The hem of the curtain fell to just below his knees.

"These curtains will help protect the scrolls from the dust and hay rising up from the stables." Samuel folded the curtain in his arms.

"Like the veil in the Tabernacle protecting the Ark." Hannah stepped to the shelving and placed the other curtains on the middle shelf.

"Until it did not." Samuel placed a hand upon one of the scrolls.

"You saw it taken from the Holy of Holies?"

"I did not see it removed from the Tabernacle. I was on the ground behind the crowd tending to the High Priest. It was hard enough to see the empty cavity where the Ark had been, the veil and pillars tossed aside in the Holy Place."

"My son, you have not told us all that took place after we left Shiloh."

"What did Shira tell you?"

"That you returned early the next morning before we had risen and that you were no longer the child of the vow." Hannah began to smooth out the wrinkles on the pile of curtains she had placed on the shelf as if she were gently rubbing a child's face. She recalled every word Shira had spoken to them that morning. "You told her that you were now the son of the vow, the firstborn son of your parents, the ransomed price confirmed the night before by the voice of Yahweh. The voice had spoken to you out of the flame of the altar in the Holy Place. The Almighty confirmed all your father had spoken the day before, that the line of Eli would end with the death of his sons. I remember every word Shira said, they are burned into my heart. I did not sleep for days after we returned home. Only prayed, prayed for my son, that Yahweh would protect him." She gripped the edge of the shelf and lowered her head. She could not keep the tears from spilling out of her eyes.

"Shira said nothing about my appearance?"

Samuel's question surprised Hannah and she raised her head.

"Your appearance." Hannah wiped her face with her sleeve. "She said nothing. What of your appearance?"

"Another time, Ima, when we are all together." Samuel went back to the crate and scooped up another armful of scrolls and placed them next to the others on the shelf.

Hannah chose not to pry. There would be another time. What her son had confirmed with his own lips was that Yahweh had appeared to him, had spoken, confirming her vow made those many years ago. Yet she wanted to know a little more. She would risk her son's patience for a little more of his encounter with the Almighty.

"You said Yahweh appeared to you in the fire upon the altar."

Samuel said nothing as he neatly straightened the scrolls on the shelf. Hannah thought he might not have heard her, then she thought he might be ignoring her. But once the scrolls were ordered to his satisfaction, he held onto the edge of the shelf and stared at the rolled-up scrolls of Yahweh's words.

"I did not see an image, Ima. No physical appearance. It was just the voice, the immense power contained in the voice. The voice of the Almighty that spoke creation into existence as it is written in the scrolls of the beginnings."

Her son paused. She saw a slight nervous twitch on the side of his face, then he swallowed. She too felt the impulse to swallow.

"This voice spoke my name. After years of silence, Yahweh came out from behind the veil and confirmed displeasure with the house of Eli. That was all. Nothing more. Yahweh's scorching words terrified me. I wanted to flee. I wanted to play false with Eli, pretend I heard nothing, but I could not. I did not know how or when it would come to pass. I was only obedient to deliver the unspeakable message, and then to bear witness of Yahweh's divine will...it was a terrible thing to watch. Yahweh has been His own witness."

"What do you mean?" Hannah studied her son's glassy eyes as they stared at the scrolls on the shelf.

"The prophet Moses writes that two witnesses confirm a truth. Yahweh spoke to Father and me the same truth, and it came to pass. The Almighty is His own witness."

"For the Almighty to confirm His word through my husband and my son is beyond imagining." Hannah braced an arm upon the shelf to keep from collapsing.

"It began with your vow, Ima. And your prayer when you left me at the Tabernacle as a child. Who knew. Who knew."

Samuel's whispers of wonder were echoed by Hannah and then faded into silence for both of them.

Hannah took a deep breath and laid a firm hand on Samuel's forearm. "Will you write of this?"

"I must. This is Yahweh's story. Not mine. It must be written for our people."

Hannah reached up and gently placed her fingers beneath his trembling chin and directed his face toward her. She could see the pain this story had written upon him, and that it would cause more pain when he transcribed it onto the scrolls of Yahweh. She saw clearly now what her vow had done, the pain it caused her son. She was not prepared for this. She had known only the pain it caused her, but had not considered what pain her son might have when she gave him over to Yahweh. She knew this story would be one of many that would cause anguish to the heart of her son. But there had been no turning back for her all those years ago, and now she knew what was ahead for her son—one esteemed by Yahweh to speak and record His word, but with an uncertain future, and a continual wounding of his heart. The son of the vow had turned his face toward Yahweh, and with the speaking of his name, had begun living for Yahweh. And now she knew he would always tremble at the word and will of Yahweh.

"I am glad you have come home, my son. At least for a while."

Hannah opened her arms, and Samuel allowed her to embrace him.

Fourteen

FREED FROM ALL LEVITICAL RESPONSIBILITIES, SAMUEL RE-mained sequestered in the room above the barn. He wanted to feel safe and protected. He began to appreciate his father's peculiar behavior leading up to his prophesy on that first Day of Atonement and to understand what he meant when he told Samuel that he did not belong to himself. He never did belong to himself. He most certainly understood his father's need to be alone while his soul wrestled with Yahweh.

Samuel studied the scrolls of Moses and the fathers he brought from the library of the Tabernacle. He scribbled notes as he began to collect his thoughts for writing a more comprehensive history of Yahweh's interaction with the chosen, from the death of Joshua until the present day. There were so many stories that needed to be documented in an orderly form. The act of writing would force him to focus his thoughts and perspective to gain a better sense of the history and destiny of Israel. And he prayed, cautiously. What could you say to the Almighty after He had spoken to you? Yahweh would speak again. Perhaps there would be a visitation. There was historical precedence for such.

Samuel used the silence to heal his mind and heart, to regain a semblance of order of what seemed impossible to comprehend or reconcile to human experience. If Yahweh spoke again soon, and Samuel had not fully recovered from the first encounter, he might expire.

But it was her voice that began to evaporate the turmoil in his soul.

> "When you ride on your horses;
> When you sit in your saddle;
> When you walk along the road;
> Sing of Yahweh's righteous acts."

Samuel stopped writing in the middle of a sentence. It sounded as if she were in the room. He got down on all fours and crawled to the center of the room. He found a separation in the flooring where he could see with one eye a sliver of the stables below him. And there she was working in the stables, feeding the horses and cleaning out the stalls. Singing of the Almighty. He rolled onto his back and just listened.

Her voice was impossible to ignore, as though she were singing just for him. The beauty of it frightened him. The beauty of the sound. The beauty of her face that appeared when he closed his eyes to listen. Once last week he had heard her singing off in the distance, and he could not help himself. He had to follow her voice. He had exited his room and descended the stairs. It was drawing him like a spell. He followed the sound down the path next to the corral until he came into the open pasture. He hid behind the corral fence and watched as she sang to a newborn colt getting onto its wobbly legs and taking its first steps. He had never heard anything like it. He had never seen anything like it. Singing in the open, a song of spontaneous worship of creation. It had been too much for him, and he had hurried back to his room.

He rolled back onto his stomach and spotted her leaning against a stall door.

> "The earth shook, the heavens poured,
> The clouds poured down water.
> The mountains quaked before the Lord, the One of Sinai.
> Before the Lord, the God of Israel."

The poetic phrases were haunting. He quietly crawled over to the shelving and began to look through the collection where he kept individual records not yet complied into a single story. While he looked through the records he found himself humming the tune she sang. He knew the poem was familiar, that he had read those words before. When he found the record he was searching for he unrolled it and saw the words Shira sang written out. It was a song attributed to Deborah, the only female judge to rise out of Israel. The "Song of Deborah" celebrated a victory for Israel over her enemies and Deborah's insight into Israel's tribal relations.

He had grown-up in the Tabernacle hearing the musicians and Levite priests singing and chanting praises to Yahweh, but never these words, in such original melodies, and never with such passion. Samuel's heart blazed as Shira sang these lyrics, and he committed to include the lyric poem in his written history of the judges of Israel.

The sound of his father's voice calling for Shira broke the trance her singing had put him under. Samuel crawled over to the window and raised his head just high enough to see the courtyard below. What he saw amazed him. Elkanah rode into the courtyard on his horse and pulled hard on the reins for it to stop. He tossed the reins to Shira as she came out of the stables. He dashed into the house, and when he emerged he held a leather satchel.

"Deliver these documents to Mushi in the south pasture. The buyers of our filly are impatient to be off."

From the safety of his window, Samuel watch Shira yank the hem of her robe above her knees—she wore leggings like a man—leap onto the horse, take the satchel from his father, and barrel out of the yard. Samuel moved away from the window and leaned back against the wall. He did not want Shira or his father to see him watching from the window. This was an extraordinary sight. He realized there was so much of the wider world he had never seen and he longed to be part of it.

One night Samuel was startled awake by a sound outside his door. He had fallen asleep on his writing table. After eating his supper and setting his food tray outside the door on the steps, he had decided to write a while longer before going to bed. He looked about the darkened room. The light had gone out in the clay lamp, yet the room was illuminated with the moonlight flooding through the windows. The clay vessel was cool to his touch. How long had he been asleep?

He stood up to stretch and that was when he heard the footsteps racing down the stairs and moving briskly out of the stables. He scooted over to the window with its view of the courtyard and saw the form moving across the yard toward the family dwelling.

"Shira, is that you?" The words flew from his mouth before he realized he had spoken; before he could second-guess the impulse and refrain. It was too late. The form stopped, the moonlight casting its glow upon the shape. There was not another soul around. The form waited, motionless in the moon's bright light. It must be her, Samuel thought, and he climbed out the window and stood upon the roof.

"I hope I did not startle you."

When the form did not speak, he was about to jump back through the window to avoid embarrassment, but he stopped when the form turn to face him.

"I'm sorry if I disturbed you. I thought you might be asleep when I came for your tray. There was no light in the window...and...well...good night."

She started to turn back toward the house.

"Please, don't leave. I'm coming down."

Samuel did not wait for her to object or dash away. He did not crawl back through the window into his room to take the stairs. He did not want to lose sight of her. Instead, he crawled over the edge of the roof and wrapped his legs around the center post. He shimmied halfway down the post and then dropped to the ground. Samuel had forgotten whatever discomfort he imagined he might feel when he finally summoned the courage to approach Shira. He did not seem to mind being in close proximity to the one whose face was never out of his mental imagery, whose voice was a constant sound in his mind. The fear with which he had wrestled in his own imagination, of feeling less than a man—of appearing as someone she might think as weak and cowardly and want nothing to do with if she knew how he had been treated by Eli's sons—had vanished. He was all action, every muscle alive, every intention clear and focused. His body was strong. When he looked at her in the moonlight, his fragmented heart felt knit together.

"Are you the one who delivers my food and picks up after me?"

"Not always. Your mother has come a few times."

"Neither of you should have to do this. My isolation has imposed upon you both."

"I don't mind, really, I..."

Samuel startled Shira when he took the tray from her and set it on the ground.

"I've lost all sense of time and don't know the day or the hour except by the sun and moon. I am sorry to have done this to you."

"We knew you were working on the scrolls and that those last days in Shiloh were very troubling." Shira caught herself, putting her hand over her lips.

"You remember what my face looked like when I came to the tent that morning. I have been afraid that you would think less of me if you knew... knew what..."

"I would never do that." Shira had not allowed him to finish.

"I've been watching you from my window and listening to your singing." Samuel wanted to change the subject. "It's not all I've been doing. I've been writing as well."

Samuel wanted to tell her about his writing. He wanted to tell her so much, and did not know where to start. He didn't know where it would lead if he did start. He had been startled awake and his body released from its confines, his vibrant soul free of all inhibitions. Was he dreaming? He must be dreaming for him to feel so liberated, and if so, he did not wish to awaken.

"That's good...I mean about the writing...that is good."

"I saw you ride my father's horse." He blurted out the words, the ever-changing topics racing through his mind too quickly for his mouth and tongue to keep pace.

"I did. I do."

"I've never ridden a horse. I've never ridden anything." He spoke as if Shira riding a horse was the most astounding thing he had ever seen. Perhaps it was considering the restricted world he inhabited all his life. "You ride animals. I sacrifice them."

Samuel paused to allow the comparison of what he had just said to sink in. "Is it difficult to ride? It looks difficult."

"I can teach you if you promise not to sacrifice the horse after you've ridden it."

It surprised them both when they laughed together.

"I remember my father riding a horse when I was a small child. I think it was brown with a white blaze on his forehead. That was a long time ago."

"It must have been Efrain."

"Who is that?" Samuel was perplexed by the name.

"Efrain was the name of your father's horse many years ago. He rides one of his offspring now. Efrain was very...fruitful. He left behind a great legacy."

"My father names his horses?" Samuel shook his head in disbelief.

"Only the ones we do not sell. People come from all over to buy his horses. Your father knows how to break and train well. A prince from Damascus once bought one."

Samuel looked at the house, then back to the barn. He looked past the stables to the expanse of corrals and pasture in vivid shadows from the moonlight. What few memories he had of living at home were saturated by fog, no solid recollections to dredge up that elicited any feeling, good or bad. It was almost as if this location, his parents, Shira, were characters in a story located in a far-off place of some ancient tale located on the other side of the world. How could he have come from the place where he now stood?

"Where have I been?" He turned back to Shira. "Why did I not know?"

"I've got just the horse for you."

Samuel appreciated her cheerful attempt to reengage his attention.

"Her name is Aviva, a five-year-old mare. Nice and gentle, perfect for beginners."

"I've been a Levite and priest all my life. I was offered to Yahweh and... and...my father names his horses." It made him weep, and Samuel lowered his head, hoping Shira did not witness the swipe of moisture off his cheek.

Samuel heard voices and they both turned to see Elkanah and Hannah walking toward them, illuminated by torchlight. Samuel moved to go, but felt Shira's hand touch his arm. He looked down at her fingers looped over his forearm, a gentle pressure applied to hinder his exit. He did not pull away, nor did she release him.

"Don't leave. They will want to see you."

Elkanah swung the torch in Samuel and Shira's direction. They both covered their eyes from the brightness of the light.

Samuel heard his mother's muffled cry of alarm. Both his parents were shocked to see him.

"You've come out of hiding." Elkanah pulled the torch away from their faces.

He saw his mother clinging to his father's arm. "I don't know what to say."

"That is a rare moment."

These words drew an immediate jab into Elkanah's ribs from Hannah.

Samuel was too flustered by his parents' discovery of him in the courtyard to see the humor of their interaction, and he bent down to pick up the tray of dishes.

"I was stretching my legs." Samuel stood with the tray and handed it to Shira. "Shira was collecting my tray at the same time. You're out late."

"The tribal leaders called us to meet in the village square. They report that the Philistines are moving the Ark from one city to another," Elkanah explained. "The Philistines are gloating. The Five Lords parade the Ark in their cities to provoke us. And we Hebrews do nothing."

Samuel felt the sting of Father's words. He was not sure how to respond. "What should I do? Perhaps I should meet with Eleazar. I feel my presence here puts all of you in danger. Perhaps I should leave?"

His mother's impulsive "No!" was echoed by Shira's quieter one. He watched his father put his arm around his mother's waist.

"Son, sometimes it is better to do nothing. You must continue your work and you are safe here. Yahweh will direct you."

"Yes. Yes. But when, Father?"

"When Yahweh sees fit. The Almighty is not unaware of us or any of His chosen."

Samuel knew his father's words were true and it settled his heart. He felt his body instantly begin to relax.

"It's late." Elkanah handed his son the torch. "See that Shira gets home."

Once Samuel took the torch from his father, Elkanah took the tray from Shira. He nodded to Hannah in the direction of the house, and they both hurried toward the door.

His parents slipped into the house and closed the door. Samuel looked at Shira, not sure what to do. When she began to walk in the direction that led to her home, Samuel's legs unlocked and he caught up with her. Shira set a slow pace, which Samuel honored. He was in no hurry to part from her, but was unable to engage in conversation. When they reached the path leading to her house, she turned to him.

"Yahweh spoke my name." He had to stop her from taking the path to her home, and it was the first thought that came to him.

"I know. You said He spoke to you in the Tabernacle."

Her affirming smile helped him to relax. He knew he wanted to share with her those experiences and the feelings that came with it. He believed she might understand. He hoped she would understand. He could not contain all this in one heart, his heart.

"Yahweh spoke, and when I spoke the words of the Almighty to others and they came to pass, a great power was unleashed. After I spoke those words, what followed was beyond what I could have imagined. It frightened me. I just needed to tell you."

"I understand."

"Do you? I hoped you would. When I came to the tent the next morning and you did not run away when you saw my face, I thought you would understand me."

Shira examined his face and head in the torchlight. "Your hair is growing back and the bruising is gone."

"My parents do not know what happened. Thank you for not telling them."

"I do not know what happened. You said only it was the enemies of Yahweh."

"Yes. Yes." Samuel looked away and took a deep breath. "The bruise may be gone and my hair is growing back, but I still feel the pain on that side of my face. I don't know why. It has been long enough now for it to have subsided."

Shira raised her hand to the side of his face that had been injured. She began at the top of his head where the hair had been cut from his scalp and gently traced her fingers along his skin from the temple all the way to his jawline.

"You have healed well." She dropped her hand to her side and started up the path.

Samuel stood still and watched her ascend the stepping stones to her front door. She turned and waved before she slipped inside. Samuel ran his fingers down the side of his face as Shira had done, a slow descent, a caress. There was no pain. This human connection was unlike anything he had ever experienced. Her touch had released something far off inside him, a mysterious secret he could not comprehend, and a rushing stream of delight began to flow through his blood, washing away the fear that had lodged in his heart.

Fifteen

SAMUEL WAS WAITING AT THE STABLES THE NEXT MORNING when Shira arrived, greeting him with her bright smile.

"I have been awake since before sunrise. To be truthful, I do not think I ever slept. The writing can wait. Teach me to ride."

Samuel's room above the barn had suddenly become too confining. An urge to spend time outdoors had awakened a new life force inside his heart. Instead of listening to lectures from Levitical scholars, he would learn to properly ride Aviva, under the tutelage of Shira. Instead of cleaning out the ashes from the altar fires, he would clean out the stables. Instead of leading animals to slaughter, he would learn to husband them. Instead of sitting in classrooms studying the laws and stories of Moses, he and his father would study the business ledgers.

Home for Samuel had always been something in the abstract, but in time it became a satisfying reality. Falling into bed each night exhausted, his muscles sore from heavy labor; the hours spent on horseback mastering his riding skills; the joy he shared with his parents; the constant happiness of being in Shira's company, these experiences he never dreamed were possible. He saw in his parents how a different life, separate from the duties of the Tabernacle, could still be a life devoted to Yahweh.

And then there was Shira. The blazing fire of Yahweh suspended above the altar in the Holy Place was steadily merging with Shira's smiling face. The sound of Yahweh's voice was being echoed in the songs Shira would sing. The powerful memory of the one-time appearance of Yahweh was being reinforced by the everyday company of this delightful, young woman. These joys gave him a new sense of purpose in writing the stories of Israel, to show the fullness of what life on earth could be when in relationship with the Almighty. He never felt so alive. He was newly born; everything and everyone was worthy of his curiosity. His mind burned with a vibrancy to combine the world of the divine with the world of domestic bliss. This balance of life had to be Yahweh's gift.

She thought the racket of hitching the two-passenger wagon to the donkey and leading it out of the stables would be enough noise to roust him out of bed, but it took tossing pebbles through his window to finally get him to appear.

"I was up late writing." Samuel stretched and vigorously rubbed his face.

"Hurry. I have something I want to show you." Shira stood in the seat of the wagon and pointed to the east.

Moments later they were seated side by side, Shira on the reins, driving them beyond the corral and pastures and vineyards.

"Where are you taking me?"

"You will see." Shira looked eastward and snapped the reins. The donkey bolted and settled into a swift gait.

The clear eastern sky was beginning to glow with the rising sun, gradually extinguishing the light from the stars of the night. The sun had not yet broken the horizon, but it would not be long. Shira guided the donkey up the pathway's steep grade that circled around the hill. They had ridden up to the olive groves on horseback before, but not in time to watch the sunrise.

The ground leveled off when they reached the top. Shira drove the wagon to the middle of the grove and turned the animal to the east, bringing them to a stop right at the edge of the tree line before the hill begin to descend into the valley below. They sat in silence until the horizon revealed the outline of the arch of the sun and the white sky began to turn the colors of red and orange. Shira climbed out of the wagon and moved over beneath an olive tree. The sun began to claim more of the sky and she began to sing.

> "Arise, O Yahweh. Arise.
> Let the light of your face shine upon us.
> Let your glory fill the sky like the sun.
> Let your majesty cover the earth.
> May the praises of your people come from Zion.
> May the praises of your people proclaim
> All that you have done among the nations.
> Arise, O Yahweh. Arise.
> Let the light of your face shine upon us."

Shira kept her eyes on the horizon. She felt Samuel move in beside her and watch the sun make its way above the line of the earth.

"Your singing gives my spirit the sense of floating in midair. You have made me realize that praises to Yahweh can be sung outside the confines of the Tabernacle and not just by trained musicians. You have made me realize many things I never thought I would learn, ever thought it was possible for me to do."

"And I never thought I would watch the sunrise with the prophet of Yahweh." Shira smiled, but did not turn her eyes from the sunrise.

"Life has been so peaceful in this place. The time spent here has taught me so much. You have taught me so much. How is it that you sing so beautifully?"

Shira did not respond. She knew there was no answer to his question.

"You just open your mouth and these praises burst forth." Samuel shook his head as if in wonder at Shira's ineffable gift.

"And how is it you hear the voice of Yahweh, that the Almighty communicates with you and your father?" She bowed her head and clasped her hands in front of her. She did not want to sound irreverent or doubtful. She did not doubt. She was accustomed to sensing the Presence of Yahweh stir her own heart whenever she sang, when she rode her horse in the fields and pastures, whenever she came to the olive grove to be alone, to watch a sunset. Yes, Yahweh often stirred inside her own heart, but this was different.

"It has only happened once, for the both of us. To my father in his pastures and to me in the Holy Place. And the outcome was not comforting. My heart still breaks when I remember what was said, and I took no pleasure in witnessing the fulfillment."

"Perhaps the Almighty expressed His heart through you. Perhaps He shared with you the burden of His heart when He gave you His words. If they are the words of the Almighty, then once spoken, they must come to pass. Perhaps the heart of Yahweh takes no pleasure in giving you His words and watching the ending. Maybe it is why you were chosen to hear His voice and to speak His words. The Almighty desires a companion."

Shira could not believe she was saying these things. She had never had such thoughts of Yahweh before. Her mind had never been pressed to consider the greatness of Yahweh beyond the scope of her world. Now, after spending so much time with Samuel, could it be that her heart might be awakening to something new for her, a new breath of spirit in which to see the world, some small blaze of Yahweh to share with a companion.

"That Yahweh's words might be as painful to Him as to me. That Yahweh desires a companion. You force me to ponder something beyond my priestly training."

"I do not mean to speak for Yahweh or you. I do not pretend to know what all is in my own heart. How could I know the heart of Yahweh or know your heart?"

What she realized in this moment was that the spirit of this man had been moving upon her heart for some time like the spirit of Yahweh had moved upon the waters of the deep, pondering a new beginning. Was this a new beginning for her? A new beginning with the prophet of Yahweh? She could imagine it. She could believe it.

"I have studied the scrolls of Moses, the stories of the fathers and the judges of Israel, how Yahweh dealt with them. I secretly yearned for the companionship of the Almighty, and when it came to me, it was fearful."

"I believe it will not be the last time. Yahweh will speak to you again."

"You believe that, truly?" Samuel looked at her.

Shira knew he sought her reassurance, and she knew she wanted to give it. "I do. Yahweh will speak again."

"I fear it and yearn for it. Perhaps next time it will not be so burdensome."

"Will you return to Shiloh?"

"If the reports are to be believed, there is no Shiloh to return to. I would not want to return, not after the time spent here at home...with my parents...with you."

Shira felt Samuel's fingers tug on the sleeve of her robe as if to give special emphasis to her importance. She had not expected the words or the tug on her sleeve, but both coming from this man was a tug upon her heart. It was true, she had taught him many things about living in this quiet setting. And his willingness to learn and the joy he derived from it, gave her a deep pleasure she had never known. She had devoted her life to caring for the world around her, and had never considered what that might include beyond the limits of what she had seen. She too had within her soul a yearning that, until Samuel's unexpected arrival, had been reserved for what she believed was Yahweh.

When she opened her mouth to sing it was for the Almighty, about the Almighty. So it was to the Almighty that she felt a true belonging. But when this prophet of Yahweh entered her small realm, it awakened her heart to new horizons. It made her imagine that she might also sing for someone else, someone who would be a companion on this earth. Yet she was unsure. She struggled to see how she could...how she might be approved by Yahweh for His prophet.

Shira released her clasped hands and dropped them to her side. When Samuel took the hand closest to him and lifted it to his lips, her breath was suddenly called back. He gently pried open her fingers and kissed her palm and then began uncurling each finger and kissing each fingertip. When he returned her hand she held it against her breast, pressing it into her flesh if only to help her heart stop beating so fervently. He placed his hand upon her shoulder and turned her to face him.

"I have seen your hands at work. They care for your mother. They labor in the stalls. They harvest the vineyard. They comfort a foaling mare. They are strong hands, and I hope only to honor them with my kisses. But my highest hope is that you would honor me by becoming my companion for life."

He leaned forward and gently pressed his lips to hers. She did not flinch, but she did not yet respond in kind. She waited to be sure that what she had felt for some time—that the beginnings of love for this man might become fully known—was now rising up in her heart and streaming out in every direction. She felt just born, on wobbly legs, like the just born filly or colt, and the heat from her heart rose up to her lips and burst forth into a returned and passionate pressure upon the lips of the prophet of Yahweh. When they finally paused for the fresh intake of air, she looked into his eyes.

"If my mother approves. If your parents approve. If Yahweh approves. Then my heart and soul gladly approve of being your companion."

Shira took a step back and kept a slight resistance to his desire for a second kiss.

They had been almost inseparable once Samuel had emerged from his self-imposed exile: working together, riding together, eating together, getting acquainted in uncommon ways that went against the grain of the accepted cultural practices. She knew her heart was being steadily drawn to him. The looks they shared, the laughter, the joyful reaction when they came into view each morning after a night apart was a constant and growing pleasure for her. But these were new eyes with which she looked upon this man. This man had heard the voice of Yahweh and spoken the words of Yahweh. She knew these encounters with the Almighty would occur again and she must be prepared for that. But how? How did one prepare for such?

"Are you afraid?" Samuel asked.

"Yes." Shira only knew to be honest.

"As am I." Samuel gave her a wistful smile. "But I am less afraid with you at my side."

When she felt his fingers under her chin and her face being drawn to his, she began to fully believe that she was being invited into this divine union.

The principal line from her heart to his lips was now straight. Heated by desire, Shira threw her arms around Samuel and kissed him like a strike of lightning, then kissed him again, igniting her breastbone, igniting the wonder of human love, igniting the flame of Yahweh.

Sixteen

SABA SAT BEFORE HIS WORK STATION IN THE MIDDLE OF THE night, staring at two golden objects. He couldn't sleep, so why not study his handiwork in the quiet of the night when the shop was empty and the citizens of Aphek were asleep? If any of the Philistine citizens really could sleep. Rest had been impossible for the nation since Prince Namal and the other Lords of the Seren captured the Ark seven full moons ago.

"Remember our Egyptian ancestors. Remember the Pharaoh and the hardness of his heart." Saba mumbled to himself this admonition from the priests of Dagon.

What had been exuberant revels after crushing the army of Israel had quickly turned to panic once the rats began to appear. Months before, Lord Namal had led the Philistine army against Israel and had crushed her. The capture of the Ark of the Covenant had been a premium bonus the Five Lords of the Seren had not anticipated when they slaughtered over thirty thousand men of Israel and sacked the city of Shiloh.

Lord Namal had proven a valiant warrior with nineteen kills by his own sword. He refused to stay back with the other lords safely on the hilltop overlooking the valley. The young lord wanted blood on his hands. He wanted to win the respect of his soldiers. He wanted to earn the scarified marks of battle on his body. He wanted to risk death. He wanted to sow death.

When he led his troops back to Aphek astride his stallion and covered in the blood of his enemies, he was hailed as the new champion of the Philistine nation. All the citizens gathered to welcome the conqueror, and when Lord Namal entered the city through the Archway of the Gods, he had leapt from his horse onto the wagon carrying the Ark of the Covenant, stripped off his clothes, tossed the blood-soaked garments to the adoring throngs, and danced naked around the Ark. It was then that the adoration of the people turned to worship and they hailed the young lord as a new god. Seven months later this god lay in his bed of pain along with most of the Philistine population, suffering from what the young lord referred to as, "a smiting in the secret part of my posterior."

But no one was thinking of a devastating plague seven months ago when the Five Lords of the Seren and all the citizens of the Philistine nation were celebrating the defeat of Israel and the capture of the Ark of Yahweh. Saba remembered his uneasy feeling when the Seren had the Ark taken to the temple and placed beside it the statue of the Dagon as an act of superiority over the defeated god of their enemies. Saba's fear proved true the next morning when the priests of Dagon entered the temple and found the statue lying face down before the Ark. Lord Namal summoned Saba to the temple to see if the statue had suffered any fractures or cracks from the fall and to advise in the process of setting the god back in its place of prominence. There was no damage done except to the pride of Dagon's priests, and Saba spent most of the day in the temple overseeing the laborers re-erect the statue onto its pedestal.

After a second night of celebrations, when the priests returned to the temple to offer sacrifices to their victorious god, they were stunned to see Dagon's image not only horizontal before the Ark, but its head and hands broken off with the body parts lying on the threshold of the entrance into the temple. Saba had been awakened from a sound sleep and escorted to the temple by a dozen soldiers. His blood froze when he stopped at the entrance of the temple and looked inside at the prostrate statue with its head and hands broken off. Saba would not cross the threshold into the temple, nor would he have anything to do with the repairs; other artisans could have that job. No amount of coin was worth risking what he was beginning to believe: Dagon had fallen victim to the dominance of the god of Israel. Who was to say this overt act of vengeance by a superior god would not spread beyond Dagon's temple?

And then there came the infestation of rats followed by a devastating plague that struck the Philistines with bleeding boils and ulcerated tumors. Those who died were considered fortunate. The rest of the population wished for death.

"Remember our Egyptian ancestors. Remember the Pharaoh and the hardness of his heart," Saba kept whispering as he gingerly removed the warm poultice of herbs and medicines from the tumor on his right hip. This hourly practice only brought temporary relief. He had been doing this for months, but nothing brought healing. At least his tumors had not spread to his arms and hands. It would have made it too painful for Saba to work preparing this strange offering to this strange god of Israel.

The priests of the Philistines had summoned all their theological powers, poring over their sacred books and searching desperately for any incantation or spell that would kill the rats or a potion to heal the tumors. They prayed and sacrificed and chanted and prayed again, but no amount of praying or sacrificing to the gods of the Philistine pantheon could rid them of the plague of rats or bring a cure of the bloody flux. If no cure was found soon, Saba knew he would soon be dead along with half the population.

After months of anguished debate, the greatest religious minds among the Philistines concluded that they should try to appease the god of Israel with an offering. It was not an admission of guilt, the priests argued; their choice of action was pragmatic, based solely on the survival of the populace and not from any spiritual enlightenment. The objects to be offered to the god of Israel were very specific: five golden rats and five golden tumors representing the Five Lords of the Philistines. The rat was the carrier of the plague and the tumors were the cause of suffering and death to the people. Each lord would be responsible for contributing one rat and one tumor apiece.

When Lord Namal came to Saba's studio, covered in tumors, he offered Saba the job along with a chest of gold coins. Saba took the commission but refused the compensation, much to Lord Namal's surprise. Saba told the young lord he believed that his generous offer of payment might not be helpful in appeasing the god of Israel. If this god required a personal sacrifice, then he was glad make it. He also felt he had a hand in bringing about the initial victory and the ensuing plague. He had agreed to the request of Lord Namal's father to spy on Israel and draw the sketches of the city so the lords would best plan their attack. And, if he was to die, no amount of coin would make any difference. Saba thought it ridiculous to believe that any offering would placate the god of Israel. He believed this god had little interest in rats and tumors, gold or otherwise. He just wanted his Ark back.

It was impossible for Saba to sit in any position for long, and he pushed his weak body out of the chair and shuffled over to the work table. He extended his hand just above the golden tumor. It measured five fingers in length. Next he measured the tumor on his hip. He had designed the golden one after this fleshly one, and the fleshly one had grown in size since he calculated the original dimensions. The tumor on his hip had grown another two fingers in length.

"This must work." Saba turned his eyes from the repulsive sight on his hip.

He placed the golden objects inside a wooden chest and closed the lid, then shuffled over to the window and saw the glimmer of light in the east. Lord Namal and his entourage would be here soon and he needed to pack his medicines and dressings and extra clothes for the journey ahead. They would depart for Ekron that morning. The Ark of the god of Israel waited in Ekron; the Five Lords of the Philistines would meet in Ekron; and from Ekron the offering would be made to Yahweh before returning the Ark to its rightful owners.

The Five Lords followed behind the lumbering cart pulled by two female cows that had just calved and had never been yoked, another stipulation the priests of Dagon insisted upon, along with the construction of a new wagon to carry the Ark. Just any cart would not do. Saba did not understand all these provisions, but if these details were important to the priests, so be it. If these details appeased the Hebrew god and rid them of the plague, that was all Saba and the entire Philistine nation cared about.

Behind the Five Lords followed the five artisans who had created each lord's golden tumor and rat. Saba and the other artists did not have the benefit of being carried by slaves on comfortable litters as they followed the Ark all the way from Ekron to the border with Israel. They had to limp and hobble under their own power. The Five Lords were carried on litters to within sight of the border crossing that marked the territory of Israel. Just over the border was the village of Beth Shemesh. The advanced stage of the disease had debilitated the strength of the lords, but they did walk the last paces to the border, propped up on either side by a priest of Dagon as a show of humility. Priests and lords together would see it through to the end.

The wagon was a simple flatbed design, nothing ostentatious to compete with the splendor of the Ark. No driver's seat. No driver was necessary. That was part of the stipulation. The cows must be guided by a divine hand for this to work. The railing around the bed was high enough to keep the objects from vibrating off onto the road. No one wanted to handle these objects once they were on board. A long wooden tongue was attached to the front axle so the team could be harnessed on either side. Five jeweled chests were placed behind the Ark, each containing the offering of a golden rat and tumor.

The procession kept a respectful distance behind the slow moving cart. Saba had to admit the priests of Dagon had devised an ingenious plan, nothing complicated about it. Once the cows were put in position and set in the direction of Beth Shemesh they were to be released and allowed to plod down the road of their own bovine freewill. Should they maintain their course and cross into the territory of Israel, it was believed the god of Israel had brought this deadly disease upon the Philistines.

If however, the cows veered off the chosen path and went in any other direction, the priests of Dagon would say that the god of Israel had not struck the Philistines, but that this pestilence was mere chance. Either way, the priests would be able to hold to their theology with the people, although not for much longer, because they would be dead if this plague was not soon lifted.

All eyes watched the cows lumber straight down the road toward the border crossing, turning neither to the right or left. It was a hopeful sign. A ditch lay on one side, and open ground on the other. When the cows paused at the boundary line and began lowing as though announcing their arrival to those on the other side, the political and religious leadership of the Philistines held their breath as they watched and waited.

Saba's heart was pounding as he could see laborers in the distant fields pointing in the direction of the Ark. Some ran toward the Ark poised at the border. Others ran in the opposite direction, taking the road toward the village of Beth Shemesh. Others remained in the fields singing and shouting. Saba could not make out the foreign tongue they spoke, but from their exuberance, it appeared they were rejoicing at the unbelievable sight of the Ark of the Covenant sitting in a wooden cart in the middle of the road.

The cows bobbed their heads at the approaching field hands. The workers stopped short of the boundary line and would not cross. They would wait and not step into a foreign land even to retrieve this holy object stolen from them. It was as if they too were testing the god of Israel to see what would happen.

Saba wanted to scream for the dim-witted cows to move forward. If they did not cross the border, he and the entire population were doomed to die.

The cows lowed once more, a duet bellow of triumph, and then tightened the leather harness as together they strained forward, finally crossing into the territory of the god of pestilence and death. Still, the field workers did not approach the cows, nor did Saba and the Philistines breathe a collective sigh of relief. There was still more that must happen, more required before all fear could subside and lives return to normalcy.

Not until the cows stopped beside a large rock inside the undisputed land of Israel, not until Saba saw the village elders running down the road from Beth Shemesh and ordering the team released from its tethers, not until the field hands removed the Ark and chests containing the pair of golden objects and set them both on the massive rock, and not until the wagon was chopped into pieces and the two cows slaughtered on the spot and sacrificed in the flames of the wagon did anyone on the Philistine side of the border think there might be reason for optimism.

Once the altar flames were consuming the flesh of the two cows, the task was done, and the Five Lords and priests of Dagon would return to Ekron and wait together with the entire Philistine population. They would wait for the lifting of the judgment of the god of Israel or prepare themselves for their final journey into the afterlife.

Saba paid little attention to the Five Lords and the priests returning to their litters to start back to Ekron. Saba was not ready to depart just yet. He took a few cautious steps closer to the border, his eyes riveted upon the Ark and the jeweled chests perched upon the immense rock. He watched in awe as the animated praise coming from the men of Beth Shemesh turned suddenly to a dark slaughter. A deadly over-excitement gripped the field hands and they ripped the lid of the Ark from off its gold case. Some of them began to lean over and look inside and others began to fight over the contents. No sooner had they done so, then the bodies of these men began to fly into the air, catch fire or evaporate into dust before ever hitting the ground. The horror of the scene compelled him to step toward the border line, but he did not cross. He suddenly felt like rejoicing. This strange god was no respecter of worshipers. This god would destroy the people called the chosen as quickly as he would inflict a plague upon the Philistines.

Saba could not count the number of men who died right before his eyes. The terrific speed with which it happened caused him to fall to his knees. This was justice. This was deserved. This, for Saba, was vindication for his brave act to spy for his country against his enemy. He took a deep breath and then another and then another to be sure. He could not remember when he was last able to take a deep breath without flinching in pain.

His nose detected the smell of fresh air. He had breathed the stench of the plague for so long he knew it would be the last odor he would ever inhale. He filled his lungs with this pure aroma, rose to his feet and began to walk toward Ekron with a little more strength in his legs and a little less limp in his step. Yes, he would spy again, gladly.

Seventeen

SHIRA SAT ON THE EDGE OF THEIR BED, CLOTHED IN HER CERE-monial wedding garments. The table had been pushed into one corner of the room, the bed in the other. One lamp was placed upon the table, its small flame adding an indistinct light to the space. Beside the lamp lay a wineskin and two goblets next to it drained of their contents. Shira stared at the volumes of scrolls and parchments stacked floor to ceiling with the newest writings rolled up and in large clay pots along the far wall. The collection of blessed writings copied and passed down through the generations by the priests and Levites of Israel. Before her was the library of the words of Yahweh, the story of the covenant relationship of the chosen people with the Creator of heaven and earth.

"My life's work." Samuel stood nearer to the shelving and waved his hand over the sacred writings. "It is difficult to imagine how the scrolls and I came to this room."

"It is a heavenly wonder." Shira marveled at the awesome sight.

"Yahweh must reveal to me what is to happen next." Samuel lifted his shoulders and hands in a gesture of bewilderment.

"You must write, my husband. You must preserve these words until the time of revelation." She rose to her feet and moved toward the shelving.

"My wife believes the Creator of heaven and earth has more to say to me."

"Yahweh has more to say than could ever be written, and more for you to do." Shira bowed her head. Perhaps she presumed too much.

Samuel turned his eyes away from the stacks of parchments and looked at his wife's smiling profile.

"What a wonder you are."

Shira open her arms and motioned for him to approach her. She took Samuel's hands and placed them upon the hem of her veil. Samuel did as instructed and raised her veil. Silver earrings dangled from her lobes. A garland of White Broom flowers crowned her head.

"You must help me, my queen." Samuel held the hem of the veil in his fingertips.

"It would be an honor, my king." She guided his hands over her head and he released the veil, then Samuel rested his hand upon Shira's shoulder. She took his hands and kissed the back of each one. "May I be a crown of splendor in your hand. May you rejoice over your bride."

"You are like a royal diadem in the hand of Yahweh."

Shira removed the flowered crown of White Broom and set it upon the nightstand next to the bed. She would dry and press this garland to preserve the memory of this day.

"The first of seven days, my king."

"The first of seven nights, my queen."

Samuel pulled back the quilts from the bed. Then he reached to her veil and released the clamps that attached the veil to her hair and folded it before dropping it upon the floor. Shira reached to remove her earrings, but Samuel stopped her. He loved watching their motion at the slightest move of her head. He loved their reflective flash cast from the light of the oil lamp. Then he loosened the straps that secured her wedding dress, first one shoulder, then the other. He closed his eyes and inhaled the scent of myrrh in the air, the spikenard fragrance of his bride, the trace of wine on the flow of her warm breath. He paused to savor the banquet of aromas. When he opened his eyes he beheld her shining face as she laid her cheek against his forearm and gave him a smile, encouraging him to continue. He gently pushed the straps over the slope of her shoulders, but held onto the dress, guiding it down her body.

"Do I see pleasure in your eyes, my king?"

Samuel could not speak at first; the smile on his lips prevented him from shaping the words. He worked his jaw to unlock it so he could answer her.

"In my eyes. In my body. In my heart, my queen."

He removed the vial from his belt and poured the liquid into his hands. The myrrh dripped from Samuel's hands as he placed them on Shira's neck, rubbing the scented mixture into her skin until he was light-headed from the aroma.

Shira loosened the knot of the purple headband, lifted it off Samuel's head, and let it fall to the floor. Untying the gold sash around his waist, she allowed it to drop as well. She untied the three leather bows down the front of his robe and opened the collar, helping him slip one arm and then the other out of the sleeves. As she began to untie the ribbon belt of his underclothes, she watched him watching her delicate fingers loosen the ribbon and stretching out the waistband so the garment could fall unhindered. Shira took the vial of myrrh from his hand and poured the remainder over his head and shoulders, shaking the last drops from the vial before tossing it onto the bed. The myrrh flowed off his head and down his face and neck. Her hands worked the liquid into his scalp and face, her fingers massaging the perfume into his skin. When she finished her task, she stepped back in admiration.

"Do I see pleasure in the eyes of my queen?"

"I am consumed with pleasure in all that I see, my king."

Samuel pulled back the curtain. He took a scroll off the middle shelf and let the curtain fall back into place. He tiptoed over to the table and picked up the clean, neatly folded change of clothes and set them on the floor. He then pushed aside the tray of dirty dishes and brushed the crumbs away before he sat down. He decided not to light the lamp, but instead, unhooked the curtain on the window, allowing the natural light to illuminate his reading. He swirled his finger over an empty plate, mixing the bread crumbs with a glaze of apricot syrup. The flavor exploded onto his tongue, which only increased his ravenous hunger. Each day, they had eaten like starving beggars, devouring every meal left at the door as if their appetite would never be sated.

Samuel looked at his beautiful wife asleep on the bed, her head resting on the pillow, the sunlight reflecting off her as she calmly rose and fell with each breath. How many days had they spent in this room? How many hours had they spent in each other's arms? How many words had they spoken? How many dreams had they shared? What had happened to the outside world since the wedding ceremony? Would they even care?

A quick glance out the window and Samuel saw Elkanah racing across the yard. He carried no tray of food, which was a disappointment. When he heard Elkanah's lumbering footsteps climbing the wooden stairs, it then dawned on Samuel that maybe the seven days of bliss were over and Elkanah was coming to the bridal chamber as the bridegroom's witness to collect the bride and bridegroom for the wedding feast. But why was he coming alone? Why was his mother not with him or the wedding guests gathering in the yard for the feast?

Samuel jumped out of his seat, knocking over the chair with a crash. Shira flinched and tucked her head beneath her pillow. Samuel barely had time to slip into a robe before he got to the door. When he cracked open the door, he put his finger to his lips for Elkanah to keep his voice low.

"I have news."

"What is it? Is the wedding feast today?"

"No. It is not until tomorrow, but this could not wait."

"What is it, my love?" Shira groaned from underneath her pillow.

"Nothing, go back to sleep."

Samuel stepped outside, closed the door, and looked into Elkanah's excited face.

"Son, the Ark...the Ark has been returned. The messenger just brought word. The Philistines have returned the Ark of the Covenant."

"The Ark? Is it safe? Where is it?"

"It is safe. It has been taken to the house of Abinadab."

"The Ark of the Covenant in someone's house?" Samuel could not believe what his father was saying. "Abinadab, father of Eleazar. They have hidden the holy instruments of the Tabernacle. Of course. Of course that is where it is." Samuel came near to wonder and amusement at where Yahweh had brought back the Ark. "But how did the Ark get there?"

"It first arrived in the village of Beth Shemesh, just over the border, but there were no priests in the village so they sent word to the Levites living in Kiriath Jearim to come immediately and collect the Ark. Several men from Beth Shemesh have died."

"Died? How? Why?"

"Field hands. Farmers. The messenger said they had opened the doors of the Ark to look inside and..." Elkanah's voice trailed off.

"I understand, Father." Samuel gave his father's arm an understanding squeeze.

"They need you, my son. The people need you."

Was this true? What his father just said, was it true? Did Israel need him? Did Yahweh need him? Was this the beginning of new revelation, a new direction?

"We will need to eat something. We're starving."

"At once." Elkanah turned and dashed down the steps.

Samuel stepped back inside the room and closed the door. He pulled aside the curtain in front of the shelves and stood motionless before the records of Yahweh and His chosen people.

"Is this true, Yahweh? Is this the new path I am to follow?"

Samuel heard his bride stirring behind him.

"Come back to bed, my love."

He turned to see her rubbing her hand over the rumpled quilt. He smiled at the shaft of light that brightened her sleepy face.

"My love, Yahweh has come back to us."

It was impossible for Samuel to keep Shira from going with him to Kiriath Jearim even if he had wanted to, which he did not. He wanted her by his side at all times. She had bound out of bed the moment Samuel told her about the Ark, and began to dress.

"I shall take the scroll that describes the design of the Ark." Samuel was checking the catalog numbers to confirm the right scroll. "And what should I wear?"

"Your Levitical robes." Shira pointed to his clothes laid out on a rack in a corner.

"How did you know I would need these?" Samuel shook his head in wonder.

"I did not know, but I believe in being prepared. Now get dressed." Shira kissed him on the cheek and dashed out of the room.

When Samuel met her in the courtyard, Shira had two horses waiting. He handed her the scroll. They both embraced Hannah and Elkanah and climbed onto their horses.

"You are returning, aren't you?" Hannah pressed her hand against the backside of her son's horse.

"Yes, Ima, as soon as we are able."

"Yahweh is with you, my son." Elkanah drew his wife to his side.

"Go," his father said.

Before the wedding, Samuel spent time with Eleazar and his father, making sure the holy objects of the Tabernacle were safely hidden. Foreign spies were reported to be looking for these hidden treasures. People with no loyalty could be bribed. Those with no scruples would trade their spiritual heritage for "a mess of porridge." The Philistines may have captured the Ark of the Covenant and decimated the army of Israel, but Samuel would do all in his power to safeguard what remained.

The nation of Israel was despondent over their crushing defeat at the hands of the Philistines. Who knew how long it would be before Israel could rise up to defend itself against another invasion? Without a central government and no city with a Tabernacle for the people to worship and sacrifice, Samuel had taken it upon himself to see that Israel's most important treasures and the sacred writings were kept safe until some future day when the Ark would be returned and Israel's glory could be restored. Perhaps the day had arrived.

When Samuel and Shira arrived in Kiriath Jearim, Eleazar met them at the bottom of the hill. Former guards of the Tabernacle patrolled the perimeter of the property at the base of the hill. It seemed to Samuel that every Levite in the region had gathered at the home of Abinadab overlooking the village from its place on the hilltop. When Eleazar escorted the couple through the crowd, Abinadab rushed to Samuel from out of the door of his house and dropped to his knees at his feet.

"Give thanks to Yahweh for He is good."

Samuel and his fellow Levites responded with, "His love endures forever."

Abinadab held out his trembling hands to Samuel. The man's silvery gray beard was wet and his dark eyes streaked with red. His face was gaunt from exhaustion.

Samuel took his hands, knelt down, and began his prayer with Abinadab leading the Levites in response.

"Let Israel say..."

"...His love endures forever.

"Let the house of Aaron say..."

"...His love endures forever.

"Let those who fear the Lord say..."

"...His love endures forever."

Abinadab wrenched his hands away from Samuel's grasp and fell prostrate before him, pressing his face into the ground.

"I don't know what to do, Samuel. Yahweh is in my home. Men have died. Yahweh struck down the men of Beth Shemesh for touching the Ark of His holiness, and now the Divine, the Blessed, the Almighty is in my house. I sent my family away. No one dares enter. I have not eaten. I have drunk no wine. I have not slept since Yahweh crossed my threshold. It is a fearful thing. Help me. Help me know what I am to do."

Samuel placed his right hand upon Abinadab's head.

"Be comforted. You are worthy. Yahweh has returned and honored your house to be the house of the Almighty for this time. The Lord's right hand has done mighty things! Yahweh's right hand is lifted high; the Lord's right hand has done mighty things!"

Samuel saw that he was surrounded by priests all looking down at him. He stood and took in the dense crowd. Samuel saw about him a sea of faces—faces of fear, of bewilderment, of desperation, of helplessness. They were lost. Yahweh had been found, but Israel was lost. Their faces and eyes were expectant, and Samuel knew their hearts were waiting to hear from him words that might explain the return of the Ark; how the "right hand of Yahweh" had done this mighty act.

And the words filled his spirit, overflowed from his lips. "We must open our eyes. We must see what Yahweh has done. Our own stained hands had given our enemies the Ark of the Covenant, our greatest treasure, the Mercy Seat of the Presence, and with no help from His chosen, Yahweh returned to His people. Yahweh is not dependent upon us. We are dependent upon the Almighty. What was impossible for us proved possible for Yahweh. We did not retake the Ark, Yahweh returned. Yahweh returned to His chosen people by His own power and His own choice. The weight of His glory is returned to us and there is no other god before Yahweh."

Samuel searched for his bride. He raised his hand and the Levites parted to reveal Shira standing at the outer edge of the crowd. Her smile was an inspiration to continue.

"We are people of the covenant. We must remember Yahweh chose our ancestors not from out of the great nations, but from the desert wanderers. We must not abandon Yahweh for He has not abandoned us. We do not want for Yahweh to depart from us. We do not want Yahweh to be taken from us. We must never forget the holiness of Yahweh and turn our backs on Him. We must not wander. We must repent. We must return and serve Yahweh, the God of Gods, the God of the Covenant, the God of our nation."

Samuel stepped back to Abinadab and lifted him to his feet. He motioned to Eleazar to join them. He placed his arms around father and son.

"The Ark of Yahweh has come to the house of Abinadab, and there it shall remain until there is a day for Yahweh to be praised and worshiped in the assemblies of the tribes. And Eleazar, his son, shall be the guardian of the Ark. He shall protect the Ark, revering its holiness and continually offering praise to the Presence on the Mercy Seat."

When he had finished, Samuel stepped over to Shira and took her hand in his. "I must go inside."

"Yes. Yahweh awaits you."

Samuel moved closer to her, whispering words for only her to hear. "My heart trembles before Him. I can hardly swallow. My legs have hardened and cannot move. Yet I know I must enter the house and worship Yahweh."

"You will be safe. Yahweh wishes to bless you and reveal Himself to you. He awaits you, and I await your return."

Samuel brought her hands to his lips. If these were to be his last moments on earth, it was the face of his bride he wanted before him. He turned and approached the front door, paused, and then stepped inside.

Shira watched as Samuel disappeared into the shadows of the house.

She knew she had not lost her husband. Yahweh had appeared to her husband. Yahweh had spoken to her husband. Yahweh had opened His gate of righteousness to her husband, and she would give the Almighty her praise. Samuel was not his own. He was not her own. But in His kindness, Yahweh would share His prophet with her. She knew deep in her heart, Yahweh trusted her. The Creator of heaven and earth had entrusted His prophet into her care. His presence began in their bridal chamber and would last for all their marriage. She would give thanks to the Lord, for He was good; His love endures forever.

PART FOUR

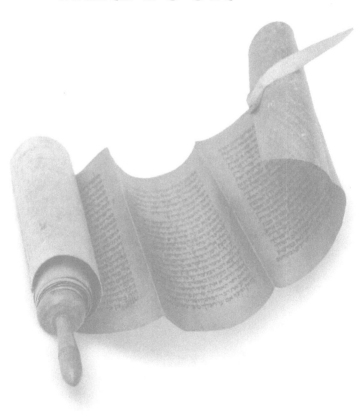

Eighteen

SAMUEL STOOD UPON AN OUTCROPPING OF ROCK. HE NEEDED the height it provided to see and be seen by the great assembly gathered on this stretch of land just north of his home in Ramah. Shira stood just behind him while his students from the prophet school were gathered below him on the ground. This was a perfect moment for Samuel's students to be out of the classroom to witness the prophetic call on the Seer's life. The nation of Israel let it be known that they wished to repent and seek a new commitment to Yahweh. So Samuel issued the summons, and he stretched out his arms to embrace the throng.

"We are here at the Mizpah, the tower of watching, the place where our ancestor Jacob made his bond with the father of his wives. He swore to care for them and their sons, the fathers of our nation, the chosen of Yahweh." Samuel began to raise his arms to the sky and address the Presence. "Yahweh has sworn to care for His chosen people. The Almighty has been faithful to His covenant. It is we, your chosen, who have broken the bond, and we wish to return to you. We have rid our tents, our homes, and our whole hearts of foreign gods. We commit ourselves to you, O Yahweh, to serve you only. For only you, the Almighty, are able to deliver your people from the hands of her enemies."

For years, Samuel had been unable to persuade the people of the covenant from compromising with their enemies. They thought if Israel was more tolerant and would embrace the gods of the Philistines along with Yahweh that this inclusion might gain them some favor with the Five Lords, but it did nothing to relieve the tyranny. The knee of the Philistines was a constant pressure on the neck of the Hebrews. Even now the Philistine army camped at the western border with Israel within sight of Mizpah. They were prepared to attack this assembly called for by the tribes of Israel.

"We come now before you, Creator of heaven and earth, with tears of sorrow, in weakness, powerless against those who oppress us. This day, we have refrained from food and drink so that our bodies might be afflicted, so that our hearts may be purified, so that our minds may know the truth, and our mouths speak of the knowledge of our sin against you. As atonement, we pour out to you that which cannot be taken up again."

Samuel lowered his arms and called by name each tribe and her tribal leader. The twelve leaders stepped forward, each one bearing on his shoulder a large clay jar filled with water. They formed a circle in front of the stone outcropping where Samuel and Shira stood. Close enough for Samuel to bear witness of their penance and far enough away not to get soaked by the offering.

Each tribal leader, one by one, lifted the clay jar off his shoulder, raised it before Samuel and Yahweh, and made his offering for his tribe: "O Yahweh, giver of life, we cry out in sorrow for our sins, and pour our sacrifice upon this ground." Once Samuel nodded his approval, the tribal leader emptied his jar of water upon the earth.

When the last tribal leader stepped forward, he lifted the jar from his shoulder, but did not raise it before Yahweh and Samuel. Instead, he set it upon the ground beside him.

"Samuel, prophet of Yahweh, before I pour out the water of penitence for the tribe of Benjamin, I wish to address you."

Samuel dropped his head and mumbled under his breath. "Benjamites. Yahweh spare us."

The only one able to hear Samuel express his annoyance at the interruption to this religious ceremony was his wife standing behind him. Shira quietly shushed her husband.

"Jeush, son of Bela, head of the tribe Benjamin, speak your mind." Samuel grit his teeth to minimize the vexed tone in his voice. The only thing Samuel wanted to hear was a confession, not a speech, especially not from someone of the tribe of Benjamin.

Jeush had inherited the honor of tribal leader from his great, great grandfather when he was appointed to lead the tribe after the civil war nearly decimated the male population of the tribe. He was a head shorter than most men but twice as broad. His thick body covered in the skins of wolf and wild boar, doubled the size of his frame.

"My lord, we are the least and the smallest tribe of the nation of twelve." Jeush spoke as if this was a point of pride, not in shame.

"There is good reason for that." Samuel shook his head but did not raise it.

Shira shushed him more forcefully.

"Much time has passed since our enemies returned the Ark of the Covenant, and the tribe of Benjamin rejoices that the Mercy Seat of Yahweh rests in the promised land of the chosen. But having the Ark in our possession has not spared us." Jeush paused for Samuel to acknowledge him, but he did not bother to raise his eyes. "Since the return of the Ark, the hand of the Philistines has been oppressive upon us. Our enemies took advantage of Israel's lack of an organized military and no central government. They control the trade routes to the Great Sea and captured the smaller cities along our borders. Those cities under their domain are levied with burdensome taxes. Even now, as we stand here, their army is poised at our border ready to strike." Jeush reached inside his garment of wolf skin and removed a small clay statue of the Ashtoreth goddess and extended his arm in the air for all to see. "My lord, prophet and judge of Yahweh, this little clay statue cannot be the sole reason we suffer under such oppression."

Now Samuel raised his head. He saw the clay goddess in Jeush's raised hand and heard the murmuring of the crowd as they responded to his stopping this ceremony. The Philistines had marshaled. What was he doing?

"You had been warned not to embrace the pagan culture of the Philistines, and you did not listen. Now in your despair you come to the one person in Israel who could intercede for you." Samuel glowered at Jeush, and did not conceal his disgust with this affront. How dare Jeush bring this idol into the ritual of repentance? How dare he stop this ceremony with the army of the Philistines prepared to attack them?

"You are correct, my lord. You are the great intercessor with Yahweh and have served us well. But your gray hairs increase and your years rise in number. You leave no one behind with your great wisdom to judge and power to intercede with Yahweh."

Samuel took a step closer to the edge of the rock outcropping. His heart was beginning to boil. He felt the hand of his wife upon his shoulder.

"My years and gray hairs mean nothing. You must rid yourselves of these idols."

Jeush spit on the statue of the Ashtoreth, and then hurled it over the heads of the clan chieftains of his tribe standing behind him. "I do not worship these little graven toys. They mean nothing, but more needs to be done for our safety and survival. We need new leadership. Who will be raised up to replace you?"

"My sons have been trained in the ways of Yahweh and serve as judges in Israel."

"Your sons are scoundrels. None among the tribes of Israel want that yoke placed upon their necks. It would be worse than the Philistines."

Now it was Samuel's turn to be the restrainer. He felt Shira begin to move up next to him, and he held a firm arm in front of her.

The roar that erupted from the Philistine army stationed on the western border cracked open the sky. Everyone looked to the west. Everyone except Jeush and Samuel. The two men glared at one another.

Then Jeush bent down and picked up the clay jar beside him. "O Yahweh, giver of life, we cry out in sorrow for our sins, and pour our sacrifice upon this ground." Jeush upended his jar, pouring out the contents upon the saturated ground.

The twelfth water offering completed the ceremony. The twelve tribes of Israel were united in repentance. Just as a second howl from the Philistines burst upon the air, Samuel called for the sacrifice. The young prophets hastily erected a stone altar below the outcropping of rocks and lay upon it bundles of dried wood.

"Bring forth the lamb." Samuel snapped his fingers at the young prophet who held the leash on the bleating lamb.

Jeush stood firm in his place. Everyone around him seemed unnerved by the impending attack while he kept his face toward Samuel.

"That is the second roar of the Five Lords. Upon the fifth, the Philistines will charge." Jeush calmly spoke and calmly withdrew his sword from its sheath. "May you live long, my lord, and appoint a righteous ruler before you join our fathers in Sheol. Until then, do not stop crying out to Yahweh for us, that the Almighty may rescue us from the Philistines."

Samuel hopped down from the rocky outcropping onto the ground near the altar. While he felt a shooting pain heat up his spine, he was not about to show it on his face. He did allow the third cry from the Philistines to cover the grunting sound he made as he limped over to the altar.

"Hand me the knife." Samuel held out his hand and the hilt of the knife was placed in his palm. He folded his fingers over it. He took a few deep breaths to calm himself before he placed his hand upon the head of the lamb.

At the fourth roar, more of the assembly of Israel were looking at the advancing Philistine army than were watching Samuel.

Samuel raised the knife. "Yahweh, God of the nation of Israel, the chosen of the Almighty, come and save us. Our enemies are set upon us, and only you, O Yahweh, can save us from their hands."

The combined sounds of the last bleat of the lamb as Samuel slit its throat, the fifth cry of the Philistines as they broke into a run toward the frightened and disoriented army of Israel, and the deafening thunder that shattered the atmosphere on the plains of Mizpah caused everyone, Philistine and Israelite alike, to fall to the ground.

Samuel went down on his knees beside the altar, his hands gripping the large stacked stones that now flowed with blood from the dying lamb. He looked up to see Shira lying prostrate upon the ledge of the rocky outcropping. She raised her head and smiled at her husband.

"Yahweh is faithful to His faithful prophet."

When Samuel ordered the torches to be tossed onto the altar, the dried wood burst into flame. He climbed back upon the rocky ledge and helped Shira to her feet. Together they turned to look across the landscape. The plain was covered with prone bodies lying upon the ground. There were no clouds in the sky. The sun was bright and hot. There was no cause, human or earthly, that could explain the thunder. It was the voice of God that had created the earsplitting sound, the voice of Yahweh, the God of Israel.

"The voice of Yahweh has tumbled down upon us and shattered our enemies. They are routed. Arise and pursue."

From his position on the rocky ledge, Samuel could see the violent agitation among the Philistines as they got to their feet in confusion and panic. They began to gore themselves with their own weapons while many took flight back inside their borders.

Samuel looked at Jeush lying on the ground, his sword fallen from his hands. He watched as Jeush gradually got to his knees and raised his head toward him.

"I will not be joining the fathers in Sheol just yet." Then Samuel took Shira's hand and made their way back to the carriage that would carry them home.

Nineteen

SAMUEL COULD NOT AVOID HIS VISIT TO BEERSHEBA ANY LON-
ger. Were his two sons as bad as had been reported? Were they as corrupt
as the rumors indicated? Did their conduct bring dishonor? He had to see
for himself. He had to bear witness. But he dreaded the prospect of confronting them face-to-face. It was a fearful thing to face the Almighty, to
hear the voice of Yahweh in his ears, to read in the scrolls of Moses of
the wondrous acts of the Creator of heaven and earth. But to confront his
sons—to discipline his sons, to accuse them of being wicked in the sight of
Yahweh—would be a heartbreaking task.

The fault must be his. He would not even lay responsibility upon
his dear wife. He was absent much of the time either on his circuit rides
performing his duties as judge, or when he was home, he devoted himself
to the education and training of the young men recruited to his prophet's
school from all over the country. When his sons had gained his attention
he was often too strict, scolding them for misbehaving or having too high
an expectation of their academic excellence when they became of age and
were enrolled in his school. He had done all he had known to do.

But he had to admit it was possible that he was closer to Yahweh than
any other man, including his sons. When Samuel delved into such realities
it brought only turmoil to his heart. Each journey into those troubling

memories was too painful, and the possibility of ever finding a path back, too fearful.

On the final stretch of his annual tour of the cities of southern Israel, Samuel took a detour to Beersheba. It had been years since he had been to the city, and he decided to leave his horse and pack mule stabled in a village just to the north of Beersheba, and leave behind all professional vestiges of himself: the robes of a judge, the scrolls of a prophet, the implements of a priest. A half-a-day's walk, through the foothills to the base of the southern mountain range near the border with the Philistines, and he would arrive in Beersheba. He departed the village well before dawn so that most of his walking would be done in cooler temperatures, and were he overwhelmed by his sons' ill-actions, he could slip out of the city without being noticed.

The road leading up to the city was long and gradual. Beersheba had been built on a hill by the bank of a dry riverbed which allowed the flow of winter waters and ensured a regular supply of water. Samuel followed alongside the scaffolding for construction workers building a mud brick outer wall as he approached the main entrance. The harassment from the Philistines required a circular defensive barrier around the city.

Just before entering the city gates, Samuel noticed two separate piles of stones. He stepped off the road and circled around the two piles of rubble. At one time these were stones of remembrance, shaped into altars to recall the promises and visions of Yahweh to the fathers of Israel. Samuel prayed in a low and quiet voice.

"We have forgotten your promises, O Yahweh. We have forgotten your promises to the fathers to make for yourself a chosen people without number, without end, to a thousand generations."

Samuel knelt down between the piles and picked up a stone. He ran his fingers over the rough and jagged edges of the rock.

"We have forgotten your command to not be afraid. You, the Almighty, sent us into Egypt. You, Creator of heaven and earth, brought us back again. You, O Yahweh, brought us into a land of Promise, made us into a great nation, and this is how we honor you, in the rubble of forgetfulness."

Samuel saw that his tears were dripping through his beard onto the stone in his hand. The dry wind evaporated much of the moisture, and Samuel rubbed the traces of his sorrow into the porous surface before placing the stone inside his travel bag. He stretched his hand toward the second pile of rocks, selected a stone, and placed it also inside his bag. He would have a stone from each altar. He would remember if no one else would. Then he went back to the road, and before he joined the human flow into the city, he lifted the hood of his travel garment over his head to conceal his identity.

The last time Samuel and Shira were in Beersheba was at the ceremony for Joel and Abijah. That was when Samuel passed on to their sons the authority to hold court and act as judges for the towns and villages in the lower southern district of Israel. He had not returned since that day. He had no desire to do so.

His sons could have set up their court in the local Levitical school, or they could have used a structure adjacent to the local synagogue as well, but Joel and Abijah chose to hold court in the village square where residents and travelers could watch their judgments out in the open.

Samuel remained on the periphery of the crowd gathered before the two seats and a large table placed on a raised platform. Two Levites stood on either side of the table and began to blow their shofars when his sons emerged from the front entrance of a large house a short distance from where the court had been set up. Many in the crowd began to cheer, though most remained silent, their sullen faces marked with expressions of either anxiety or disdain. The two men lumbered toward the seats with heavy awkward steps, their pace slowed by layers of flowing robes and protruding bellies. They were accompanied by armed guards with several Levitical scribes carrying pouches and scrolls following behind. When the two men took their seats, Samuel gasped.

"It cannot be. It cannot be them." Samuel's quiet whisper was in stunned recognition of Joel and Abijah. What had become of his sons? When he and Shira last saw them, they were lean and dressed in simple garments more appropriate to the sons of the supreme judge of Israel. The layers they wore were made from multicolored fabrics with bejeweled turbans on their heads and rings on nearly every finger. This was what happened when a judge was unsupervised. They got fat and overdressed.

When the first case was called, Samuel watched a man step out from the crowd. He squeezed the arm of the woman next to him and patted the head of the young boy standing beside her. A younger girl stood on the other side of the woman, as a third child squirmed in her arms. The man cradled an old clay jar in his hands. He was dressed in clothes of a laborer with a leather apron tied around his middle. He did try to approach the table with a sense of calm self-respect, and not the cocky assurance of his opponents. These two men were well groomed and similarly dressed to the presiding judges. One carried a document in his hand and the other held a silk pouch of coins in each hand.

Joel and Abijah smiled at the two well-dressed men who approached the table where the Levite scribes had spread out their parchments and writing utensils. Samuel's sons completely ignored the other man as he approached. When Abijah gave a bored wave of his hand, a scribe stood and read the complaint between the opposing sides. Once the complaint was read, Joel nodded for the man holding his clay pot to speak.

"I am Gehazi the potter. Everyone in Beersheba knows of my family. We have been potters in this city for four generations. I am training my son to be the fifth generation." Gehazi pointed to his son standing next to his mother. The young boy stiffened his back when the eyes of the crowd shifted to him.

"My descendants fought beside Commander Joshua in the wars of conquest. My fathers belong to the tribe of Simeon. When the tribes divided the land of Promise, my family settled here in the territory of Simeon inside the borders of Judah. When we left our tents to become citizens of Beersheba, my great grandfather began to make his pots and sell them from his shop beside his house. The shop remains to this day, and the quality of work of the family of Zaccur, the son of Hammuel, the son of Mishma, my family name, all of the tribe of Simeon, is known in the territory for its excellence. I teach my son today to excel in his craft and be honest in his dealings."

Gehazi reverently raised his pot into the air with both hands to show the beloved object to the judges, who, to Samuel's eyes, appeared uninterested in the man's story. Then the potter turned to show the crowd, and a few responded with tepid applause, but most were silent. The Levites seated at the table below Samuel's two sons raised their hands to hush the crowd and were quickly obeyed.

"This is the first pot my great grandfather ever made." The potter carefully set his clay pot on the Levite's table, removed the lid, and took out a tattered and worn scroll. He gingerly unrolled the scroll and read the contents, stating that on such a date nearly a century ago, his great grandfather had registered his business with the city council for the amount of five shekels. And each year since, the family patriarch paid the tax to the city to update his license.

"For the last three years I have been unable to pay my city taxes because of the decline in my sales. These two have come all the way from the tribe of Dan with their caravans of cheap pots made in Gezer. Their sole purpose is to have dominion in the trade from Beersheba as far north as the city of Joppa on the Great Sea. They want only to control the trade and care nothing about our city or our citizens or my family."

At this point Joel raised his hand for the potter to stop his argument, and pointed to the Levitical scribe at the table.

"Read what this man owes to the city."

In a monotonous voice the scribe announced to the whole assembly that the potter owed the city of Beersheba the staggering sum of almost seventy-five shekels, an amount impossible for the potter to pay.

"That is not what I owe. It is not even half of that amount. You have inflated the price to line your pretty robes with the excess." Gehazi began pounding his fist on the table with such force that the scribes had to hold onto their parchments and writing implements to keep them from bouncing off the table.

A guard stepped between the potter and the scribes and pushed him away from the table. Once Gehazi was subdued, the man with the two silk coin pouches tossed one onto the table where it dropped with a clack like the snapping of a bone.

"For what the potter owes to the city."

Gehazi was clearly stunned to hear these words, as was Samuel. Could this be a change of heart? Samuel noticed sly smiles appear on the faces of his sons. He supposed it was not at the pleasure of witnessing some unexpected benevolence on the part of the two business traders from the tribe of Dan.

Then the man tossed his second pouch onto the table. "For the purchase of his business and his property."

At this proposition both sons defied the weight of their corpulence and jolted to their feet as the crowd gasped in astonishment.

"It is ruled this day that the potter is now free of all obligation for what he owes to the city of Beersheba."

One Levitical scribe began immediately to write down the words of Joel, while a second scribe wrote down the words of Abijah.

"It is also ruled this day that the potter will forfeit his business and his property and vacate its premises within thirty days of this day. And because we are feeling particularly free-handed, we rule the potter is not responsible for covering the costs of today's trial."

Gehazi howled as he pushed aside the guard who stood in his way and rushed to the table to retrieve his clay bowl. He slammed his deed of property down on the table. "This document condemns your judgment. This document condemns your perversion of justice. This document is sacred in the sight of heaven."

"Take him away, and call the next case." At Joel's command the guards went to grab the potter, but he grabbed his bowl off the table and wielded it like a weapon, causing the guards to stop in their tracks. Then Gehazi raised it above his head and smashed it upon the ground into pieces. The crowd, the guards, even Samuel's corrupted sons froze at the sight of the potter's vivid action.

"May Yahweh smash you like the pieces of this bowl. May your wicked judgment be heard throughout the land of our fathers. May the justice of heaven be brought upon your heads." Then Gehazi turned to his family, a broken man, and began leading them out of the hushed assembly.

Samuel witnessed one trial after another, justice perverted every time in favor of the wealthy over the common citizen. When he saw his sons approve the city council's petition to tear down a neighborhood where poorer citizens resided in favor of a new commercial district, it was too much to bear. Samuel put his hands on the shoulders of the people blocking his way and began to push them aside. But then he felt an invisible shield press against his breastbone, preventing him from moving forward. His breathing became labored. He knew he should speak, that he should shout above the heads of the crowd that his sons were corrupt, evil men, with no fear of Yahweh. They did not walk in the paths of righteousness; they served neither Yahweh nor men, but their own appetites. They offered perverted judgments, their greed blinded their eyes. But his mouth was shut.

Where was the courage of his father, who denounced the wickedness of Eli and his sons in the courtyard of the Tabernacle? The courage of his father had not passed down to him. He imagined Joel and Abijah riding on the death-cart, their lifeless bodies driven from the battlefield, just as he had seen Hophni and Phinehas. The sons of Eli and the sons of Samuel were lost to their fathers.

He dropped his arms to his side and began to walk out of the city square. How could he tell their mother what he had seen? When Samuel walked through the main gate of the city, he glanced over at the two piles of stones where the altars of Isaac and Jacob once stood. He pulled the two stones he had taken earlier in the day out of his bag and held them in his hands. He was not worthy of taking these stones. How could he tell Shira what he had witnessed and then confess that he had not confronted them? The potter had shown more courage by speaking out against the dishonorable judgment of his sons.

Just as he was about to toss the stones back onto the pile of rocks, he felt a jolt of strength that banished his initial weakness and shame. He could not walk away. He did not want to remember this day with this ending. He could not be silent. He dropped the two stones back into his pouch and marched back into the city square.

The court had closed for the day and crowds were dispersing. Samuel stopped before the judicial tables. The Levites and scribes were organizing the court documents and counting the fees that they had collected for each case. Samuel's two sons were standing near their judicial seats, conversing and laughing with victors of the petitions they had ruled in their favor.

"The court is adjourned for the day. You must bring your petition next week." The Levite who spoke did not look up, but continued to count his pile of shekels.

"I bring no petition," Samuel said, and took the two stones from his bag and dropped them on the table.

The pile of shekels scattered. The copying of the court documents came to an abrupt stop. All of the scribes and Levites were unnerved and began to shout at the hooded stranger standing in front of their tables.

Abijah and Joel were distracted by the commotion and directed their attention his way. "Stranger, what is your issue with the court?" Joel moved in front of his chair.

When Samuel picked up the stones, the Levites hired to protect the court and the two judges drew their swords and approached him.

Samuel did not cower. He did not even acknowledge the guards. His focus was on his sons. He had come for his sons.

"Do you know these stones?" Samuel held out the stones toward his sons.

"Identify yourself." Abijah stepped over to his chair beside his brother.

"These are stones from the altars of remembrance now in ruins outside the city. One stone from the altar of Father Isaac and the other from Father Jacob. Each man built their altar after Yahweh had appeared to them and promised to create a great nation from their offspring. The practice of your court and your judgeship is also in ruins."

"Who are you, old man?" Joel demanded.

Samuel set the stones back down upon the table. When he removed the hood of his robe from his face both Joel and Abijah collapsed into their chairs.

There was silence in the city square. The eyes of the citizens of Beersheba were riveted on the court and the two sons of the prophet of Yahweh slumped inside their chairs, all pomp and self-assurance deflated from the bodies.

"My sons. My sons." Samuel ignored the stares from the crowd. He looked only at the two men collapsed in their seats and struggled to recognize what they had become.

Certainly he knew they were his offspring, but what he saw beyond the flesh of his flesh was a reflection of his dark and cast-down heart. He knew he had ignored them, but the demands of his work had required such devotion to Yahweh. He had looked the other way for so long that the two souls who sat before him now were almost unrecognizable, heavy-shaped ghosts that bore only a distant resemblance.

"We are your sons, Father. Look upon your handiwork." Abijah spoke, almost in the tone of a plea.

"You rarely looked at us before." Joel opened his arms to provide a fuller vision. "So look now and see what we have become."

"The reports are true. The reports are true." Samuel could only repeat himself.

"I do not know what you heard, Father, but at least you have come," Joel said.

"We wondered how long it would take before you came to see for yourself," Abijah added, leaning forward in his chair.

"The life I gave you. The life I wanted for you—"

"We never asked for that life, Father!"

"It was to train you, to prepare you for a life devoted to Yahweh."

"And you treated us like your students, worse than, in truth, not sons."

Samuel saw that Abijah's hands began to tremble and he gripped the armrests on his chair to control them.

"Perhaps I was too harsh, too demanding, but the burdens of being a prophet of Yahweh are difficult. You had to be prepared to receive the prophet's mantel."

"Yes, the mantel of the great prophet Samuel, 'whose words never fall to the ground.' If we heard that phrase once, we heard it a thousand times." Joel could not avoid a tone of mockery.

"That was too great a burden to bear, too heavy a mantel to place upon the shoulders of your sons." The quivering in Abijah's hands transferred to his voice. "We could not live up to that, so why even try?"

"Why should we even listen to you? You never listened to us, never really saw us, never even acted as if you cared we were around. That is, when you were around." Joel stood up as if to be more assertive in his case against Samuel. "You were more present when you were absent. Ima spoke well of you while you were on your travels, but then you were never the man she painted in our minds once you came home."

"I gave you all I knew how to give."

"Except yourself." Abijah lowered his head, no longer able to look at Samuel.

"The son of the vow made no such vow with his sons." Joel appeared to lose strength in his legs and held onto the arm of his chair for support.

This was too much for Samuel to bear. One son stood in defiance. The other son sat in brokenness. Samuel became conscious of the crowd of people staring in wonder at this scene between father and sons. He bowed his head and looked at the stones resting on the table. What he thought would be a rebuke of his sons had become a rebuke to him as their father. Without warning the gnarly edges of these rocks became smoothed over by his tears. He picked up the rocks and returned them inside his bag. He looked at his sons once more. It took everything within him to speak with a steady voice.

"May Yahweh forgive me, my sons. May Yahweh be with you, my sons."

The crowd parted for Samuel as he passed through. When he came to the main gate of the city, he glanced at the two piles of stones where the altars of Isaac and Jacob once stood. He walked back to the crumbled piles and pulled out the two stones. He was about to drop them back onto their respective pile when he changed his mind. He would take them home. He would add them to the altar stones he had gathered for the offerings he made at his home in Ramah. He would make an atoning offering to Yahweh for his failures. He would make an offering on behalf of his sons. He would remember this day, painful as it was, and hope the forgiveness of Yahweh would descend upon father and sons in equal measure.

SAMUEL DID NOT FEAR TRAVELING AT NIGHT. HE PREFERRED IT, especially when the moon was full as it was this night. The moonlight illuminating the wide, desert valley to the west and reflecting off the mountains to the east made for excellent visibility along the empty road that wound its way through the foothills in the territory of Benjamin. Traveling at night for normal people was folly. The chances of falling victim to bandits or nomadic raiders were great. But Samuel did not fall into the category of the normal person.

When he rounded the bend on the road at the base of the hill he saw moonlight reflecting off the top of the sharp-toothed, stone pillar rising out of the ground. He stopped his horse and the pack mule in the middle of the road. In the far distance, he could see a faint glow of light shining from the city walls around Ramah. While the city slept, he knew he could ride around the walls undetected, make his way home, and crawl into bed beside his sleeping wife. How he longed to sleep in his own bed, next to his wife, to take pleasure with his wife.

After all the years of travel, there was little pleasure to be had in the long absences from home. A good night's sleep was rare without Shira next to him. He needed to sleep, to rest his mind and body, to restore his strength for what he knew lay ahead.

He dreaded the coming days. The discontent from the tribal leaders continued to grow. Complaints from his Levitical brothers led by Eleazar had become impossible to ignore. Despite the victory over the Philistines at Mizpah—despite the retaking of the cities captured by the Philistines, despite the peace, albeit fragile, that Israel enjoyed, the people of Israel were growing bitter and discontent. Something must be done. After what he had witnessed in Beersheba, he could not stall the inevitable much longer.

At the end of his annual circuit ride through the heartland of Israel, it had become his ritual to stop and pray at the "Stone of Help." Samuel had the local stonemasons cut the pillar from a large outcropping of rocks at the base of the mountain overlooking the stretch of flatland between Mizpah and Ramah. For Samuel, this unpolished, rough-hewn tower was erected to commemorate Yahweh's divine help. It was more sacred to him than the Tabernacle or any man-made object, except for the Ark of the Covenant.

Samuel guided the horse off the road onto a path through the trees until he came to a clearing where the pillar stood like an enlarged fang growing out of the earth. Samuel dismounted and approached the chiseled stone.

"O Most High. O Eternal One. The Name above all names." He stopped in front of the stone and braced his hands upon it.

"God of my fathers. This is the stone of Ebenezer, the stone of your help. Israel had sinned against you and embraced other gods. When they came to me, I cried out to you, Lord of heaven and earth. I cried out for you to throw off the yoke of our enemies."

Samuel began to circle the sacred column, scraping his fingers along the sliced rock and causing soft granules to fall to the ground.

"Here on this blessed ground, on that day, we confessed the sin of Israel against you, the Almighty. On this blessed ground, on that day, we cried out to Yahweh, the Almighty for rescue."

Once Samuel completed his circle, he placed both hands upon the stone.

"You heard our cries, O Lord. You heard our cries and rescued us. When the Philistines drew near to destroy, you thundered with a devastating thunder and scattered our enemies. The God of our fathers fulfilled the prophetic word of my mother—may she abide forever in your Eternal Presence. You fulfilled the words she spoke when she brought me to the Tabernacle and left me that day, 'The force of man shall not prevail. Yahweh will shatter those who oppose Him. Against them will Yahweh thunder in heaven and the ends of the earth will be judged.' The Ebenezer, the Stone of Help, is the remembrance that the I Am heard the cries of His people and came to their rescue."

He fell to his knees and wrapped his arms around the pillar. From crown to sole, he was claimed for life, avowed possession of the Almighty for all of his days.

Samuel detoured off the main road into Ramah and made his way toward home, toward his bed and Shira's loving arms, toward rest. He did not know how long he would have the strength to make these journeys. Winters were spent at home, but the rest of the seasons Samuel woke up in different cities throughout the land. Even when he was home, he never got much rest. There were the demands of the prophet's school, overseeing studies, copying new scrolls and parchments to be given to Levites and rabbis in each city and village he traveled. Plus the new collections of stories of Yahweh's people being compiled. There was always the need for his judicial and prophetic authority, but at least he got to sleep in his own bed every night.

In the early years, Shira would go with him on his annual, north-to-south circuit rides through the major cities of Israel, building altars, offering sacrifices, presiding over judicial cases, leading retreats, establishing Levitical schools for priests, and gilds for prophets. Her companionship made these trips endurable. But when Samuel's parents, Mushi, and Shira's mother had died and the boys were growing up, Shira needed to stay home and oversee the family business. She was more than capable of handling those responsibilities.

When he returned home and rejoined the administration of the prophet's school, he had engaged the boys in the school hoping this vigorous on-the-job training would provide insight and wisdom for Joel and Abijah to use as future judges and leaders for the people of Israel.

At the proper time, Samuel sent his sons as far away as possible while still within the relative safety of the country, thinking perhaps the separation would help them come into their own. Beersheba had a good Levitical school and the city was in need of judges. When Joel and Abijah finished school at home, Samuel appointed them surrogate judges in

Beersheba. This would keep him from having to travel so far south each year and give a chance for his sons to establish themselves. But what he had seen on this latest trip broke his heart.

Before Samuel rode into the yard, he whistled. He knew Moses and Zipporah would be sleeping at the entrance of the house, and he did not want their barking to startle Shira. The two mongrels recognized their master's whistle and dashed in his direction. Samuel slid off his horse and was almost knocked to the ground by the shaggy pair's enthusiasm.

To his amazement, Samuel saw a light coming from the window as he rounded the corner of the house. An even greater surprise awaited him at the front door.

"You stopped at Ebenezer, didn't you?" Shira was leaning on the doorframe dressed in her night clothes.

"It is the middle of the night. Why are you awake?"

"Sleep is impossible knowing you might be home any day now."

Samuel dropped the reins and moved to embrace his wife when he tripped over the dogs swirling around his feet. Were it not for Shira catching him, he would have fallen on his face. Samuel growled and threatened the dogs, which had no effect on them. They both reared up on their hind legs and laid their front paws on Samuel's chest, vying for his affection.

"Stay here with the children." Shira kissed him as she breezed by. "I'll stable the animals."

Samuel wrestled with the dogs in the courtyard while Shira led the horse and mule off to the stable.

When she returned, Samuel was sitting in the doorway with Zipporah and Moses resting their heads in his lap. He had finally gotten them to calm down and was scratching behind their ears.

"Take off your clothes and come into the house." Shira had the leather saddlebag containing the scrolls and Samuel's writing slung over her shoulder.

"That's the best greeting I've had in months." Samuel groaned as he got to his feet.

"We will leave the rest of the travel bags for tomorrow." Shira rubbed her hand over his cheek and opened the front door.

The dogs instantly trotted into the house in front of her. "Out, both of you."

The dogs stopped immediately. Moses and Zipporah looked back at their mistress to see if they might have misunderstood the tone of her voice. "You have been sleeping in the house for months. Now it is your master's turn." She kept her arm up and finger pointing beyond the door and into the outer darkness. Moses and Zipporah dropped their heads in submission to this banishment and trotted away, whining with every step.

Samuel climbed into the over-sized tub in the middle of the common room, raising the water level to his waist. He leaned back in the warm, soothing liquid and watched his wife dip a pitcher into a pot of steaming water heating on the fire. Tired as he was, he dared not take his eyes off his wife. He wanted to be sure he was not dreaming, that this was not a vision but Shira in the flesh. He knew if he closed his eyes he would not wake until midmorning, and he did not want to dream of her. He had to settle for dreams of Shira for months. Now, he wanted the reality of her touch, her voice, her kiss.

Shira tested the water in the pitcher. It was a little too hot, so she set it on the table to cool and took a vial of oil and poured a portion into the tub and the rest over his head. After rubbing the oil into his scalp, beard, and around his neck, she checked the temperature of the water in the pitcher. Satisfied, she poured it over Samuel's bowed head. He groaned in pleasure as the hot water cascaded over his head and down his chest and back. Shira turned to go refill the pitcher from the pot on the fire, but Samuel tugged on the back of her robe, gently pulling her back to the tub. She playfully tapped his hand away, then quickly disrobed and stepped into the tub. Shira curled inside Samuel's embrace and laid her head upon his chest.

"Sing." He ran his fingers along the curve of her arm. "I need to hear you sing."

Shira raised her hand up to Samuel's head and ran her fingers down his face.

> "How comely you are, my beloved.
> How fair, O how fair.
> Behold you are my beloved.
> I lie down in the comfort of your arms.
> Like the cedar beams in our dwelling.

Like the mighty bow of the cypress.
The strength of your arms protects me.
I lie down in the comfort of your arms."

Sleep was too heavy a weight for Samuel's eyes. His hand slipped off the rim of the tub and sank beneath the water.

The morning after his return and while he still slept, Shira hitched the small wagon to a horse with enough room in the wagon bed to include the two of them, a basket of food and skin of wine, water bucket and feedbag for the horse, a pot with smoldering coals to start a fire, blankets to lie on and under, and Moses and Zipporah. The dogs would not be deterred on this occasion.

Each year that passed, Shira could tell that it took longer for her husband to recover from his travels; the fatigue a little harder to shake off. He moved a little slower; his hearing was a little worse; he slept longer than usual. His mind was as sharp and nimble, but after every journey he came home with another layer of weariness covering his body. The demands on him were great, and she took it upon herself to do everything she could to restore him body and soul.

Shira picked up her husband in the courtyard once he stumbled out the front door. She snapped the reins on the horse's rump and called for the startled animal to move forward. Moses and Zipporah leapt into the back of the wagon as she sped past the stables. Her husband nearly fell off his seat into the bed of the wagon. This sudden rush of speed surely got the blood pumping through his veins. It was exactly the jolt he needed to dispel the sleep and remember life with her could be fun and unpredictable.

When they arrived at the top of the highest hill on their property, Shira pulled into a grove of massive fig trees with their expansive branches intertwined from tree to tree, blocking out the sky. The gnarled base of each tree was like giant claws digging into the earth. Years ago, Elkanah had abandoned the grove planted by his great grandfather for a more lucrative business of horse breeding, and instead of transplanting the trees in the valley below, had allowed them to become an overgrown forest.

The dogs leapt out of the wagon, their noses leading them in duel directions. Samuel unhitched the horse and hobbled it beneath the tree's shade. Then while Shira arranged their picnic site, he watered the horse, and then slipped the feedbag over its head. Then he gathered some dead-fall branches and built a fire. The dogs had lost interest in following the scents they caught when they arrived, and were now stealing pieces of the dead limbs Samuel had gathered and broken in the effort to get their master to play fetch until Shira lured them over to the blanket with an offering of food.

They ate and drank and napped away the afternoon. When Shira woke she saw Samuel stirring the embers of the fire with a long stick, his eyes staring into the blaze, looking at something on the other side of the world.

"What is troubling you?" Shira crawled over next to him.

"It's worse, much worse than we imagined or the reports we heard." He never took his eyes from the flame.

She dreaded speaking it, but it had to be spoken. She dreaded the pain it would bring, but it had to be faced.

"The reports are true then?" Shira knew in her heart what the answer would be, and knowing that when Samuel spoke it, her heart would break again.

"They did not even hide the bribery, had armed guards to protect them."

The blood rushed into Shira's face as she listened to her husband relay his encounter with their sons. She knew Yahweh would not allow this to continue. Change would come soon, and their lives would never be the same. Shira wrapped Samuel into her arms, and they sat silent before the fire until long after the sun had gone down.

Twenty-One

SAMUEL HOPED FOR A LONGER PERIOD OF TIME BEFORE IT WAS discovered he had come home, but every few days a new messenger arrived. New messenger, same message: "The people can no longer tolerate the current situation." He ignored each request for an audience. The latest delegation from the tribes assembled from around the country had waited for days in Ramah and was growing weary of the rebuffs.

"They can wait in Ramah until the Salt Sea dries up," Samuel announced to Shira.

To avoid the harassment, Samuel left the house before daylight and did not come home until well after dark. He would go about on the property, checking on the vineyards and livestock. Or hide in his old room above the stables, studying, writing, and preparing for his upcoming, week-long assembly with the young priests and prophets he was training.

Shira could cover for him. He would never tell her where he was going so she would never have to lie. She could honestly inform whatever emissary came on whatever day representing whatever tribe of the twelve, that her husband was not at home and she did not know where he was and was uncertain of his return. Samuel knew the tribal chieftains and priests, fathers of households, and men of age and authority from his decades of traveling the countryside, and it was impossible for him not to feel the growing tidal wave of resentment at his delaying tactics.

"A faction from Asher arrived today." Shira dished Samuel a bowl of onion broth with potatoes and goat meat after he returned home one night.

"All the way from Asher." Samuel chuckled. "The absurdity of the Asher delegation traveling so far only to end in disappointment."

He sat on a stool by the front door soaking his feet in a water basin, his worn and dirty sandals cast off beside the stool. "Haven't they got anything better to do?"

"Apparently not." Shira handed him his bowl and spoon, then planted herself in front of him, arms folded, watching him cool his first bite of stew with his breath.

Samuel might ignore the steady stream of tribal delegations coming to his house, but she would not let him ignore *her*.

He sighed. "What?"

"You know they are not going to leave Ramah."

"Good for them, and good for the innkeepers and the eating houses in the city. The business community in Ramah will thank me when this is over. I can hear them counting their shekels now." Samuel cocked a hand over his ear as if listening to the sound of clanking coins.

"Don't be so sure." Shira dropped her arms and sighed. "And when might this face-off be over?"

"When they tire of their foolishness and go home." He shoved his first bite of stew into his mouth. It was apparently still too hot, given how he sucked air through his teeth.

"I'm the one tiring of the foolishness, and I can't go home." Shira spun around, frustrated by Samuel's stubbornness, and returned to the stew pot to dish out her own bowl of stew.

Moses and Zipporah lapped at the water in the basin until Samuel gently nudged them away with a wet foot. They moved away and planted themselves in front of the fire, their snouts pointing in the direction of the cooking pot.

Shira sat down at the table and started turning over spoonfuls of stew in her bowl in quick strokes. She allowed the crackling of the fire, the bubbling of the stew, the panting of the dogs, and the repetitive tapping of her spoon against the clay bowl as she cooled her food to amplify the emotional tension in the room.

"I'd love some bread, please."

Her husband's grumpy request did nothing to ease the strain between them. Shira dropped her spoon onto the table and grabbed the loaf of bread out of the basket, tore off a chunk, and lobbed it at her husband. The flying bread bounced off Samuel's chest and landed inside the cradle of his arms. Shira did not even acknowledge her husband's look of surprise at her tavern manner of serving him. She watched Samuel slowly brush the crumbs off his lap. She knew he was stalling his response.

"So what do they want?" She shifted her body in the chair to face him, her food forgotten. "What would bring delegations from all over the country to our front door?"

"They want what can never happen, what can never be approved."

"And that would be..."

"They want to return to Egypt. They want to be enslaved again."

"What does that mean?" Shira threw up her arms in annoyance. "Nobody is going back to Egypt. No one is going to be a slave. Don't talk in riddles."

Shira was not about to let him avoid her question. She glared at him, waiting and watching as he took the hunk of bread, dipped it in the stew, and then bit off the soppy end. He could finish chewing the bite of food tumbling around in his mouth, but she was not about to let him so much as take another whiff of stew without answering her.

"They want a king. The people of Israel want a king of their own."

This was not the answer Shira expected. Perhaps deep in her heart she did know why the delegations had come to Ramah after all. In all their years together only one thing had tested their marriage—not the long absences, not the commitment to his work, not the demands of Yahweh—that one thing that both of them found so difficult to admit. They had done everything they knew to do to raise their sons into becoming godly men, but the lure of the world had been too much of a temptation. And now Shira knew the consequence of their sons going astray had come back to visit their doorstep.

"And this 'in-gathering' in Ramah from the tribes of Israel, has it anything to do with our sons?" She asked but did not want to hear the brutal truth, that their sons were a national disgrace.

"The nation of Israel has a king. Yahweh is their king. And I am His prophet. Yahweh will never approve of this. I will never allow it."

Shira propped an elbow on the table and rested her forehead in her hand. Then picked up her spoon and filled it with stew. "I am just as much to blame in this as you."

She lifted the spoon out of the bowl and stared at the bite of meat floating in the dark broth in her spoon. Would he say more? Would he rise from his seat and place a comforting hand upon her back? This was, after all, a shared burden of failure. But her husband only stuffed more food into his mouth. Best to change the subject.

"The stonemason delivered your new altar top today." She nibbled on a piece of meat inside the spoon.

"How does it look?"

"Like an altar. A horn in every corner, just like you requested."

"Good. I've lost count of the number of altars I've built, at least one in every city where I judge, plus all the others scattered on the hills in between. I want this to be my last altar, and I want it on my own property. I've been going to the people all these years. Let them come to me. So where do you think I should erect it?"

Shira would not give him an answer. Instead, she took her next bite of food and cast her eyes away from him, forcing Samuel to answer his own question.

"I was thinking at the top of the hill in the grove of fig trees. It's a beautiful location overlooking the valley. You know, where we ate the other day."

"I know." Her sullen, two-word reply was all she would give him.

"Yes, I like that spot. Let them come to me for a change. My body is beginning to feel the years and the miles. Let them come to me."

"You are repeating yourself. They *are* coming to you. They have been coming to you, and you run and hide, and I have to deceive them by making excuses for you."

The dogs suddenly broke their vigil before the cooking pot and made a mad scramble for the door, barking wildly. They leapt in the air and scratched their nails across the door in mid-flight.

Samuel jumped up so fast his feet slipped in the basin, splashing water all over his legs and robe and the floor and knocking the stool onto its side. He growled at his clumsiness and the frantic barking of his dogs, but his harsh scolding did not diminish their fury. He plunked his bowl onto the table, grabbed the overturned stool, and opened the door ready to defend hearth and home.

The dogs bolted around Samuel's legs, but came to an abrupt stop as soon as they realized they were outnumbered by a much larger contingent of potential foes who happened to be carrying flaming torches. Two in front of the group swung their torches at the dogs, forcing a snarling retreat and held them at bay.

"What is the meaning of this?" Samuel raised the stool in the air like a weapon.

Shira came up beside him and called the dogs to heel.

"Samuel, it is I, Eleazar. Do not be alarmed. We come in peace."

There stood so many men in the yard, several holding torches above their heads it could have been a mob. Levites, a few military commanders dressed in corselet armor and brass helmets, and those dressed in costly garments, which Samuel recognized were tribal chieftains. He did not lower the stool.

"Eleazar, what are you doing here?"

"I am sorry for the late hour." Eleazar separated from the group and took a step closer to the door. "We had no choice. May we come in?"

Samuel almost laughed at the thought of this horde crowded into his common room, but he was too angry to be amused. "There is no room. Don't be ridiculous."

"My father and I, and Ahiah, the High Priest, then; the rest wait outside?"

"They can wait back in Ramah, or better yet, go home all together."

In the light cast by the torches, Samuel could see eyes glance around his legs and look away. He looked down to see a large wet spot around the hem of his robe and a pool of water around his feet. The humiliation only intensified his anger at the unexpected intrusion. He went to shut the door in the faces of this rude mob.

"Samuel, please, we have all traveled a great distance to council with you."

Samuel watched Eleazar raise his hands in supplication and the gesture stopped him from slamming the door.

"We represent all of Israel. May the three of us enter?"

"I see you are well-armed with witnesses." Samuel stuck his head out the door.

"I learned this wisdom from the prophet of Yahweh." Eleazar bowed his head.

Samuel did not move from his guardian position at the door until he felt his wife's hand upon his shoulder. He had used the door to keep her semi-concealed from the eyes of those who stood outside in her front yard.

"Don't be stubborn, Husband. Let them enter."

His muscles relaxed at his wife's whispered chastisement, and he lowered the stool in his hand. Samuel called for the dogs to come inside. When they obeyed, Shira nodded to Samuel. He stepped back and allowed the uninvited guests to enter.

Eleazar entered, followed by his father, Abinadab, and Ahiah, the High Priest. Once they were inside, Samuel closed the door on those left standing in the yard. He set his stool against the wall where he had sat soaking his feet and then leaned his back against the door, glaring at the men standing in the middle of the common room, all three looking down at the ground. Samuel did not mind making them uncomfortable.

"How dare you come to my house uninvited?"

"Where else would we find you?" Eleazar nervously shuffled from side to side.

"How dare you come to my house uninvited in the middle of the night?"

"When else have you been at home? During the day we found only your wife who kindly explained your constant absences." Eleazar nodded to Shira in admiration. "And it's not the middle of the night. The sun has barely set."

"You come to my house uninvited, in the middle of the night, with a show of force as if to threaten me."

"The force was not to threaten you, but for our protection."

"There are many dangers from without and within." Abinadab's face held a solemn expression.

"There are no dangers between Ramah and my home." Samuel pushed off from the door, moving closer to the trio of men. "Except perhaps a pack of jackals."

"Our enemies are always prowling, looking to strike." Eleazar deflected Samuel's insult.

"The Philistines, the Ammonite hordes, the Amalekite raiders, all sorts of nomadic mongrels. You know this as much as you travel."

Shira could have excused herself, but she chose to stay. She crouched between Moses and Zipporah—who had begun to growl at the strangers in their home—and stroked the tops of their heads, quietly shushing them. The growling ceased, but they kept their eyes focused for any threat against their masters from these unfamiliar persons.

"But we are not here just to discuss our common enemies." Eleazar thanked Shira with a nod of his head for subduing the dogs.

"Then why do you come now when I just saw you a few months ago in Kiriath Jearim on my last circuit? Something wrong with the Ark? Does it need to be moved?"

"The Ark remains secure in Abinadab's home and is well cared for." Ahiah tucked his quivering hands behind the ephod to conceal their trembling.

"The Divine Presence is welcome in my home forever." Abinadab raised his hands upward. "May the Eternal One be pleased to dwell in my humble abode."

Shira would have preferred to go unnoticed, would have loved to slip outside and gone for a walk with the dogs except for having to pass through the crowd of visitors milling about in their yard. She could vanish into another room in the house or vanish altogether. But there was no way to make a graceful exit, and she knew she needed to do something to defuse the growing tension. Her husband should have been the first one to offer food and drink to their guests, invited or not, or, at least, gestured for them to take a place at the table, but his manners were nonexistent. So she stood and pointed for the three men to take a seat. She ignored Samuel's look of surprise as if she had committed an act of disloyalty, and stepped over to the shelf to fetch some bowls.

"Food and drink, my lords?" Shira looked over her shoulder to see who might accept her offer as the men quickly took their seats. "We have plenty of both."

"We dined earlier, and we need to be of sober mind tonight." Eleazar answered for all of them.

Shira came over to join her husband who stood at the table.

"Ahiah, you wear the ephod and the breastplate with the twelve stones. Is this a way to honor me in my house, I wonder?"

"We wish to honor the prophet of Yahweh in all things." Ahiah strained to hold a weak smile. He was youngest of the three, his golden beard, rounded shoulders, and kettle belly clothed in his High Priestly robes, gave him an impressive bearing.

"The tribal leaders have gathered in Ramah, as you know." Eleazar continued drawing Samuel's attention. "There has been growing frustration among the people. You must be aware of this truth."

"Enlighten me."

Samuel looked to the men on either side of Eleazar. Abinadab kept his eyes closed and head bowed as if in an attitude of prayer. Ahiah's eyes darted about the room as if he might be looking for a place to hide. It was up to Eleazar to speak to him. Samuel watched Eleazar's hands grip the edge of the table with his fingers and take a deep breath before he spoke.

"You are getting older, my friend."

Samuel immediately raised his hand to stop him. "Eleazar, you come to my house to insult me with the obvious. We were students together in Shiloh, need I remind you."

"I am aware. May I continue, please?"

Samuel lowered his hand to his side and Shira slipped her fingers inside it.

"The last time you were on your circuit, you confessed to me how tired you were. I could hear it in your voice, see the fatigue in your eyes. You cannot deny it. Riding the judge's circuit takes its toll on one's body and mind. Being the prophet of the Almighty is a great responsibility you have shouldered for many years. All Israel acknowledges your faithfulness—"

"But I am still old, in your opinion."

"In the opinion of all the people." Eleazar pointed directly to the twelve-stone breastplate worn on Ahiah's chest.

"Are you saying my age has something to do with my ability to do my job? That somehow my age disqualifies me from performing the duties of my divine appointment?"

Samuel was not going to make this an easy conversation. He looked at Abinadab and the High Priest who offered nothing to the discussion. They seemed content to remain mute.

"We are sure, after decades of serving as prophet and judge of Israel, that you have a wisdom and experience in mediation and in hearing and speaking for Yahweh that cannot be equaled. There is no one like you in all of Israel, not since Moses, the greatest of all prophets. And there is no one in all of Israel who can be found to replace you."

Samuel straightened his back. He did not mind the comparison with Moses.

"But I'm old. You are saying I'm old." Samuel was insistent for a blunt answer.

"I'm saying you are not immortal. Who is? Even the prophet of Yahweh can't live forever. Unless you know something the rest of us do not."

Eleazar paused for Samuel to reply but he did not speak. By remaining silent, Samuel was forcing Eleazar to continue on his own.

"Shira, I believe I will take your offer for a cup of wine."

Shira felt a slight trembling in her husband's body and noticed him digging his toes into the floor beneath them.

"Right away," she said, and released her husband's warm hand and wiped the perspiration from her palm onto her robe before taking three cups and a wineskin from off the shelf. She was thrilled to be doing something, anything besides standing before this tribunal. Shira set the cups on the table, but Abinadab and Ahiah put their hands over their tops. Eleazar alone invited her to fill his. She removed the plug in the skin and filled her guest's cup. He allowed her to determine the amount, and she stopped halfway to the brim. He smiled and nodded his approval. Shira placed the wineskin back on the shelf and noticed Eleazar staring at the cup in his hand before he spoke.

"I wish you could live forever, because there is the matter of your sons."

"You come to my house and insult my age and now you insult my sons."

"Your sons do not walk in your ways. Their greed exceeds their ability to judge with fairness and impartially." Eleazar held the cup aloft in his hand, poised to drink, but not yet ready to bring it to his lips.

"You have been conferring about my age, my fatigue, and my children all behind my back."

"I and all of Israel." Eleazar pointed once again to the breastplate with his free hand. Eleazar used the twelve stones as his silent ally.

The twelve stones of Israel glistened in the lamplight of the room, reflecting colored sparkles on the walls and ceiling every time Ahiah made the slightest move.

"Abinadab, I let you keep the Ark in your house. How many years now? How many years have you and your household been blessed with Yahweh abiding under your roof? I could have brought the Ark here; set it up in my own home. I could have enjoyed such blessing as you for all these years. But no. And now you turn on me like this?"

Samuel waited for a response, but the old man did not even raise his head or open his eyes to face him. His lips moved, barely perceptible beneath his thick beard, so Samuel turned his attention to Ahiah.

"Ahiah, you are the great grandson of Eli, my mentor and High Priest. You know the curse Yahweh pronounced on his family line, that all Eli's progeny would die in the prime of their life. Against my better judgment, I anointed you High Priest. And this is how you repay me."

"My lord, I accepted the anointing with a full knowledge of my destiny. You have enjoyed advanced age, while I know my life will be cut short, blessed be the name of the Almighty. So it is with that urgency that we come before you now."

Samuel had not expected such a bold response from the young priest, so he turned his gaze to Eleazar once again.

"Eleazar, I appointed you guardian over the Ark of the Covenant. You are the guardian of the most sacred item of our nation, the very heart of Yahweh. And now..." Samuel had one final appeal, one final hope that the heart of Yahweh could touch the heart of the guardian of His Holy Ark.

"...And now I and all of Israel wish to invoke the law of the king."

Eleazar finished Samuel's sentence, and raised his cup to his lips.

Shira turned to her husband and gasped. She clamped her hand over her mouth. Everyone in the common room assumed her reaction was because of what Eleazar just announced, but it was not. Shira saw the shadow of her husband's soul begin to turn, a dark turning, a new possession, not of deeper humility or claim of holiness, but an ominous, vindictive mood showing itself in Samuel's fluttering eyelids and intensified curl of his lips. The Samuel she had always known had taken wing, leaving behind a poisoned and poisonous creature. She moved away and stood between the dogs. They also sensed the change in their master's demeanor and began to whimper in fear.

"Yahweh is your king and I am His prophet."

Shira watched Samuel's eyes turn to slits, sharpening in his harsh face.

"This is not an easy request for us to invoke, my lord, but we have no choice."

"You have a choice, Eleazar. You have my sons."

"If you had only confronted your sons with their sins, my lord." Ahiah leaned forward over the table. "My great grandfather confronted his sons—"

"To no effect. They did not turn from their wickedness."

"True, but still he confronted them. He may have been helpless to change them, but he was not blind to their sin. You know this. You witnessed this in your time serving in the Tabernacle."

"And the character of your sons are proving to be the same, and you have done nothing."

Samuel felt the point of Eleazar's spear driving home the point of his negligence toward his sons' waywardness.

"You could have also been looking to appoint different judges, but you have groomed no one."

Abinadab tried to tamp down the rising tempers and volume in the room. "We do not wish to insult the prophet of Yahweh."

Samuel leaned over the table, his whole body a menacing threat. "You reject me, you reject Yahweh."

"We are not rejecting you, my lord." Ahiah offered his opened hands in supplication to Samuel. "You have been a great leader for Israel, and now we seek your guidance in giving us a king."

"You just want pomp and splendor." Samuel looked fiercely at the three men seated around his table. "You want the trappings of a king: palaces, a royal court, the grand retinue. Your desire exceeds your judgment."

"We need a king to lead us in battle. Not one who just wears a crown of gold."

"And what of the victory over the Philistines at Mizpah?" Samuel rapped his knuckles on the top of the table.

"My lord, no one can forget that day." Abinadab curled his fingers around his empty cup and shifted his weight in his uncomfortable chair before he continued. "It was a great victory, and we have the Ebenezer Monument to remind us, but our enemies have increased in strength and number since then."

"And what if the sons of your king turn out to be as corrupt as you accuse mine of being? They will be much harder to remove. What will you do then? Will Yahweh hear your whimpering, your cries for help then?"

"So you admit your sons are corrupt?" Ahiah rose from his seat, but when he saw Shira's reaction of surprise and hurt at his blunt question, he softened his tone. "Please, accept my apologies for my words. I should be more sensitive in your house and under your roof. Forgive me."

Samuel did not dare to show weakness before these men, and hoped that Shira would remain by his side, a united front. But he watched as Shira knelt down between the dogs and rested her hands on the heads of Moses and Zipporah. She turned her head from the room to shield from view the tears Samuel knew were welling in her eyes. The anger in Samuel's heart only blazed with more heat.

"Moses made provision for us at Sinai." Eleazar placed his hand on Ahiah's arm and directed him to sit back down. "We've all read the scrolls, my lord. Moses foretold of a time when we would need a king, and the time has come."

"Because of the hardness of your hearts. Because of the stiffness of your necks." Samuel struck back hard, wanting to shame these men for the pain they caused Shira. "Moses made these provisions because of the foolishness of your judgment, not because it was the will of the Almighty."

Samuel enjoyed seeing his words hit the three men like a hammer, immobilizing them in their seats. He knew he spoke the truth. He knew their hearts were hard and their necks were stiff, but Samuel also knew in the recesses of his own heart that while he might espouse his rightful place as the prophet of Yahweh, his righteousness and moral values were not shared by his sons.

Eleazar took a deep breath, looking at his father then the High Priest before casting his eyes up to Samuel.

"My lord, something has to be done if the nation is to survive. The prophet Moses did not leave Israel without a leader before entering the land of Promise. Before climbing Mount Nebo for the last time, he appointed Joshua, a man of valor and faith. Our current situation, may I beg your forgiveness for the implication, is not the same. We need a 'Joshua,' a king and a commander to organize a standing army and lead us. The Almighty has spoken through you ever since the destruction of Shiloh and the death of Eli. You have been His great prophet and judge. None of your words have fallen to the ground. You have traveled the land bringing Yahweh to the people, praise be to the Eternal One, and now we come to you—"

"I shall inquire of Yahweh for you." Samuel did not allow Eleazar to finish. He pushed away from the table. He would not be humiliated in front of his wife. He would leave, escape.

"My lord, it is for the sake of Israel that we have come to you." Eleazar forced his point.

"I shall inquire of Yahweh for you."

He watched helplessly as Samuel grabbed a skin of water and his over-cloak.

"My lord, this is a great burden for all of us." Eleazar rose to his feet in an attempt to stop Samuel from leaving. "We need to know that you are—"

"I said I shall inquire of Yahweh for you. How many times must I say it?" Samuel jammed his feet into his sandals, jerked open the door, and stormed out into the yard, shouting at his dogs to follow, which they obediently did.

Shira remained on her knees, looking down at the floor. She did not want to get up. She no longer had the dogs to protect her. She did not want to face the three men around her table. She wanted only to be hidden from public sight. Through the open door she could hear voices respectfully greeting her husband, but she heard no reply from him. She heard the three men shuffling around her table, attempting a quiet exit. She heard a muffled blessing from the High Priest before he closed the door, a rumbling of voices became fainter with their departure. Then for a moment, it was all silent, and she held her breath to be sure the silence was genuine. She held it and held it. If she did not, her voice would erupt in a convulsion of pain. She held it and held it until no ears but hers could hear the discharge of anguish inside her shattered heart.

Twenty-Two

SAMUEL DROVE THE HORSE LIKE A MADMAN. THE FOUR-HORNED altar top bounced inside the wagon as it sped along the dirt road. He snapped the reins, shouting for the horse to go faster up the hill toward the grove of trees. Moses and Zipporah ran full speed beside the wagon. The pair had started out riding in the bed with the altar. They'd jumped inside it while Samuel hitched the horse to the wagon. But soon after Samuel pulled out of the stables it was not safe for the dogs to ride with a bouncing altar piece dangerously shifting its weight with each bump in the road. They leapt out of the wagon when Samuel had to slow down for the horseshoe turn in the road leading up the hill.

When he reached the top, Samuel yanked on the reins, and the horse's legs nearly buckled, responding to the demand to stop beneath the thick canopy of overgrown fig trees. The stone altar slammed into the back of the wagon seat, cracking the wooden frame. He leapt out of the wagon not bothering to inspect the altar for damage or to tie-off the horse that stood on wobbly legs, panting, with foaming saliva streaming over its bridle. Moses and Zipporah stood beside the horse, their own rib cages barely able to contain their heaving chests, and watched as their master stormed off into the darkened grove of trees, driven by an inexplicable lunacy.

"How dare they. How dare they insult you like that." Samuel thrashed his arms about in the air. "They want a king. 'Let us have a king to rule over us,' they said. 'A king so we can be like other nations,' they said. If they want a king, let them go back to Egypt. If they liked Pharaoh so much, he can rule over them. They would never make it back to Egypt. They would die in the desert before they got there. Let them go. Let them all go back. See if Moses or Joshua comes back from the dead to lead them. They revere those men so much, Yahweh, you bring them back from the dead."

Samuel passed under a stout limb just above his head. He jumped up and gripped it with both hands and began to repeatedly pull his chin up to the limb and then lower himself the full extent of his arms.

"I am old, they said. I'm not old. I have the strength and vigor of a man half my age. I'm not old, Yahweh. I'm not."

His hands slipped off the rough bark of the limb, and as soon as his feet hit the ground, he took off again. This was not a late night stroll to settle the mind before going to bed. This was a forced march fed by an ugly truth.

"You heard them, Yahweh. They accused me of being blind to the realities around me. I'm not blind. They are blind and have a short memory. Have they forgotten who I am? Have they forgotten all I have done for them? How much I have sacrificed? And now they want to toss me aside. They say I'm old and want to toss me aside."

Samuel began to circle a large tree in the center of the grove. He kept a hand connected to the massive trunk to keep from stumbling over the hard, lumpy roots spreading out like tendrils from the base of the trunk before plunging into the earth.

"Look at what they're doing, Yahweh. Look at what they are saying. Their craving to have a king and a royal family has driven them mad. They are turning their backs on me. They are turning their backs on all the good that has been done. All these years our arrangement has been working and now...now the world is turning over."

His circling of the tree came to an abrupt end when his left foot slipped and he smashed the toes of his right foot against a root. Samuel smote the tree trunk with the beefy part of his hand to distract his mind from the pain that came streaking up his leg. He pushed away from the tree and began an erratic, limping dance in a clearing in the grove until the pain subsided. He knelt down and felt his toes. They were chafed and bloody and throbbed when he massaged them. He rested his arms on his bent knee.

"This is wrong. This is all so wrong. What they want is wrong and they will pay for it. They will regret it. You know they will, Yahweh. You know they will regret it."

He stood and began to hobble toward a different tree, one with branches low to the ground, easy for climbing.

"And who do they think they are? 'All of Israel wishes to invoke the law of the king,' Eleazar says. Is Eleazar 'All of Israel'? Are Ahiah and Abinadab 'All of Israel'? Are the tribal chieftains 'All of Israel'? How dare they presume to represent all of Israel."

When Samuel reached the branch lowest to the ground, he secured his footing and hoisted himself onto a higher branch and started clambering up the tree. He climbed and climbed, reaching the top branches before he stopped, unable to climb any higher. He wiped the sweat from his brow and looked into the sprawling curtain of black above him, the crescent moon in the shape of a smile cut into the face of the night sky. A breeze began to blow through the trees, causing the branches to sway and leaves to flutter.

He leaned his back against the tree trunk and wrapped his arms around the branches on either side of him. Suspended above the earth, Samuel listened to the powerful sound of the wind filtered through the foliage of the grove. He rocked from side to side on the branches as though he were adrift at sea. The night felt bottomless, the expanse around him, endless. There was no normality of thinking in this moment. Only one hard fact: his emotions were primal. The truth of it had lodged in his soul from his earliest memories and now rushed back into his heart in a quick convulsion. This feeling of disconnection was still familiar. In the long ago, he remembered lying alone at night, his soul heavy with the weight of misplacement.

"I am lost, Yahweh. I am being cast away, Divine One. I am being left on the portico of the Tabernacle surrounded by strangers. I am waking to a world I no longer recognize. I am awake and I am listening."

He closed his eyes. He no longer wished to view the external world he left behind at home or the world he saw from his leafy perch. He wanted to shut out the sound of hostile, dissenting voices. Even the sound of the breeze in the trees was an irritant, though he liked the feel of it on his hot skin. He wanted no sound to penetrate. He wanted no sight to distract. He wanted only to sink into the darkness of his soul. There it would be quiet. There he would not even be able to hear the beat of his heart.

"I am bound to you, O Eternal One. I am bound to you only. We are bound together to the end." Samuel's whispered prayer faded upon his lips as he yielded to the force of exhaustion.

The rays of the approaching sun were rising above the eastern hills when Samuel awoke with a start, causing him to lose his balance.

Samuel cried out and gripped the limbs on either side of him. He was surprised to find himself in the top of a tree looking out over the valley. It took him a moment to remember what had driven him there.

When he shifted his weight on the branch where he sat, he felt shooting pain in his lower back and legs. He looked down at his foot with its chafed toes covered in dried blood. When he gingerly touched his swollen toes he was reminded of how he had smashed them against an unforgiving root.

He slipped off the branch and began to lower himself down the tree. The muscles in his arms barked to the strain he exerted as he carefully made his way down the middle of the tree. Every muscle in his body was in revolt to every move required in his descent.

When he reached the final branches, Moses and Zipporah were waiting at the base of the tree. The dogs did not allow Samuel to get both feet on the ground before they were jumping all over him. He wished "All of Israel" were so loyal.

He gently planted his wounded foot on the ground. He tried to avoid further damage to his toes from the flailing paws of dogs excited to be reunited with their master. He knelt down and wrapped his arms around their necks, allowing them to lick his face.

He limped out of the grove over to the horse and wagon. Samuel stroked the horse along his snout and scratched under his chin, apologizing for his rough treatment the night before. He promised a breakfast of oats and barley once they got back to the stables.

When Samuel painfully climbed into the back of the wagon to inspect the altar top and cracked seat the wonder struck him. A summons to listen so powerful he fell flat upon the altar. A pure reverence weighed down upon his back, pressing his chest into the stone surface. He gasped as a flame without burning clutched the face of his soul.

"Yes. Yahweh. Yes. I am the sacrifice. I am the slain one. Take my life. Do not withhold the knife. Do not restrain your angel. Do not be silent."

He was bathed in the pure brightness of the light.

"The cries of my chosen have come to me. Listen to my chosen. My chosen have rejected me, not you. As they have done since I brought them out of Egypt, they have forsaken the Almighty as king to serve other gods, so have they done this to you. Listen to my chosen, but warn. I have listened to their cries, but warn them of what a king will do."

Samuel's cry came forth from his solid body which yanked him up to his knees in a sudden jolt as if coming from deep within the earth.

"Your heart, O Yahweh. Your heart is always for your chosen. Your heart is always for me. You hear the cries of your people. You hear the cries of your servant. Forgive me, O Yahweh. Forgive my foolishness; forgive my pride that eats my heart with bitterness; forgive my anger that makes me dead and untouchable."

He fell back upon the altar and lay there until the cadence of his sobbing had been exhausted. He pulled himself upright. He looked down upon the altar, the bed of his death, and made the decision that here in this grove it would remain. Here the stones would be laid, including the two stones brought home from Beersheba. Here the altar piece would rest upon the Ebenezer stones, the fires lit, the offerings made. He would erect the altar in the coming days before it was time to host the prophet's symposium.

Samuel crawled out of the back of the wagon. He gripped the wooden railings to keep from falling as he inched along the side of the wagon to the front. Samuel's tired body and throbbing head made him wince with every move, but he had to move. He had a message to deliver. Before he could rest and nurse the pain pulsating through every muscle layer in every limb, he must deliver the message from the Almighty.

"Yes, Yahweh. Yes," Samuel repeated as he unhitched the horse and patted its neck. Then he leaned into its ear to whisper, "We must first go to Ramah, my friend, and then you will be fed and watered."

When Samuel entered through the gates, he rode straight to the center of the city. Moses and Zipporah trotted faithfully beside him. He could not go home yet. He could not see his wife or eat and drink or bathe or change his clothes. He could do nothing for himself or for his animals until he had spoken.

It was still early in the morning and most of the population had not yet begun the business of the day. He made his way through the streets toward the city well and the olive presses. Those few venders opening their shops along the street had to look twice before they recognized him as the prophet. He did not come into town that often and when he did, it was never this early in the morning nor did he appear with his clothes torn, or twigs and leaves stuck in his hair and beard, or an exposed foot covered in blood. Samuel's appearance was more like that of one who dwelt in the mountains or desert, not a prosperous citizen of Ramah, not the exalted prophet and judge of Israel. Samuel ignored the shock and wonder from those he passed.

Samuel stopped at the well in the center of town with olive presses built below it. He dismounted and guided his horse over to the watering trough for livestock. His horse and dogs plunged their tongues into the water, lapping rapidly. His own thirst was raw and painful, but it would not be quenched before he was done speaking for the Almighty.

"Yes, Yahweh. Yes." Samuel ran his hand across the arch of the horse's back, the bubbling sweat soaking his fingers. He wiped the moisture from his hand onto his clothes and climbed the steps beside the olive presses to a landing that overlooked the center of the town. He waited in silence as citizens of Israel rushed out of their abodes and into the streets, many still putting the finishing touches on their grooming preparations for the day. He watched as men and women gathered, children too, pressed against a mother's side or held in her arms or a young boy secured on his father's shoulders. Beggars and thieves, innkeepers and trades folk, operators of fruit and vegetable stands and traveling merchants began to convene. Highbrow and lowborn streamed into the city square, and rabbis and Ramah's civic and political leaders. And those delegations that had come from the four corners of Israel with their unanimous complaint, he especially wanted them to be present, in particular Eleazar, Ahiah, and Abinadab. It was these three men who would explain to "All of Israel" the meaning and consequences of their demands.

Once Samuel saw the High Priest, the curator for the abode of the Ark, and the guardian of this sacred item hustled through the crowd with their armed escorts, he knew "All of Israel" had been assembled.

Eleazar, Ahiah, and Abinadab took their places in the front of the platform and looked up at him, the prophet and judge of Israel, the mountains and sunlight at his back.

Samuel went back down the steps to speak to the three men. "Last night my heart was full of dross. It has since been burned away. Still, forgive me for being hostile to you in my house." Samuel had spoken just to them, just for them, and in unison, they offered forgiveness.

Samuel went back up the steps to the platform and surveyed the crowd. "What I must say displeases me, for it displeases the heart of Yahweh when you demanded a king and were unyielding in your desire to be like all the other nations. Have you forgotten that Yahweh is your king?"

Samuel paused to allow the question to sink deep into the collective mind of the crowd. Everyone stood still, leaning toward him, expectant, a thousand eyes watching, a thousand ears listening.

"But I have kept my word to you. I have kept my word and sought the Eternal One on your behalf. I have listened to the Divine One, the One you have been forsaking since the day the Almighty brought you out of Egypt to this exact day. I have kept my word and sought the Lord on your behalf, and the Divine One says, 'I, the Lord, have heard the cries of my chosen. I have listened to them, but solemnly warn them, let them know what a king will do when he reigns over them.'"

Samuel held out a small hope that, once he explained to "All of Israel" what a bad scheme it was to have a mortal king reign over them, they would surely see the error of their judgment. Surely when they realized that this king could become a heavy yoke, that "All of Israel's" sons would be forced to serve in his court and army and their daughters would serve as maids and cooks, that the independence they now enjoyed could be taken from them, that they would turn away from this demand.

Surely they could see the potential for their individual autonomy to turn into servile exploit under the tyranny of an earthly king. Surely they must know that this king would wield arbitrary power over them, and that unless the heart of this king was inclined to Yahweh, he could turn them into slaves with a life of bondage. Surely they must know that the will of this mortal king was random and could turn against them at any point, that he would take the best of all they had; that to pay for his royal court, he would take a percentage of all they owned—property, livestock, their fields and vineyards, their servants and employees—and force them to work the lands this king had confiscated for his personal use.

"Is this the king you want, one that rules a kingdom of slaves?" Samuel swept his gaze across the crowd, but no one replied, no one moved, no one seemed to understand the disadvantages he had laid out. The only reaction he got was the reflection of blank faces. He might as well have been speaking to a gathering of the deaf and dumb.

"And the day will come when you will cry out for relief from your bondage, but the ears of Yahweh will be shut. When that day comes the answer from the Almighty will be silence."

Samuel thought surely the fear of Yahweh not hearing them when they should cry out from the oppression of their mortal king like their forefathers had cried out from their bondage in Egypt, surely this reality would be powerful enough to make them see this foolishness. But "All of Israel" was silent, returning the same silence of Yahweh Samuel had threatened them with.

He had lost. "All of Israel" would remain adamant. The morning sun was turning hot. Trickles of sweat ran down his back. His empty stomach and dry mouth made him faint. He dared not show any weakness, so he moved off the platform and started down the steps when Eleazar stepped out of the knot of humanity and stopped him.

"My lord, we have heard your words, but our answer is the same. We want a king to rule over us. We want to be like the other nations. We want a king to lead us, to go before us and fight our battles."

Samuel nodded and continued down the steps. The people made a path for him as he made his way back to his horse waiting at the trough. Samuel gritted his teeth as he mounted his horse, but he was not about to let anyone know his body was sore and aching. He turned the horse around and started to move through the crowd, but stopped when he came to Eleazar, Ahiah, and Abinadab.

Perched upon his horse, Samuel looked upon the three solemn faces looking anxiously up at him. "Yahweh has listened to you. I have listened to Yahweh, and the Almighty says to give you what you want. You shall have your king. You shall have the king you desire. Now go back to your hometowns."

Samuel snapped the reins. He looked neither to the right nor the left as he departed the city center. He rode upright, a proud procession of one. A gusty wind blew against his back and his robes billowed like the sail of a ship snapping around his back and legs as Moses and Zipporah trotted along beside him.

Twenty-Three

SAUL HATED STANDING IN LINE. AND THERE WAS A LONG LINE waiting to get water from the well that served the villagers living outside the walls of Ramah as well as the nomads and travelers who did not want to enter the city and pay the high fee charged to non-citizens.

The city water might be cleaner but not worth the cost. Saul hated waiting for anything, especially when there was a crowd at the well, a stench from mounds of animal dung scattered around the premises, and the threat of bandits and marauders who would use force to break line or commit worse atrocities upon those gathered. But the water was free, and Saul could not argue with free even if it meant holding your nose while you waited.

He hated being on this trip. He hated being away from his family. He had never been away from home for more than a day, and this was the beginning of the fourth day. To Saul and his servant, Ezbon, it felt like an eternity, and on a mission Saul considered futile. When the two of them arrived at the well that morning, judging from the length of the line of beasts and humans waiting their turn, Saul determined it would be some time before Ezbon would get to water their horses and fill their depleted water skins. So Saul chose to wait under the shade of a mushroom-shaped rock on the northern side of the well. He tucked himself under the dome out of the sun and tried to relax in the rising heat after drinking the last few drops of water from his skin. When it was Ezbon's turn at the well he would join him to refill his container.

There was little breeze that morning and the smell made Saul nauseated; an empty stomach and a parched tongue did not help. He thought of home. If he did not return soon, the vultures would be making a meal out of his body. To air his perspiring glands, Saul pulled up his leggings above his knees and slipped his arms out of the sleeves of his long shirt, baring his chest. He untied a piece of cloth secured onto his leather sword belt and shook it in the air. He used it to wipe the moisture off the brass armlets he wore on his biceps, each with the carving of a wolf head on its front.

Before departing, Ahinoam had given him this cloth that she had been working on for weeks in the evenings. She had sewn the names of their family on it, their sons and daughters: Jonathan, their first born, followed by his girls, Merab and Mikal. Both daughters had flowered into beautiful young women. And then there were the twins, Ishvi and Malki, boys about to be young men. Saul and Ahinoam had discussed the possibility of trying for a third daughter to even out the sibling ratio, but as of yet, that had not happened, and Ahinoam's time for bearing children was rapidly coming to an end.

Saul recalled with fondness and longing the images of his wife and each child as he ran the tip of his finger over the stitching of their names. Why in the name of the Almighty were he and Ezbon wandering the desert and mountains on this fool's errand commissioned by Saul's father? He and Ezbon had spent enough time and near enough money searching for his father's stray donkeys separated from the drove during a strong thunderstorm than the cost to replace them. It had gone from a good idea to an exercise in futility halfway through this odyssey, and even though they had only been traveling for a few days, to Saul it felt like weeks, and he was ready to turn toward home.

A shout from Ezbon brought Saul out of his daydream. At first, he thought his servant had made it to the head of the line and was calling for Saul to meet him at the well. But when he looked out from the shadow of the rock, Saul saw Ezbon waving from the middle of the line, and three raiders circling the well on horseback wielding their swords and frightening people away. Saul rose to his feet, tucking Ahinoam's stitchery into his belt and began jogging toward the well. He neglected to pull down his leggings or slip his bare arms back inside the sleeves before making his way toward the well.

Saul paused to wait for the raiders to sheath their weapons and dismount. They were clothed in fragments of fur and hide crudely sewn together with snug-fitting leg coverings protecting their skin from blistering from long periods on horseback. Their wild faces were layered in desert grime, and highlighted for vicious effect, were smears of red color around their eyes.

Saul stopped and called to the three men, hoping they might clear away from the well, but they just laughed and began to lower the bucket into the well while their horses drank from the trough beside it. Saul strode toward them, two steps for every step of a normal man.

At a distance, Saul knew he appeared like any other man, but as he drew nearer the larger he loomed, and Saul watched the eyes of the raiders begin to widen to fit his increasing stature. None of the three would be able to stand eye-to-eye with him. They froze in place, unable to move. He inflated his chest for effect just to confirm in the minds of these rabble that they had never seen Saul's equal in physical presence.

"I bet you liked the odds of three against one until I got a little closer. Now your hands are too weak to grip the hilt of your sword. I see only two choices." Saul kept his voice calm and assured. He anchored a fist against each hip and allowed his posture to flaunt the muscles and scars his body earned from laboring on his family farm handling livestock, not from battle, but these scoundrels had no knowledge of that fact. Saul let his expansive prowess make its impression felt. The sweat trickling down his shoulders onto the brass armbands made the wolf faces etched into the metal glisten in the sunlight.

"Go to the back of the line to wait your turn or poison this well with your blood."

The raider holding the rope attached to the bucket released it. When the bucket hit the water deep inside, a faint splash could be heard in the sudden stillness around the perimeter of the well. Consensus was reached without speaking a word. The raiders remounted their horses and began riding away to the jeers and ridicule of the crowd they had just terrorized. The three raiders chose thirst rather than humiliation of having to go to the back of the line.

It was only after the raiders disappeared from sight that Saul felt foolish. He realized he looked as strange as the raiders with his leggings rolled up around his knees and the long shirt hanging from his waist exposing his bare chest. He hastily stuck his arms back into the sleeves and pulled down the legs of his pants. By then people began to praise and thank him for his bravery and insisted they draw water for him.

Saul tried to go back to his hiding place beneath the rock outcropping, but the crowd would have none of it. They encircled him, pulling on his arms and slapping his broad shoulders and tapered back in appreciation for his heroism. Women started to remove their jewelry. Men took coins from their pouches—all offerings to their hero. He and his servant were invited to stay overnight in a dozen homes. But Saul declined all offerings. He just wanted to go home.

Before arriving at the well, he and Ezbon debated whether or not to continue searching for the lost drove of donkeys. They had traveled these days without success and concluded that by now the donkeys had either perished in the wild or been absorbed into new herds. Now, Saul and Ezbon's families would be more worried about their safety than concern for the donkeys. In only a matter of a few days, they had gone through their food and were down to their last shekel. The expectation to locate the donkeys should not have taken three days.

"Let's make short work of this, Ezbon." Saul handed off his empty water skin. This much attention was making Saul squirm with discomfort.

"Master, you know the Seer, the prophet of Yahweh, lives in Ramah."

Saul and Ezbon smiled at the people congregating around them. Someone took the water skins out of Ezbon's hands to fill them with water from the bucket. Two men took their horses and led them over to the trough. They were happy to oblige every stranger's need to repay Saul's gallantry.

"The Seer is highly respected and everything he says comes true. I learned he is in Ramah now. Would it hurt to ask him which way we might go to find the donkeys?"

"I don't know, Ezbon." Saul looked up the hill to the city. Confronting the raiders seemed much easier than the prospect of facing the Seer. "We have nothing to give him: no food, no money. We have no gift for the Seer."

Ezbon propped his foot upon the rim of the well and stuck a finger into a flap inside his leather shoe. He worked out the single coin and held it up.

"A shekel for emergencies. Give it to the Seer so he can tell us which way to go."

Saul hesitated, so Ezbon took his master's hand and placed the coin into his palm.

"What does it hurt to have the Seer inquire of Yahweh for us? If he can't tell us, then we go home. What does it hurt?" Ezbon's eyes were bright with optimism.

Saul curled his fingers over the coin in his large hand. He scanned the smiling faces of the crowd in front of him. "Yes, Ezbon. What does it hurt?" Saul spoke with a tone of resignation, not any hope for a positive outcome.

When their horses had drunk their fill and their water pouches were full, the two men waved to the people, and began leading their horses up the hill toward the city gates of Ramah.

Samuel stood in front of the raised platform in the middle of the synagogue, looking inside a large chest placed upon a table on the platform. The doors on the front of the chest were open, revealing the shelving inside with parchments lying flat on each of the shelves. Scattered about on the long benches in front of the platform were students who had come from all over the region to study with him, the prophet and judge of Yahweh. Samuel had met these young men and their families in the different cities where he traveled throughout each year. They served as students to the rabbis in their local synagogues, but Samuel had handpicked the ones he believed would be good candidates for learning to wait on and communicate in deeper ways with Yahweh beyond the normal Levitical training. On his very last circuit ride around the country, Samuel announced his intention to host a prophet's gathering and had extended the invitation to these young men to join him in Ramah for an extended time of study and prayer.

The room was quiet except for some whispering coming from the back of the synagogue. Samuel did not need prophetic skill to know who was doing the talking. He did not even bother to turn around to summon the culprits.

"Gad, Nathan, since you are so fond of talking, please come forward and read."

Samuel continued to examine the contents of the chest.

The two young men could not have produced a full beard between them. Wisps of blond fuzz patched Gad's face, while streaks of a browner hue covered Nathan's. Gad had been well-fed as a child and had the roly-poly body to show for it. Nathan was leaner, but spindly and awkward. The two had grown-up together in Bethlehem, both born into prosperous families who attended the same synagogue, both with above average intelligence, and while mischievous and fun-loving, there was nothing sinister about them. They might have both been spoiled as children, but it had not ruined their characters. Samuel judged them teachable and, with the proper guidance, could see them becoming something beyond what they or their families ever imagined.

The two boys had not moved from their seats. They sat mute and wide-eyed while their peers enjoyed their uneasiness.

"Any time now." Samuel lacked any hint of a scold. He pulled a sheet of parchment out of the chest, glanced at it, but decided to put it back. Then he turned to face the group. "We're waiting."

Gad was the first to stand and make his way to the aisle. When Nathan got to his feet and took his first step, his leg knocked against the bench in front of him and he bounced into the back of his friend, causing Gad to stumble forward into the aisle. This spectacle made it even more difficult for the others to keep silent.

Samuel dropped his head back and guffawed. He had felt listless most of the morning, his mind drifting. But seeing Gad and Nathan tumble into the aisle energized him and re-engaged him with the present moment.

"Do you think it is possible for the two of you to approach the platform without inflicting personal injury on yourselves or others? I dare not hope you could approach with any measure of solemnity."

It was hard for Samuel to be stern while laughing at the mortification of these two students. He struggled to regain his composure and restore calm. If anyone was listening outside they would have heard the rare sound of laughter coming from the synagogue.

"We are sorry, my lord." Gad's face was a spasm of shock.

"Yes, my lord." Nathan slapped his leg as if in punishment for lack of discipline.

"Please come to the platform." Samuel waved them forward.

Joined at the hips, the two boys made it to the front without further incident.

"Now, Gad, you choose the parchment, and Nathan you will read from it." Samuel pointed to the parchments inside the cabinet.

This broke with precedent. Each day of the public reading, only Samuel chose the text and only Samuel read his selection before he began his teaching. Samuel kept the flat parchments stored in this portable cabinet. Two of the students were chosen by lot for the honor of carrying the cabinet from Samuel's home to the synagogue each day of the assembly and back again. However, no one had been allowed to select a scroll, only Samuel would do that, and only by random selection. Then he would teach extempore. Now one student would choose the text and another would read it.

The two students on either side of the table were unable to move; their eyes locked on each other's startled expressions at what Samuel had instructed them to do.

"Go ahead, Gad, make your selection, and Nathan, you take your position." Samuel knew his instruction had caused a small panic in his students, so he tapped the small wooden podium next to the chest to free them from their paralysis.

Nathan circled the table and stepped onto the platform, gripping the podium with his perspiring hands.

Gad looked inside the chest but was hesitant.

"Reach in and take one, Gad." Samuel would not let his student delay.

So Gad lifted his trembling hands to the top shelf and carefully removed the first parchment, then handed the fluttering document up to his friend.

Nathan carefully positioned the sacred writing on the podium, cleared his throat, and read the heading above the passage.

"This is the story of a man named Micah from the hill country of Ephraim who made idols for personal use with money stolen from his mother."

Samuel raised his hand for Nathan to pause.

"A mother's curses and a thieving son's personal vanity—making graven images of himself. Unsettling times for Israel. Samson, the last of the great judges was dead, and there was no one to replace him. Where was righteousness to be found? Everyone did as they saw fit...unsettling times."

Samuel ambled toward the west window of the synagogue. He paused at the candelabrum to adjust a candlestick tipped on its side dripping wax onto the floor. After straightening the candle, Samuel ground the hot wax into the floor with his sandal before making his way over to the west window.

"You may begin, Nathan." Samuel would listen to the reading from the window.

Samuel rested his arms on the window frame and gazed out the window lost in thought. He felt his robes illuminated by the light of the sun streaming through the window, giving him a radiant glow.

"My lord, I am ready."

Had he said those words or were they spoken by Nathan who was ready to begin the reading?

Samuel did not respond. He was waiting and watching. He had forgotten where he was, what he was doing, and who was present. At this same window the day before about the same time the revelation had come, the voice had whispered inside his heart. Samuel had just finished reading the story of Gideon, the judge, to his students.

"Israel was constantly being invaded and impoverished by the surrounding nations because she kept worshiping the foreign gods in the land of Canaan."

Samuel expounded on the text as he stared out the window the day before. "But Israel would not listen to the prophet Yahweh had sent them. The prophet of Yahweh had come to teach and exhort, but Yahweh did more. The Almighty heard the cries of His people and sent an angel of Yahweh to confirm the words of the prophet and to appoint a deliverer. And when the angel of Yahweh appeared to Gideon while he was threshing his wheat, the angel called him a 'mighty warrior.' The angel of Yahweh saw within the character of Gideon something this bumbling farmer never saw within himself, and so a man of the soil became a man of the sword."

Samuel had paused at that moment once he had made his point to give time for the thought to sink into the minds of his students. It was important to understand the role the prophet played in relation to Yahweh and Israel. It was in that quiet moment while Samuel was staring out the window that Yahweh uncovered Samuel's ear. He heard Yahweh whispering in his heart: "Their cry has reached me," the hushed voice spoke. "I have looked upon my people. About this time tomorrow, I will send you a man from the tribe of Benjamin. Appoint him leader over my people Israel. He will deliver my people from the hand of the Philistines." And when the voice had finished, Samuel recoiled, unsure of what he had heard.

A Benjaminite? Appoint a king from the tribe of Benjamin?

Samuel became immobile. He listened for more. Perhaps he misheard.

When there were no more words, Samuel leaned out the window, peered into the bright sky, scanned the marketplace, then looked back through the interior of the synagogue before dropping his eyes to the floor. The declaration had ceased. There was no codicil from Yahweh, no additional clarification. How could this be? From the tribe of Benjamin, the tribe nearly annihilated by civil war because of its evil actions, Yahweh would choose Israel's first king. Why not choose a king from the tribe of Judah or Reuben or Manasseh and Ephraim; any tribe but Benjamin?

In the silence of Yahweh, Samuel had to stew on this unfathomable message for over a score of hours. In that space of time, instead of Yahweh's words tumbling through his heart, Samuel kept remembering Eli's personal denunciation regarding anyone from the tribe of Benjamin: "Never trust a Benjaminite. They are a disgrace to Israel. They will be forever remembered as the tribe who brought the wrath of the Almighty upon itself. A Benjamite is never to be trusted."

Samuel knew this prejudice had been taught him. Would he inflict such narrow-mindedness upon Yahweh's chosen? Would his bias be passed onto the next generation?

"My lord, I am ready." Nathan cleared his throat again. "May I begin?"

Stillness could be a furious motion, and Samuel did not respond. He stood unmoving before the window, his countenance brightened by the quivering daylight. Samuel was giving himself over to Yahweh, inviting every young man in the room to share this unspoken, collective sense of wonder. Samuel wished for the natural alignment of the student's heart with his own to join in reverence for the Almighty.

"Yes, Yahweh. Yes." Samuel braced his arms on either side of the window before leaning through the opening until his head disappeared from sight. Samuel was captivated by his vision. He knew from experience and his teaching from stories written and spoken, that a prophet of Yahweh could always expect the unexpected. Now his students were to witness a demonstration of such a phenomenon.

"My lord," Nathan blurted.

"Yes, Yahweh. Yes." Samuel pushed himself back into the room, whirled around, and slammed his back against the wall. He was trembling. His legs were giving way. He slid down the wall, his breathing rapid and labored. He reached out his arms.

Nathan and Gad made a mad dash for him, each one taking an arm.

"I must get outside without delay." Samuel ignored the faces of the students crowding behind Gad and Nathan, staring in amazement at him squatting on the floor. "Help me up. I must get to the west gate at once." Samuel's gruff directive set Nathan and Gad into action, and they lifted him to his feet.

Samuel's footing was unsure. He accepted the aid Gad and Nathan provided as they braced him on either side. But by the time they reached the door of the synagogue, Samuel jerked his arms free and blasted out of the entrance, his strength fully restored. What he had seen from the window, he would face under his own power. There was no weakness. All previous signs of distraction witnessed by his students had given way to a vigorous focus. Samuel marched down the street toward the western gate with Nathan, Gad, and the other students following at his heels. They would witness a life lesson in the prophetic arts, something to tell their children and grandchildren.

When Saul and Ezbon met a group of young women coming down the hill from Ramah, they stopped them to ask if the Seer was in town and was told he could be found in the synagogue. Saul was not accustomed to receiving such fawning interest from others, a result of never venturing far from home for any length of time. The people in his hometown of Gibeah were used to seeing him around the city and no longer awed by his impressive height and build, his rugged and handsome features. To them, he was just Saul, son of Kish, husband to Ahinoam, a reliable friend, and proficient farmer. But from strangers the looks of wonder made Saul uncomfortable. He did not like being the object of attention, admiring or otherwise.

They tied the reins of their horses onto a long railing at the entrance into the city alongside other horses. They could not stretch Ezbon's coin enough to properly stable them and pay the Seer for his prescient knowledge. Saul rubbed his empty stomach as he and Ezbon approached the marketplace. The smells of fresh bread, fruits and vegetables, roasted goat and lamb wafting from the vendors' stands made him salivate.

"If we don't find the Seer, I say we spend your last coin on two kebabs of lamb and go home." Saul scanned the city square for the location of the synagogue. "If we ride hard we should get home shortly after nightfall."

Saul felt Ezbon grip his arm, directing his attention to the approaching mob.

It amused Saul to see a middle-aged man marching toward him with a bevy of young men following behind him. He spun his head around to see who might be coming through the gate worthy to receive this greeting committee. People in the street were stepping to the side, giving way to this fast-moving troop; it was either that or be trampled for the man had a no-nonsense expression. Saul thought perhaps they were headed out of the city, and he and Ezbon stepped aside to make way for this parade to pass in front of them. He never expected the group to halt in front of him.

Saul looked down into the man's resolute face, his nostrils flaring with each heavy breath. His dark eyes glared up at him, darting rapidly, and strands of hair stuck to the side of his perspiring face. Saul might have been amused at the sight of this puffing, clammy man, but instead he felt a tingling of fear begin to stir at the base of his spine, a sensation he did not experience when facing down the three ruffians at the well.

He looked at the boys huddled behind the man. He was not an adequate shield to protect them from this towering, armed figure, and they began to back away. Saul knew if he so much as growled at them, they would scatter like fleas. He looked at Ezbon who responded with a puzzled expression. Then Saul looked back at the man who did not appear he would start the conversation, so Saul decided to speak first.

"Sir, I am Saul, son of Kish, tribe of Benjamin, from Gibeah. I'm here... we're here... We're here hoping to find the Seer. Would you know where he might live?"

When the man replied that he had found the Seer—that, in fact, he was looking right at him, that he was Samuel, prophet and judge of Israel—it was Saul who now took a step back, his left hand creeping up the sheath of his sword and coming to rest upon the hilt. His hand never came near his sword when he confronted the raiders. Why now? What instinctive vulnerability did he feel deep inside that made him think he might have to use force to cut free from the man's grip?

Samuel felt no threat from this man towering a good head and shoulders above him. He detected in the man's eyes a sense of recognition. Samuel too felt that this was not the first time they had met. Their paths had converged. But where? Samuel knew this indeed was Yahweh's choice, the one with whom He would share the leadership role. The man to whom all of Israel would now turn in their desire to have a king. But why a Benjamite? Samuel had to swallow hard and force down the temptation to turn his back and walk away. He too must be submissive to the will of Yahweh though with grudging reluctance.

"Come to my home. You will dine with me. I will sacrifice for you at my altar on the high place. I will tell you everything that is in your heart, and then in the morning I will let you go."

Samuel beckoned for Saul to follow him, but he did not move. Samuel had not said enough to reassure this man that in spite of the mysterious quality of their encounter, Samuel was only reacting to the will of Yahweh and it would be carried out whether or not either of them understood what it meant. More needed to be said, so Samuel chose to give the future king a sign of his credibility.

"The donkeys lost three days ago are found. You need not worry about them."

Samuel watched as the muscles in Saul's face began to quiver and his hand released its grip on the hilt of his sword, falling powerless at his side.

Samuel's modest display of clairvoyance set the hook, and should help convince the future king that he was on the cusp of something beyond his understanding. And while Samuel might concede that this tower of a man was chosen by Yahweh to replace him, the power and influence so long enjoyed by him, the prophet and judge of Israel, would not be easily relinquished or overlooked. It would be an ever-present force.

"Upon you all of Israel has set its desire. Upon you and your entire family."

Samuel could see that Saul was not prepared for such a declaration. Samuel looked over his shoulder at the amazed, bright faces of the young men clustered behind him. He wanted to be sure they were watching. This was a lesson of Yahweh, and that whatever Saul might say or do now would be remembered all of their lives.

"My lord, I am a Benjamite, the smallest tribe in Israel, and my clan is the least of all the clans in the tribe of Benjamin. Why do you say such a thing to me?"

Samuel frowned, knowing he could blurt out a thousand responses. "That is a question only the Almighty can answer. Now come with me." Samuel whirled around and began marching back up the street, forcing his students to scatter in every direction to avoid being run down by their teacher.

Samuel secretly hoped Saul would not follow, that Saul would turn around and go back to whatever pastoral life he had with his clan among his despicable tribe. Then this nonsense to appoint a king could be stopped before it could gain any traction, and Samuel could go back to the tribal leaders and tell them that this was a bad strategy from the beginning, that the one appropriate candidate for the job turned out to be unsuitable. He could then go to Yahweh with the same point and say, "The one you chose refused the job, so may we pick up where we left off?" But then he heard footsteps racing up behind him and there was Gad panting as he kept pace.

"Is he following us?"

Gad glanced back over his shoulder and put a hand above his brow to shield his eyes from the glare of the sun. "Yes, my lord."

The course was set. There was no turning. Samuel knew the transition of power had begun and the certainty of the coming days struck his heart with a shuddering fire.

Twenty-Four

SAUL WARMED HIMSELF BY THE FIRE BURNING INSIDE THE LARGE metal basin set on a stone table in the center of the rooftop. He watched the prophet and judge of Israel amble along the perimeter of the roof, occasionally taking an object from a pocket of his robe, bouncing it in his hand before returning the item to the pocket. The night was clear and cold. In the light of the stars and a half-moon, Samuel appeared like a murky spirit taking his measured, silent steps around the edge of the roof of his house. It was just another peculiar scene at the end of a long day of strange occurrences.

That day, Saul had shared the chief seat next to Samuel at the head of the long table in a dining chamber. It was next to the prophet's library and academy where they and Samuel's students were served a lavish meal of roast lamb and fresh vegetables. Saul had never experienced so formal a gathering. He could not believe his eyes when a platter bearing the right shoulder and breast meat of a lamb, the choicest of cuts, was set before him. No one received such a large portion. While a student poured steaming broth over the meat on Saul's platter, Samuel explained that this was the portion set aside for him just for this occasion, that the choice selection of meat symbolized the strength to bear the burden of governing the people and fighting in their defense. Saul could not fathom how the prophet knew he was coming to Ramah and why he was eating a meal so laden with

262

meaning. But when Saul reached out with his left hand to take his first bite, he could see the prophet look askance and grunt in disapproval. Samuel did not speak to him the rest of the meal, and Saul ate cautiously, unaware of how he might have offended the prophet.

After the meal, the prophet led a procession up the steep hill on the back side of his property to the altar and there the sacrifice was prepared and offered, and though Saul walked by Samuel's side from the dining hall to the high place and returned down the hill afterward, they never conversed. It was not until nightfall when Samuel bade his students good night and instructed Saul to accompany him up the outside steps to the rooftop of his house that Saul thought he might get some explanation for this strange turn of circumstances. Saul had followed the prophet around all day like an obedient pet, and by now he was growing weary watching him trudge around his rooftop. The fatigue he felt began to weigh heavy upon his eyes.

Samuel paused in a corner of the roof and pulled the ram's horn vial of oil out of his pocket. He had Shira fill it with balsam oil before he and Saul took to the roof. He looked over his shoulder at Saul slumped in his chair, his head pitched forward, eyes closed, and chest rising and falling in a slow rhythm.

He turned back and held the ram's horn in the moon and allowed its subdued radiance to glow onto the horn. The anointing of sacred oil had only been used by the priesthood of Israel. Not Joshua, not any of the great judges of Israel were anointed when they took their places of leadership. Only the priests of Yahweh received this special consecration. Samuel would be the first to break the ancient custom and anoint a king, a man of Yahweh's choosing, not his. He would not have chosen this man or any other man. Samuel might have gone to his grave without ever confronting the issue of leadership and succession or waited until his last days before taking any action.

There was still plenty of life in him. He was still capable of leading. It was the people he blamed. It was the fear and ignorance of the people that had brought them to this point, and he had been forced to bend to their will. He would use a common oil to anoint Israel's first king, not the expensive mixture of myrrh, cinnamon, cane, cassia, and olive oil used by Aaron to anoint the Ark of the Covenant and all the sacred articles of the Tabernacle as well as the successions of priests since Aaron.

Samuel slipped the ram's horn of oil back inside his pocket and looked again at Saul. This transition of power was not to its equal. This man asleep on his roof was not equipped for the task that lay before him. Yahweh had chosen him, yes, but Samuel would give the Almighty a little more time to change His mind, if He would. Surely there was someone else in all of Israel Yahweh could find who would be more suitable. Someone other than a Benjamite. Surely Yahweh agreed with his assessment of this man and would inform him of a different choice before it was too late. Samuel would give Yahweh a little more time. He would give Yahweh until daybreak.

Samuel moved noiselessly over to Saul. In the firelight he examined Saul's sword and sheath lying on the table beside him. He had noticed it earlier that day slung over the back of Saul's chair at dinner but had not gotten a good look. Samuel had not seen its like until he ran his fingers over the Egyptian symbol for eternal life carved into its sheath.

His hands suddenly began to tremble as he quietly turned it over and saw the symbol of the setting sun between two mountains. It was difficult to believe there might be another sword like it. It was difficult to believe that this was originally Samuel's sword, the sword of his family. It was difficult to believe that this sword, his sword, was now in the possession of the first king of Israel. But it was true.

Samuel pulled the sword all the way out of its sheath. He held the sword of his fathers in his hands. How did this young man come into its possession? Surely this was not the man he had given it to at the battle of Shiloh against the Philistines when they captured the Ark. This man was too young. Could it have been his father? Samuel wondered. His father who had acted bravely and honorably. He had not fled once the battle had been lost. When every man was fleeing to his home, this Benjamite acted nobly. He had taken up the bodies of the sons of Eli and carried them upon his broad shoulders until they could be placed upon the death cart. He had been true to his word and delivered the message Samuel had entrusted to him, to tell the High Priest that his sons had been killed in battle defending the Ark of the Covenant. If that brave man was the father of this young man, he would have come from good stock, he would be the inheritor of an honorable bloodline, he could be worthy. Might Samuel have misjudged this young man and his capabilities?

Samuel put the sword back into its sheath, turned from the future king, and walked back to the edge of the roof. He raised the sheathed sword to the sky.

"Yahweh. O Yahweh. What have I done? You have returned to me the sword of my fathers by the hand of the first king of your choosing, and I have scorned him. I have scorned the one of your choosing. My heart is full of shame at the thought of despising your chosen. He has not asked for this appointment. He has not been prepared. I, at least, the son of the vow, had been promised to you before you knit me in my mother's womb and prepared me in your service. But you have plucked him from the least of your people and brought him to me. O Yahweh, forgive my foolish and stubborn heart."

Saul groaned in his sleep and shifted in his chair. Samuel lowered the sword to his chest, embracing the legacy and the future in the same moment. "Your will, Yahweh. Your will alone be served."

Samuel slipped over to where Saul had his legs outstretched, lay the sword back on the table, and gently tapped Saul's sandaled foot. Saul jerked awake, sucking in a deep gulp of air and gripping the sides of his seat.

Samuel picked up a pitcher and poured some water into two clay goblets.

"Drink this." Samuel offered a goblet to Saul who looked around blinking, his eyes trying to rouse himself from his deep slumber.

Samuel sipped the water from his goblet and watched as Saul drained his goblet with loud swallows.

"Walk with me." Samuel set his goblet on the table. He did not wait for Saul, but started moving back to the edge of the roof.

Saul set his goblet on the table, wiped his mouth, and stumbled to catch up with Samuel. They took several revolutions around the roof line without speaking. The only sound was the scraping of their feet over the hard clay roof and the occasional howl of a lion far in the distance.

"You really do not understand what is happening, do you?"

"No, my lord."

They continued on in silence, looping the roof, until Samuel paused and looked into the night sky. He pointed to the northern sky. "The Shepherd's Belt. Do you see it?"

Saul followed Samuel's finger into the northern sky until his eyes caught sight of the constellation of stars. "Yes, my lord. It is beautiful."

"My wife and I enjoy sleeping on our roof watching the stars."

"My wife and I too enjoy—"

"How many wives do you have?"

"Only the one." Saul looked surprised by Samuel's quick change from stargazing to the number of potential wives in his household.

"That is good. That is good. One wife is good. It is wise for the king to only have one wife. Too many wives can confuse a man's heart."

"I am blessed with the wife of my youth. I'm quite happy, and we have many children, but I do not understand the reference about the king having one wife."

Samuel looked into Saul's face as though the lines around his eyes and the few scars not concealed beneath his thick, dark beard might tell him something about Saul's character he had not yet noticed. "Have we ever met before?"

"Not to my knowledge, my lord. You have passed through my hometown of Gibeah on your judge's circuit, but I have brought no case before you. I rarely venture out. Life on our farm and the demands of family have kept me close to home all my life."

Samuel nodded his head and continued to lead their stroll along the roof.

"Unusual sword you have." Samuel nodded toward the weapon on the table.

"Yes, my lord; a gift from a Levite my father met when Israel retreated from the Philistines after they destroyed Shiloh and captured the Ark years ago. He asked a favor of my father. In the chaos of fleeing the enemy, my father never saw him again."

"I'm sure the stranger does not regret his gift to your father." Samuel then turned his head toward Saul. "And your father has given it to you."

"He often told me the story of how he received it from a mysterious stranger who asked him to carry a message to the High Priest in Shiloh. How the High Priest died when he heard the news of the death of his sons. To bear my father's sword is a great honor."

"Since you were given the sword, have you ever used it in battle?"

"I am thankful that I have never had to use this sword against man or beast."

"That is unusual given the constant threats from our enemies."

"My enemies consist of weather and wild beasts that attack my livestock. My home is tucked into a valley north of Gibeah and overlooked by potential dangers from man. I know the threat from the Philistines is constant. They have captured several small towns along our western borders, and have an outpost not a half-day's ride from my farm. But since our defeat at Shiloh, I have not been called upon to defend my hometown."

"That could change. These are unsettling times."

"I am aware of that, my lord. The danger is serious."

"You are aware of the great pressure on me to appoint a king. The tribal leaders are insisting Israel have a king. They say our nation needs a king to lead them in battle against our enemies."

"I have sat in councils and heard those words discussed by my tribal leaders."

Samuel noticed that Saul rubbed his stomach as if surprised by a sharp pain.

"Is that why I am here, my lord? Is that the reason for this unusual moment?" Saul removed his hand from his stomach and waved it in the air.

Samuel looked at the one chosen by Yahweh. His appearance was striking and he gave off the aura of a warrior, someone who men could follow into battle. Samuel had given Yahweh time to change His mind. He had hoped Yahweh might change His mind regarding his selection. But now, it was Samuel's heart that was changing. Once Samuel held the sword of his fathers, he knew his heart harbored a foolish bias, yet it was a stubborn bias. The nudge from the Almighty for a changed heart was a nudge to his own heart. The spirit of the prophet was subject to the control of the prophet, so he continued to give Yahweh more time to break the prejudice in his heart and replace it with compassion.

"Have you ever read the final recitation Moses gave to the people of Israel before he ascended Mount Nebo?"

"My lord, I am a man of the soil, not a man of the word."

"The Almighty, the Creator of heaven and earth, the Divine and Eternal One, has chosen Israel as His portion and His inheritance. Israel is the apple of His eye. It is a great mystery why Yahweh makes His choices, but once made, the Almighty cannot go against His word. I have been tempted to believe Yahweh might alter His mind, even attempted to persuade Yahweh to do so, but regretted my folly. Moses sings of this and much more before he climbs Mount Nebo to die."

"Then I must read these great words."

"I shall have copies made for you. Read it and remember what you read."

"That would be a great blessing to me and my family to have such a document."

"You know the stories of how Israel turned to other gods once the great prophet Moses led them out of Egypt. You know the stories of Yahweh's anger against those who sought after other gods, how Yahweh hid His face from them, turned His back on them in His jealousy, and allowed them to perish because they lusted after detestable and worthless idols. You know this."

"Yes, my lord. I know the stories."

"Do you keep idols in your home like so many have done and still do?"

"No, my lord. I have never—"

"Your wife or children, do they worship idols?" Samuel did not allow Saul to finish, and Samuel saw the flash of anger in Saul's eyes at his invasive questions.

"My lord, my daughters may have some images, some figurines in their room, but they are harmless collectibles, I assure you."

"Destroy them in any case when you get home. The first commandment shall not be compromised by you in any way."

"Yes, my lord."

Samuel detected no deep conviction in Saul agreeing to his theological directive. "These words of Moses, these blessed words given to the great prophet from the Divine and Eternal One is a source of life and strength for the people of Yahweh."

"I am sure you are correct, my lord."

Samuel looked to see if Saul was just agreeing with him for the sake of agreeing or if he valued the importance of what he said, but Samuel could not tell from the blank face and weary eyes looking back at him if any of what he said made any impression on Saul's heart. Centuries of governance was about to be turned over in the life of the nation of Israel, and he and Saul would be the two men who would forge this new direction. If Samuel was honest with himself, he too could not comprehend why Yahweh had agreed to take this course and what it would mean in the future.

"I have seen these words, written by the scribes and placed beside the Ark, beneath the Mercy Seat of Yahweh, inside a golden chest."

"Yes, my lord."

"And I have seen the fire of Yahweh, the Almighty. He has appeared to me."

"Yes, my lord."

"And I have heard Yahweh, the Almighty. He has spoken to me. I hear Yahweh, the Almighty. He speaks to me."

"Of that, I have no doubt, my lord."

From badgering questions, to insistent directives, to boasting of his high standing with Yahweh. Saul had to control his irritation with the prophet in order to absorb all that he was hearing and try to formulate clear answers in response. He found himself backing away from Samuel with each statement asserting his status and authority in Israel. There was no question in Saul's mind as to his place, but he did not understand why Samuel had singled him out and spoken to him with such intensity and why these points he made were so important that they should be made to Saul alone as if he himself had become the embodiment of all Israel.

Saul was receding into the shadowy light of the night with the feeling of panic intensifying in his gut. The prophet indicated for him to sit on the ledge of the roof.

Saul obeyed, clasping the weathered edges of the raised ledge built around the circumference of the roof. It was all he could do to keep from making a mad dash for the stairs, or worse, leaping from the roof and taking his chances with landing on the ground. The urge to escape was near impossible to resist.

"Do you know Moses's final words to Joshua and to all of Israel before his death?" Samuel positioned himself closer to Saul.

"I'm sure they are very important, my lord." Saul dug his fingers into the disintegrating clay ledge. He kept his head and eyes lowered hoping to conceal his trembling fear in the presence of the prophet and judge of Israel. Saul glanced at the dying fire and wished to be near its warmth to stop his shivering.

Samuel squatted down in front of Saul. The effort was painful to his joints and knees, but he was willing to endure the discomfort for the sake of these boiling words that must be spoken. The night was waning and light was breaking in the eastern sky. This cowering man in front of him had to understand. It must be made clear to him that he was to be Yahweh's inevitable choice. That unless Yahweh changed His mind, and Saul was to receive the anointing, he would be given power that could potentially destroy him. Samuel looked again to the east. Yahweh was running out of time to change His mind if He was ever going to do it.

"After recording all the inspired words of Yahweh, after pronouncing the sacred blessing over each of the twelve tribes, after singing his account of Israel's story and praise for Yahweh's divine atonement, Moses said to Joshua and to all the people, 'Take to heart all the words I have solemnly declared to you this day, so that you may command your children to obey carefully all the words of this law. They are not just idle words for you— they are your life. By them you will live long in the land you are crossing the Jordan to possess.'"

Samuel gripped Saul's powerful arms and forced him to look into his face.

"Do you understand what I am saying to you? Is it clear to you? You must understand. It must be clear to you before you become...before you can become..."

Samuel could not speak the word. He could not pronounce the word that would change the course of Israel's history. He placed his hands upon Saul's shoulders and braced himself as he stood back onto his feet. He turned to the east and his eyes squinted at the sight of the sun. He cocked his ear for any whisper from Yahweh, but all was silent. It remained silent until the sun crested above the hills.

"Until what, my lord? Until I become what?"

Samuel had no answer. The night had come and gone and there was no change of heart from Yahweh, which must mean it was Samuel's heart that had to change. Still, because of his ingrained bias against anyone from the tribe of Benjamin, he could not tell this man in no uncertain terms that Yahweh had chosen him out of all the men of Israel to be her first king with a free heart. Samuel removed the ram's horn of oil from his pocket. He squeezed it inside his hand, pressing it so hard he thought he might crush it.

"Before I become what, my lord?"

Samuel looked down into Saul's face, a man's face and yet bearing an innocence, bewildered and frightened, and yet inquisitive, anxious to understand, eager to please. But Samuel discerned that the heart of this man measured himself too low, doubted any ability he might have, a heart alarmed by a world he could find too overwhelming.

"The sun is up." Samuel returned the vial to his pocket. "Get ready, and I will send you on your way."

Samuel heard Saul scramble across the roof. He glanced over his shoulder to see Saul grabbing his sword as he dashed by the table and nearly stumbled down the steps, his feet were moving so fast.

When Saul reached the bottom stairs, he went straight to Ezbon waiting at the gate of the courtyard and instructed him to get their horses. Samuel raised his head and held his breath. All he heard was the morning songs of the birds, breezes blowing off the hills into the valley, neighing horses in the distance. He heard his wife's voice coming out of their house, scolding Moses and Zipporah for growling at her guest. Samuel knew she had no idea who was standing in their courtyard. A time was coming when she would bend her knee to this man.

He turned to cross to the stairs and a rush of new words filled his heart, Yahweh's words, words confirming the will of the Almighty. He paused and listened, rubbing his hand over his chest. New words. New signs. New instructions. All from Yahweh. All to be fulfilled. All to be obeyed. And Samuel knew that the prejudice he felt toward the Benjamite, toward Yahweh's choice, the future king of Yahweh's chosen, was draining from his heart. The heart and mind he had hoped to change had changed his instead.

When Samuel walked around the corner of the house, Saul and Ezbon were about to mount their horses. Samuel came up beside Saul, placing his hand upon his shoulder.

"Please bid your servant to go ahead of you." Samuel whispered his instruction, not wanting Ezbon to hear what he would say to his master. "Meet him on the road outside the entrance to Ramah. You and I shall walk together. I have a message from Yahweh for you."

Samuel turned his back and went over to Shira, cupping her face inside his hands.

"I have not slept." Samuel held on to Shira's face, lingering to enjoy the width of her smile. "I have one more instruction to follow and I shall return to you."

"I shall prepare something to eat." Shira rubbed her cheek against his hand.

"Only a little fruit. I haven't much appetite. I just want to sleep." Samuel kissed her head and started walking toward the road to Ramah.

Samuel waited for Ezbon to ride his horse past where he stood. Samuel waved for Saul to join him, and they watched as Ezbon rode at a clipped gait and took the road that circled around the city instead of the one that led into the city center and headed south toward Gibeah. There was no one else on the road. It was too early in the morning for there to be much activity.

The two of them walked in silence until they reached the split in the road. Samuel pointed to a clump of wild jasmine bushes and a small abandoned olive grove just off the road. Samuel removed the ram's horn from his pocket as they began to move toward the grove and held it in the palm of his hand for Saul to see.

"What is this, my lord?"

"Tie off your horse there." Samuel pointed to the first olive tree they came to. Its massive trunk was split in the middle with half of the tree lying on the ground. Samuel sat down on the dead tree trunk and watched as Saul tied the reins of his horse onto the trunk that was still standing, and then he indicated for Saul to come before him.

"Kneel, my son."

When Saul hesitated, looking around to see if anyone was watching, or coming down the road, Samuel had to reassure him.

"There is no one, my son. No one is watching but Yahweh. I am doing the bidding of the Almighty. Do not be afraid. Please kneel and remove your head covering."

"Yes, my lord." Saul slipped the covering from his head and scratched his scalp, ruffling his thick hair before he got down on his knees.

Samuel removed the stopper from the ram's horn and stretched out his hand above Saul's bowed head. Once he began to pour the oil onto this man's head there would be no turning back. The man's fate would be sealed. He would be on the path of becoming the first king of Israel, and Samuel's rejection by the people would be complete. Neither of them had asked for this to happen. Neither of them had ever imagined this moment would happen. Neither of them was prepared for this moment. Yahweh's secret intentions had caught them both by surprise.

Samuel's hand began to tremble and he could feel a tingling in his fingers. It had to be done now, no more delay, and Samuel tipped the ram's horn over, allowing the balsam oil to freely pour onto Saul's head. Samuel held it up until the contents were empty. The Spirit of Yahweh thus bestowed, now flowed down Saul's head and poured into his beard.

"What does this mean, my lord? What have you done to me?"

Saul's voice was raw with inquiry, plaintive with concern, and Samuel felt a flood of sympathy for this man quivering and kneeling before him. Samuel set the empty ram's horn, empty of Yahweh's Spirit, upon the dead tree trunk. Then he leaned forward and kissed Saul on either side of his face above the line of his dark beard.

"My son, you are now the prince of Yahweh. The Almighty has anointed you leader of His inheritance." Samuel raised his hand for Saul not to open his mouth. "Say nothing. Only listen and know what is happening to you is true and the will of Yahweh."

Samuel locked on to Saul's eyes. Samuel was ready to speak the truth and will of Yahweh. He would bolster the king's mind with truth, he would encourage the king's heart by conveying Yahweh's will with the compassion spilling from his own heart. The course of a nation would turn on this moment between these two men, and Samuel wanted nothing to stand in the way of Saul's kingship.

"On your way home you will meet two men near the tomb of Rachel, the mother of your tribe. They will tell you that the donkeys you were looking for have been found and that your father is now worried about your safety.

"You will go on till you come to the great tree of Tabor, the giant oak under which the prophet Deborah sat to judge the people and where she is buried. You will meet three men on their way to Bethel to sacrifice at Jacob's altar with three goats, three loaves of bread, and a skin of wine. They will greet you and offer you two loaves of bread. Accept the offering.

"Finally, you will pass the Philistine outpost you spoke of on your way to your home in Gibeah. As you approach the town you will meet a procession of prophets and scholars coming down from the high place. While they are worshiping and giving praise, the Spirit of Yahweh will fall upon you in power and you will join with them in their supplications and you will be changed into a different person."

Samuel placed his hands upon Saul's lips.

"All these signs will happen to you today and you will know and be known by Yahweh. You will know that the Almighty is with you and that my words are true. Once these signs are fulfilled, do whatever your hand finds to do, for Yahweh is with you. To whom is all the desire of Israel turned, if not to you and your father's house?"

When Samuel dropped his head, Saul looked around the ancient grove, his gaze bouncing off the olive trees, overgrown jasmine bushes, rock formations, his horse, the sky, every visible object in sight. His eyes could not rest on a single object or focus upon it until he caught sight of the empty ram's horn lying on its side on the dead tree trunk. He pulled at his moist beard saturated with the holy oil of Yahweh and his own drenching sweat. He tucked his wet hands under his arms and pressed them against his side.

"I am to be changed into a different person? How is this possible?"

"This kind of transformation is rare. I cannot explain it. Yahweh knows all things. You are His now. It is done."

Saul kept his eyes on the empty ram's horn. "It is done? Am I to go now?"

Samuel nodded, but he did not raise his head to look at Saul.

"In seven days you must come to Mizpah. I will summon all of Israel to witness the one of Yahweh's choosing, the one to whom all the desire of Israel shall be turned."

"In seven days."

"Meet me in Mizpah in seven days. I will come and tell you what to do."

"Yes, my lord. Thank you. Thank you. Am I to go now?"

"Yes, go."

Saul sprang to his feet and saw the ram's horn. Samuel's head was still lowered with his eyes shut tight, and Saul snatched the horn off the tree trunk and dashed away without saying another word.

"It is done, Yahweh. Your will has been done. May our king be worthy. May he be a man of righteousness. May he serve the chosen people of the Almighty with honor."

Samuel listened to the sound of the horse's hooves pounding against the hard, packed ground as it raced down the road. When the sound had faded, Samuel opened his eyes and reached for the ram's horn but it had disappeared.

Twenty-Five

EZBON AND SAUL SPOKE LITTLE ON THE RIDE HOME. SAUL DID not want to explain what had happened with the prophet. He allowed the predictions of the prophet to unfold on their journey home, and with each prophecy fulfilled down to meeting the procession of prophets, Saul began to wonder if he had not moved into an altered state of being.

The day began by the prophet anointing him as the first king of Israel, and at the gates of Gibeah, after he and Ezbon parted company, Saul found himself surrounded by a group of prophets all of whom were given over to divine exuberance. Overcome by the precision of fulfillment, he became caught up with the prophets in their joyous outburst of dance and worship, losing all sense of time and place. All the prophet had foretold had come true. Was this really proof of Yahweh's appointment, of Yahweh's full blessing? The prophet had said it was so. He could give an accurate account of the details, but why had such amazing things transpired and why had they happened to him?

Saul could identify one thing that felt real in this unreal experience... the change in his heart. His soul expanded with each fulfilled prediction. The boundaries of his physical world had enlarged, yet he had done nothing to change his way of life. He had been quite happy and saw no need to ever change, but since Samuel confronted him in the streets of

Ramah, everything about his existence had been disrupted. An unsettling premonition descended upon him. His conventional life had ended. If anyone could make sense of it, Ahinoam could. His wife would be the only one he could trust with such a secret, one that would have to be kept for the next seven days.

He dismounted a good distance from the family compound and stealthily moved off the road, leading his horse through a thicket of trees toward the clearing buffeting the perimeter of the compound wall. It was not safe for Saul to come home after being gone for several days. There was plenty of time to plot against him, to design strategic plans, devise cruel tortures that would prove painful. The Philistine army stationed all along the border with Israel kept everyone in the area constantly on the outlook for potential danger. But it was Saul's own home that posed the greatest threat to life and limb.

He was ever alert. The enemy could be hiding behind the trees, lurking in the branches above him. They were a cunning lot. He paused at the edge of the thicket, scanning the open space between the tree line and the waist-high rock wall encircling the compound. Over the wall he saw a couple of old men examining the flower beds inside the gardened courtyard leading into his house and pointing wildly at one another. He could not discern the cause that had set off this argument between his father and his uncle, probably whose day it had been to water the flowers.

Uncle Ner's mental capacity had long been in decline. What was not in decline was how the two brothers liked to argue, their only pastime since neither of them did any work around the property. Saul caught sight of Merab, his oldest daughter, coming from the house. She brought a quick end to the heated exchange by handing each man a cup of goat's milk. Merab had a beautiful calming effect on everyone.

Saul was distracted by movement around the vegetable garden. The thick limbs of an avocado tree were shaking, and he saw Mikal, his younger daughter, picking ripened avocados for the evening meal, a task he knew Mikal was loath to do. She was quite the spitfire and hated getting her hands dirty with work she deemed beneath her. Mikal would find the transition from farmer's daughter to princess an easy one.

He caught a whiff of what Ahinoam must be cooking for supper: fresh pigeon roasted in wine sauce. The aroma made him salivate. Jonathan must have had a good day of hunting. Saul scanned the compound for the twins,

Ishvi and Malki, but did not see them. The sun was descending in the west so they could be coming in from the fields or stabling their horses. And where was Abner, their uncle? He knew better than to leave the compound unguarded and vulnerable to attack. This was unacceptable.

The area seemed clear to make his approach. Saul checked his horse to see if she detected any danger. Her muscles did not ripple with any sign of skittishness, so he led her across the clearing. When he reached the wall he followed it around to the back of the compound where the stables were located. That's when he heard the whirring sound followed by the whip snap. He should have leapt over the wall, but instead he spun around and faced the clearing, toward the surprise attack. The object hit him square in the chest and the brown powder exploded all over his face and head. He would never live down the humiliation.

The flax pouch of flour struck with enough force to knock him off balance. He dropped the reins, and when he plopped on top of the wall, two bodies jumped him from behind, forcing him back onto his feet. His horse immediately drew back. Through the brown powder caked on his eyelids, Saul could see the slinger leap onto his horse and start riding around the clearing, shouting in the pleasure of conquest.

A third body flung itself into the back of his legs and Saul fell backward. The three attackers quickly pinned him to the ground as a blond giant leapt upon the compound wall, his sword drawn and pointed down at Saul who lay helpless on his back.

"Does the enemy yield?" The blond giant's eyes were slit like a viper preparing to strike if Saul gave any indication of hostile intent.

Just then the attacker on his horse jumped from the saddle and withdrew his sword, turning it upon him. "Does the enemy yield?"

Saul looked about at the faces of his assailants. He looked back at the blond giant every bit an equal to Saul in stature and strength: lean, tall, and muscular except for the long blond hair he wrapped in braids that fell over his rock-hard shoulders and secured with a leather headband bearing a wolf's head crest on the front piece.

The blond giant scratched his scruffy beard in irritation. "Yield. I'm hungry and it's near dark."

"Yield. Yield. Yield." The young captors drummed upon Saul's chest accompanying their chanting.

The rider of his horse joined in the chant, jabbing his sword at him.

But Saul refused to yield. He could hold off until the savory aromas from the house made their hunger unbearable.

"Yield. You heard him. Yield." A young woman gripped Saul's beard, thick with brown flour.

Saul's howl of pain as the young woman tugged at his beard elicited squeals of laughter from everyone including the blond giant.

Just then a woman stretched her body over the wall: the black and silver hair flowed over her shoulders, thin lifelines creased across her forehead, and the small crow's feet beginning to extend beyond her large brown eyes, created a pretense of anger.

"Yield like the lady says or no one gets fed tonight." She pushed herself off the wall and folded her arms in front of her.

It was all up to Saul, but the patience of the group had reached its limit and with one voice they cried, "Yield!"

"I yield! I yield!" Saul roared before heaving the young people off his chest, scattering them over the ground like bouncing rocks. He scrambled to his feet, growling and grimacing, arms and hands ready to strike like a wolf, but no one felt threatened. Then Saul stretched over the wall next to the blond giant and tried to kiss his wife.

"Go on with you." Ahinoam shook her head at Saul's filthy appearance and pushed his face away in disgust.

Saul feigned disappointment at her lack of affection. Then he addressed the blond giant standing high above him on the wall.

"Abner, you were lying in wait. How did you know I had arrived today?"

"Helez the baker told us when he delivered our bread that he had seen you this morning dancing in front of his shop with musicians from the prophet school. He said the crowd was so thick he could barely get his cart through to make his deliveries." Abner returned his sword to its sheath.

"I did not notice any crowd, Abner. People were watching?" Saul blinked his eyes in bemusement. He remembered only a strange, new power pouring into him, not the hundreds of eyes looking in wonder at the son of Kish celebrating in worship to Yahweh.

"Just the whole city of Gibeah, Cousin. Helez thought it so incredible he asked, 'Is Saul also among the prophets?' as if you had given up the life of a herdsman."

"Helez delivered our bread in the morning, and you are just now arriving?" Ahinoam pointed toward the setting sun and studied Saul with quizzical eyes.

"I did not come straight home, but went back with the prophets to the high place. I was captivated by what was happening to me, to us, and lost the sense of time."

"I accused Helez of tipping into his wineskin. 'My cousin would never be dancing with the prophets,' I said." Abner's words momentarily routed Saul's memory of his time with the prophets, and he playfully shoved his cousin off the wall into the compound, then he raised his long arms toward his children and they rushed to his side.

"Saul!" a high-pitched voice called from the front entrance to the house.

Two old men waved at him from the courtyard with Merab standing in between, escorting them toward the family gathering at the wall. Ner, Abner's father, was stooped and feeble, requiring Merab to support him. Kish, Saul's father, used a staff for balance, but was too proud to accept help from anyone. He quickened his pace toward his son, distancing himself from his feeble brother aided by his granddaughter.

"My heart was sharp with worry. Let me touch you and know you are real." Kish stretched out his hand toward Saul, reaching over the wall that prohibited the embrace of father and son.

Saul released his children and approached the wall opposite his father. He took Kish's hand and held it firmly against his bearded cheek. "I am real, Father. Let your heart be at ease."

Kish's face, eager for this confirming touch, relaxed into a thankful smile. His exhaled breath quivered with relief.

The children returned to their father, all huddling around him like anxious chicks until he pulled them once again into his side.

"Where have you been? Where have you been?" Uncle Ner wagged his gnarled finger at Saul as Merab gently guided him toward the wall beside his brother, his raspy chastisement drawing smiles from the family.

"You were lost in the world. Where have you been?" Ner's voice was a treble of squeaks and whistles.

"In search of your brother's donkeys, Uncle Ner," Saul replied.

Ner's face became a jumble of confusion. "You lost the donkeys? Kish, he lost your donkeys."

"Hush, brother." Kish waved his hand for Ner to keep silent. "The donkeys wandered away days ago. Saul went to look for them."

"Did he find them? Did he bring them home?" Ner pointed an accusing finger at Saul. "You lost your father's donkeys."

"Ner, would you stop babbling, you deranged old man."

"We were about to send out a search party, Cousin. We thought you were swallowed up by the great wilderness." Abner chuckled and circled his arms as if the wilderness was the whole world.

"Were you lost, Father?" Jonathan's eyes widened at the prospect.

"I was never lost."

"The donkeys. The donkeys." Ner began to wring his hands, on the verge of tears.

"We never found the donkeys, Uncle Ner. We searched for days and were about to give up when Ezbon suggested we seek out the prophet Samuel."

The energetic bustle of the family abruptly stopped when Saul mentioned the name of the prophet. The sound of the name repeated on the lips of the family echoed faintly; a name that carried the weight of mysterious wonder. Only Ner appeared not to be awed by the mention of the Seer's name. Perhaps in his baffled mind the name was just a name with no more value to the vagueness of his identity.

"Tell us what he said to you."

Saul read the trepidation behind his wife's question. Then he looked into the faces of his family. What could he tell them? Samuel had said so much to him. He had sought out the Seer for a little information on the lost livestock, and a day and a night later, he left the Seer with his head dampened from balsam oil and with streams of prophetic words—regarding a future that would cause upheaval in the lives of everyone who stood before him—boiling inside his head. What donkeys? Had not his uncle Ner mentioned it, he might never have remembered why he and Ezbon had set out days ago.

"There is time enough for that later. You look famished, my love. Let's all go inside and eat." Ahinoam waved to the family to head inside the house.

Saul could see the shadow of uncertainty cast over her face. He nodded to her knowing that he would give her details not shared with the rest of the family.

No one made a motion in the direction of the house. All wanted to hear from Saul. All wanted to know what the Seer of Israel had said to the designated head of this clan. All had completely forgotten about supper and their empty stomachs.

"You saw the Seer?" Kish was aghast to hear of this. He scooted closer to his son, his staff braced against the ground for balance.

Saul reached out to take his father's arm and hold him up from the sudden weakness in his legs.

"You spoke with the Seer? You stood before the Seer?"

Saul could have given many answers to this question: I stood. I knelt. I ate. I spoke. I trembled before the Seer. I looked into the eyes of the Seer and saw the truth of my own inadequacy as a man reflected back upon me. Finally, I ran from the Seer.

"Yes, I met with Samuel, and he assured me the donkeys had been found."

"Two days ago. They were brought home two days ago."

Saul knew his cousin was calculating the time. He knew it did not take two days to travel from Ramah to their home.

"Yes, well, there you have it."

Ahinoam stepped in to intervene. "He's called 'The Seer.' He sees things and they come true. Now, the donkeys are home. My husband is home. Dinner is served."

Mikal and the twins elbowed each other as they scrambled over the wall and raced toward the house, but Jonathan remained beside his father.

"I'm glad you're home, Abba."

Saul flung his arm around his son's neck and pulled him into his chest. "I have some tales to tell you."

"Stable your father's horse, Jonathan," Ahinoam said and extended her hand over the wall to bid her husband come.

Saul released his son, and Jonathan climbed onto his father's horse and trotted around the wall to the stable behind the compound. Abner took over for Merab and helped guide his father back to the house. Merab took the opportunity to embrace her father before she and her grandfather began to follow the others into the house.

"I have missed you," Saul whispered into his wife's ear and dropped an arm over her shoulder.

She responded by latching her arm around his waist as they began to move toward the house. "I sense you are changed."

"Much has happened on this trip." Saul pressed closer to her. "Once everyone is asleep, I will tell you everything."

Ahinoam looked into his dirty face and patted her husband's chest. A puff of flour-cloud rose into the air. "And after you have bathed."

Saul stood on the ladder, the upper half of his body protruding out of the opening of the roof, eyeing the sky for the first sign of stellar activity. His official duty was to keep everyone honest. Jonathan, Ishvi, and Malki lay or sat on their woven mats, each with his blanket wrapped around him, their eyes latched onto the firmament above in this competition to be the first to spot the flying star.

The first two who picked out the burning orb would be exempt from disposing the contents of the buckets of night waste from both houses in the compound in the morning. Each week the degrading job had to be assigned. No one ever volunteered. The girls were automatically exempt, but the boys had no choice. However, Saul devised competitions for his sons to keep the selection process evenhanded. Jonathan was in favor of a slingshot contest, which he always won. His twin brothers howled in complaint of their big brother's unfair advantage. But on clear nights picking out shooting stars equalized the competition.

Tonight the stars appeared fixed in their positions, none of them willing to let go of their place in the universe to streak across the sky. Ahinoam had called twice from the ground floor that Saul's water was nearly ready for his bath and for him to come down.

"Hurry, boys. I'm tired and want to take a bath."

"Let's play, 'Pick a hand.'"

Malki was ready for a new game and rolled over on his stomach.

"I don't have anything with me...for that...game."

Saul patted up and down his garments with his hands in search of an object suitable for the game. Then he felt a solid object in his left pocket and pulled out the ram's horn of oil Samuel had emptied over his head, holding it in his open palm.

"Where did you get that, Father?" His sons were curious but not awed by the horn in his hand.

Saul had to think of how this object found its way into his pocket.

He could not remember. He did recall seeing it in the prophet's hand, and remembered the oil being poured over his head, but the next thing that came to his mind was the memory of racing to catch up with Ezbon who waited for him on the outskirts of Ramah.

"It is a ram's horn that once contained the Spirit of Yahweh." Saul spoke in a hoarse whisper. His fingers began to tremble. His reaction was quick. He slammed his hand with the horn against his chest.

All three boys jumped when they witnessed their father's reaction. Then they burst into laughter at the emergent fear that gripped their father's face.

It took a moment for Saul to realize that his sons were laughing and why they might be amused at his antics. He was trying to frighten them and they were not about to get taken by the ruse. It was a great relief to Saul that his three sons believed he was just trying to scare them. He did not have to confess his renewed fear at the sight of the horn.

"All right, Malki is first." Saul put his hands behind his back and shifted the horn back and forth in his hands before telling Malki to make his selection.

Malki chose his father's left hand and cheered when Saul brought his arm around to reveal the horn. Ishvi also won when it was his turn. At Jonathan's defeat the twins leapt to their feet and danced on the roof, jeering at their older brother who groaned in dismayed by the thought of the foul chore awaiting him at sunrise.

"Good night, boys. Go to sleep now." Saul slipped the horn into his pocket. He grabbed the wooden door and put it in place, closing off the boys on the roof, then climbed down the ladder to the second floor.

Once he stepped off the ladder, he turned around and looked below at Ahinoam stacking clean dishes on the shelving built into the south wall of the common room. When he caught her eye, he waved toward the girls' room on the opposite side from where he stood to indicate he was going to check if they were asleep. His wife pointed sternly at the tub, and he smiled. Then he tiptoed over to the girls' room and stuck his head around the edge of their privacy curtain. They were both asleep and had neglected to extinguish the oil lamp perched on the raised bench attached to the back wall. He exhaled in frustration at such senseless waste of oil. This was a chronic issue with these two, one about which he was constantly harping.

He stepped around his sleeping daughters over to the bench. Propped against the wall was the collection of cloth dolls and clay figurines the girls and their mother had made or purchased over the years. Surely the prophet did not mean for him to take these away from his girls. Surely they could never be considered idols in the sight of the Almighty. Saul patted the horn in his pocket and decided Samuel's directive to rid the house of any would-be idols could be put off for another time. He would broach the subject again with Samuel, perhaps when he was in a different frame of mind. He bent over the lamp and blew out the flame.

Saul descended the ladder from the second floor into the ground floor common room. He went to the front door as Ahinoam moved a small table covered with bathing oils and grooming tools over by the tub. Before closing the door, Saul looked across the compound at his cousin's house. It was dark. No lamps burning in any window, the result of having no wife or children with which to contend. But Abner did have two old men to care for, which, in Saul's mind, evened the hands of balance. Kish and Ner could be a handful. Abner had taken on the responsibility of his father and uncle, though daily care for two widowers was really shared among the whole family. Saul did wonder what might happen to this arrangement if Abner ever did decide to get married; convincing a prospective wife to care for two additional old men might prove difficult.

Saul heard Ahinoam clear her throat, and he looked back into the room over his shoulder. She stood behind the tub, motioning for him. The low light of the fire and the steam rising off the hot water in the tub made the image of his wife vibrate. He would need her now more than ever, but he still could not find the courage to explain the drastic change that was coming in their lives. Saul knew Ahinoam did not like surprises. He could not take her to Mizpah in seven days and astonish her with Samuel's proclamation that she and her husband were to be the king and queen of Israel. He had to tell her.

Saul closed the door. He shed his clothes as he approached the tub but removed the horn from the pocket of his robe before dropping the garment onto the floor. He patted his wife's bottom before stepping into the tub, which caused her to shake her head and smile in amusement. He tried to kiss her, but she blocked his advance with her raised arms. Not until he had been scrubbed clean from days of travel and the residue of flour from their children's ambush.

Saul gave a disappointed sigh and eased down inside the tub, allowing his skin time to adjust to the temperature of the hot water. In spite of the tub's excessive size, it was impossible for him to completely submerge his body. When Ahinoam pushed Saul's head under the water, his knees rose well above the rim of the tub like two hairy mountain peaks. The thick hair on his legs lay plastered over the bold contours of his muscled limbs.

Saul held his breath and felt the strength of his wife's hands digging into his scalp and through his beard, loosening the grime and flour he had been unable to remove with the wet towel she had given him before they sat down to eat their supper earlier that evening. The oil Samuel poured over his head in Ramah was being diluted in the bath water, water that would be dispensed by the bucketful the next morning throughout the flower and vegetable gardens. A part of him wished the ointment could never be washed out, that a thin sheen of the holy emollient would always cover his head as a reminder of its purpose and the symbolic presence of Yahweh.

His muscles began to relax in the heat of the water, and he allowed himself the pleasure of the moment, a calm release of bodily fatigue that only came when he felt completely safe. Never before had a day taken so long to complete its cycle of time or been so full of strange events, and now, finally, it was nearing its blessed end. Yet it was not completely over. There remained one more task: recounting the events to the most important person in his life.

Saul felt Ahinoam's fingers gently tugging his head to the surface. He sucked a deep breath of air into his lungs the moment his mouth rose above the water line.

"Your hair and beard were more oily than usual." Ahinoam took the towel from off the table and wiped her hands. "Did you stick your head in a bucket of olive oil?"

"Sit down, please." Saul rubbed water out of his eyes with the back of his hand.

"But I haven't finished yet. I still have—"

"Please, pull up a stool. I need to tell you something."

Ahinoam looked at Saul, his hair plastered down the sides of his face, his beard dripping water like thawing ice. "You are water-logged. It is hard to take you seriously."

"I know. But this is not play." His tone of voice and the fixed glare of his eyes, not upon her but upon an object he held in his hands, made his wife take notice.

Ahinoam went over to the loom he had built for her years ago and grabbed the stool in front of it. She placed it beside the tub and sat down.

The two of them were silent, listening only to the crackle and hiss of the fire, the gentle rippling of the water in the tub, and their breathing—in sync just as their whole life had been. Their conversations on serious matters usually centered on familial subjects and were resolved with time and patience. This was different.

"On the roof tonight, the boys asked what this was and where I had gotten it." Saul opened his hand that held the ram's horn, and then offered it to Ahinoam. She raised the hollowed-out vessel before the firelight for a clearer examination.

"You said you saw a change within me. It is true. I am changed. The prophet has changed me, and I fear it will change everything we have ever known."

Ahinoam lowered the horn away from the light of the fire and placed it upon the towel draped over her lap. "I'm listening."

Saul took a few deep breaths to calm his heart. He reached down and took the horn that lay on the towel in Ahinoam's lap. He held it with both hands.

"Yesterday this horn contained an anointment, not a healing anointment or perfume or seasoning for cooking. The prophet referred to the contents as the Spirit of Yahweh. He poured the oil on my head and told me that the Lord Almighty had anointed me leader over His people, 'Yahweh's inheritance,' to be exact."

Saul took his eyes off the horn and looked at his wife. Her lips began to unfurl, but when they started to quiver, she bit down on them. Yet she never took her eyes off of him. She gazed at him with a look of unknowable wonder.

"The day before this, Samuel met us in a street in Ramah. We had come about the lost drove of donkeys. I did not recognize him, and after he identified himself, he said the donkeys were found. Then he said something mystifying, 'To whom is all the desire of Israel turned, if not to you and your father's house?' It was so absurd...our family? Benjamites? The smallest clan of the smallest tribe of Israel? How could this be so?"

"We knew the tribal leaders were begging the prophet to appoint a king, but..." Ahinoam could not finish her thought.

"I know, but whether a king or prophet or judge were to lead us, it would not affect our quiet life. We would go about life...go about..."

Ahinoam placed her hand upon Saul's open palm covering the horn. "...Go about life as normal. What happened once the prophet spoke this to you?"

"He took us to his prophet school built on his estate and prepared a great feast with all his students. Afterward, the prophet and I spent the night on the roof of his house. I watched him pace and pray upon the roof. I know that it was hard for me to remain awake.

"At dawn he instructed Ezbon to go ahead of us, and the prophet and I went into a wooded area off the road. That is where he anointed me and kissed me in a sign of reverence for my new station in life. His kiss felt fatherly, but distant, unsure." Saul dropped his head at the memory of Samuel's gesture, only a customary sign of esteem. "Without real affection."

"How could there be affection. He does not know you." Ahinoam came quick to her husband's defense.

Saul placed his other hand on top of hers and gently caressed it. "There is more. Everything the prophet foretold would happen to us on the way home came to pass exactly as he said it would, down to the last detail of my being caught up in the adoration of Yahweh with the prophets from Gibeah. Up until then, I had only felt this fear, confusion, and wonder at each turn of events. But there, in front of Helez's bakery, I felt this unforeseen rush of power that propelled me into the gathering of prophets. At first I resisted, but it felt as though I were tied to the end of a rope pulling me forward by an invisible force and then whipping me around. I suppose you might call that dancing or worshiping. We've seen the prophets perform such."

Saul gently removed Ahinoam's hand covering the horn. "From there I went with the prophets to the high place outside the city where they have their school time, and we continued to worship around the altar until... until I found myself coming home...as if I had found a portal and exited out of a trance."

He touched the horn with his fingertips. "Such strange events, wondrously strange, all from the contents of this small vessel."

Ahinoam stared at the empty vessel as her husband stroked the rough horned surface with his fingers. Saul's silence meant he had spoken most of what he needed to tell her, but perhaps not everything. Her husband had captured the story in its startling clarity, but she knew the heart of her husband, his retelling left no doubt in her mind that there were no patches of mist in his memory to cloud the facts. He would not alter the sequence of events or slant the accuracy to influence her understanding. Yet she believed he was not finished. The settlings of truth still lay at the bottom of his heart.

It was not until Ahinoam heard the chattering of her husband's teeth that she realized he had stopped speaking. She had been staring down at the horn, watching her husband rubbing his fingers over it, listening to his words, imagining their meaning, marveling at the scope of the effect. She looked up to see her husband shivering. Ahinoam stuck her hand in the water.

"The water has turned cold." She flung the water drops off her hand and stood up.

"You should have said something."

"I have been saying something."

She took the horn from his hand and set it on the side table. Then she pushed his head beneath the water one last time for him to scrub out the residue of grime and flour. Ahinoam held out the towel when he raised up. As he stood, she draped the towel over his body and helped him out of the tub. Together they moved beside the fire to allow its heat to warm him. The fire sizzled as the water droplets fell onto the hot embers.

Ahinoam was suddenly aware of the oils and grooming utensils lying on the table along with the ram's horn—empty now, its divine contents diluted by the bath water.

"I need to trim your beard...cut your hair."

"Another time."

Ahinoam left the warmth of the fire and slipped out into the courtyard when Saul stepped behind the curtain of the bedroom to fetch a clean robe. After a few moments, while she gazed into the heavens, she felt her husband's strong arms wrap around her and they both scanned the vast, black expanse above them.

"I go in search of lost donkeys and return home a king."

Ahinoam turned inside his strong embrace to face her husband. "Then it is so. You will be king."

"I will be king." Saul pointed to a star streaking across the sky like an arrow shot from a bow, its long, flaming tail making an incision on the darkness.

She laid her head upon his chest, ignoring the blazing star. Her voice was a somber echo of its normal bold quality. There it was. Her husband had spoken the last swallow of truth she had been waiting to hear...he would be king.

"I am more fit for the loom and the care of my family."

"And I for plowing a field and being a herdsman."

Ahinoam raised her head off his chest and looked about the compound. "What do we do now?"

"In seven days we are to meet the prophet in Mizpah. He is summoning the people. All Israel will be there, he says."

She pressed herself back into his warmth, nestling her head again upon his chest.

"All of Israel will be there." Behind her closed eyes she could not imagine such a gathering.

Twenty-Six

SAUL HAD TO SCRATCH HIS HEAD TO REMEMBER THE LAST TIME they had been to Rainbow Cave.

"Years. Not since the twins were born." Ahinoam pointed a playful yet accusing finger at him. "I doubt you can even find it now, it's been so long."

Saul smiled at her teasing indictment and blame for the gradual misplacement of a romantic side to their life. But Saul had shocked her when he proposed the idea the day after his return from Ramah.

"Let's take some time for ourselves, no work, no family...a whole day... just us...before Mizpah." He took great pleasure at his wife dropping the wooden bowls she was putting back on the shelf after supper.

"The whole day? What will we do all that time?" she asked that night in bed after the house was asleep, and she pressed her body against his back.

Saul rolled over and brought his lips right up to her earlobe. "We'll think of something," he whispered.

The laugh that burst from her mouth could have awakened the children sleeping on the floor above them.

The day before the trek to Rainbow Cave while going about the everyday household chores around the home and gardens, Ahinoam fielded questions from her inquisitive daughters about where their parents were going that would keep them away for the entire day.

"Why do you call it 'Rainbow Cave'?" Merab had grown tired of her mother's slippery evasions to the more personal questions.

"There is an underground stream running deep inside the cave, and at some point, I don't remember how far we had to walk, but at some point the cave opens into this cavern. Underground streams have created a large pool of water on one side of the cavern, and the water is funneled along the wall and disappears back into the ground. The stream comes to the surface again near the entrance and flows out of the mouth of the cave. Inside the cavern, there is a sandy area beside the pool, and high above the pool there are cracks in the walls like gashes, allowing in the sunlight. At a certain point in the day shafts of light cut through the slits above, and as the mist rises from the water for that brief moment a rainbow appears. Once after some heavy rains, the mist was so thick, we saw a double rainbow, one on top of the other."

"Why haven't you ever taken us to this place?" Her mother's story had sparked Mikal's romantic nature.

"I don't know, really. So much has happened. You children started showing up and farm life took over. We just sort of forgot about it, I guess."

"You will be gone the whole day?" Merab's face was pinched in bewilderment.

"What could you be doing all that time?" In spite of her curiosity, such a dramatic break in routine family life was too disconcerting for Mikal.

Ahinoam opened her mouth to respond to her daughter's questions, but then caught herself with a sudden influx of impossible answers. Both girls had come of age and their young bodies had flowered. They were showing signs of wakefulness on matters of the heart, but Ahinoam decided this was not the time for a conversation on the consequences of romantic attraction to the opposite sex.

"We'll think of something." Ahinoam was quite happy to leave her daughters in a state of confusion concerning their parents' private lives, and by the befuddled look on her daughters' faces, she knew she had deflected a discussion of the pleasures they might have with their future husbands to another day.

That same day, Saul was sitting on the wall while Ahinoam trimmed his beard and cut his hair when Abner and Jonathan returned from the field. That morning Saul had informed Abner and Jonathan that he was not going with them. He would be staying home all day. When Abner stormed out of the stables, Saul knew that his cousin was having none of it.

"Prepare for the coming wrath," Saul muttered to Ahinoam under his breath.

"You stayed home this morning for a haircut?" Abner circled around in front of the wall.

"Ahinoam was beginning to confuse me with the donkeys." Saul picked up a handful of his freshly cut hair from the top of the wall.

"You stayed home for a haircut." Abner grumbled as he paced in front of Saul.

"And I will not be working tomorrow either, Cousin. Ahinoam and I will be going to Rainbow Cave in the morning."

Abner stopped in his tracks, bent over and stared into Saul's large brown eyes as if he could divine his cousin's malady.

"You were gone for days looking for donkeys. You're not home a day from Ramah and you decide you are no longer going to work, that you can just take off anytime and play. What is wrong with you, Cousin? Did the Seer put a spell on you?"

Saul let out a nervous chuckle at Abner's question. Perhaps Samuel had put a spell on him. The prophet and his words from Yahweh had certainly changed his life.

"This may not be the best time to tell you, but the family needs to travel to Mizpah in a few days, and I must prepare for it."

"Mizpah? Prepare? What in the world are you talking about? You just got back from traveling." Abner stood up straight.

"I am sorry, Abner. I will be no use to you. Take the twins to the fields."

"The twins are no use to me in the fields." Abner threw up his hands in disgust and, as he marched back toward the stables, he passed Jonathan and blurted, "Your father is under a spell. He will not work with us. Come with me."

Saul waved for his son to go back to the stables with Abner. "You will understand soon enough, son. Just go with your uncle."

"Should we not tell them?" Ahinoam said.

Together they watched their bewildered son shrug his shoulders and trot off to the stables after his uncle.

"I think it is best to wait. What if something changes? I do not want to tell them and then find out someone else is chosen. We wait for the prophet to announce Yahweh's decision in the manner in which he sees fit." He grabbed his wife's hand and kissed it. "Until then, we are going to Rainbow Cave."

Saul underestimated the time it would take. He was sure they would find their favorite spot on earth, or rather under the earth, by mid-morning and be having a breakfast of figs and honey cakes at the entrance of the cave. But the sun was well on its way to the top of the sky and they still had not found the cave. The terrain had changed significantly since their last visit, a landscape that no longer matched their memories. His wife could not conceal her amusement when Saul led them on two different trails with one ending in a farmer's field and the other at an overlook with a steep drop-off. If they ever did find it, the dark cave and its cold streams would be a welcome relief from the rising heat of the sun.

Saul was about to admit defeat when the main trail opened onto the face of a cliff. He was sure they had reached another dead-end, but in the quiet of the surroundings they both could hear the sound of running water.

Saul slipped off his horse, handed the reins to Ahinoam, and disappeared in the undergrowth. He began hacking his way through the foliage with his sword. After a few minutes, he stopped. "I've come to the edge of a stream." His disembodied voice rose in the air. "It might lead to the mouth of the cave."

They led the horses through the cold stream beneath a thick canopy of lush foliage. Saul cut a sprig of lavender growing wild on the ground underneath the foliage and handed it to Ahinoam who tucked it behind her ear.

It was not far before they came to the opening of the cave. They stood before it looking for specific signs that this was indeed Rainbow Cave.

"It does look familiar, but I don't remember this overgrowth of trees and shrubbery in front of the cave. I thought it was clear around the entrance."

"It has been a long time." Ahinoam jabbed him in the ribs with her finger.

Saul pretended to be in pain from the jab before taking the reins from her hand. He led the horses out of the stream and tethered them to a tree in the shaded area near the entrance of the cave. He removed the blankets from the horses' backs and scattered some straw on the ground that he brought from home for them to munch on while they waited. Saul helped slip the bag of food over Ahinoam's shoulders, and then he lit the torch from the smoldering coals he had collected from last night's cook fire. He blew his breath on the coals inside the metal capsule to heat them up. When the torch ignited, he tossed the blankets over his shoulder and they entered the cave.

Just beyond the entrance into the cave they came to the source of the stream bubbling up from the ground. Saul took Ahinoam's hand and helped her jump over the fountainhead. With one long step he got to the other side. They continued on, with the torch extended at the end of Saul's long reach. The ground went from loamy to hard-packed until it became all sand as they moved out of the tunnel and into the open cavern.

"It feels smaller. I remember it being larger." Ahinoam released her husband's hand and moved toward the pool of water. She looked up at the shafts of sunlight coming through the gashes in the earth above them. "Put out the light. We don't need it."

She stopped at the edge of the pool and did not take her eyes off the rocky slits in the ceiling above her.

Saul extinguished the torch in the capsule of the coals, and then spread the blankets on the sand. Once he unbuckled his sword and dropped it beside the blanket, she felt him beside her. She slipped her hand into his and pointed upward. Saul followed her lifted gaze until he saw the light along the craggy underbelly of the earth as the sun moved across the sky.

"We just made it." Their eyes were fixed on light shafts coming through the cracks at the high point of the cavern.

And there it appeared in the rising mist, the multicolored arc shimmering through the vapor and water droplets collecting on the ceiling before falling back into the pool below. The dispersion of color through purified water radiated over the whole space, illuminating every cranny of rock, and for a few brief moments, removed all shadows from the world. There was no flickering of light. The straight beams cut through the top of the earth and offered them shelter beneath a bright path to the world above. Saul and Ahinoam were entranced, their gaze clear and steady until the light shafts slipped down along the cavern wall and plunged straight into the rippling pool of water. The sun was now directly overhead, burning away all traces of the rainbow's colorful brushstroke pattern.

Saul turned toward his wife and cupped his hands beneath her neck. "I am safest here with you. I fear nothing here with you. My soul is at rest here with you."

He removed the stem of lavender from behind her ear and ran the tip of the flower across her forehead, down the bridge of her nose, her mouth, her chin, and along the ring of her neck. He suspended the sprig between their noses long enough for them to enjoy a shared whiff of the sweet aroma, and then he tossed it onto a blanket. Saul pulled the bow of ribbon tied around the top of Ahinoam's robe until it was free of its knot. No rainbow, no light of the sun, no pool of pure water, no natural wonder carved out beneath the surface of the earth by eons of time could compare to the beauty he saw in his wife.

Ahinoam held the sleeves of Saul's robe as he pulled his arms out. All the dark nights and cold days, the sorrows and joys, the fears and apprehensions, stopped at the edges of the blankets by the heated touch of skin to skin. The world was above them, awaiting them—those to charge, those to keep safe, those to control. But for now, all conscious knowledge of what lay before them was banished. They were unshackled, free to indulge, released to become the sole translators of the meaning of joy, leaving behind only the fleeting impressions of their united bodies pressed upon the sand beneath them.

After the summons from the prophet and judge of Israel had gone out, all tribal chieftains and heads of clans began gathering in Mizpah. Saul did not want to travel with the other clan representatives living around Gibeah, or leaders of the tribe of Benjamin when they left for Mizpah days ahead of the event. He saw no benefit in spending all that time in Mizpah waiting for the prophet's public statement of the king's coronation and listening to gossip and speculation on the qualities and nature of the man chosen. Some people were sure to be disappointed, so why should he subject himself to grumbling before the fact. His family would be a bulwark of support against the negative reactions sure to arise once Samuel made known who would be Israel's first king. Given the other tribe's generational prejudice against Benjamin, the one tribe that caused the first civil war in Israel's history, Saul expected the worse, and his family would be a comfort. They could make the journey in a day, there and back, traveling at a moderate pace.

The children were thrilled. They had never traveled beyond Gibeah, and it meant a day without chores. At supper the night before it was all any of them could talk about. Abner, however, resented having to be gone from the farm when there was so much work to be done, especially since the work had been hamstrung by his absent cousin.

"I have more important things to do than listen to an old prophet rave about selecting a king." Abner washed down his last bite of roast quail with a swallow of water.

"You have been acting a bit strange, Abba," Jonathan offered.

The family had taken their meal outside around a fire.

"I have needed some time for reflection, son." Saul gave Ahinoam a quick smile.

"You cannot reflect behind a plow, Cousin?" Abner tossed the quail bones in the fire and wiped his greasy fingers on his shirt. "You cannot reflect while you move the donkeys from one pasture to the other?"

Saul found it difficult to tell his cousin how his heart was changing, getting him ready to take on the leadership of the nation. What had once preoccupied his time and energy, no longer interested him. How could he explain this to Abner or anyone other than his dear wife.

Once his hands were clean of quail grease, Abner grabbed Saul's hand and pulled it toward him. He raised it to the firelight so he could see. "You get your hair and beard cut, and then Ahinoam cleans and trims your nails. What sort of madness was this?"

Abner dropped his cousin's hand and leaned back against the perimeter wall.

Saul did not respond to the grumbling of his cousin. It was better to remain silent, and the family was willing to allow the cousins to keep the dispute between themselves.

"What's a king going to do for us?" Abner said, breaking the tense silence.

"I need you to be there with me...for me. I am going to need you."

Saul had to convince Abner to come with the family without telling him the real purpose for the trip. But Abner just glared at him for his mysterious answer.

"I need you here, working with me, on our farm." Abner leaned in to the light.

"Abner, it is just for a day. The prophet has summoned us, all the tribal leaders. We must represent our clan and witness the coming changes for our nation."

Abner rose to his feet and kicked at the dirt. Then he bent down and tucked his arms under an arm of Ner and Kish, lifting them to their feet.

"I will go." Abner made no attempt to conceal his exasperation. "But life better be different after this. You have not been right since Ramah. Life better change."

"Life will change, Cousin. I assure you."

Abner looked at his house, and turned Ner and Kish in that direction.

"I must get the fathers to bed." Abner started leading the old men to the house.

"We leave at first light, Cousin."

"First light." Abner tossed his grumbling response over his shoulder.

How might he lead a country when he could not even lead his own cousin. Saul's heart was changing to take on the leadership of the nation and not just personal, domestic interests. The new heart Samuel spoke of was awakening, a heart fit for a king, not a farmer, and surely his cousin would understand once Samuel announced Yahweh's choice for king. So a new heart would be required of him, a heart full of wisdom to rule a people, no longer concerned just for his kith and kin, but for the welfare of a nation.

The rest of the family bade their parents good night and went off to bed. Once alone around the fire it was safe to talk.

"That did not go well." Saul snapped a twig and tossed the pieces into the fire.

"He will understand soon enough." Ahinoam laid her head on Saul's shoulder.

"It's not him I worry about. It's me. I expect Abner's reaction to this king business to be the common response. It doesn't build confidence."

Ahinoam leaned up and kissed her husband's newly trimmed cheek. "He will come around. They will all come around."

Twenty-Seven

SAUL'S CHILDREN WERE WIDE-EYED FROM THE TIME THEY climbed into the wagon until they arrived at the Stone of Help monument erected on the road between the hilltop city of Mizpah and Samuel's hometown of Ramah. Ahinoam drove the wagon with Ner and Kish perched on a bench attached to the back of the driver's seat. Saul and Jonathan rode their horses in front while Abner rode behind.

Saul kept glancing over at Jonathan as they rode; his son's eyes focused straight ahead, his face an expression of maturity beyond his years. This boy was a source of consistent pride. Almost from the time Jonathan could walk and speak, every task, every chore, every command given, every request made of him, he performed with no objection and completed without requiring his father or Uncle Abner or anyone to come after to correct.

He was the consistent peacemaker between his siblings, even negotiating filial truces when arguments arose between his elders. Yet he had a warrior's heart, fearless when fending off attacks from wild beasts who threatened their livestock. No citizen in Gibeah could match his skill with a sling. He was deadly accurate, known to hit quail in flight. It pained Saul to think Jonathan's skill with a sling would eventually be tested in combat, but having him at the king's side was worth the risk. He was an inspiration to anyone who stood in his presence. Saul could see in his son the qualities of leadership he felt he lacked. He knew he would be relying on Jonathan in ways that neither of them could anticipate. The thought of Yahweh choosing him to be king in order to prepare Jonathan to assume the throne calmed Saul's heart and gave him a clarity of purpose. The moment he became king, Saul would begin to groom this first prince of Israel to be his successor. He would be king if only to make his son a true king.

Saul reached his long arm across the divide between them, landing a playful punch on Jonathan's shoulder almost knocking him off his horse. Saul burst out laughing at his son's startled face. "Your face has been scowling at the world for the last hour. What are you thinking?"

"I have never been this far away from home. Everything is new."

"Yes it is. It is all new. Everything will all be new." Saul reached over again this time to place a tender hand upon his son's shoulder. "I am proud of you, son."

Campsites began to appear around the outskirts of Mizpah, lining both sides of the road leading to the monument. The outside circumference around the Stone of Help was reserved for the representatives of the twelve tribes. For the last several days, these delegates had been streaming into Mizpah ahead of the ceremony, setting up their official booths and raising their tribal banners so that the chiefs of each clan would know where to register once they arrived. It was Samuel's explicit instruction that all tribal leaders and heads of families be present at this auspicious occasion and that there should be a record kept of all the designated officials in attendance.

Inside the circle near the Stone of Help was an area reserved for the priests and Levites. Their private tents, makeshift offices, and the listing booths all looped around the great Stone. The appointed tribal leader was to register his delegation with the scribes at a listing booth once their contingent arrived.

Beside the monument, a tent was pitched for the Ark of the Covenant surrounded by an honor guard of heavily armed soldiers. Eleazar had transported the Ark from his father's house for this occasion. Ahiah, the High Priest, had overseen the construction of a raised platform from which he and Samuel would stand before all the assembly. On this day, the Ark of the Covenant would be carried out of the tent and set before the platform once Samuel and the High Priest had taken their place on the stage. It was important for the people to see that the Presence, the Almighty, the God of their fathers, was in attendance for the selection process. Next to the platform was a stone table for the preparation of the sacrifices and an altar. There were to be sacrifices made after the king was chosen.

Merchants were allowed to erect booths along the road leading to the great ring of twelve tribes, but forbidden beyond that point. This was a somber moment in the history of Israel, and Samuel would not allow commerce to overshadow the event. Buying and selling were necessary to help sustain this influx of people but it was not to become a festive occasion.

Jonathan was the first to spot the Benjamite banner with its wolf head insignia flapping in the hot wind above the tribal tent as the family made their way along the road toward the great circle. When he pointed it out, Saul waved for Ahinoam to follow them. Father and son cut off the road and dismounted. The area was crowded with tents and booths and hordes of people, so they led their horses the rest of the way, clearing a path for Ahinoam. Once she parked the wagon near the tent of Benjamin, all the children leapt out. They had never seen anything like this great assembly. This was no simple trip into town, or attending services at the synagogue, or spending a day at the harvest festival each year in Gibeah. All the peoples of the world had gathered at this spot.

"You boys help your grandfather and uncle out of the wagon." Ahinoam stood in the wagon and stretched her back. "Your father will find out what we are to do now that we're here."

Malki and Ishvi climbed back into the wagon to assist the two old men.

Saul gave the reins of his horse to Jonathan for him to tie off onto the side of the wagon and then went to help his wife from her seat.

"Do you see him anywhere?" Saul waited as Ahinoam looked over the bustling crowd to see if she spotted Samuel anywhere.

"I'm not even sure what he looks like."

"He is unmistakable." Saul reached out to help her down. "I should go into the tribal tent with Father and see what we should do."

"How will the prophet know you are here?"

"I don't know. His instructions were for me to come to Mizpah." Saul lifted her from the wagon and set her on the ground. "I am here. Now it's up to him to find me."

The twins brought their grandfather and uncle to Saul as Abner and the girls trailed behind.

"Ima, this must be all the people in the world." Mikal locked onto her mother's side. Merab followed her sister's example and latched onto Ahinoam's other side.

"Come, Abba, we should let them know we are here." Saul pointed Kish in the direction of the entrance to their tribal tent.

Abner followed Saul and Kish while the rest of the family stayed behind.

The three men moved through the crowd toward their tribal tent, taking in the view of the whole area around the Stone of Help. The tent of Benjamin was the smallest of the twelve and the least adorned. The other tribal chieftains had tents designed to dazzle the eye and envelop as much ground as possible. If this was the moment for Israel to receive her first king, then each tribe intended to vie for maximum preference. From tent peg to tent peg, from center post to the top of the tent where tribal banners proudly flew, every effort had been expended to attract the eye of the king by its elaborate and colorful decorations. First impressions were of vital importance. Chests overflowing with precious stones and tribal artifacts, gold and silver, and finely woven rugs and tapestries were placed in front of each tent. Once the king was chosen, these gifts would be presented to him. Whoever was given the crown, all the tribes would compete for the king's favor, and its leaders would seek ways to benefit by having the ear of the king.

The puny size and the drab gray colors of the goat-haired tent of Benjamin could not compete with the elaborate measures taken by its eleven older brothers. The only gift on display in front of the tent of Benjamin for the future king was a magnificent, black stallion, sixteen hands in height from hoof to shoulder top with a white blaze running down its long snout. Whoever rode this beast would be seen from a great distance. Three guards were posted to keep curious onlookers from approaching the horse.

"What are we doing here, Cousin? What have you gotten us into?" Abner was taking in the expanse of tribal opulence as they marched toward the tent of their clan.

"Not me, Cousin. The prophet summoned us. This is his staging."

The three of them paused at the entrance of the tent of Benjamin. Saul caught the eye of the stallion giving him a look of dark knowing no human eye could cast. The beast had recognized its future rider. The beast knew. The beast flung back its head, surprising the attendant who held the reins, nearly yanking his arm from its socket and scattering the skittish guards. Saul smiled that this beast seemed to acknowledge the future king by rearing up on his hind legs and pounding the ground with his forelegs.

"The family of Kish has finally decided to make an appearance," a voice boomed from inside the tent. "We expected you days ago."

Saul stepped inside the tent and saw Jeush rise from behind a table and start pushing the clansmen out of the way as he came around to greet the new arrivals.

"Good to see you, my friend." Jeush, the leader of the tribe of Benjamin, threw his arms around Saul and kissed his cheek. The intensity of his embrace forced them back outside the tent. The space inside the tent expanded when the two of them spilled out of the interior.

"Is this your beast?" Saul pointed to the stallion.

"Indeed it is."

"Your stock is the best in Israel, my friend." Saul slapped Jeush's broad shoulders.

"And I have the dented face and broken nose to prove it." Jeush pointed to his face and laughed. "This brute could face down the Destroyer himself."

Jeush marched toward the obsidian monster rearing back on his hind legs. The terrified attendant scrambled away the moment Jeush jerked the reins out of his hands.

"Calm. Calm." Jeush stood before this high-strung beast without flinching, his voice composed and strong. "Calm yourself. You'll make a bad impression on our king."

The horse's forelegs crashed onto the ground, rippling the muscles from neck to flanks. Jeush held his hand upon the horse's head and every muscle in its body relaxed.

"There, there. That's my beautiful one. That's my noble one." Jeush turned his back on the creature, letting the reins slip from his hand. The horse followed Jeush as he headed back to Saul. "Adara. I named him Adara...beautiful, noble. Fit for a king, don't you think? Whoever the prophet may choose, Adara will—"

Before Jeush could finish his boast, the blare of trumpets and shofar began to sound from the inner circle around the monument. Shouts from the crowd directed Saul's attention toward the open carriage rumbling down the road toward the monument.

Samuel and Shira were seated in the back with two young students riding beside him. A second wagon followed behind filled with Samuel's other students. Saul knew that Samuel and his entourage of young prophets were a purposeful reminder to implant in the conscious of the king, and every king who would follow, that no matter who held the throne of Israel, the prophets of Yahweh would always be present to speak for the Almighty. They would always be a force for Yahweh. If the day proved Saul was to be king, then he hoped Samuel would help his heart remain steadfast.

Saul watched in wonder as the carriage and wagon passed near where they stood.

"What a pompous entrance." Jeush and Saul stood side by side and Adara thrust his head between them. "So you want to see the delusional old man put on his show." Jeush put his hand under Adara's neck and began to scratch it.

"I think not, my friend." Saul felt the reverence of the moment growing deeper within him. "The prophet is worthy of being the mouthpiece for Yahweh. None of his words have fallen to the ground."

"He was so opposed to the idea of appointing a king. He finally came to his senses or was forced to. Any king will be better than his two sons."

"And the king will need his wisdom," Saul whispered as he watched Samuel's carriage stop beside the Stone of Help.

"Next time, don't stand there like a naked chicken." Jeush grabbed the arm of the attendant and slapped the reins back into his wary hand. "Adara knows when you're afraid. He can smell it on you."

Saul looked back at Jeush, thinking that he might be referring to him, but saw the attendant leading Adara away.

Jeush turned to Saul. "I must go to the inner circle to hold the banner of our tribe. Join me as soon as your father has put his family name on the scroll. The prophet wants a record of all clan chiefs who attended this day."

Saul took the arm of his father and ushered him into the tent to sign his name as Jeush and the other clansmen marched away.

Kish took the metal cylinder from the Levite administrating the record of the presence of every clan and bent over the scroll to scratch his name, "Kish, son of Abiel," next to the insignia of the profile of a wolf's head inside the circle of a yellow sun.

"A great day for Israel." Kish handed the small rod back to the Levite.

"May it be so." The Levite spoke as if reserving the right to judge the greatness of this day after the results were made known.

Saul handed Kish off to Abner once the two emerged from the tent.

"I guess you and the family can follow Jeush and join him in the inner circle reserved for the tribe of Benjamin," Saul said to Abner.

"Front row for the show." Abner could not hide his full measure of scorn. He curled his bottom lip inside his mouth and blew a sharp whistle toward the clan of Kish milling around the wagon. He waved for all of them to join him. The children raced up to their uncle and grandfather while Ahinoam took her time escorting Ner.

Saul instructed the children to follow their uncle and that he and their mother would follow. The twins took over and helped Ner toward the Benjamite section.

Once they were out of earshot, Saul took Ahinoam's hands and placed them upon his chest. "You feel that? My heart is racing like Jeush's horse at full gallop."

"It is a horse fit for a king. One you are worthy to ride." She stood on tiptoe to kiss his cheek, and then led him to the sector of the inner circle designated for their tribe.

Saul and Ahinoam took their place beside the family clumped together and craned their necks to see all the activity happening by the platform and monument.

Samuel waved for Ahiah, the High Priest, dressed in full sacred garments, to precede him up the stairs of the platform while he waited at the bottom. Ahiah dangled the golden chain of the censer, puffing white smoke into the air as he walked the four corners of the platform. The twelve precious stones in the Breastplate of Judgment sparkled in the sunlight. Most of this crowd had rarely, if ever, seen the High Priest. Not since the sacking of Shiloh and the destruction of the Tabernacle had there been any of the national celebrations where the High Priest would make a public appearance, and Samuel wanted this momentous occasion to reflect the reverence of Yahweh.

Once Ahiah completed his loop around the platform, Samuel waved to

Gad and Nathan who raced to the back of the wagon to fetch a wooden table. The other students took positions at the foot of the steps. Samuel smiled at Shira who chose to remain in the carriage to watch the proceedings. He then climbed the steps and onto the stage. Gad and Nathan followed behind carrying the table and setting it in the middle of the stage.

After the two young men exited the stage, a Levite walked up the steps carrying a silver tray that held a leather bag. He approached Ahiah who stood at the edge of the stage and knelt down, holding the tray aloft before the crowd arranged in a circle around the dais in twelve tribal clumps. Each tribal leader stood in the forefront of their section, holding a long staff with their tribal banner attached to the end and raised well above the heads of the crowd for all to see.

When Ahiah placed the censer on the tray, he removed the leather bag and attached it to the inside of his breastplate. The Levite descended the stairs, leaving Ahiah and Samuel alone on the platform. Ahiah then turned to the Levites standing before the tent of the Ark of the Covenant and raised both hands in their direction. The musicians brought their shofar to their lips and blew a sustained detonation of sound. The curtains of the tent were withdrawn and Eleazar, guardian of the Ark of the Covenant, emerged holding a golden jar. Behind him came the Ark, suspended between two poles hoisted on the shoulders of twelve Levites, six in front and six behind.

When Eleazar led the procession out of its protected area beside the Stone of Help and into the open, the honor guards fell in behind, golden shields braced against their chests, their spears raised in the air. Soon as the Ark came into view, the tribal leaders began to wave their banners as the shouts of sustained praise and the rolling percussion of applause from the people began to drown out the penetrating blare of the shofar.

Eleazar led the Ark around the circle of the twelve tribes so that all the people could see the Presence. As the Ark passed before the individual tribes, the level of praise increased from sector to sector, one tribe attempting to outdo the other with its volume of adoration. The Ark was then set on a thick carpet in front of the raised platform. Eleazar approached the front of the stage with the golden jar and held it before the High Priest. Ahiah opened the leather pouch and removed two gemstones, raising them before the Ark and the people. The crowd instantly ceased their praises, and Ahiah waited for the final echoes of worship to fade before he spoke.

"The Urim and Thummim, the eyes of Yahweh." Ahiah shouted to be heard, and then he dropped the precious stones into the golden jar and took it from Eleazar.

Eleazar ordered the honor guard to surround the Ark in front of the platform. He was then handed a spear before taking his position at the center of the protective circle. He shouted a command and all spears were thrust forward. No one would get near the Presence, no one but the honor guard and the Levitical priests.

Once Ahiah saw that all was in place, he nodded to Samuel who moved to the opposite side of the table and raised a hand. Samuel scanned the hushed crowd, a long, steady survey, his gaze clear, no flickering his eyelids. He looked into the clear, vibrant sky. It seemed to Samuel that he had the approval of the people and the Almighty to proceed. Samuel detected nothing in heaven or on the earth would stop this course of action. All requisite instructions had been met. All the tribes had gathered and were prepared. And from his elevated position in the center of the assembly, Samuel caught sight of the grave face of the future king standing head and shoulders above his fellow tribesmen crowded into their tribal enclave. He had arrived, and Samuel would delay no longer, yet he would not allow Ahiah to cast the first lot until he had delivered one final reminder that Yahweh would always be the God of the chosen.

"Yahweh is the God of Israel. It was the Almighty who brought you out of Egypt, and delivered you from the power of Egypt and all the kingdoms that oppressed you."

Samuel paused for these words of Yahweh's power and intervention to sink into the hearts of the people. They were silent, so Samuel stepped down to the front of the platform and stretched out both arms, his entire span, to encompass all twelve tribes, all the Levitical clan, all of Israel. "And now you have asked for a king. Yahweh has heard your cry and will grant the desire of your hearts. He will set a king over us."

Samuel held his arms aloft. The people of Israel were now an inclusive group complicit in their decision to become like every other nation in the world. He had hoped never to see this day. He had hoped that the displeasure he felt and expressed on behalf of Yahweh might be enough to prevent this day. But this day was the will of the people and would be honored by Yahweh. And if honored by Yahweh, then he too would bring honor to Yahweh by being his prophet, faithful to the desire of the Almighty.

"So now present yourselves before Yahweh by your tribes and clans." He raised his hands toward the first tribe. "The tribe of Reuben, come forth."

The leader of the tribe of Reuben raised his arms, holding the staff with its banner and stepped toward the platform. Then Samuel turned to Ahiah, took a deep breath and gave the order to begin.

Ahiah shook the golden container before upending the jar, allowing the two precious stones to fall upon the table. He and Samuel studied the Urim and Thummim lying on the table top, Yahweh's answer staring them in the face, and then Samuel turned to the crowd. "Yahweh says, 'No!'"

The leader of the tribe of Reuben lowered his staff, removed the banner, and stepped back into the designated area with the other chieftains of his tribe.

Saul and Ahinoam stood tucked inside the relative safety of their family and the chieftains of the Benjamite clans all riveted by the elimination process. Beginning with the tribe of Reuben, Samuel would call out the name of one of the twelve sons of Jacob, oldest to youngest, and each tribal leader would step forward, banner raised proudly to the heavens, until the answer from heaven was given.

"Yahweh says, 'No!'"

Samuel would shout after he summoned the elected leader to approach the platform for the casting of the lots. Each tribe received the same answer, and the leader would lower his staff and remove the tribal banner in deference to Yahweh's rejection. When eleven tribes had been eliminated, all the clan chieftains and their families that gathered in the area designated for the tribe of Benjamin remained silent in communal awe, unable to comprehend what was happening to them.

But for Saul, it began to feel more like the physical manifestation of a nightmare. He felt a sharp pain in his head and the light of the sun made his eyes water, mixing with a profusion of sweat streaming from his scalp and forehead. When Samuel summoned the tribe of Benjamin to approach the platform and he saw Jeush's watery figure step forward, his hands gripping the staff bearing the tribal banner, Saul yanked the soaked headdress off his scalp and began wiping his eyes.

Samuel only confirmed the obvious; that the king would come from the tribe of Benjamin, but he had to adhere to the rules of order and have Ahiah cast the lots. "The tribe of Benjamin."

Samuel looked with Ahiah at the result of the gemstones lying upon the table. "Yahweh says, 'Yes!'"

The Benjamin delegation erupted. It was official. Jeush hurled the staff into the air, danced in a circle before his tribe, and caught the staff before it touched the ground.

That was the moment Saul knew he had to escape. It was all coming to pass. It was happening just as the prophet said it would. Of all the people in the nation of Israel, the eyes of the Almighty were focusing on him.

Saul watched as Samuel raised his hands for silence. While his tribe was making a joyous clamor, other tribes were protesting, raising their voices in opposition of Yahweh's choice. Saul had expected this response from some of the people. How could Yahweh select a king from a tribe so base and small a tribe, so scurrilous of reputation in the history of Israel since coming to the land of Promise? There must be something faulty with the Urim and Thummim. The prophet must have misinterpreted this final cast.

"Peace. Peace. We are not done. Yahweh has spoken. The king will come from the tribe of Benjamin. Now we continue clan by clan."

Jeush calmed the jubilation within his own tribe with his raised hand, and then he spun around, stiffening his spine, the banner of his tribe flying high in the air.

Saul began to shrivel inside as Ahiah continued to cast the gemstones onto the table, and one-by-one, each of the chieftains from the tribe of Benjamin was eliminated. He felt himself reverse in scale, becoming smaller instead of larger. He took advantage of everyone's distraction with Yahweh's rejection of clan after clan and broke away, heading back to where they had parked the wagon, but his wife caught sight of him trying to run.

"How can you leave?" Ahinoam was astounded by his sudden departure.

"I feel...I need a moment. I have a raging thirst. I'm going to the wagon." He retied his headdress around his head and trotted toward the wagon just as Samuel called the name of his clan.

"From the tribe of Benjamin, the clan of Matri, Yahweh says, 'Yes!'"

Saul made it all the way to the wagon before he bent double and spewed out the contents of his stomach. He staggered between the horses, braced himself against their flanks, and retched again.

"From the tribe of Benjamin, clan of Matri, family of Ner, Yahweh says, 'No!'"

Saul wiped his mouth, stumbled to the back of the wagon, and began digging through the baggage, searching for something to drink. His thirst was excruciating.

"From the tribe of Benjamin, clan of Matri, family of Kish, Yahweh says, 'Yes!'"

Saul ripped off the top to the water skin and began to guzzle from its neck.

"From the tribe of Benjamin, clan of Matri, Kish, head of his family, Yahweh says, 'No!'"

Yahweh was upon him. Yahweh was crashing down upon him. There was no one left, no one else to be called. Saul dropped the water skin onto the ground and allowed the contents to spill onto the soil.

"From the tribe of Benjamin, clan of Matri, Saul, son of Kish, Yahweh says..."

Saul scrambled into the wagon and began covering himself with the bags of clothes and baskets of food.

"...Yahweh says, 'Yes!' Yahweh says, 'Yes' to Saul, the son of Kish, of the clan of Matri, from the tribe of Benjamin."

Through the gaps in the wooden panels on the wagon, Saul could see Jeush hurl the staff with its tribal banner straight into the sky and fall to his knees, screaming at the top of his lungs. His voice soon was drowned out by the blasts of trumpets and the blaring shofars and uproar from all the people.

It was Ahinoam's face that first appeared around the back of the wagon. She held out her hand to Saul who was frenetically trying to conceal his large body beneath the baggage, but then she was distracted by the raucous babble coming from the crowd.

"They don't know I'm here. We could leave now. You could drive the wagon away, and I could stay hidden under the baggage." Saul pleaded with Ahinoam to escape.

"Jeush is running around looking for you." Ahinoam was amused by Jeush's panic. "I can't imagine what he is thinking."

"What are they doing now?" Saul's own heart was storming through his body.

"It looks as though Samuel is instructing the High Priest to cast the lots again. They are not sure if you are here." Ahinoam looked back at her husband, a smile on her lips. "You already know Yahweh's answer to that question. Come now."

Saul could not reach out from beneath the baggage and take her hand. His arm was stopped, and every conscious effort to raise it was blocked by wilting fear.

"You are my love, my life, my heart and my soul. My eyes are clear. I see as Yahweh sees. When I see inside my husband's heart, I see a king. I see the king Yahweh sees. I see the king you can become. You are my husband, and now you are my king."

Saul felt a rush of power. The pain in his head vanished. The glare of the sun no longer hurt his eyes. The knots in his gut dissolved. The clamp on his lungs released its grip and he took a deep breath. The strength in his legs returned and he began to get to his feet, the baggage tumbling around him as he stood his full height. He commanded his arm, his first command as king, and he reached out to take his wife's hand. Just as their fingers touched, Abner and Jonathan raced around the side of the wagon.

"Father. Father. You are king. Yahweh chose you. You are king. You are king."

"What are you doing in the wagon, Cousin? The people want to see you. Come."

The rest of Saul's family gathered behind the wagon along with the clan chieftains of Benjamin. His children could not stop bouncing off the ground, leaping in and out of each other's arms.

"Make way! Make way for the king!" Jeush shouted as he led Adara around to the back of the wagon to present his gift to the king, tears flowing from his eyes. "For you, my lord. The honor of our tribe has been restored. Yahweh is praised."

Saul leaned over and kissed Ahinoam. "I must go."

They both winced after their kiss. This parting was of a different kind, a different dimension, a different weight to the separation. They both sensed that this was the first of countless partings that would prick like the piercing of a thorn into their hearts.

Saul slung his leg over the back of Adara and stretched over the stallion's long beautiful neck to whisper into its ear, "You are fit for a king."

Saul sat up and nodded for Jeush to lead the way.

"Make way! Make way for the king!" Jeush shouted, and the throng began to part as Jeush led Adara back to the inner circle where all of Israel awaited the king.

Saul turned to look at Ahinoam one last time. She had both hands over her mouth and when she lifted them from her lips, hurling an invisible kiss toward him, the king, Saul felt reborn, alive with power, a blood surge pouring into every dark corner of his being.

It was a short parade, the first king of Israel led before each of the tribes ending at the steps of the platform where Samuel and Ahiah awaited him. Not everyone expressed unabashed exuberance for Yahweh's selection. Not every tribe bent the knee as Jeush led Adara and the king before them. Not everyone cried with approval or waved enthusiastically as he rode past. If those so displeased by Yahweh's choice had known a Benjamite would be a king, they might not have been so insistent on having one.

Saul dismounted Adara and embraced Jeush, and then threw his arms around his sons and daughters, kissing each of them. Finally, he grabbed his cousin by his beard.

"You will be my first appointment, Cousin!" Saul had to shout into Abner's ear to be heard above the vocal fray. "Prepare to be Commander of the Army."

Abner smiled, then bent his knee and bowed his head before his cousin.

Saul bound up the steps. When he reached the stage, Ahiah immediately bent his knee. Saul was not sure what he should do or say to the High Priest so he waited until Ahiah rose to his feet and looked him in the eye. When he did, the king smiled and placed a hand upon Ahiah's shoulder.

"I will need you. You will keep me in the Presence of Yahweh."

Then Saul looked at the prophet to present him to the people. He felt the slight quiver of fear began to stir, but he resisted its grip. He would not allow the emotion to overtake him. Yahweh had made His choice, and the growing clamor of the people seemed to approve. He moved beside Samuel. The prophet and king faced each other.

"It has now been publicly confirmed." Samuel pointed to the Urim and Thummim on the table beside the golden jar.

"There is no changing Yahweh's mind?" Saul's question was meant to give the prophet a measure of respect for his understanding of Yahweh's mind.

"The lot is cast, but its every decision is from Yahweh."

"I had hoped Yahweh might see it differently, but now Yahweh be praised."

"Yes, Yahweh be praised."

Samuel turned from Saul and looked out upon the boisterous crowd.

Saul looked at Samuel's face, the blending of his graying hair into the curls of his graying beard. He could not read what the prophet might be thinking behind the wrinkles of his skin or the sagging eyelids.

"My lord, you have been the mouthpiece for Yahweh. I must hear from the Almighty through you. I do not desire to usurp your place. Do not think me a rival, but as one entrusted to your care and guidance so that I may wisely lead once the prophet of Yahweh rests with his fathers."

"Your tongue is skilled in flattery and persuasion." Samuel turned back to Saul. He appeared impressed by what the chosen king had said.

"It is a country, unschooled tongue, my lord."

"Man is swayed by outward appearances, but Yahweh looks upon the heart."

"I speak only from my heart."

"Then Yahweh will be your judge."

"And you?"

"The choice was Yahweh's. In all things, I obey Yahweh."

All of Israel was impatient for a public declaration from the prophet and the king, the vocal waves of adoration and acclamation were becoming choppy and dissipated.

"My lord, show me the way of Yahweh." Saul raised his hand to the crowd in salute of their praise. "For my sake and for the sake of Israel teach me to be a great king."

Samuel began to back away from Saul, moving across the platform to the far end of the table. The crowd went silent at the sight of the prophet giving ground. Then Samuel raised his arm and pointed at Saul, the prophet's eyes swamped by mercy.

"You see the man Yahweh has chosen?" Samuel paused to steady himself. Everyone waited to hear which way the prophet's tongue would cut it. "There is no one like him among all the people of Israel." Samuel bellowed his affirmation, and then he lowered his head in honor and esteem to the king of Israel.

Trumpet and shofar split the sky, Levites began to dance, soldiers around the Ark beat their shields with the shafts of their spears, and all of Israel began to shout, "May the king of Yahweh's chosen ones live forever!" turning the phrase into a paean of praise.

Saul looked at the young prophets positioned at the base of the steps and watched them mimic the bowed head of the prophet in honor of the king. Saul understood there would be this tension between them, but perhaps not forever. Saul then raised his eyes to the heavens, his limbs, trunk, and head all throbbing, every pore of his skin exultant with joy at his striking transformation. He was a new brand of flesh and blood. He turned his palms upward, a supplicant's request for guidance to rule the people of Israel, a humble gesture for Yahweh's pleasure, and added his own voice of praise rising into the heavens.

Epilogue

SAUL HAD INSTRUCTED JEUSH TO MEET THE LEVITICAL EMISSAR-
ies at the city gates of Gibeah. He did not want them brought through the
city. He did not want any great fanfare of their arrival given the temper-
ment of the indigenous Gibeonite population. They still resented their servile position among the people of Israel, even though it was their ancestors
who shackled them to this menial station with their deceptive treaty with
Commander Joshua when he led Israel into the land of Promise.

Now that a king had been chosen, more and more Israelites were
coming to the city. Contingents from several of the tribes were arriving
every week, bringing their tribute. The historic conflict between Israel and
the conquered Gibeonite citizens was beginning to escalate. Some tribal
leaders argued that if Gibeah was to be the seat of power for the king and
residence for the royal family, then Israelites—not foreign ethnic groups—
should populate the city and surrounding region. Saul feared tensions
could get out of control. He did not want to mar the beginning of his reign
with the expulsion of the native Gibeonites or worse, unleash a genocidal
assault.

Jeush escorted Ahiah, the High Priest, Eleazar, the guardian of the
Ark, and the entire Levitical parade around the city and up the hill toward
Saul's compound. At the crowning ceremony in Mizpah, Eleazar suggested
moving the Ark from the home of Abinadab to Gibeah to be near the

king. Saul and Samuel's reaction was the same: keep the Ark where it is until Yahweh instructs otherwise. While Saul wanted close connection to Samuel and Yahweh, he needed time to become his own man.

Gad and Nathan, two of Samuel's students, trailed behind Ahiah and Eleazar on two donkeys. They had brought with them chests of scrolls and documents for the king, copied out by the prophet's scribes.

On either side of the road, the officials of the various tribes had established their camps in the forested ground from the city limits all the way up the road to the clearing around Saul's compound. Tribal banners flew before the encampments of Asher, Zebulum, Issachar, Manasseh, Gad, Naphtali, and Ephraim. When the Levites blew their shofar, sounding the arrival of the High Priest and guardian of the Ark of the Covenant, all the delegations lined up on either side of the road and voiced praise and blessing to the Almighty as the Levitical honor guard moved past.

Saul was proud of his family and how they had adjusted to this abrupt change in their former uncomplicated lives. He wanted to show them off and insisted every member be present at the arrival of the High Priest, the guardian, and their Levitical retinue, scrubbed and dressed in their finery. All of Saul's family huddled excitedly behind him with Ahinoam at his side as they watched Jeush escort Ahiah and Eleazar into the compound. When Ahiah and Eleazar approached the royal family, Jeush reared up on his horse and heralded the new arrivals.

"My lord and king, I present Ahiah, High Priest of Yahweh, and Eleazar, guardian of the Ark of the Covenant." Jeush's booming voice projected over the compound. "I give you King Saul, the family of Kish, the tribe of Benjamin, Yahweh's anointed, and the first king of Israel."

Silence followed Jeush's drawn-out announcement. No one was sure what to do next. This formal introduction had never been done before. Saul smiled and applauded. When the royal family joined in, the crowd quickly followed the example with applause.

"I am not sure of a proper greeting to our king." Ahiah dismounted from his horse and smoothed out his robes.

"We discussed possible options, but came to no conclusion." Eleazar dismounted and passed off the reins of his horse to a Levite.

Ahiah and Eleazar had been the first to confront the prophet with the need for a change in Israel's leadership by insisting on the right to have a king. While they had no role in the selection, it was their intention to support this king regardless. There were so many responsibilities heaped upon Saul in such a short time that he was grateful for any assistance they could provide.

"Let's not stand on ceremony." Saul extended his arms toward the two men as he moved toward them. "These things will come in time."

Saul placed a firm hand upon the shoulder of each man as they stood in a tight clump between the two horses.

"Yahweh has blessed me with your support. All of Israel knows that I have not been groomed for this honor. Organizing this new form of governing and uniting twelve independent tribes into one nation will be a challenge. Your help will be invaluable."

Ahiah and Eleazar bowed their heads before the king.

"My lord, answer me something." Ahiah raised his head and cast his eyes back toward the road. "As we traveled the road we saw no representatives from the tribes of Simeon, Judah, Dan, and Reuben. There has certainly been enough time since the ceremony in Mizpah for them to send a delegation. Why aren't they here?"

Jeush chose not to wait for the king to respond. He took it upon himself to answer for his sovereign. "I don't know the proper ways we commoners are to honor our king and show our allegiance, but those tribes have chosen not to send an official delegation."

Jeush leaned over the opposite side of his horse and spat in the dirt.

Saul raised his hand to Jeush for him to restrain himself.

"The leader of the tribe of Benjamin is quick to my defense." Saul looked back at Eleazar and Ahiah. "His manner may be crude, but his loyalty is without question."

"But why have they not yet come, my lord?" Eleazar was puzzled by this lack of courtesy from the four tribes.

"It is not that they have not come. It is that they will not come." Saul lowered his eyes. "Dear friends, it will take time for everyone to learn to accept Yahweh's choice as king. We must not hold them in contempt until they come around."

"My lord, the priests of Levi and the guardians of the Ark will do everything in our power to bolster the king in all he does." After Ahiah spoke these words he knelt before the king. Eleazar immediately went to his knee in solidarity.

Saul placed his hands on their bowed heads. "And I hope to be a better king for your love. Now, please rise."

Once Ahiah and Eleazar stood on their feet, Saul noticed two lads perched on their beasts. They were dressed in robes of black and gray, identifying them as prophets of Yahweh. Their young faces belied an apprehension and lack of surety as to their place in this moment.

"You are students of the prophet, I see. Samuel said he would be sending someone. I am sure he has trained you well in the prophetic arts and the sacred writings."

The young men's eyes twitched timidly. Given the physical stature of the king, they sat eye level with Saul though they were mounted on the backs of their donkeys.

"Yes, my lord." The two spoke at once, surprising both of them.

Saul smiled at their united awkwardness. The two young prophets' discomfort was made more humorous by one's unsteady wobbling on the back of his donkey, his large head rolling like a melon on a barrel top, and the other's toes dragging the ground, his legs were so long. They both nervously squirmed in their cloth saddles until realizing they should dismount and take a knee before the king, which they hurriedly did so.

"What treasure do you bring in your chests?" Saul pointed toward the pack mule tethered behind them.

The unsteady one glanced at the long-legged one and shook his head, then he dropped his eyes to the ground.

"The scrolls of the fathers and copies of some new documents on the first judges of Israel written by the prophet Samuel."

Saul noticed the obvious note of pride in his voice.

"We also bring a record of the ceremony in Mizpah and a list of clans and tribal leaders who attended." The first overcame his nervousness to make himself more present.

"That is a treasure." Saul placed his hands upon the chest of writings.

"And scrolls with the regulations of the kingship. That is all, my lord."

"Excellent." Saul opened his arms to the two neophyte prophets. "Will you be staying with us or are you just dropping off the chests before returning to Ramah?"

The taller one looked over at his companion, whose gaze had returned to the ground.

"If my lord will have us, we are here to serve the king in the prophetic matters of Yahweh and on behalf of the prophet Samuel."

Saul knew these two were too young to have in-depth knowledge regarding the matters of Yahweh. Saul might try to take advantage of their youth, testing them in some way to see how deeply they had fallen under the spell of Samuel's massive personality. Saul would admit he certainly had. The prophet was persuasive. But perhaps these young men were impressionable enough to be open to another perspective on this whole new world they all found themselves inhabiting.

"Please rise." Saul wanted to redirect them away from the scripted answers they had rehearsed before arriving. "Where is your home of origin?"

They rose to their feet and traded a sidelong glance but kept their heads bowed and did not answer.

"It's a simple enough question. You both look like you come from good homes. What is your tribe?"

"We have been under the prophet's instruction and living in Ramah with my lord Samuel for some time now at the prophet's school." The taller one spoke with genuine pride. "But we both come from the town of Bethlehem."

"Ah, the tribe of Judah." Saul looked at Abner and Jeush. "Glad someone from Judah will be among us."

They were so young. Saul glanced at Jonathan standing upright and proud beside his mother. His son and these young prophets were about the same age.

"And what names did your parents give you on the day of your circumcision?"

The one who had been unsteady on his mount answered first. "My name is Gad, my lord."

"And I am Nathan, my lord."

Saul pondered the meaning of the two names. Then he looked at Gad, "Your name means 'good fortune,'" and then turned to Nathan, "and your name means 'Yahweh has given.'"

It would be to Saul's advantage to keep these young men in court.

"So it must be my 'good fortune' that 'Yahweh has given' you both to the court of the king. You will make a great addition and be invaluable help."

Saul walked back to his family and stood next to Ahinoam. "You must be patient as we find our way in this kingly business. There is much for all of us to learn."

Then he lifted his arms to encompass all the new arrivals.

"The king and his family are honored by the coming of the High Priest, the guardian, and the young prophets from Ramah. We welcome all of you."

Acknowledgments

GRATITUDE BEGINS WITH MY PARENTS, HENRY AND BERNIE, AND ends with my wife Kay and daughters, Kristin and Lauren. Everyone else lies in between.

Michael Blanton, Steve Brallier, Michael W. Smith, Jim Davis, and John Brewer. These men of God gave of themselves to me for decades. They sacrificed their time and treasure on my behalf just because they loved me and believed in me even when I didn't believe in myself.

Beverly Mansfield for giving me my first real shot at writing books and Esther Fedorkevich for landing my first two co-authored book deals.

Dr. Steve Guthrie, professor of Old Testament, who listened to my initial dream to write these stories and handed me an armful of books to start my research.

Brian Mitchell, President of Working Title Agency/Media. When everyone else said "no," he said "yes." When rejections from publishers began crowding his inbox, he said, "I believe." When I gave him the option to throw in the towel, he said, "Keep your towel." Brian brought this book across the finish line. And to Dave Schroeder, marketing guru extraordinaire also of WTA/Media.

Steve Taylor and Ben Pearson for including me in the creative team to write the screenplay for *The Second Chance* and *KABUL24*.

The father/son team of Ben and Derek Pearson for their work on the promotional videos, and to Jillian LaFave for her fabulous web design work.

My siblings and their families. They saw all the warts and still loved me.

Jim Reyland, and the studio team at Audio Productions, Inc./Nashville for making my audio book sound terrific.

All my threatre artist collaborators and friends who inspired me to be a better storyteller.

Whitefire Publishing for taking the risk on an unknown. And for Roseanna White's insightful and "gloves-off" editorial guidance. This book has achieved a higher level of literary craft because of her.

And finally, to God...I have been carried between His shoulders all my life.

HENRY O. ARNOLD

Henry O. Arnold has co-authored a work of fiction, *Hometown Favorite*, with Bill Barton, and nonfiction, *KABUL24*, with Ben Pearson. He also co-wrote and produced with Steve Taylor (director) and Ben Pearson the film *The Second Chance* starring Michael W. Smith, the screenplay for the authorized film documentary on evangelist Billy Graham, *God's Ambassador*, and the documentary film *KABUL24*, based on the book which is the story of western and Afghani hostages held captive by the Taliban for 105 days. He lives on a farm in Tennessee with his lovely wife Kay. They have two beautiful daughters married to two handsome men with three above-average grandchildren. For more information please visit: www.henryoarnold.com

Made in United States
Troutdale, OR
12/04/2024